also by jessa hastings

The Conditions of Will

The Magnolia Parks Universe
Magnolia Parks
Daisy Haites
Magnolia Parks: The Long Way Home
Daisy Haites: The Great Undoing
Magnolia Parks: Into the Dark

Never
Never

time of your life

jessa hastings

ORION

First published in Great Britain in 2025 by Orion Fiction
an imprint of The Orion Publishing Group Ltd.
Carmelite House, 50 Victoria Embankment
London EC4Y 0DZ

An Hachette UK Company

The authorised representative in the EEA is Hachette Ireland, 8 Castlecourt
Centre, Dublin 15, D15 XTP3, Ireland (email: info@hbgi.ie)

1 3 5 7 9 10 8 6 4 2

Copyright © Jessica Rachel Hastings 2025
Internal Design © 2025 by Sourcebooks
Cover art and design © Emmy Lawless

The moral right of Jessica Rachel Hastings to be identified as
the author of this work has been asserted in accordance
with the Copyright, Designs and Patents Act of 1988.

All rights reserved. No part of this publication may be
reproduced, stored in a retrieval system, or transmitted
in any form or by any means, electronic, mechanical,
photocopying, recording, or otherwise, without the
prior permission of both the copyright owner and the
above publisher of this book.

All the characters in this book are fictitious, and any resemblance
to actual persons, living or dead, is purely coincidental.

A CIP catalogue record for this book is
available from the British Library.

ISBN (Hardback) 978 1 3987 2830 1
ISBN (Export Trade Paperback) 978 1 3987 2831 8
ISBN (Audio) 978 1 3987 2834 9
ISBN (eBook) 978 1 3987 2833 2

Printed and bound in Great Britain by Clays Ltd, Elcograf S.p.A.

www.orionbooks.co.uk

For me, actually. You needed this. You did it.
Don't let anyone make you feel how you began to again.
You're good at this. *We* are good at this.

Pronunciation Guide

Ysolde: ih-ZOLD (rhymes with "cold")
Featherstonhaugh: FAN-shaw

Joah: JOE-uh (like "Joe" with a soft "uh" at the end)
Harrigan: HAR-ree-guhn

Caravella: KAH-ruh-vel-luh
Evanthe: eh-VAN-thee (stress on the second sylla-
ble, "thee" rhymes with "key")

Mancunian Word Guide

Alright?	Hello
Bellend	Dickhead
Bladdered	Drunk
Boozer	Pub
Div	Idiot
Fag	Cigarette
Fit	Good-looking
Gip	Throw up
Hench	Muscular
Knackered	Tired
Manky	Dirty
Melt	An idiot/wimp
Mithered	Angry
Nowt	Nothing
Owt	Anything
Pants	Underwear
Piss-take	Something done to make someone look stupid or mock them
Quid	Money
Rubbish	Bad
Summat	Something
Toffy	Snobby
Vest	Tank top

part one

ONE

ysolde

I DIDN'T THINK YOU COULD tell in the moment—I didn't know you could feel the gravity of your life changing around you when it is, in fact—I always had sort of felt as though you became aware of it in retrospect. Like, after the fact, you think back and you're able to identify "oh yes, that moment did actually change my life"—but I have it here now, straightaway.

Straightaway from the other side of an impossibly crowded room full of people I was sort of pleased to see not five seconds ago, who now only stand as an obstacle between me and the pair of impossibly blue eyes that I can't look away from over across the bar.

I've been in New York a lot lately; it was NYFW. And I once accidentally had sex with Mitchell Montrose-Bowes back in December because it was Christmas and Christmas is always weird at home, so I lied and said I had to work in Paris, but then I was just in Paris alone, and I couldn't spend it with Lala and her family because her mum would tell my dad and then my charade would be up, so I had to stay in Paris and pretend to be busy which is a recipe for a disaster, especially when your ex-boyfriend is filming a Jean-Luc Godard film (which, let's be honest, I'm not going to see) and like, fuck it—it's Mitchell Montrose-Bowes and it's nothing you haven't done before, all the while definitely being something you shouldn't do again because he did cheat on you, after all. With Meghan Miller, of all people, for the love of god.

And when I came to from my terrible Parisian delirium and had the wherewithal to run away from MB, I ran right into the arms of the other one, and I know you don't blame me, because how could you, because it's Fletch. And he's him. And 1994 was such a mindfuck of a year with what happened back in September and he was there for all of it, and he's good and safe, but it's always a bit messy with us—I don't know why. Me probably.

Anyway, London's shit that time of year. February's not really cold enough for snow anymore, but it is in New York, and February's one of the best months for snow there. I don't love cold—I actually don't love the hot either. Lala says I'm Goldilocks when it comes to temperatures, but I just want to be okay, really. I like to be comfortable. And if I have to be uncomfortable, I want it to be for a reason. I don't much love to be sweaty, but I'll get hot to go brown. Similarly, I certainly don't love being cold, but if it's snowing, it's pretty enough to be worth it—do you know what I mean? Uncomfortable things have to be worth it, worth whatever discomfort they bring you, otherwise they're just…uncomfortable for no reason.

"Oh my god," Lala whispers to me. She's spotted those blue eyes on the other side of the room herself now. "Is that—"

"Yes," I cut her off.

Lala is my best friend. We've been best friends since we were fifteen and we were both sent to one of those terrible model houses in Paris for a month for a million casting calls. I don't know what happened—maybe because we were the only non-white girls in the house. Both of us biracial, and it could have been a disaster and all competitive because modelling often is like that, but yay feminism, or something—because we just sort of fell in love. We also don't look the same. I don't need to tell you who she is, because I know

TIME OF YOUR LIFE

you know, but Lala Caravella—fiercely beautiful, chocolate-brown eyes that match her skin, strikingly angular.

Lala grips my arm with some urgency now. "He's staring at you like no one's ever stared at you before in your whole entire life."

"That feels untrue, considering our profession, and all—" I tell her without looking away from him. I can't look away, not first at least. If I do, it'll imply I'm afraid and maybe, if there were a gun to my head—which there isn't, but if there were—I'd possibly admit that maybe, I am. Just a tiny bit. But that's only because I've never before felt my life changing in a moment, and I've had some really obvious-in-retrospect life-changing moments.

When my mother died, that was one. When Jilly E. Edwards approached me in Selfridges when I was fifteen which led to Rain Models signing me a week later, that was another. Lala, a big one. None of them I realised were changing me in the moment, but then here, now, it's strange—there's like a bubbling in me. As though living inside my blood there's a trillion tiny little north magnets and he's a big, old south one.

Our eyes are still locked from across the room—his friends noticed now too I think, because he whispers something to him, taps him in his chest. And whatever the friend says—he's a pro-ducer, I think? I recognise him—Blue Eyes chuckles at, and glances away, and all at once I feel victorious because he looked away first and also a bit like I'm free-falling through space and time because I swear to god for the past minute and a half, that man's gaze was the thing that was anchoring me to the planet. Gravity.

My bodyguard gives me an exasperated look—we've been down this path before, or so he thinks. I get crushes on men rather easily. Sue me.

"Come on, Juliette," he says, a tired look on his sweet, young face.

That's not my name, by the way, he's just—professionally tuned into everyone who stares sideways at me or, like, blinks in my direc-tion. He has to be. I don't want to talk about why, but he does have to be. You can know that much.

Aleki moves Lala and I deeper into the Groucho Club, and a couple of people whisper and point, but I don't much worry about it because if they're whispering and pointing in the Groucho Club, they're probably about to be thrown out of the Groucho Club.

We're led to a table of people we know. I guess I'd call them our friends? Lala probably wouldn't; she says really I'm her only friend, but if she was going to have other friends, the ones sitting around the magnum bottle of Moët would be them. Riley West, the former child star, current cinematic darling (who just got out of rehab and is celebrating in—arguably—an unideal way), American, obviously. I don't think we have child stars in the UK, not how they have them over there anyway. And next to her is Chloe Bosworth, also American, also doesn't need an introduction but in case you've been living under a rock, she's Max Martin's latest musical sensation. Can't really step outside right now without seeing a photo of Chloe Bosworth and her wonderful, bare midriff. Probably could say the same thing about me though, so I shan't point fingers.

Riley stands, opens her arms. "Angels!" she squeals. "You're back!"

When Lala doesn't move in towards her embrace, I do on both our behalf.

Lala gives Chloe a nod hello, because Lala is suspicious of everyone, but she's particularly suspicious of Chloe. I'm not sure Chloe knows that though.

"How was it?" I think Chloe asks me, but I don't hear her properly because he's watching me again.

We're on the same side of the room now. He's had to reposition his body to do so, but he *is* watching me, and it *is* him, because his brother's here too. Actually, I'm not a lip reader, but were I one, I believe I might have just lip-read his brother say, "Just go talk to her."

"—Hello? Ysolde." Chloe pokes me in the arm. "I'm talking to you."

I blink twice. "Sorry."

TIME OF YOUR LIFE 7

"You opened that show. Like, what the fuck!" She beams at me. "Did you lose your mind?"

"I love Gianni, always—but, I mean, what he's doing right now?" I breathe out all the awe I hold in my chest at any given moment for that beautiful genius of a man. "Heaven."

"Are you talking about Versace's Spring 1995 collection?" Riley injects and I nod, smile because I'm proud—proud to have walked it and worn it, and I love Gianni so much, so this has nothing to do with him, but I'm not really listening again because I think the thing that's about to change my life is walking right towards me, but I can't completely confirm because I can't look up in case it's true.

And I need you to know something, okay—? I'm not shy. I never don't have anything to say, I don't tend to back away from a fight. Once when Lala and I were fresh, a very mean Brazilian model who was technically, at the time, much higher on the food chain than Lala or me (but also technically definitely not as pretty as either of us) tried to steal Lala's dress backstage for a Galliano show, and I physically fought her. It's the only time I've ever gotten into a physical altercation in my entire life, and of course it was over a dress, but my point is, I'm not some shy, precious wallflower, but the very thought of that man crossing a room to speak to me, for whatever reason, has my heart in a state of gallop.

I had sex with that actor who was arrested for trying to accidentally bring a gun on a plane. A week ago. Which, to be clear—that was an accident. He told me. So, just, like—god, keep that in mind, please? I don't get struck by stars, I am, technically, a star myself and rest assured, stars are incredibly unstriking most of the time.

I'm not starstruck; this isn't me being weird because he's him and he's from that band. I'm being weird because I can feel the earth shifting under my feet.

"Oh my god—fuck! Shit!—Oh my god—" Lala whispers very quietly a thousand times before I drive my index finger into her rib to shut her the fuck up, because now he's in front of me.

Obscenely tall, oh my god. You can never be too sure with

famous people; they're crafty. Always making themselves look taller on film and television, standing on boxes, making their co-stars stand in holes, shoe lifts—you name it—and whatever, no judgment, I get it. Men like to be tall, and I, a woman, like men to be tall because I'm tall. 5'9". It's in the job description. But sometimes you'll meet a man who's made himself look incredibly tall on-screen, and I won't name names (Gilbert Grape) but you might find yourself feeling vaguely misled, is all.

But not him here in front of me now. I'm sitting, sure, but even still, I can tell. 6'3" maybe? Could be taller, even. And if it wasn't obvious from what I said before—shockingly blue eyes. Light. Like, icy blue. There's something else about them though—something else behind that makes me sit up straighter. A confidence, maybe? Some kind of self-assurance…? Or maybe it's just good, old-fashioned pride, I don't know. He is famous for his ego, I do know that much… But then, like—fuck. *Look at that face.* Of course he has an ego, he *should* have an ego. All of him is spectacular. He has fair skin by nature but it obviously sees the sun a fair amount. A shaggy mop of brown hair, iconic to the band and, I suppose, the time in which we live. Straight-legged blue jeans and a well-oversized plaid jacket, white T-shirt underneath with some Adidas Superstars that are too worn for someone with as much money as I know he must he have. All in all, he's somehow completely spectacular by being, technically, entirely underwhelming. Except I'm not underwhelmed at all. I am in fact, very, very whelmed.

He says nothing for a good three seconds, which is weird and actually draws attention to us in an annoying way. The conversations around us all go quiet to watch on, because of course they do—why wouldn't they? He's him and I'm me and if you could listen in, wouldn't you?

"Alright?" he says, nodding his chin at me, his extraordinarily thick Mancunian accent well in tow.

I glance from him to my friends, back to him. "Hi?" He eyes Aleki. "That your boyfriend, then?"

TIME OF YOUR LIFE

I shake my head. "Bodyguard."

He looks past me to Aleki, then nods towards the bar.

"I'm gonna take her over there for a chat, yeah?"

Aleki looks at me to check. I don't nod but I give him my *yes that's fine* look with my eyes, and then the biggest hand in the world is offered to me. It's like a baseball mitt, just right there in my face, waiting for me to take it, so I do. I don't know why I do because I'm perfectly capable of getting up on my own, but I do, and if I had to pinpoint a moment where sometime in the future we'd say that the chemistry of me as a person was empirically altered, it's now—the first time we touched in this sweetly banal way, my hand in his as he leads me through a crowd of 150 of London's biggest celebrities and most questionable people.

He's 6'4", by the way. Because I'm in heels and he's still got some inches on me. A tower of a man.

He leans over to get the attention of the bartender, who double takes him. They're not really meant to do that here.

"You got Boddington's?" he asks. The bartender shakes his head. "Fuck me," he groans like it's personal. "Just gimme a lager, then—whatever you got." He looks back at me. "What're you on?"

I give him a careful look before I lean over the bar to tell the tender myself.

"Tom Collins, please." Because I shan't be spoken for.

That makes him smile a bit though, which wasn't my intent. He stares at me for a few more seconds and I feel my cheeks going pink in a way they never have before for any man.

"You know who I am, don't ya?" he eventually says.

"Everyone knows who you are," I say, even though that's exactly what the front man of Fallow wanted to hear. I say it to him anyway because sometimes it's nice to be nice. Joah Harrigan smirks a little. He's sort of famous for that smirk, I suppose. Famously troublesome. Maybe it's the "meteoric rise" of the band, how they were sort of nothing boys from Manchester, brothers, who started a band and kind of found success absurdly quickly, despite not even having had a record out yet. They both just have those kinds of faces. Like, faces you want to stare at. Him, the one in front of me—Joah—he especially has one… And a face like that—? It's not good for a man to have a face like that and also be talented, I don't think. And to be a white male? Fuck. It's a recipe for trouble. He is, inherently, a recipe for trouble. And rather infamously, I suppose at least allegedly, it does follow him everywhere he goes.

I straighten up, remind myself that whilst he might be in the biggest band in the world, I myself have been lauded *the face of the decade*.

So I counter. "Do you know who *I* am?"

"Most beautiful girl in the world," he says without skipping a beat.

"Obviously," I say, and his head pulls back—a bit surprised, but nevertheless, on board.

"Obviously?"

"*Obviously,*" I repeat myself, but then I wonder. "But do you not know my name?"

"I know your face is fuckin' everywhere…" Then his face pulls into something that almost looks like he's sorry. "But…I dunno your name."

And that's enough for me, like fucking fuck him. I'm fucking everywhere. Every bus, every magazine, every runway, every campaign, you cannot get away from me right now, not even if you tried.

I give him a filthy look as I go to move past him, but he grabs my arm, shaking his head like I'm being silly.

"I don't give a fuck about fashion and models and all that shit—"

Which—just to clarify—I *am* that shit. That shit is me. I am fashion. I am models. I am eponymous with both all over the world, so I say to you again, *fuck him*, and I snatch my arm away once more, and this time with fierce conviction.

"—Till now!" he says quickly; his eyes look sincere now and his face looks almost a bit panicked even. "Till now," he says firmly, nodding. "Now it's fuckin' suddenly the most important thing in the world…"

I roll my eyes slowly and dramatically, and he sort of smiles, shaking his head a bit as he swears under his breath.

"Fuck."

"What?"

"Reckon I'm a bit in love with ya, that's all."

The bartender passes us our drinks. I thank him before I turn to Joah. "You're ridiculous."

"I ain't ridiculous." He pulls a face, then changes his voice to make it sound like he thinks it's all a joke. "I'm *famous*."

"So am I," I remind him, which I completely hate because what the actual fuck? "And they're not mutually exclusive."

"Come back to mine," he says, completely straight-faced.

"No!"

Joah frowns. "Why not?" As though it doesn't make sense to him, a girl saying no to him.

"Because."

"Cos you're *not that kind of girl*—?" he offers.

I shrug. "I am for certain people?"

He looks mildly discouraged, but only for a second before he tries again. "You not gonna be her for me?"

I laugh airily. "No."

He frowns again. "Why not?"

"Well, I have a feeling you're quite big trouble…"

He gives me a proud, little grin. "Fuckin' time of your life, but…"

That makes me laugh. I wish it didn't, but it sort of snuck out of me, so I let it go and shake my head, so he doesn't think he's pleased me too much.

"My life is…" I trail. "I'm happy with my life, thank you."

Joah Harrigan shakes his head now, sure of himself. "Yeah, just you wait…"

I lift an eyebrow. "For what?"

He shrugs like that's easy. "Till your life's got me in it like."

I pinch my eyes. "But I don't *want* you in it."

He stares at me for a couple of seconds, and there's something about it, I don't know why, but it really is like I'm see-through and he knows it, so he calls it.

"Liar." He points at me with conviction.

"Sol—" Lala pokes her head into our conversation. "We're going to Hertford—"

I nod at her. "Coming."

Joah shakes his head again. "Oi, don't go."

I pull a face as though it's awkward between us. "I think I will…"

"Then I need to see you again, don't I?" he concludes.

I concede with a shrug. "Okay."

He blinks a few times, almost surprised. "Okay?"

He swallows—first time I've seen him look nervous, actually. He waits for the more I don't offer him, then he says, "…How?"

I give him another shrug. "That feels like a you problem…"

"What's your number, then?"

"I suppose you could, yes." I smile at him pleasantly, then say nothing else.

He lifts an eyebrow as he waits, and then I shake my head as though he's silly.

"Oh, I'm not going to give it to you."

"Why?" He's frowning again.

I straighten up. "I'll give you my number if you can tell me my name."

He groans. "Well, fuck! That ain't fair, is it? Cos you never actually told me, did ya?"

"Do you know—" I give him a small smile that's equal parts encouraging and condescending. "—Nevertheless, I have a tiny bit of faith in you that you may just still figure it out…"

"I'm gonna," he tells me, sure.

I give him a curt smile as my best friend pulls me away. "We shall see…"

TWO

joah

MY BROTHER, RICHIE, GRIMACES AS I stroll back over to him and the lads. He's older than me by three and a bit years and never fucking shuts up about it. Plays lead guitar in Fallow. He's the one people reckon is me sometimes if they spot him on the street, but they shouldn't—like, yeah, maybe he's got an inch on me, but I got the face, know what I mean?

"She turn you down?" Chops—Davey Tschopp, drummer of the band, you know who he is—pipes up, grinning like a dickhead.

"Fuck off," I snap, giving him a proper glare. No one turns me down.

Well, except her. She sorta did. Not sayin' she did all the way, but yeah…a bit.

"What happened?" Rich asks, brows halfway up his forehead.

"She got fucked off cos I didn't know her name?"

His eyes go wide, proper dramatic. "You went over to that *actual* supermodel—a fuckin' *supermodel*—and didn't know her name?" Fuck, he's annoying.

"Well, do *you* know her name?"

"Ysolde Featherstonhaugh, you fuckin' bellend."

I scrunch my face up. "How the fuck do you know that?"

He shakes his head. "How the fuck do you not?"

I growl under my breath.

"Well, it's cooked now anyway. She's off."

Richie and Chops exchange a look between themselves as I throw meself back down in a seat between Fry—Ewan Talfryn, our bassist—and Harley Parks, our producer.

Harley pats me on the back. "Plenty of fish in the sea, man."

Shrug like I don't give a shit man, cos I don't—well, fuck—maybe I do like. Probably shouldn't but, you get me? He is wrong like, though. Plenty of fish, sure, but I've never clapped eyes on one like that before.

Richie's watchin' me in this way that pisses me off. It's too close, all knowing and shit.

"You look…" He struggles to find the word. "I dunno—Sad—?"

"Piss off," I spit.

Richie's actin' a tit now though, ain't he? "Are you sad about this girl turning you down?"

"Why would I be sad about that girl turning me down?"

"I dunno, Jo, why would you be?" Pauses for dramatic effect. Knob.

"It's alright to catch a feeling every now and then, mate—" He claps a paternal hand on my shoulder. "You can set some other goals for '95, you know, besides shagging your way through all of Chelsea."

Roll my eyes at him. "Alright, Dad."

That was a low blow, and I knew it the second it left me mouth. Our dad's shit. But winding Richie up? That's just a laugh, innit?

"Fuck you." Rich skulks off, proper annoyed. Mission accomplished.

Catch feelin's—Me? Fuck off. From one conversation?

I'm just in a weird mood, that's all. And she was stupid fit.

And now me night's proper fucked, you know what I mean? Like, birds are eye-fucking me left, right, and centre in here, but

I don't want a bar of it—All I can think about is Ysolde fuckin' Featherstonhaugh, fifteen minutes away on Hertford Street.

Should I go? Nah—I shoot the thought down the second it flies across me head. I don't go places for girls. I don't chase girls.

But I dunno. Got this feelin', don't I? Can't lump her in with other girls. Because she's not other girls, is she? Fuckin' clearly not, cos look at me… I'm walkin' towards the exit now, almost without realisin' it. Didn't stand up and decide to go after her, but here I am—stood up already. Reckon I'm gonna go get her.

"Where you off to?" Chops shouts after me.

Richie goes a lifts one of them fuckin' annoying eyebrows of his, the prick. Like he fuckin' knows he's right. *Well done, Rich—there's a girl I wanna shag.* Ain't exactly news, is it?

Except—for me it is, and the cocky little shite knows it.

And I won't hear the end of this come tomorrow, will I? Lads night out tonight. Or was meant to be. Richie's on the long leash from Loxy, and we're all in London which is a bit rare these days—we have a show at the end of the week, that's why—so tonight was meant to be *a night.* And yeah like, probably at the end of it, I might've taken a bird or two back to my bed as I've been known to, but this—Fuck me, I'll be eatin' shit for this for days.

"Good luck!" Richie shouts, grinnin' like the cunt he is.

I flip him off.

Grab a cab—don't need a driver, I ain't a fuckin' div—thirteen minutes door to door. And fuck—I know this is gonna make me sound like a soft lad, but when I pull up outside—? Feel a bit relieved, don't I? Closer to her again like.

Head inside. Ask a few people if they've seen her—this place is a fuckin' maze, innit? Rooms and corners and little pockets everywhere.

Bottom floor, the club bit. That's where I find her. Right bang in the middle of the bar with her mate (who's pretty fuckin' fit herself, know what I mean)—Ysolde's tipping champagne straight into Richard Ashcroft's mouth, laughin' her fuckin' head off. Then our eyes meet, and hers go wide.

Makes me happy, that. Always had that effect on girls to be fair, but it's gone mad since the band like. Properly mental. Don't really give a fuck about it in normal life, you get me? Thing is, don't reckon this Featherstonhaugh girl is normal life, but.

I head over to her, watch as she goes all stiff, nervous as anythin'—palms off that bottle of champagne to her mate. Sidle up beside her, casual as you like.

"Alright," I say, givin' her a cool grin.

"Hi." She stares at me, lookin' a bit thrown. "Did you…follow me?"

"Yeah." Toss her a look. "I'm stalkin' ya."

Her mate pipes up, stickin' her nose into it. "We don't joke about stalkers round here," she tells me.

I glance between 'em, make sure they know they're being daft—cos they are.

I nod at the mate but keep me eyes on Ysolde.

"Who's this, then?"

"Oh, I forgot—you don't know about models and fashion and shit—"Ysolde rolls her eyes. "This is Lala Caravella. Only *the* most famous model in the world."

I tilt me head at Ysolde. "Thought you was the most famous model in the world…"

Lala flicks her eyes, proper unimpressed. "And I thought *you'd* be taller."

I scoff. "I'm 6'4". What d'you want me to be—a fuckin' lamppost?"

The mate catches a laugh she don't want to give me, tries to squash it, but I clock it.

Ysolde straightens up, arms crossed, proper impatient now, like she ain't havin' a bar of it.

"We are *both* the most famous models in the world," she says, all sharp. "What are you doing here?"

TIME OF YOUR LIFE   17

I square up now, dead pleased with meself. "Ysolde Featherstonhaugh."

Hits me with a massive eye roll, she does. Clicks straightaway— that don't land how I thought it would, know what I mean? Shouldn't be feelin' so proud of meself like.

"Oh, I'm sorry—were you after a prize?"

I shake me head, lookin' right at her. "You're the prize."

She lets out this half-scoff and brushes past me, but it ain't for me to fuck off, I can tell that much—nah, it's to get away from the crowd, for me to follow her.

"I get your number now," I say, catching up with her. "That's the deal."

"Claridge's," she says, settling into a quieter corner of the bar, all casual-like. "Call for me there."

Give her a look, raising a brow. "You live at Claridge's?"

"Yes."

"You ain't got a number? Like, your own?"

"A mobile phone, do you mean?" She starts picking at her nail, then stops herself, like she's remembered who she's meant to be.

I nod.

"Well, I suppose I do have one, but I never use it?" She shakes her head. "They're so big and clunky. Who on earth is carrying around a bag large enough to house one of those? Also, my god— who wants to be contactable *all* the time? I barely like to be contacted *any* of the time."

Fuck me, she's class. Cooler than someone with a face like that should be. Fuckin' hell.

"Why d'you live in a hotel, then?" I ask, straight to the point.

"None of your business," she snaps back, sharp as owt, but I shake me head, proper firm.

"Nah, fuck that. You—everythin' about ya—that's all my business now."

Hits me with that look again, the one where she reckons I'm talkin' shite. Does summat to me, that. Proper scratches this itch I ain't even know I had. She's got these looks just for me like—seen 'em more than once now—reckon they're just mine. Dunno how I know, but I do.

"Oh, is that right?" she asks, shoulders square and proud.

Nod like I'm sure cos I fuckin' am. "That's righ'."

Our eyes lock, and there's somethin' electric between us, like you could bring the dead back to life with the spark. Step closer—wasn't much distance to begin with, you know? Whatever gap there was—gone now. My hands are on her face now, holdin' it. Ain't never held a girl's face before. Like fuck, sure, probably I have. Twenty-three, fucked 'round a bit, so yeah I've probably had me hands on a girl's face before, but it weren't like this, you know what I mean? Holdin' her face cos I can't look away. Starin' at it like one of them glass prisms that shoots rainbows and colours and fuckin' all sorts about. Hold her face up to the sun if I could. See if the light bounces off her too. Feels like it might just…

She's got a mouth on her, this one. Like it, but. I meant, like an attitude, you get me—? But fuck, like the actual proper mouth on this girl? Art. Michael-fuckin'-angelo himself carved it from stone.

Gone quiet now, she has. And like I said, I got that effect on girls—they go all quiet, get a bit shy and shit. Used to that. But this? It's different, innit? Ain't used to a girl messin' with me like this. Ain't used to me feelin' all…fuckin' lost, like I've gone and stepped outta me own skin or somethin'.

Never fuckin' followed after a girl before… Never had to. Never chased one down, never left where I wanted to be to go to some fuckin' yuppy, toffy members' club—and shut up and fuck you, Groucho's not the same, and you fuckin' know it.

Her face is still in my hands, eyes locked.

"Where'd you come from?" I say, not thinkin', just slips out.

"What?" She blinks, looks at me like I've gone mental. S'pose I have.

"Like, what the fuck was I doin' till now?" I shrug it off. "Who the fuck was I singin' about?"

And she looks lost for a second, caught in the same windstorm I guess I'm in, but then—fuck—gets a handle on herself, doesn't she? Takes my hands off her face—which makes me heart fucking ache in my chest as she does it—like, what the fuck is that—? What's happening to me right now?

Ysolde straightens up.

"Yes, Joah." She gives me a look. "Who *were* you singing about?"

"I—" Oops. I chuckle. "—Fuck, I dunno. They don't matter anymore, though."

Rolls those eyes of hers again, like she's going for some kind of record here. Or maybe I'm just exasperating.

"You're incredibly full of shit," she tells me. "Do you ever give a real answer to anything?"

I sigh, then shrug again. "My ex. And my brother's—fuck, I don't know what they are—? Sometimes girlfriend, sometimes not-girlfriend, always a fuckin' pain in my arse..."

She nods, thinking. "Who was your ex?"

"Just a bird from back home." I shake my head, like it don't matter. "You won't know her."

"What's her name?"

"Pippa," I tell her. "Sparrow," I add, dunno why. That's her name, innit.

Ysolde's face twitches, like she's tryin' to figure it out. "She sounds pretty."

"Yeah. She is. Nowt on you, though..." I throw it out there, hopin' it lands right.

She's not havin' it, though. "Hardly a fair comparison..."

I snort a laugh. "What, with you being a supermodel and shit?"

"*And shit*, yes." That has her givin' me this fed-up smile, but ain't really fed up with me. I can tell. "Why did you two break up?"

"Because I'm a piece of shit," I tell her, dead serious.

"Oh." She stares straight at me, flat as owt. "*Brilliant.*"

"Or—fuck!—I was," I clarify. "*Before.* Till I met you. And now I'm—"

I stop talking there because to finish that sentence would make me a proper fuckin' melt, but she goes and says it anyway, in a voice like she thinks I'm being stupid.

"—*a new man?*"

I don't say nothin' back, just nod. Yeah. Fuck yeah, I'm a new man. There was me before Ysolde Featherstonhaugh, and then there's me now, after.

She laughs, shakes her head like I'm a bloody idiot—which, yeah, fair play, I am. But no one knows that, except my brother. And her, apparently.

"Oi, can I take you home?"

She pulls a face. "That feels as though you're inviting yourself over to *my* home?"

"I am." I nod.

"Why aren't you inviting me to *your* home?"

That makes me chuckle, but it's fucking sharp, yeah? Makes me think for a second.

See, I bring girls back to mine all the time, no problem. Don't even think about it. But with her? Now I suddenly don't wanna do that. Don't even know why... Don't want her to be just another girl, I s'pose. Don't think she is one. And if I bring her back to mine, maybe she will be or she could be, and no—can't be having the likes of that.

Folds them arms of hers. "Wife and kids?"

"No, just don't reckon my sheets would be up to your thread-count standard..."

"Oh!" Her cheeks go all pink. "We're getting into bed now, are we?"

I tilt my head, proper smirk on my face. "Ain't we?"

"You're very cocky."

"Aye," I admit, no shame. "For good reason."

"Well, maybe I don't want you in my fancy sheets..."

"Right, first"—I throw her a look, like she's mad if she thinks otherwise—"you do. But second, that's sound. We can—I dunno—do it on a fuckin' table or summat... I'm easy."

TIME OF YOUR LIFE

She laughs. Proper laughs. Best sound I heard since that first time me mum showed me "Here Comes the Sun," which is funny now that I think of it. I reckon—somehow—them boys wrote that one about her. Feel like science might one day prove it that she, in fact, is the proper fuckin' sun. Shove me hands through my hair because my brain is stressin' me out. I don't fuckin' think about girls like this. I ain't a poetic lad—don't breathe a fucking word to anyone, but me brother writes most of the songs, and like, happy days, good for him, he can't sing for shit. Not compared to me anyway. We all need summat to get up in the morning for.

I'm not out here thinkin' about girls how I keep fuckin' accidentally thinkin' about her, know what I mean?

She's beamin' away at me though—it pulls me out of me head for a sec.

"How very big of you," she says, all cheeky.

"Well." I grin right back at her. "I am very big."

She blinks twice, her eyes flicker down—like, *down*, you get me?—just for a second—bit cheeky—then they meet mine again, and fuck, her eyes hit like a punch to the gut.

"We shall see," she says, her eyes all sparky.

Feels like there's electricity in my blood, like a fuckin' engine roarin' in me stomach, and I want her—fuck, I want her more than I've ever wanted anyone, ever.

And then I'm fucking kissing the daylights out of her, right? Because how the fuck could I not?

Girls' mouths are always soft but her lips are pillows, and I don't know how many girls I've kissed at this point of my life—arguably, some might say too many—doesn't matter anyway, because fucking none of them hold a candle to this.

I don't believe in fate; I don't believe in all that shit about "the one"—or I didn't. Might do now. Now that I've kissed her and it's like, what the fuck was I doing kissing other people before? Waste of my fucking time, wasn't it? Didn't know bodies could slot together like hers does as I'm holding her against me now.

It's about a ten-minute walk from 5 Hertford Street to Claridge's but walkin' would mean I'd have to stop kissing her, so fuckin' fuck that. Just pull her downstairs towards a cab—and if you can believe it, that security lad of hers, he grabs me—fuckin' grabs me arm, he does.

I fling him off me without a thought and give him a proper shove. "Fuckin' touch me again, lad, let's see what happens."

She shakes her head at me quickly like, puts a hand on me chest to calm me down—like that. "He's just doing his job," she says. "It's his job to keep me safe."

"She's fine, mate. In good hands." I pull her into the taxi, and that fucker's face? Looks proper worried, and it's startin' to wind me up like.

What's the fuckin' problem, you know what I mean? Either he cares too much about his job or he's bollocksed in love with her. Neither's grand, but one of 'em's proper pissin' me off right now.

"I'm okay," she says to him, voice mostly steady, but then she turns and looks at me. "Right?"

It's a genuine question, that, and it fucks with me a bit. This girl's askin' if she's gonna be alright with me. Like, she's not sure if I'm gonna fuck it all up, and for a split second, I start thinkin' maybe she's got a point.

I nod once, feelin' this weird responsibility that wasn't there three seconds ago. Don't know if I'm ready for it or even want it, but fuck it. Heavy is the head, and she's the fuckin' crown.

"I'm right behind you," the bodyguard tells her before he slams the cab door shut.

I sit back, arm slung round her like I own the fuckin' place.

"He's a bit intense."

She gives me some Mona Lisa–PR smile, doesn't say a word. Can't tell if she's happy or sad, but there's somethin' there, innit? Something she's not sayin'.

Mood shifts after that, not for the better. It's only a three-minute drive to her hotel, but she's holdin' my hand the whole way, playin' with it like it's nothin'. Kinda like it, but.

TIME OF YOUR LIFE

She says hi to the doorman and the bellhop like she's fuckin' Eloise, all casual and confident.

We take the lift up to the seventh floor, follow her down the hall—still hand in hand—towards some fuckin' big, posh door.

She swings it open and chucks her bag on a chair.

I glance 'round. "Being a model pays well, huh?"

"Oh, haven't you heard?" She leans back against a table. "We don't get out of bed for less than ten thousand pounds."

"Ten thousand quid to stand there and look pretty—? Fuck off." Like, come off it... That's fucking annoying.

She stares at me unapologetic. "Ten thousand pounds to stand there and look pretty and convince you in a singular frame that whatever I'm touching or wearing or representing is something you must possess at all costs."

And fair play to her, I don't know what the fuck she's peddlin' right now but, yeah, I'd take ten of 'em, so I guess she's worth every penny.

Fuck, she's fit. I go to say somethin', but then there's a bang at the door.

I glower over at it, and she rolls her eyes.

"It's just Kekoa. I'll only be a second."

And I watch her the whole way. How she moves across the room, how she slides the brass door chain unlocked, how she opens the door. All proper mundane shit, but I can't take my eyes off her.

"Everything all good in here?" I hear that fucking bodyguard say.

"I'm fine," she says, all calm.

"You sure?" the nosy prick asks.

She lowers her voice, like I ain't supposed to hear. "I think he's quite sweet."

That proper throws me. Fuckin' shits me, even. Sweet? I ain't sweet. What the fuck is she on about?

And to his credit, the bodyguard backs up me point. "He isn't. But I'm down the hall. Panic button if you need me."

Panic button—? What the fuck?

"Good night—" she calls to him before she slams the door shut and walks back towards me, all ginger like, like I'm gonna bite her or somethin'.

"What's his deal?"

"No deal," she says all cool.

I give her a look like I ain't buyin' it, which I'm fucking not, by the way—I'm no muppet. But she just gives me that same look back, only this time it's a bit more stubborn, more defiant.

I breathe out, fuckin' annoyed. "You still wanna do this?"

It's starting to feel complicated, and thank fuck it is, cos I ain't lovin' these fuckin' butterflies, and honestly? Probably be a bit relieved if she said she don't wanna do it no more.

"Yes." She nods. "I'm just a tiny bit in my head now."

"Yeah—" I jerk my head towards the door. "Your mate's a right fucking mood killer."

She goes stiff at that. "I'll be sure to tell him."

I stare at her, press my lips together, and think—*fuck it. This ain't fun no more.* Only do what I want, don't I? I only do fun shit. And feelin's? Nah, fuck 'em. Ain't for me. That's why I don't get 'em.

What the fuck am I doin', but? What am I even here for—passive-aggressively havin' a go at some girl I just met 'bout her fuckin' bodyguard—who's just doin' his job, fair play to him?

Too much drama, this.

Don't want it.

Nod toward the door. "Right, yeah. I'm off."

"Fine." She shrugs, acts unbothered, but I see it—she's bothered some, cos then she says, "You know, *you* chased me…left where *you* were to find *me*, asked *me* to come back to *my* place—"

"Yeah." I nod. "And?"

Shakes her head, looks over my shit she does, but grand cos I'm fuckin' over hers too and I only met her an hour ago.

"And nothing. I was just reminding you." I nod once, turn on me foot, and walk out her hotel door, slammin' it behind me.

TIME OF YOUR LIFE

Regret. *Instantly*. Fuckin' slap to the face, it is. Me head drops back, and I silently scream *fuck* at the ceiling. Drop me face to my hands, tryna make sense of what the fuck is goin' on with me now.

I don't fuckin' regret things. Don't have arguments with girls I don't even know cos the night ain't going how I fuckin' daydreamed it would an hour ago when I first saw her across a club. Mate, I don't fuckin' daydream at all.

But now? I've got this fuckin' weird feelin' like—I dunno, if I just walk away, I'm gonna fuck up the rest of me life. Which is mental. Like, proper mental, I know—like, man, get a fuckin' grip, yeah? But like…I don't got one no more. Not since I saw her, lost it the second I did. Which is why I find meself doin' somethin' I ain't never done before.

I turn back 'round and knock on her door.

About ten seconds and it's just fuck-all silent. Me heart sinks, if you can believe it. The state of me, man. Then I hear her on the other side—door creaks open—she don't even fill the frame. Yeah like, she's tall for a girl, but Christ, she's tiny—all frownin' at me like I pissed her off, arms crossed tight over her chest.

Her brows are up, proper annoyed. "What?" she snaps, impatient as fuck.

And then I rush her. One hand in her hair, the other on her face cos that face, man—

Her lips part in surprise as mine smash into hers again. Don't even know why we stopped in the first place. Happy to be back. Ain't gonna make that mistake again.

Different this time, innit? We're behind closed doors now. More lean-in from her, and it's mad, cos I thought we were made from the same fuckin' stone the first time. But now? Now she coils 'round me, presses herself into me as I carry her through the toffiest room I ever stepped foot in in me life. We're stumblin' towards her bedroom, movin' backwards, sideways, bangin' into walls, and I dunno when me jacket and shirt came off—but they're gone now. And her hands? Fuckin' everywhere—my jeans, my chest, my hair—her hands in my hair, holy shit! Heaven. Like, yeah, Charlie's good, but this? This is fuckin' summat else.

I fall backwards onto her bed, bring her down with me—she pulls back for a second, eyes blurry and heavy how eyes go when they're cloudy with lust, know what I mean? She tilts her head, staring at me.

Prop meself up, give her a bit of a smile. "What?"

She puts her hand on me cheek.

"I get it," she says after a sec.

Give her a look. "Get what?"

"You." She shrugs. "Why people lose their minds about you. I get it now. Your face is—" She stops talking, scoffs, a bit like she can't properly believe it.

"My face is what?" I push. Wanna see where she's goin' with this, don't I? Know I'm gonna like it…

A little frown flickers over her face, goes all serious. I'll write songs for the rest of me life about how her mouth goes when she's serious, I swear to fuck I will.

"A masterpiece," she says, but all solemn about it.

Now if you ask anyone who knows me proper well, they'll tell ya: I already got a pretty big head, don't I? But when she says that, I'm buzzin', man. Chuffed.

"What's this from?" Her finger traces the scar by my right eye. Girls love scars, don't they? Fuckin' eat 'em up, you know? Dunno why.

Give her a half smile. "Don't worry about it," I tell her because that's not a part me life I want her to know about, you get me? No fuckin' way is that part of me ever gonna make sense to her.

Lie back down on her pillow—smells like her, right? How the fuck do I already know what she smells like, is what I wanna know. It's lemons, by the way. She fuckin' smells like lemons, and I'm mad for it. I ain't never paid much attention to how a person smells before. Like, sure, I've smelled girls before, probably—in passing, yeah? They all just smelled like…I dunno, *girls*?

TIME OF YOUR LIFE   27

But she smells like lemons.

Catch meself sniffing her hair, and she catches me. Starts laughin', shakin' her head.

Now, look—I ain't one to take too well to people laughin' at me… Might let her laugh at me forever, though. Maybe. Just cos I like the sound.

"What are you doing?" She grins.

"Why do you smell like lemons?"

She brushes her hair over her shoulders—dark, long, wavy— and I'm hit with another wave of lemon. She shrugs.

"Only smell I like."

Tilt my head, offer her me neck. "Like how I smell?"

She breathes me in and her eyes pinch playfully. "You smell like…cigarettes. And beer."

I flash her a grin. "Yeah, I fuckin' do."

She smiles down at me, and I push some hair back behind her ear. Eyes go soft 'round the edges, hers. And if I'm honest? All of me's soft 'round the edges for this girl now. Like a right fuckin' melt. Tell meself to snap out of it. I'm Joah fuckin' Harrigan.

In one move—worked a fuckin' treat on other birds before— flip her so she's underneath, me on top. Stares up at me, blinkin', patient as owt. Like she's got all the time in the world. Maybe she does, I dunno. Either way, I'll give her all mine.

"Ready?" I check, cos let's be honest, lads, consent matters.

"You talk a lot…"

"Alrigh'—" I roll my eyes, holdin' back a chuckle. The fuckin' nerve, know what I mean?

She bats her eyes at me bold as owt so I push into her, and that little breath she takes—? Fuck, I'm done for. No two ways about it. Thirty seconds inside her, and I know—I'm so fuckin' in over my head with this girl, it ain't even funny. And you know what? Happy fuckin' days. Never liked shallow water much anyway.

KING OF ROCK CROSSES PATHS WITH RUNWAY QUEEN

By Fiona Tate, Entertainment Correspondent, The Daily Sun

It looks like rock 'n' roll's reigning bad boy Joah Harrigan has traded his usual chaos for a bit of class. The Fallow front man was spotted getting cosy with supermodel Ysolde Featherstonhaugh during a raucous night out in London's trendiest haunts.

The pair were first seen at Soho's notorious celebrity hangout The Groucho Club, where insiders say Harrigan, 22, was "on top form," downing whiskey and charming the room in his signature scruffy style. But it wasn't long before his attention zeroed in on the impossibly glamorous Ysolde, 20, who had arrived earlier with her entourage of fashion-world glitterati.

An eagle-eyed source tells the Mail: "Ysolde was holding court in her usual way—elegant, untouchable, completely captivating. Joah made a beeline for her as soon as he spotted her. It was like a moth to a flame. And who could blame him?"

By all accounts, the pair exchanged a few words before Ysolde made a swift exit, reportedly heading to the members-only club 5 Hertford Street.

Did that stop Harrigan? Not a chance. The Mancunian rocker, dressed in jeans and one of his signature jackets and looking every bit the rebellious artist he's known to be, followed her across town.

A witness at the Mayfair hot spot dished: "Joah wasn't even subtle about it. He walked in like a man on a mission and headed straight for her table. It was electric—she didn't seem surprised to see him, but she wasn't exactly throwing herself into his arms, either. He sat down anyway. Classic Joah."

The duo spent the rest of the night deep in conversation, with Ysolde sipping champagne and Joah nursing yet another whiskey.

TIME OF YOUR LIFE

But was it love at first sight—or just another chapter in Harrigan's long list of fleeting flames?

"She's not one to waste her time," one insider remarked, "but Joah? He loves wasting girls' time. That's his favourite pastime."

Adding fuel to the fire, the two were later spotted leaving 5 Hertford Street together, sharing a cab back to Claridge's, where Ysolde reportedly maintains a private residence.

Whether this is the start of a whirlwind romance or just another late-night misadventure for Harrigan, one thing's for certain: the London social scene is in for a show.

THREE

joah

RIGHT, SO HERE'S THE THING—KISSIN' Ysolde Featherstonhaugh? That was a proper headfuck on its own, yeah? But havin' *sex* with her? Christ almighty, that was out of this fuckin' world. No lie. Like, I wasn't high tonight or owt—not even a cheeky spliff—but might as well have been.

Thing is, I'm not the biggest fan of what comes after sex, you know? Girls don't always know what to do with it—fair enough, it's a weird adjustment, innit? Before sex like, and even during, there's this—I dunno—haze? Warps how close you are actually to the person you're with, crazy close like—and it feels real, don't it? Right up until you come and then—gone. Like someone switched the lights on and you're lookin' round thinkin', *What the fuck now?*

Weird, innit?

Some girls hang about, yeah? Try and stretch that closeness out longer—but me? Once I'm done, I'm done. Ready for 'em to sling their hook—just want 'em outta there, you get me? But her? Lyin' there in her bed tonight…mate, you couldn't pay me to get up and go.

And here's the mad part—she ain't even doing owt sexy, nowt wild or over-the-top. She's just there, you know? Just—existing like.

TIME OF YOUR LIFE   31

Leant back against the fuckin' thirty-five pillows on her bed in nowt but a white vest that—thank you, God—is real fuckin' sheer, and some lacy knickers that are different to the ones I took off her just before, so fingers crossed I get to take these ones off her too, know what I mean?

She stares over at me and plucks the cigarette that's hangin' from me mouth. Takes a drag, bats her eyes calmly, like she doesn't have a fuckin' care in the world.

Never done this before—not since Pip, anyway. And that was different, wasn't it? Proper relationship, started seeing each other when we were eighteen, on and off for two years. Bit of a circus, that. But this? Here, now? This ain't the same. It's... I dunno. Lying in bed with her shooting the shit is par for the course of a relationship like that, but this—here—it's something else.

"Do you have any secrets?" she asks, battin' them lashes like she didn't just go and lob the most diabolical question fuckin' known to man right bang into the room. Sounds cute comin' from her, but. Everythin' do though, don't it?

Give her a suspicious look. "Yeah."

"Tell me one?"

Nod me chin at her. "You first."

"There are like three different boys that all believe I lost my virginity to them."

I squint at her. "Why?"

"Because I told each of them that I lost my virginity to them." She shrugs. "Men go mad for it. I'm not sure know why—"

I start laughin'. Fuck, that's pretty funny, innit? She's not wrong, I guess. Summat about it.

"So who'd you lose it to?" I ask.

She stares me in the eye, face all proper straight. "You."

Makes me laugh, that, and that makes her happy which makes me happy because I don't know, suppose I am a soft lad now, aren't I?

"Now you go," she tells me.

Push me hands through my hair as I have a think. "Dunno—I kind of wanna join the Twenty-Seven Club."

"You want to… *die*…by the time you're twenty-seven?" she asks, dead serious.

I shrug. "Maybe."

Her eyes do this quick sweep of my face, up and down, like she's sizin' me up. "How old are you now?"

"Twenty-three."

She don't look confused, not really—nah, she's more pissed off than owt. "So you'd like to *die* in *four* years?"

Another shrug from me. "Pretty fuckin' rock and roll."

"Pretty fucking stupid," she fires back, ain't even a pause there to think about it.

Takes me back a bit. Hope she don't catch that on me face— feel like she might have but, so firstly, fuck her for that, you get me? And second, fuck it—I would really fancy fuckin' her for that. There's summat about being called on me shit, you know?

I lift a brow. "You callin' me stupid?"

"If you want to die in four years purely for the sake of *rock and roll*, you don't need me to call you stupid—your desires are doing that for you."

Scratch me neck, don't look away from those eyes of hers. "Rock and roll is me whole fuckin' life, you know what I mean?"

She gives me this smile—annoyin', man—almost like she's sorry for me or summat, you know? Then she fuckin' uppercuts me again with a little whisper. "Well, perhaps you should find something else to live for, then."

I stare over at her—best face I ever fuckin' saw, and I've seen a lot faces—wonder to meself if maybe I have just—? Found somethin' else to live for, I mean. Maybe I found her on some shite Sunday night, end of Feb 1995.

She watches me closely as she takes a drag of my cigarette. "What's your favourite element?"

Give her a bit of a frown. "What?"

TIME OF YOUR LIFE

Take back my cig from her.

"Element," she says, her little eyebrows arched up. "You know, like earth, wind, f—"

"It ain't obvious?" Give her a look for not fuckin' knowin' that about me already as I take a drag. "Fire."

"Oh," she goes but she don't look all that happy with me answer—and you know what's fuckin' weird? Don't like it. Don't fuckin' like that she ain't happy with my fuckin' answer, but why the fuck do I give a shit, know what I mean?

Nod my chin at her. "What's yours?"

She pursues her lips. "Water." She fights off a bit of a smile. Fuck, she's cute. Ain't never called a bird "cute" in me fuckin' life, but here we are.

She gives me an awkward smile. "Which bodes rather well for us…"

I let out a "hah," like it means fucking shit—know what I mean? Girls go funny about shit like that, but it don't mean owt.

"Oi." Nod my chin at her. "Here's an actual important question, yeah—What's your favourite song?" I ask her.

"Of yours?" she asks the ceiling.

Shrug like that ain't fucking exactly what I was fishin' for. "Sure, go on—"

She glances over at me, grimaces a bit. "I don't…know…a lot of your music?"

Sorry, wait—what the fuck?

Scrunch me face up at her. Can't believe it, can I—is she havin' a laugh?

I scoff. "What the fuck?"

Everyone knows our music. Like, everyone. I mean—fuck me. *Probably Never* is literally the fastest-sellin' debut album in the history of British music. That ain't just big—mate, that's fuckin' massive.

She gives this little shrug, all apologetic-like. "I just know the big ones…"

I glare at her, full-on scowl. "They're all fuckin' big ones."

Rolls her eyes at me, fed up. And, swear to god, her lookin' done with me might be the best drug I've ever had. Proper rush. Gives me this weird, fucked-up thrill, having to try hard to impress someone, you know—? Cos these days, I don't gotta try at all, do I? I could cough in the drink of every other girl on the planet, and they'd probably thank me, might even ask me to do it again.

Not her, but. Nah, she'd probably fuckin' cough right back—and then chuck the whole thing straight in me face.

"Go on." I nod at her. "Favourite song ever then…"

She purses them lips of hers, thinkin'.

"I don't know. It's a tie probably. Between 'Crimson and Clover' and 'Unchained Melody.'"

"Whoa," I say—and shit. Didn't mean to say that out loud, did I—but fuck, here we are, all the same.

Surprises me, then. Dunno why that surprises me—just, I had this weird dread in me that she was gonna like, break my heart and say a fucking Take That song. Maybe Celine Dion—? But Tommy James and the Righteous Brothers? I can work with that, know what I mean?

"What?" She frowns defensively.

"I dunno." I shrug, and that much is true. "You. Everythin' about ya… It's all whoa, innit?"

Her cheeks go pink, and she rolls over, face down, into her pillow.

"That was a very cute thing to say," she says, voice muffled now by her pillow.

"No, fuck—" I shove her—not too hard but, cos I'm pretty sure if you pushed her too hard, she'd fly off like a crisp packet in a breeze. "I'm—no—I ain't cute. Fuck that."

She peeks up at me from her pillow, sly as you like, side-eyein' me. And the way she's lookin'—the way her face is just there, grinnin' even though I can't really see her gob—it's dead obvious she don't agree.

Nod my chin at her, proper eager to move on from all this cute shite, cos let's have it right, I ain't fuckin' cute, am I? Nah, I'm a fuckin' legend, man.

So I go for it—the question I've been gaggin' to ask her all night. Try to play it dead casual, though, not like some clingy fucker.

"You seen me play before?"

She rolls back in towards me.

"Once." She gives me a small smile. "Glastonbury last year."

"Oh, fuck—" My face drops, and I know I look more gutted than I should. Proper embarrassin', really like—Why the fuck do I even care? Know it wasn't my best show, yeah, but it was fuckin' Glasto. Don't need to prove myself to anyone.

But now all I can think about is her stood in the crowd when I ballsed up that one note in "Ultra Violet." Makes me want to chuck meself straight off the terrace just thinkin' about it, you know?

Try to laugh it off, dead casual. "Sounded proper shite that day, didn't I?"

She rolls her eyes. "No, you didn't."

"No, I did, yeah…" I shrug. It's true but. "We're better now."

"Well, I thought you were good then."

Shake my head at her because she's wrong—we weren't. Thought we were, but I'm fuckin' better now. Does make me happy though, that she were there, know what I mean? That she saw me up there. Me first Glasto, that's kinda a fuckin' thing, innit? Not gonna say it to her, though, like a right fuckin' nutter, but I reckon like maybe one day I might be pretty fuckin' chuffed she was there just.

"We're playin' this year again," I tell her. "Come. I'll do better."

She smiles, amused, then nods. "Okay."

"Promise?" I ask, brow up.

She nods again once. "I promise."

Then she does this half-smile thing, and fuck me, I'm prayin' she only smiles at me like that from now on. Can't fuckin' stand the thought of her flashin' that at everyone. Girls like her, but? Sometimes they're like that, ain't they? Don't even mean to be—just have this way of makin' everyone feel like they're the most important person in the world because they're paying attention to 'em. And like, let's be honest, I'm fuckin' important, fuck—maybe more than ever now that I got her attention all on me, you know? Very fuckin' aware I am that I needa fucking keep it too.

"Oi." Nod my chin at her. "We have a show this week at the Electric Ballroom."

She looks surprised. "Is that not a rather small venue for you now?"

I nod, try not to look too happy that she knows enough about what I do to get venue size.

"Yeah, it's part of this hometown-tour thing me manager's workin'—I don't know, like, we're grounded in our roots or some shite—" I roll my eyes, even though Mick's nowhere near me. Mick Sloane—good manager, proper good, but he's still a bit of a knob at times. "We've got Electric Ballroom this week, and then, end of March, we're doing two back-to-back at The Haçienda. Bit small for us now, really, but it's the fucking Haçienda, innit? Proper legendary. Come to that too."

She looks a bit taken aback, pleasantly surprised or something. "To Manchester?"

"Well." I shoot her a look, smirkin'. "Let's see how Camden goes first, yeah? You need to come to that one."

She rolls her eyes right back at me. "Need to, do I?"

"Yeah." I nod, dead serious. "Might die if you don't."

She pulls her knees up to her chest, all tucked in like a little ball, and rests her chin on one of 'em. And I've never been jealous of a fucking knee before, but here we are.

Got me sittin' here wonderin' what the fuck a bloke's gotta do to get a supermodel to rest her chin on him instead of herself.

"You're not how I thought you'd be," she says, watchin' me.

Me eyes pinch. "How'd you think I'd be, then?"

"Well, I suppose in some ways you're *exactly* what I imagined—"

I wait for her to go on.

TIME OF YOUR LIFE

"I mean—" She shrugs. "For one, you have the biggest head of any person I've ever met."

I roll my eyes. "No, I don't."

"You *literally* think you're the biggest rock star in the world."

"I *am* the biggest rock star in the world."

She waves her hand at me, like—fucking case in point.

"Oi, am I not, but?" I quip.

She straightens up demurely. "Other people wouldn't say it."

I lean in towards her with a little smirk, drop my voice to a whisper. "Well, that's because other people aren't the biggest rock star in the world, innit?"

She sniffs a laugh, tries to act like she thinks I'm an idiot and not proper sexy.

"But tell me—" I tilt my head, proper studying her now. "How I'm not what you imagined."

I watch this little battle play out on her face, like she's trying not to smile. Dead entertainin', honestly.

"*Tell me about me, Ysolde,*" she says, puttin' on this fucking daft voice that's s'posed to be me. "*Talk to me about me more!*"

"Okay—" I chuckle, shakin' me head, even though it's windin' me up a bit. Hate it when people clock me for that kind of shit. Hate it a bit less comin' from her but. Which is fuckin' weird. "Ysolde can fuck off now."

"Mmm…" She pulls a face, proper smug, playing along. "Ysolde is in her own hotel room…"

And fuck me—I want to kiss her so fucking bad, it's driving me mental. But she's being a twat, so I can't.

I decide to pivot. "Ysolde's a fuckin' weird name, innit?"

Admittedly, bit of a weird pivot but here we are.

"I suppose—" She shrugs, not precious about it at all. "My father studied English at Cambridge—" She bats away another smile, and I catch it just before it's gone. "I think he thought he'd like me more at the time he named me."

My face pulls, proper surprised. "He don't like you?"

She shakes her head, like it's the easiest thing in the world to get. "Nope."

I toss her a half a smile and look down at her, a bit pleased. Ain't pleased for her but there's summat about knowing we've got this little crack of common ground.

"Mine don't like me either," I tell her.

She sits up straight, chuffed now, like we just found out we're members of this same fucked-up, secret club. S'pose we are.

Then her eyes pinch suspiciously.

"I don't believe you. You are every father's dream—" Shakes her head. "A son who grew up to be the biggest rock star in the world—"

Point at her, dead smug. "I fucking *knew* you knew I'm the biggest star in the world!" I say, proper chuffed with myself.

Without missing a beat, she just reaches out, wraps her whole hand 'round my finger that's pointing at her, like it's nowt, keeps talkin', she does—one eyebrow arched.

"—you're in the biggest band in the world—? That'd make every father proud."

My heart sinks in me chest like a fuckin' stone, flash her a smile but feel it on me own face, how it don't reach the edges.

"Not every father." And then I feel fucking weird and exposed, and fuck that, I hate that shit, so I gesture at her. "No way with you, but. You're perfect."

Last part of what I said makes her happy.

"Actually—" Pushes her hair over her shoulders, she does. "If you think about it, I'm kind of a father's nightmare..."

I do think on it for a second. Girl like her, with a face like that, doin' a job like hers, in a world like this one? I mean, fuck—girls like her end up in hotel rooms with boys like me.

"Shit"—I try to hold it in, but a laugh slips out anyway—"you kinda are."

"I know!" Her head falls back, all exasperated and dramatic.

"Sorry—" I laugh, shaking my head. "So your old man's a bit of a cunt, then?"

TIME OF YOUR LIFE

Her whole face proper screws up. "I don't like that word."

Makes me laugh till I realise she's bein' dead serious.

"Won't ever say it again." Say that like I'm jokin', but I ain't. Want this girl's approval in me arm like a fuckin' IV drip.

"But yes." Small nod from her. "He is, but it's fine—I think it's just bad because my mum's dead, that's all."

My face drops, proper gutted. I love me mum. Best girl in the world, maybe except for this one in front of me. "Your mum's dead?"

She nods, like it's just fact. "I think if she were here, it wouldn't matter that he doesn't like me…"

I stare at her for a few seconds, tryna wrap my head 'round it. Tryna imagine how miserable and downright fuckin' sad her old man must be to not like her. Sittin' here in front of me like this, she's fuckin' perfect and she's ain't doin' owt. He's got no time for her? Fuckin' piece of shit.

I give her a small smile, soft as I can manage.

"Oi, it'd matter still," I tell her. Sound sadder than I mean to too, don't I? Maybe I am sadder than I wanna be about it meself.

"Would it?" she asks.

I nod once, like I'm an absolute authority on the matter. Am though. Unfortunately.

"Yep."

Her eyes immediately get a bit rounder and heavier, but I don't think it's for her. I think it's for me?

"I'm sorry," she says softly.

"I'm sorry too," I say back, voice low. Then I lean in, brushing my mouth over hers. Bit of a weird kiss for me, if I'm honest—no fireworks or fanfare, none of that shite. Just a kiss to kiss her because she's her and I want to.

We lie there, noses pressed up against each other's, and this is all sorts of fucked-up for me. Me heart's goin' like a jackhammer, proper poundin' in me chest like—gonna beat itself to fuckin' death at this rate, but I can't help it. It's just—her, man.

Then she rolls on top of me, and we go at it again, straight from the top, except this time it's different. Before her hands were everywhere, fuckin' everywhere, all over me, all this fucking grabbin', like this sexy sorta desperation about us that I fuckin' loved—but now her hands on me, they're slow. Measured. Sounds borin'—maybe it is borin' like, fuck if I can tell anymore. Can tell you this, though—whatever this is, she and me, I'm done for, man. I'm well fucked.

HAS ROCK GOD JOAH HARRIGAN BEEN STRUCK BY CUPID'S ARROW?

By Fiona Tate, Entertainment Correspondent, The Daily Sun

Rumour has it that rock's favourite wild child Joah Harrigan hasn't left supermodel Ysolde's private residence at Claridge's in an entire week. Could the bad boy of Britpop finally be hanging up his chaos crown for love?

Following their headline-making first encounter at Soho's Groucho Club last week—culminating in a cosy exit to Ysolde's Mayfair residence—the pair have reportedly been inseparable ever since.

Sources whisper that Joah, 22, has swapped his usual tour-bus lifestyle for the plush luxury of Ysolde's world, with insiders claiming he's been seen slipping in and out of Claridge's at all hours, often looking dishevelled but undeniably pleased with himself.

"He's barely left," a source close to the model dished. "Joah's got this way about him—he just takes over. It's like he's completely captivated her. But whether it's love or just a fleeting obsession, only time will tell."

It's a whirlwind that's got London buzzing. Some call them the city's newest "it" couple, whilst others are less optimistic about their long-term prospects.

"She's the kind of woman who looks like she has her life meticulously ordered," says a fashion industry insider. "But Ysolde's no stranger to a whirlwind romance. She's been linked to plenty of famous faces, so Joah's hardly her first rodeo. That said, he's different—more chaotic, more...unpredictable. Who knows if it'll last."

FOUR

ysolde

I WALK INTO QUAGLINO'S, ALEKI trailing behind me, and I swear his size and demeanour brings more attention to us than I inherently do myself. We spot my friends and he sits at his own table, giving us some smile.

"Oh my god, look who it is," Chloe quips as she spots me.

She's prettier in person, I think. I mean, she's pretty onstage too, but she wears too much makeup up there. In real life, with her dyed jet-black hair and dark blue eyes, she doesn't really need much else. Usually just sports a very pink lip. Last year *Rolling Stone* declared her to have taken the crown from Madonna as the queen of pop. (Who's to say whether that was taken on the chin?) (It was not.)

"Mrs. Joah Harrigan," Pixie Fife chides. Very blond hair chopped very short, skin like it's never seen the sun a day in its life. The absolute fucking worst PA you've ever met in your life, she is. Regrettably, she is mine though.

"Stop—" I roll my eyes at both of them as I throw myself down in the chair next to Lala, who doesn't say a word, just throws her arm around me and kisses my cheek.

"No—" Chloe shakes her head. "We have some questions."

TIME OF YOUR LIFE

I settle back in my chair and brace myself. "I'm sure you do."

Lala subtly elbows me because she thinks Chloe's too nosy at the best of times.

"How the fuck did this even happen?" Chloe smacks her hand down on the table, frightening away a waiter, who Lala touches the arm of and nods at me. "Tom Collins for her when you can, thanks."

"I love Fallow—" Chloe keeps going. "I've been to all their shows, and I've said so many times in so many interviews that they've been a huge influence for me." She's frowning now. "I always position myself in Joah Harrigan's line of sight, both at the shows and whenever we're out and they're like, there or whatever, and nothing—"

La gives her a judgmental look. "Well, that's probably why."

"Do you like him?" I ask Chloe.

Lala rolls her eyes. "She doesn't know him."

"Well, not biblically like Sol does now, presumably," she laments.

Lala tosses me an annoyed glance. It's supposed to be subtle, but it's not. Lala's terrible at hiding her expressions. Whatever she's feeling, it's always clear as glass. Some people hate it—lots of people, actually. I love it. I think it's funny; it can make people really uncomfortable around her, but I think it's refreshing.

"How big is it?" my PA suddenly asks.

I give her a warning look. "Pixie."

"No—" Chloe shakes her head. "I'm with her: How big is it?"

I turn to Lala, try to change the subject.

"Where's Riley?"

"Japan," La tells me. "Press tour."

Pixie's undeterred though. "Just tell me when—"

She starts with her hands close together, slowly draws them apart.

I roll my eyes at her ridiculousness. "Stop."

She does indeed stop—hands frozen—she stares at the measure between them, crestfallen. Not even two inches between her hands.

"Really?"

"What—?" I shake my head, confused by her reaction and then I realise. Roll my eyes again. "Oh, no—Pix—" I look at Joah's supposed measure again and start laughing. "No—"

"Okay, so just say when then!" Her hands start moving again, slowly farther apart. "Just say when…" The distance between her hands grows a little more. "When?" It keeps growing, her face falters. "When?" Growing still. "Oh my god—"

I take an exasperated breath. "Pix, I will take this opportunity to gently remind you that you are quite possibly *the* very worst personal assistant who exists on the planet. You barely ever assist me generally, let alone personally, so I do suggest that when I say 'stop' you do in fact…stop."

Pixie nods once with an obedience she rarely ever sports. "And zip." She mimes it as she says it.

"Well." Lala gives me a sorry look. "To be fair, I'm not your PA and I'd actually like to know how big—"

I lean in towards her, cover my mouth, and whisper. "Maybe two or three centimetres bigger than that butter knife." I eyeball the already quite-large butter knife that sits in front of us on the table and Lala snaps her head to face me immediately.

"Fuck! Off!" She stares at me in disbelief, then asks genuinely, "Are you okay?"

Chloe huffs across the table, arms crossed, a tiny bit annoyed, but I don't care at all.

"I'm perfect, thank you very much," I tell them all, my nose in the air.

"God—" Chloe shakes her head at me, a bit (albeit reluctantly) impressed. "She really does have that lovely after-sex glow, doesn't she?"

"Unzip"—Pixie mimes unzipping her mouth—"fuck, Solly, please, I just want to know everything. When did it happen? And actually, where? Every place, doesn't have to be chronological, though that would be preferable if not helpful—"

TIME OF YOUR LIFE 45

I give her a long-suffering look, as though it pains me to talk about it—as though I haven't replayed the last few days in a loop in my own mind even when Joah's been lying right next to me.

"Sunday night was the first time, like when we met—We were at Groucho. Then we left and he followed me to Hertford—"

"I didn't know he followed you!" Chloe blinks in disbelief.

"Oh my god!" Pix squeals. "Joah Harrigan following you. Fittest man in the world, go on…"

Lala gives me a silent but encouraging smile.

"And then we…went to my hotel…and we…you know…" I trail. Which evidently was not enough information for Pixie.

"Was it like, you know—on the bed?"

I think back to it. "Yes." I pause. "Well, the first time."

"And the second time?" Lala asks with a smirk.

"Oh—actually, and the second time," I concede.

Pixie's eyes pinch. "What about third time?"

"Oh my god, Pix!" I growl, exasperated. "Fuck!" I rattle them off my fingers as I think back over the past few days. "Balcony, bathroom vanity, up against a bookcase, on a piano, in my town car, in the loo of the Claridge's lobby. In Selfridges—"

"In Selfridges?" Chloe repeats back, horrified but a bit enthralled.

"Yeah, just a quickie. He's really strong."

"With the stamina of a horse, apparently," Lala adds, impressed.

"How many times is that?" Pixie asks.

I squash a laugh and try not to look too starry-eyed as I answer. "Infinity."

Chloe stares at me, not blinking. "I can't believe you've had so much sex with Joah fucking Harrigan that you've actually lost count."

I shrug a sorry.

Pixie squeals and I suppose that's when Lala deems her over-the-top, because she just slides away Pixie's cosmopolitan so it's out of her reach.

Chloe breathes out, annoyed. "I have never been so jealous of a person in my whole fucking life, like I sort of want to punch you—"

I give her a curt smile. "I would prefer you didn't…"

"When are you seeing him again?" La asks.

"I don't know—in like an hour probably? He's having lunch with his brother…"

"Oh my god!" Chloe sits up straight. "Can I date the brother? That works too."

I take a giant sidestep around the "too" in that sentence—trade looks with Lala for it though. Obviously—and shake my head, because I don't know.

"I haven't met the brother."

"Are you going to their show tomorrow night?" Chloe asks, eyebrows up.

Lala's eyes flick over all of Chloe. "You know too much about them."

"Yes," Chloe concedes with a nod before she looks back at me. "But are you?"

"Well, yeah—he asked me to go."

Chloe's eyes go wide. "Oh my god."

I look over at Lala. "But I said I'd only go if you go, Lalee."

She huffs out her nose, at least a bit because I called her Lalee and she pretends to hate it, but she doesn't really.

"Twist my arm, why don't you—" my best friend says with a reluctant smile, then she grabs my hand and pulls me up and away from the other two girls. "Okay, come on, we have to talk—"

"Wait no, that's not fair, come back!" Pixie calls to us but we're already a bit away. She pouts. "I hate it when you two leave us out—"

"Well," I remind her, "*we* are best friends, and *you* are technically my employee…"

Pix rolls her eyes and Chloe waves a hand like, *um hello?*

"Well, what about me, then?" Chlo asks.

Lala shakes her head. "You benched yourself with your enthusiasm for the boy she's fucking." Lala gives her a curt smile. "Bye."

TIME OF YOUR LIFE

She pulls me into the disabled loo and locks the door behind us, pulling a face at our friends.

"Fuck, that was a lot—"

"Them, or Joah and I?"

She sniffs a laugh before she turns to look at herself in the mirror—she glances at me through our reflections. "It is just... *fucking* though, right?"

My mouth opens to speak but nothing comes out.

Lala freezes. "Is it...?"

My brows go low, face puzzled as I look for the words.

"Oh my god, it isn't—?" She gawps at me. "You like him!"

I still don't say anything back.

"Wait—no—" She shakes her head. "Ysolde, are you in love?"

Now I shake my head quickly because—that's mad, and I haven't even pondered the thought myself because of course I'm not. I'm definitely not. Probably. I'm probably definitely not in love with him. I think. Fuck.

"Look at your face!" Lala points at me accusingly. "Oh my god, you fucking love him!"

She smacks me in the arm.

"I couldn't!"

"But you do! I can tell! Oh my god, Solly—" She reaches for me now, mildly concerned.

"La, I'm a mess. Like an addict. I hate being away from him, I hate not touching him—"

"Well." She considers this. "You have pretty big daddy issues so that separately checks out..."

I point at her sternly. "Fuck you and that's not what this is about."

She tilts her head, makes an "mmmm" sound, as though she's not so sure.

"Lala, you had two sessions with Ruth Westheimer several months ago, it's time to cut the cord."

She ignores me. "So where are we on the scale of lovers past?

Are we talking mild infatuation like when you shot that campaign with Marky Mark and you didn't leave his hotel room for thirty-six hours…? Or like…Kelly Slater, when you followed around after him for a good chunk of 1994 and wore a lot of Roxy and puka shells?"

I purse my lips. "Kelly Slater was child's play."

"Oh, fuck." Her mouth falls open in a bit of genuine surprise. "Okay."

She nods, thinking it through. Me going through a surfing phase meant that *we* went through a surfing phase, and La was okay with the bigger, more commercial islands, but she wasn't a fan of some of the weirder places we'd go. And don't tell me she didn't have to come, because all that does is tell me you've never had a codependent friend before and that's your problem not mine and actually, I feel sorry for you.

"I am properly obsessed with him, Lalee," I breathe out. "I cannot tell you what a relief it is to say this out loud, it's been eating me up inside, having to play it cool with him—"

"Why?"

"Because I need him to like me! I need him to think I'm cool!"

Lala gives me an exasperated look. "Sol, you're literally the coolest person on the planet."

"No." I shake my head with fervent conviction. "I *was*. I'm not cool anymore, I'm a complete loser now."

Lala rolls her eyes like I'm being dramatic, but I'm not. I'm just telling the truth.

"I just think about Joah Harrigan all the live long day like every other fucking girl in the world—"

"Right—" Lala gives me a look. "But—*unlike* every other fucking girl in the world, Ys—*hopefully*—you're the one he's actually, literally fucking…"

I sigh. "I suppose."

"It is mutual, right?" Her face grimaces as she asks that question and my jaw falls to the floor.

"I beg your pardon, the nerve! Of course it's fucking mutual! Obviously, it is." I give her a good glare for that one, but she just shrugs, unfazed.

"He can be fucking you and not into you. Case in point: *Heath Ledger*."

"Oh my god!" My shoulders slump. "Why would you bring that up? That just hurts my feelings—"

"Because—" She gives me a look. "You are a goddess and that is true *regardless*. But if it's not there, it's not there—"

"It's fucking there, okay? He's there."

"Okay." She shrugs again, and I can tell she's not trying to have a row, just trying to be my friend.

I reach for her hand again and squeeze it. "You will come tomorrow, won't you?"

"Oh yeah." She nods. "I want to watch the world's biggest butter knife sing you love songs, one hundred percent." She squeezes my hand. "Wouldn't miss it for the world."

FIVE

joah

"WELL, WELL, WELL," MY BROTHER says as I stroll through the doorway of the green room at the Electric Ballroom a full two hours after my call time—lost a good three in the shower of the Grand Terrace suite with Ys—and I don't wanna hear a fucking word about it.

"He's alive!" jeers Fry.

I point at him, warningly. "Shut it."

My brother walks over to me, looks me up and down, smacks me on the chest in a way that feels patronizing, even if it isn't.

"You look good, lad. Been doing extra cardio?"

Run my tongue over my teeth. Prefer not to give him the satisfaction of letting him know when he's getting on my nerves.

"No more than usual."

"Bullshit," Richie fires back, staring me down like he's Sherlock fucking Holmes. Then he turns to Fry and Chops, proper smug. "And it's with one girl too—"

Chops gawps at me like I've just told him I've given up drinkin' or summat equally daft. "Nah, no way…"

I roll my eyes at the lot of 'em, over their shite. "Can we talk about the show tonight—?"

TIME OF YOUR LIFE

"Yeah," Chops starts. "So—"

"—No," Richie cuts him off. "Can we talk about our kid and his supermodel?"

I give Richie this proper long-suffering look, cos he's windin' me up on purpose, the prick—I know he is. "She's not mine." She is, but. "What about her?"

He nods his chin at me, all knowing. "How was she?"

And it's mental, you know… A week ago, same question about some other girl, wouldn't have bat an eye. Would've told him—would've told all of 'em—happily. Any other girl, probably would have pretty happily bragged about a five-day fuck-fest. But not her…

Don't even wanna answer the question. How was she? *Fuckin' heaven, and none of your goddamn business, Rich.*

Can't say any of that though, can I? So I just nod coolly instead. "Good."

"Good!" Richie chuckles. "You 'ear that, lads? Jo's been avoiding us all week for *good*…"

I flash him a shit-eating grin. "Or maybe I'm just avoiding you because you're a prick, know what I mean?"

"*Maybe*"—Chops eyes us both—"we should talk about our show tonight."

"Is there a party later?" I ask, just to fuckin' spite him, the bossy tosser.

Chops sighs, disappointed. "Because *that's* what matters."

He's a purist, see? All about the music, nowt else. Which is fair enough, I s'pose, but we're the biggest fucking band on the planet, so let's fucking party down while we can.

"Stringfellow," Fry says, throwing the name out there like it's gospel.

I grimace, though. Me and the lads have had some proper wild nights in that club. One of my favourites, no lie. But there's this weird little niggle in the back of me mind, like maybe I don't wanna take Ysolde there? Dunno why, don't read into it. I'm not.

I nod, ignoring that fucking niggle. "Sounds good."

"Want me to tell Mick to put her on the list?" Fry offers.

Richie pulls a face. "It's Ysolde fucking Featherstonhaugh. She don't need to be on a list."

"Speaking of lists—" Chops eyes us all. "We don't have a set list for tonight yet, lads."

"We have one fucking album, mate—" Roll my eyes at him. "I reckon we'll probably just play that."

He rolls his eyes. "In any order in particular, champ?"

I shrug, unbothered. "Whatever fucking order they come out of me mouth."

My brother nods his chin at me. "She coming tonight?"

"Think so." I nod casually. Cos I am. Casual, I mean. Not like my heart beats a bit faster thinking about her. That'd be properly fucked, wouldn't it?

"Nervous?" my brother asks, and fuck him for asking it. Absolute piece of shit. Like I'm fucking nervous. I'm not. And how the fuck did he know anyway?

"Nope," I tell him. "Lox coming down tonight?"

He nods, and that's that, then. Back on again, are they? For now, anyway. For better or worse—mostly worse, let's be honest— Loxy Blythe and my brother have been carrying on since before the band was even a thing. Not quite since school, I don't think, but not far after.

Wish I could say she's like me sister, but she pisses me off too much.

Not that siblings can't do that—fuck me, no one pisses me off more than Richie sodding Harrigan, know what I mean? But Loxy—I don't know, man. You know those people who sorta just get off from annoyin' other people? That's her, and I'm other people.

She and me get into it sometimes. Which means Rich and me get into it sometimes.

Actually, Rich is a bleeding prick, so we get into it a lot of the time, don't we?

TIME OF YOUR LIFE

53

Didn't used to. But even when we were kidders like—if me and Rich were gonna scrap, we'd fuckin' scrap. Worse now we're older, somehow. Dunno why. Just is. Me mum says it's cos we're famous, but I dunno. Reckon it might just be us, you know what I mean?

"What time's your girl gettin' here?" my brother asks, and I don't know why it shits me—just does—maybe a bit because I dunno the answer. When I was leaving her place and I said to her, *"I'll see you later."* And she said, *"Yeah, okay."* And I said, *"What time do you reckon you'll be 'round?"* And she said, *"I don't know, what time does it start?"* And I said, *"We go on at nine thirty,"* and she said *"Then nine twenty-five, I guess?"*—won't lie, was a bit deflating that she wasn't—you know, like, chomping at the fuckin' bit to see me onstage, so I didn't wanna be like *come early* or owt embarrassin', like I care, you know—? Because I don't. Never have before. Feels a bit like I might do here, but. Don't need my nosy prick of a brother poking about in me business, know what I mean?

"Who are you mate, her fuckin' dad?" I roll my eyes at him as my brother raises his arms in surrender.

"Who's fucking dads?" Heddie Greer asks as she waltzes into the room, a pile of clothes in her arms and a playful grin plastered across her face.

Our stylist. Knows her way 'round an outfit, dead sharp with it. Pretty decent shag, too.

"Oh, have you not heard?" Rich starts, proper smug. "Joah has himself a—"

I'm on him in a flash, clamping my hand over his gob before he can get the words out. He shoves me off, hard enough that both Fry and Chops are on their feet instantly, ready for whatever's about to kick off. And, like clockwork, Mick pops up out of nowhere, lurking like a phantom, already braced to step in in case me and Rich get carried away. Fair play to him, we have been known to in our day.

Rich points at me, eyes narrowed. "Don't touch me, man."

I shrug at him. "Don't run your mouth."

"Heds!" Mick gives her a pointed look—says somethin' to her without saying owt, like they've talked about this before, or summat. "Why don't you take Jo to his dressing room, have him pick somethin' for tonight."

I look down at meself. "What's wrong with what I'm wearing?"

She gives me a look, all business—or supposedly. The way her eyes run over me, though, it's not just the job, is it? Nah, it's a bit of that, sure, but it's a lot because she's seen me naked. And the way she does it? There's this edge to it, like she's reminding me she has. Like, in her head, my body's half hers by default.

"Well," she says finally, proper breezy, "let's just get a jacket on you, and we'll go from there."

———

I'm standing in my dressing room, shirt off, Heddie fannying about with my belt—sounds a lot sexier than it is. Could be sexy, I s'pose. Heddie's fit, no arguing that. Proper fit, I reckon. But she ain't her, is she? Not the girl I've been shagging all week. And for the first time ever, I'm not arsed.

That's weird for me, know what I mean? Proper weird. Cos I can tell Heddie's havin' a crack, laying the groundwork for later.

The way her fingers are brushing over my skin at the top of my jeans—could probably just about pass as part of the job. But then you pair it with the fuck-me eyes she's throwin' my way, and it's not. Not even a bit.

And the thing is, normally I'd clock that, shrug, and think, *ah, fuck it—why not, like?* But this time? Nowt. Ain't even tempted.

It's not me specific, by the way. She'd have a crack with Richie just as easy as she would with me. Probably easier, to be fair, but she's gotta know Lox is knocking about somewhere.

And Fry and Chops? She's definitely tossed them a pity shag or two over the years. Not sure if they were meant to be pity shags, but that's what I call 'em, just to wind 'em up. Works every time.

Then there's a knock at the door.

TIME OF YOUR LIFE   55

"Yeah?" I call out, dead gruff.

"Decent?" Rich shouts back through the door.

I glance down at myself. Shirtless, jeans halfway on, Heddie still faffing about with the zip like it's her first time doing one up. Good enough for me.

"Yep," I call back.

The door swings open, and it's not just Rich standing there. It's Rich and Ysolde (and her fuckin' bodyguard, but he's a bit part of the furniture now. Not a bad lad, don't mind him. Can't imagine this is winning me any points with him but—fuck). Ys stops dead in her tracks, eyes go wide.

"Oh my—" Her gaze flicks from me—and Heddie's hands, conveniently near the spot she's set up camp at for the last week—over to my brother. "What would *indecent* look like?"

"Oh, don't you worry, mate—" The absolute prick gives her this smug look. "You'll find out."

He flashes me a smirk, and I know full well he's tried to throw me under the bus on purpose. Course he fucking has. Prick.

Thing is, I'm not doing owt wrong. Not really. But fuck me, it don't look great, does it? Shirt off, Heddie's hands practically halfway down my jeans.

"Fuck—" I mutter, shoving past Heddie quick and heading straight for Ys. "Hey." Put my hand on her waist.

"Hi," she says, eyes locked on Heddie behind me. Realises she's doing it, then shifts her focus to me. "Hey."

Touch her face.

She blinks a few times, like she's catching up. "Hi."

I smile at her, happier to see her than I want to be. "You alright?"

She nods. I glance over her shoulder, through the doorway.

"Where's Lala? I wanna meet her properly."

"On her way," she says, but she's barely paying attention. Her eyes have drifted straight back to Heddie, who's still standing there, bold as brass, staring at us like she's part of the conversation.

And you know what's mental?

I've ain't never felt weird 'round two girls that I've fucked about with, but man, I'm feelin' a bit ill. Watchin' Ys's brow twitchin', like she's confused or worried about shit, and Heddie's just standin' there, isn't she—? Lettin' her crack on with it, not easing the tension or my girl's mind, not even pretending to—just staring back at her like she's got all the time in the world. Proper Heddie move, that.

So, before it gets even weirder, I nod at Ys and go, "She's just our stylist. Heddie."

Chuck her name on the end, all casual, and I can see it straightaway—that's wound Heds right up. Proper brassed off, and I know it.

"Yeah." Heds flashes Ys a curt smile. "I'm just his stylist."

Ys sticks her hand out, cos that's just her. Sweet to her core, even if she don't want ya to think it. "I'm Yso—"

"—olde," Heddie butts in, sharp as you like. "Featherstonhaugh. I know. *Stylist*—" She points to herself, then flicks it towards Ys. "*Model.*"

Then Heddie spins on me, hands on her hips, looking like she's about to start a scrap. "Can we finish up?"

"Yeah." I shrug, just want her to piss off, if I'm honest. "Just tell me what to wear and I'll wear it."

Heddie gives me a look—proper pissed, isn't she? All this girl bullshit in that fuckin' look that I couldn't give a shit about, or at least I didn't till about thirty seconds ago when it started fuckin' with Ysolde.

"Right—" Heddie snaps, with this single nod that somehow screams she's raging at me.

Might as well wind her up a bit more, eh?

"Oi—" I reach for a jacket and a shirt, holding them up for Ysolde. "Which one's better? This." Hold up the blue denim jacket against myself. "Or this?" Hold up a baggy flannel shirt.

"Uh—" Ysolde's eyes flit from me to the clothes, moving about like she's sizing everythin' up, sneaking a glance at me in between. Then she nods, like she's cracked it. "Well, you've got quite broad shoulders and the seams of that denim jacket will accentuate your shoulders, cap-sleeve seam of that shirt will blunt them."

I chuck the shirt back at Heddie, keeping hold of the jacket.

"This'll do," I tell her, don't even look her way.

Dickhead, I know. Makin' a point but, aren't I?

"But—" she pipes up, starting to argue.

"This," I cut in. End of story.

"Okay." Heddie nods once, proper pissed now. And I can feel— somehow fuckin' feel it, I can, in the equilibrium of the universe, that I am going to pay for that somewhere down the line. Heds gathers the rest of the clothes she pulled for me and skulks out the room, loudly closing it behind her. Not quite a slam—that'd be fucking rude and unprofessional. Slam-adjacent though, I'll say that much.

As soon as the door shuts behind Heddie, Ys crosses her arms and fixes me with this dead serious stare.

"You've had sex with her."

"What?" I blink, proper taken aback. "How the fuck could you possibly know that?"

She shrugs, all casual. "I can tell."

I gape at her, full disbelief. "How?"

"Just how she looks at you."

"Yeah?" My eyes narrow. "And how does she look at me?"

She crosses her arms tighter, suddenly lookin' a bit...I dunno, exposed or summat. "Not dissimilar to how I look at you, I suppose."

"Well—" I slip my arm round her waist, tugging her in close. "That fucking sucks for her, then, cos I don't look at her and you the same way."

She gives me a look, half-doubting, half...summat else. "Are you really trying to tell me you haven't had sex?"

"No, we have," I admit, probably a bit mindless about it. Realise it a second later and add, "Not, like, today or owt—"

"But in general."

"Yeah." I shrug. "I mean—of course, yeah—"

Her head pulls back. "Of course?"

But I reckon she's being a bit stupid, so I say: "Why wouldn't I have?"

Didn't like that. She nods coolly. "Sure, yeah."

I stare down at her, trying to assess what the fuck is happening right now. "You jealous?"

She stares at me, pouting almost, and it's like she has to force herself to say it out loud, can see the wrestle happening live on her face, so I can. "Maybe."

I nod a couple of times—bit impressed, if I'm honest—she's a proud girl. Most birds who look how she looks are... Dunno if the shoe was on the other foot that I would've admitted to it meself.

I clear my throat, tilt me head so our eyes meet.

"You know I've had one girlfriend in me life. Fucked 'round a lot, but I don't really date girls like—Ain't an option for me, know what I mean—?"

That doesn't make her happy. Her little face goes a little darker. "Okay?"

"We met Sunday, you and me," I remind her. "Didn't leave your fuckin' side till Wednesday. Afternoon, right? We had to have my single pair of pants laundered..."

That makes her smile a bit. I keep going.

"Got invited to a party last night—couple of the United lads were gonna be there. Like, mate, I'd've binned off a bloody surgery to go to that—but I didn't, cos I'd rather be with you—I ain't never spent that much time with a girl in one go. Never," I tell her, dead serious. Then I duck down so we're eye to eye. "You don't got to be jealous, Ys."

And then—swear to god—she fucking launches at me. Jumps right up onto my waist, grabbing at my shirt, kissing the absolute life out of me.

"What the fuck are you doin'?" I ask, though let's be honest, I don't stop kissing her back.

"That was a very sexy speech," she mumbles, voice muffled cos she's got her face buried in my neck now.

TIME OF YOUR LIFE   59

Next thing I know, she's reaching for the fly of my jeans, and I've gotta pull back—

"Oi, I can't—" Shake my head. "I can't."

She stops, kinda freezes up. "What?"

"I can't do that right n—"

She cuts me off. "—Is this about that girl?"

"What?" I blink.

"Were you and her about to—"

"No." My face scrunches up. "Why would you—?"

"Are you lying to me?" she asks without missing a beat.

"No…" I say, slowly and carefully. "Why—?"

"You've just never not wanted to have sex with me before…"

"Have I never?" Me head pulls back. "We've been like fuckin' about for five days like. It ain't no great measure of never…"

"There's an implied bracketing to the never of which I'm speaking about that's contextual to you and I and the time in which we've been involved, so I would say my never stands."

Run my tongue over my teeth, bit wound up by all this shit. I should be annoyed. She's being annoyin'. This whole thing's fuckin' annoying. But for some reason, I'm well into it, so I just tell her the fuckin' truth, don't I?

"We've got a rule."

Her eyebrow shoots up, waiting for me to carry on.

"No sex. Before a show."

"What? Why?" She scrunches up her face, she's sceptical. Fair play, though—bit of a daft rule if you ask me.

I shrug, casual. "Cos I'm fuckin' shit during the show if I've had sex before."

Her face softens a bit, and I'm done for, aren't I? Fuck me, I love her face.

"Why?" She looks like she's tryin' not to laugh. Thank god, man—if she laughed at that, I'd probably have to off myself.

"I dunno—testosterone or some shit?" I roll my eyes. "That's what Mick says?"

Could be shite, I dunno. Told me it's a secret rule they abide by at United to get the best outta the lads before a game. Best way to get me to comply is to tell me those fucking lads do it, and fuck it— I'm in. Freddie Fletcher don't shag a girl pre-match? Right then, Joah Harrigan won't fuck pre-show either.

Ys's eyes pinch. "Really?"

"Yeah." I nod.

"Promise?"

"Yeah." I nod again, fight off the grin that keeps croppin' up on my face. "I'll have sex with you the minute go we're offstage…" That makes her smile. Like makin' her smile, I do… "Wait in the wings, if you want, Ys…" I duck so our eyes are level again. "Hike your skirt up a bit—we can crack on straightaway…"

Her eyes pinch. "You're teasing me."

"Yeah, a bit—" I smile. "I'm game if you are, but."

There's a bang on the door.

"Five minutes!" a stagehand calls from the other side.

"Aye," I call back, then glance at her as I tug on me shoes. "You wanna wait side of stage?"

"No—" She shakes her head. "I have to find Lalee. We can stand out there with the common man."

She says that last part like it's a joke, but all men are common compared to her and I reckon she knows it too.

"Okay—" I walk towards the door now, pause halfway out of it. "But don't stand at the side, it sounds weird—" Then I fish in my back pocket—a couple of passes for her and her friend. AAA. They'll never let her back here later without 'em. Don't even really know how she's here without one now? Maybe because she's her and she got lucky. I hand 'em over.

"These passes can you get you anywhere."

She pockets them, says thanks, and I pause again because I'm a bit in me head about where she's going to stand—wanna sound perfect in her ears, you know what I mean? "Try and stand at the sound desk so you don't think we're shit, yeah?"

She smiles, amused. "Okay."

"Okay?" I nod back. "Sound desk. Middle of the room. Not the side."

"Got it."

And then the weirdest fuckin' thing happens—like, properly mad. I suddenly clock that she's standing in my dressing room, and I like her there. Like the idea of her being the last thing I see before I go onstage just works?

My eyes dart back to her, and before I can think too much about it, I grab her face and kiss her, quick and rough. "Swear to fuck, you're unreal."

Her eyes go all soft—love it when they do that. Proper melts me. She's just about to say summat back when my brother barges past my now-open door and smacks it with his hand.

"Jo." Bang. "Fuckin' now." Bang again.

I suck in a deep breath through my nose, already fuming, cos Richie tellin' me what to do winds me up like nothin' else.

But then she puts her hand on my cheek, gives me this smile that just cuts through the rage like it's nowt.

"Go well," she tells me.

And you know what, for once I'm gonna do what I'm told.

SIX

ysolde

IT'S CONFRONTING ACTUALLY—MORE SO than I thought it'd be—seeing other people want him.

The stylist threw me for an absolute loop. That was weird and hard and I wished I didn't care—I shouldn't care—I'm a million times prettier than her but then, she's been where I've been and actually, she was there first, and that makes me hate her a bit.

Her aside, just being at his show is sort of fucked-up and crazy.

Fallow are a big band, I know that. I wasn't blowing smoke up Joah's arse when I said they're the biggest band in the world. Arguably, of all the bands in the world that are actively touring today, Fallow is the biggest. Maybe only barely eclipsed by U2, but even then, I'm not so sure because Bono doesn't look like Joah, and that without a doubt counts for something.

There's an energy and an expectation in the room that I haven't really felt anyplace else, and they're not even onstage yet.

Lala and I are led towards the sound desk by Aleki—we get stopped a few times on the way as people recognise us—no one thinks anything of it. Whatever Joah and I are, the papers haven't

TIME OF YOUR LIFE

cottoned on properly yet. Jilly said there were a few articles, but this last week, he and I weren't papped together once.

I am, to everyone here, just another Fallow fan.

And I'm not *not* a Fallow fan. I *do* know the big ones. You can't not know the big ones; they're always on the radio.

"What's their big, famous one again? 'Boys and Girls'?" Lala asks, glancing around.

I shake my head. "I think that's Blur?"

She nods like she's remembering. "Oh, that's right."

"He's quite weird about them, actually…" I shrug. "Them and some other band. Brightlines."

"Bright *Line*," she corrects me.

I roll my eyes.

She looks interested. "Is he competitive?"

"I think so." I nod. "I've really only known him in a very contained and insular environment, so I can't be completely sure, but I have my suspicions…"

She thinks about it for a minute. "That'd be kind of sexy. I like competitive men." She thinks more. "To a certain degree."

I give her a dubious look. "I'm not going to name names, but you dated an impossibly glorious man, who was incredibly competitive in his field, and you hated him in the end."

She groans. "We work in the same field! I don't want him to be competitive with *me*. I want him to be competitive with other men. It's, like, sexy and primal—"

I roll my eyes at her, and she probably would have tried to prove her point more except the lights dim, and the loudest sound I have ever heard in my entire life erupts from the mouths of everyone around us.

I mean, I jump from fright.

It's different than last year at Glastonbury. People were excited then—of course they were—everyone's excited to be at Glastonbury. But this is something else.

They let them scream for a minute or so and then a guitar rips a single cord, and somehow, the loudest sound I've ever heard gets even louder.

Lala and I trade looks, and I wonder for a second—*who am I sleeping with?*—like, I know who, obviously. And I know literally that it's Joah Harrigan from Fallow—but conceptually, who the fuck am I sleeping with?

And then—as though it is even possible—the screaming gets so loud, I feel it through my body and down to my bones, because Joah walks onto the stage, and *that's* who the fuck I'm sleeping with.

He waves at a few people screaming his name from the audience as he steps up to the microphone, spots me as he does. He subtly nods his chin at me, gives me a hint of a smile, and my heart goes entirely berserk—and that's before he's even started singing.

They open with one of their big ones—I don't know the name of it but you've definitely heard it, it's arguably their most famous one—and it's weird, you know?

How many girls stare at him like they want him—actually, how many of them stare at him like they love him—? That's kind of terrifying.

I did go into tonight sort of telling myself, *Okay, he's in a popular band, there are going to be fans there, they're going to call his name, look at him with googly, dreamy eyes, and you'll probably think it's funny and weird*—and I mean, I get it, I have fans too. It's a strange thing to navigate and I've navigated it before. I've dated other people with fans before, but I've never dated someone with fans like this.

There is this one girl, she is crying. Actually, there are lots of girls crying, but there is one in particular who is frantic, like, truly, actually shaking, reaching up for him from the pit of people in front of the band.

Lala nods at her. "That's…insane—"

"Right?" I say, unable to look away.

People with celebrities can be so weird, as though they're starving and the person themself is the only sustenance left on the planet.

It's beyond adoration and adulation.

It's not just girls either, it's men too. Granted, not as many crying manically, but eyes closed, arms in the air, singing, chanting, and yelling his name and the words he wrote, absolutely making a god out of that twenty-three-year-old boy who was on his knees in my bedroom last night, his head between my legs.

They are incredible though. Quite unparalleled in the way they perform and undeniably unparalleled in the way the audience responds to them, and still—do you know what? He kind of stares at me the whole time.

And maybe he's just masterful at his craft, maybe he makes everyone in the room feel like he's singing to them personally—but I feel like he may have been *actually* singing to me specifically.

"Do you know what?" Lala yells into my ear about midway through the show.

"What?" I yell back.

She flicks her head in Joah's direction. "I get it."

I love having her approval. I feel my back straighten, all proud. "Do you!"

"Yep." She nods. "Very sexy."

It feels strange watching Jo onstage—because lots have an onstage persona, I get it—Madonna is actually quite normal in real life. But Joah is very cocky onstage. Which—think about it—he's not *not* cocky offstage either, so think about what that's implying. But it works for him? I wish it didn't. I wish I didn't find his arrogance sexy, but I do. I want to do filthy things to that man. But I suspect at this point that that feeling isn't exclusive to just me in the room. I feel actually quite confident that given the opportunity, many people present would be pleased to do sexy things to Joah. Or Richie, I suppose.

I have gathered that there's a bit of a rivalry amongst the fans about which brother is the better brother, though I suspect the scales tilt fractionally in favour of the front man who's shared a bed with me for this last week.

His brother is attractive though. Similar height. Shorter, wavier hair. Same blue eyes though. I think he's a bit more measured. I'm not sure why I think that, that's just the feeling I get.

Anyway, they sing a couple more songs, and I don't know how many songs are on the album but I feel like it has to be wrapping up soon when Joah starts speaking.

"You know the best part about being in the biggest fuckin' band in the world—?" he says to the audience. "It's all the girls, innit?"

The crowd cheers, but Lala pulls an uncertain face. Onstage, the brother tosses the bass player a confused look.

"Fuck me, I love girls—" Joah keeps going. "Love 'em. Always have—"

I purse my lips, unsure where exactly this is going.

"You know what, man? I met a girl…" he says and there's some cheering from the audience. "This week, didn't I—?"

I go still. What's he doing?

"And you know what? It's been the weirdest fuckin' thing… but I cannot get her out of me head." He says that whilst staring directly at me. I'm not sure anyone in the room besides Lala and the band know that, but it's an impossibly and bizarrely intimate moment between us that just happens to take place in front of two thousand people we don't know.

"And I'm singin' these songs—arguably the best fuckin' songs in the world to you lot—" He gestures to the audience and they cheer. "*Undeniably* the best motherfuckin' fans in the world—" They cheer louder. "And it's my pleasure to be here with you lot, isn't it, yeah—? But I cannot—*for the life of me*—get this fuckin' girl outta my head." There's cheering again, albeit perhaps a bit less because he's undoubtedly crushing the dreams of much of his female audience who believed (genuinely, as so many of them somehow often do) that they may have been in with a shot at going home with him later tonight.

"She's like a tune in my brain, man—?" He's staring at just me again. "That I can't stop humming. Don't want to stop humming, do you know what I mean—?" He looks away, and thank god because I thought I was going to burst into flames.

"And I wanna sing her a song, but I don't have a song about her yet." The audience boos a little, I hear someone yell *Poor form!* And Joah looks at them, a bit amused. "I know—I know—shut up, man, like—we only met on Sunday, didn't we? Fuckin' calm down—"

"You had all week!" yells someone playfully from the crowd.

"Well, I was a bit busy, wasn't I—?" Joah rolls his eyes from stage.

"Doing what?" calls an audience member.

"Her, mate." Joah laughs, and the room erupts in laughter and cheering. My cheeks are so flushed—and this is crazy, because Lala is wildly protective of me. She doesn't think it's funny or endearing ever if someone's crass or vulgar about me—so let this be a testament to how irresistibly charming Joah Harrigan is: Lala laughed at that.

"Ain't had time to write one yet, have I?" Then he looks back at me. "But I will, mark my words…" My heart skips, like, thirty beats. Joah pushes his hands through his obnoxiously perfect (and now a bit sweaty) hair. "So I'm just going to sing her favourite instead, if that's alright with you lot."

The audience cheers but the band trade confused looks, and I can tell immediately, it's the first they're hearing of this.

Rich covers his mic and yells, "What?"

Joah yells something back.

I think I see the bassist say, *Are you fucking kidding me?* and then Joah shrugs before he turns to his brother. *Just fuckin' play it,* I think he says.

The brother flips him off, then stomps on the pedal in front of him a couple of times, and I'm not totally sure what's happening until I hear the guitar riff.

"Now I don't hardly know her," Joah sings, and he's back to staring at me, and I'm back to being a puddle when he unflinchingly sings the next line:

"But I think I could love her."

Girls in the audience start crying again, and it's hard to tell whether it's because it's the best song in the whole entire world, or because they're aware he's singing that song to a girl who isn't them. It's impressive, actually. How good the band sounds with not even a moment's notice to perform a song they've apparently not rehearsed.

Joah sings the whole song without looking away from me, and there's something so sexy about him singing "Crimson and clover, over and over" again and again, his eyes locked on just me the whole time.

It's the best rendition to that song I've ever heard, aside from the original, and when they finish it, the room loses their fucking shit.

Lala lets out an exasperated breath. "Ugh."

I look over at her, surprised. "What?"

"We're going to be late to the after-party…"

I look at her, unsure. "Why?"

"Well, you *have* to go backstage and shag him now, don't you?" She gestures towards backstage. "I mean, are you kidding, Sol? What the fuck was that? That was the most romantic thing I've ever seen. You should have his baby, probably. If that song didn't already make you pregnant, my god, Ys—what are we saying? Like, go—"

I blink at her twice.

"Go." She waves towards backstage again. "Go now. This is their final song."

I look at her quizzically. "How do you know?"

"This is the last track on their album? It's probably their most famous song."

"Oh."

"Wow." She stares at me, almost but not quite impressed. "You know startlingly little about their band. No wonder he's so into you." She adds that last part as an afterthought. "Go." She shoos me. "I'll find the brother or something."

The band finishes and then the crowd goes mental. I get

TIME OF YOUR LIFE 69

stopped a few more times on my way through as I navigate my way back towards backstage. Aleki's behind me again—and it's always weird when I'm trying to hook up with someone and he's just there—like of course he is, it's his job. But then he just has to awkwardly hover outside or nearby—? Awful. And awkward. So we decided fairly early on to just believe that whenever I'm doing that, *actually*, I'm just in that room playing rummy. Just a nice, little game of cards, that's all.

I hover outside Joah's dressing room, glancing back at Aleki. I give him a sheepish smile.

"I'm just going to play some cards now…"

He rolls his eyes, but there's some amusement under there. "After that—? I'm sure you fucking are."

I knock on the door.

"What?" Joah calls through it.

So I open it, peer through—his face lights up.

It's quite lovely, someone's face lighting up when they see yours, don't you think?

"Hi," I say quietly as I walk inside, close the door behind me.

"You weren't in the wings…" He gives me a playful smile.

"Were you disappointed?"

"Crushed." He fights off a smile, then he rushes over towards me, picks me up off the ground by my waist, kind of spinning me as he does it.

"Fuck, I missed you." He grins.

I'm completely delighted, but try my best "Did you?"

He gives me this *seriously?* look that frankly is too adorable for a man with his charisma and sex appeal to be throwing around willy-nilly. "Watchin' you from a distance that whole time—fuck!" He presses his lips into mine. "You like it?"

"Very much."

"How'd we sound?" he asks, eyebrows up and hopeful.

"Heavenly." I trace my thumb over his immaculate jawline. "You're very good."

"Yeah, I know," he says, matter-of-factly. Arrogant, to be sure—hard to argue with, though.

"Were the band annoyed about 'Crimson and Clover'?"

"Oh yeah—" He gives me a steep look. "I'm gonna fuckin' eat shit for that…"

His gaze settles on me, flicking from my eyes to my mouth. He swallows heavy. "Worth it, but."

My hands fall to the button of his jeans and I give him a little, tiny smile.

"I should quite like to make sure it was *so* worth it, though…"

"Yeah?" He tilts his head, blinks a couple of times, and I have to steady my breathing because everything he does is spectacular, even if it's nothing at all. "Any bright ideas?"

I reach behind me and lock his green room door.

SEVEN

joah

WE SHOW UP SEPARATE, ME and Ysolde. Do it on purpose. Paparazzi love me, love her too. Together? Be a right fuckin' circus.

Not hiding her, though. Just not sure if I'm ready for the whole world to know I reckon I'm in love with her, you know what I mean?

Dunno who gets there first, me or her, but I walk in—bit of a commotion. Standard. I'm a big deal.

I'm barely ten feet into Stringfellows when Mick grabs me. Proper grabs me, like he's got summat important to say.

He gives me a look I don't like. "You can't do shit like that, Jo."

Dunno what the fuck he's talkin' about. "Like what?"

"Announce that you're—I don't know—*fucking betrothed* without telling me. I didn't even know you fucking had a girlfriend."

I roll my eyes, can't help it. "She's not my girlfriend."

He actually looks relieved. Prick. "Thank god."

Don't like that either. "Want her to be, though."

Mick groans, proper dramatic. "No. Fuck, no." He drags me farther into the room, runs his hands through that ridiculous head of hair. "You're *Joah Harrigan*, you can't do girlfriends."

I give him a look, deadpan. "I'm Joah *fuckin'* Harrigan. I can do whatever the fuck I want."

"Mate—" He sighs like he's trying to reason with me. Fuckin' hate when he does that. Don't know if it's cos they're right—the ones who reckon I'm not a reasonable man—but whatever shite Mick's about to throw my way, I don't wanna hear it.

"Fucking do her to your heart's content, but don't run your mouth about her onstage."

I raise my brows. Don't fuckin' like being told what to do, do I? He keeps going anyway.

"You need to be single, Jo. People need to believe you could be theirs."

I stare at him like the idiot he is. "Our audience is seventy percent male."

"Right, but do you know how much that thirty percent does for you—?" He looks at me like he's made some massive point. I dunno what fucking point he thinks he's made. Flown straight over my head, whatever it is. "Do you? Jo, the sales *matter*—those thirty percent buy multiples and merch and—"

I shrug. "I don't care."

He rolls his eyes like I'm the exasperating one. "I know you don't care, but I care."

I shake my head, waiting for him to get to the point. "So?"

"And the label cares…"

"The label can fuck themselves."

Mick hooks an arm 'round my neck, draggin' me away from some familiar-lookin' lads who are definitely having an eavesdrop. Probably the label, come to think of it. Ah well.

"Jo—" Another one of those paternal looks. Can't stand 'em. Don't much like fathers. "We've talked about this… You can't go mouthing off saying shit like that, you'll piss someone off and they'll—"

"What—?" I cut him off, tilting my head, daring him to finish. "What'll they do? Unsign the biggest band in the world? Alright,

TIME OF YOUR LIFE 73

lad—"I clap him on the back as I turn to leave. "Let's see how that works out for 'em."

"Where are you going?" he calls after me.

I spin 'round, wouldn't usually bother, but I wanna see the look on his face. "To get meself a fucking girlfriend."

Make me way through the club, lookin' for that girl with the best face I've ever seen. Spot her tucked away in a corner behind a velvet rope, sat with me brother and her best mate. She clocks me from a ways off—gets to her feet—like she knows I'm upset? Dunno if I've ever felt like someone knows me like she does. Knows me just from a look across a packed room? That's some rare shit, that is, you know what I mean?

Takes her a couple of seconds to get to me. Her hands go straight to my face the second she's in front of me, mine land on her waist—summat about us, I'm fuckin' tellin' ya—pulls us towards each other. Her brows creased, proper worried.

"What's wrong?"

"Nowt." I kiss her instead.

She doesn't buy it. Maybe that's the downside of being known— they clock when you're lying.

"Are you sure?"

I nod. "Yeah, just…my manager's a fuckin' dick."

"Oh?"

"Bit pissed off about the song tonight."

"Oh…" She grimaces.

"Yeah," I carry on. "Reckons the world needs to think I'm single…"

"Oh." She says it careful, presses her lips together, not sayin' the thing she's gagging to. But you know what? I fuckin' know her too. See it written all over her face, what's brewin' in her head.

"Are you… *not*… single?" she asks, all easy breezy like.

I bat away a grin that's trying to creep onto me face, give her a look instead. "Fishing, are we, Ys?"

Her mouth opens, ready to protest. "I—"

Cut her off, don't I? "I love you."

Her eyes go wide, but she's happy. "What!"

"Sorry—" I shrug. "I do."

She shakes her head, but she's smilin' a lot now. "No, you don't."

"Nah." I nod. "I do."

More head shakes from her, proper stubborn. "What do you—"

I cut her off again. "Now say it back."

She gives me a look, bit serious. "Joah, we met on Sunday."

"And I told you then, at Groucho, didn't I?"

She flicks her eyes at me. "You were being silly."

"Was I?" I tilt me chin up, dead serious now. Maybe I was, but I fucking mean it now. "Go on—" I duck so we're eye level. "Say it back. I know you do…"

She stares at me, her eyes, her face, her mouth, all of it screaming that I'm right—I know what it looks like when a girl loves you. Fucking millions of girls love me. Don't love them, though. Love this one here, don't I? If she'd fucking say it back.

Ys gives me a proud look. "*Do* you know that?"

I nod, sure as owt. "Yep."

She straightens up, and summat shifts in her face, goes serious. "Don't cheat on me and don't lie to me."

Alright—fuck, I think to meself, but then she keeps on going.

"And if you *do* do the first one, for fuck's sake, don't do the second."

I nod. "Right."

"You won't make me look…stupid?"

Shake my head, solemn. "Never."

She breathes out through her nose, calm. "Fine. I love you too."

"Fuck yeah you do!" I lift her clean off the ground, spinning her about as I kiss her. "Now let's go have a proper snog and let me feel you up in front of Mick so he has a stroke—"

Her eyes go wide. "Joah—!"

"I'm joking!" Am I though? "Kinda."

Ysolde rolls her eyes, and I grab her hand, tugging her along towards the back.

Mad, isn't it, that she hasn't really met the lads yet? Just Rich, and barely at that. Don't even know how they met, do I? How he ended up bringing her back to my green room—?

"Ysolde Featherstonhaugh," Richie cuts in. "We know."

I nod her way. "My *girlfriend*."

"Oh fuck—" Rich laughs. "Alright."

He gets up, swaggering over all big-brother like—tosser. Leans in close, whispering so only I can hear: "How much of that was to piss off Mick?" He smirks.

"A bit." Whisper it back, but it's a lie. Fuckin' none of it, that's the truth. I want her to be my—fuck it, whatever—*girlfriend*. Just mine, really, you get me?

Ain't never fallen for a girl this quick before, have I? Not havin' 'em think I'm some wet wipe.

"We've met before. For a minute, just—" Ys smiles at him.

Richie chuckles, sticking his hand out to Ys. "Alright, good to see ya again."

She takes his hand, gives him that smile of hers—I can see it nearly knocks him clean off his feet. Not his fault. Her smile's like that, just. She's got that effect on men. Most of 'em, anyway.

Not girls though—fuck.

Loxy's glaring at my girl in a way I don't fuckin' like. Now, fair play—aside from when I was dating Pip, Lox's been the only bird 'round us from the start. Heddie's been on the team about nine months now, and they get on alright, but Loxy don't see her like she does other girls. Fallow's been Loxy's savanna, hasn't it? Ys showing up out of the blue ain't gone down too well.

I point to her. "That's Loxy."

Loxy doesn't say a word, just blinks a couple of times.

"Oi." Richie frowns, gives his girl a poke. "Don't be fucking rude."

Loxy shakes her head, mutters, "Girls like her don't have owt to say to girls like me."

Ys shifts uncomfortably, looks dead uneasy all of a sudden. If she didn't know what to say before, she sure as fuck don't now. Hate it. Proper pisses me off, Lox making her feel like shit.

"Girls like her—?" I narrow my eyes at her. "Hot ones, you mean?"

Loxy flips me off, and Rich rolls his eyes, muttering some shit under his breath.

Ys gives me a pointed look, leans in and whispers, "That can't have helped."

"Fuck her, I don't care—" I whisper back, then gesture to the lads on the couch. "That's Chops and Fry. That's the girl Chops is fucking. That's Fry's missus, Stacey. That's Harley, our producer, and that's—" I pause cos I don't recognise that last person.

But Ysolde does, apparently!

"Chenko!" Ys grins at the new bird hanging off Harley's arm. She's new. Not seen her before. Very fit.

"Ysolde!" The girl's got some kinda accent. Eastern European, maybe? Dunno.

They hug.

I glance between them. "How do you—?"

"We're all signed to Rain," Ys says, nodding over at her best mate, who's chatting up some up-and-coming geezer called Gary Lightbody. Dunno if he's any good or just full of shit.

Ys pulls me over to her mate. "Lalee—"

Lala looks up.

"I'd like you to meet my *boyfriend*…"

Lala jumps to her feet, her face lighting up like Christmas. It's cute. They're cute.

Lala turns to me. "Hello, Boyfriend. I see you wasted no time."

I shrug. "Know what I want. Went for it."

She nods, a bit impressed, I reckon. "Suppose I'll be seeing more of you, then…"

"Suppose you will." I nod back. Game recognises game, don't it? Reckon she's the most important person in Ys's life. Or she was, till about five minutes ago.

TIME OF YOUR LIFE

I hook an arm 'round Ys's neck, press my mouth to her ear. "You wanna get out of here?"

Ys looks surprised. "You don't want to stay?"

I shrug.

She lifts a brow. "Are you not, quite infamously, a bit of a party animal?"

Pretend to think about it. "I've been known to party on occasion…"

"Yeah—" Richie pipes up, sidling beside me. "And David Beckham's been known to kick a fuckin' ball about…"

I snort a laugh.

"We don't have to leave…" Ys smiles at me, encouraging.

Sort of want to, though, don't I? Can't fucking say that, though. First time in me life summat's sounded more fun than gettin' pissed and off me face. Can't say that either, so I say this instead: "Fuck it, man, let's go."

Chuck meself onto the couch, pull Ys down onto me lap, kiss her neck cos I can't fucking help it—keep at it till she squirms.

"What d'you want a bottle of?" someone shouts over. I glance at Ys.

"Don Julio," she says.

"Ey, what you on about?" I pull back, give her a look. "We shoot Johnny Walker 'round here."

She presses her nose to mine. "Not anymore, you don't."

And y'know what? Fuck it, she's right. I'll fuckin' shoot whoever she wants me to now.

JOAH HARRIGAN SERENADES MYSTERY MUSE AT FALLOW'S HOMETOWN TOUR KICKOFF

By Fiona Tate, Entertainment Correspondent, The Daily Sun

Last night, Fallow lit up Camden's Electric Ballroom for the first of three shows on their intimate hometown tour—and whilst the music was as explosive as ever, it was front man Joah Harrigan's unexpected onstage antics that left the crowd buzzing.

In a move equal parts rock star and romantic, Harrigan, 23, stunned the sold-out audience when he paused the show to wax poetic about a mystery woman in the room. "She's like a tune in my brain that I can't stop humming," Harrigan admitted, sparking wild speculation about who this "tune" might be.

Well, we've got our guesses. Rumours swirled after Ysolde Featherstonhaugh, the fashion world's It Girl and British socialite, was spotted front and centre alongside her famous BFF, Lala Caravella. Whilst Featherstonhaugh maintained a low profile throughout the night, insiders claim Harrigan's smitten gaze barely left her.

The intimate Camden show—a deliberate nod to Fallow's gritty beginnings—took an unexpected turn when Harrigan broke into a cover of "Crimson and Clover," reportedly Featherstonhaugh's favourite song. The moment was electric, with fans cheering wildly, though not everyone was thrilled. "He's ruined my life—but in the best way," confessed one tearful fan post-show.

Backstage sources reveal Harrigan's bandmates were blindsided by the song choice. Witnesses reported his brother and Fallow's lead guitarist, Richie Harrigan, throwing an unimpressed glare at Joah as the impromptu performance began. But the frontman's charm, as always, won out. "He's magnetic," said one audience member. "It felt like he was singing to just one person in the room."

TIME OF YOUR LIFE

Whilst Fallow is no stranger to performing at massive venues like Wembley, this three-show hometown tour—culminating with two dates in Manchester next month—marks a rare return to more intimate stages. Publicly, it's a gesture of gratitude to their roots; privately, industry insiders say it's a savvy move to keep their "grounded boys from Camden" image alive.

Whether Featherstonhaugh's presence signals a budding romance or a mere coincidence remains unclear, but one thing's certain: Joah Harrigan's blend of rock-star bravado and romantic theatrics has the world's attention.

The biggest band in the world, a supermodel in the crowd, and a song sung straight to her—if this is night one, we can't wait to see what Manchester brings.

EIGHT

ysolde

JILLY E. EDWARDS IS INDISPUTABLY the best agent on the planet.

She found me when I was fifteen outside Selfridges in my school uniform. I was with my older sister, Evanthe—she never said anything but I think she hated that I was scouted and she wasn't. It's not that she's not beautiful; she is—but I probably am more so in a conventional way. Beauty is a funny thing, isn't it? The only way I've ever really been able to approach it is to treat it like it's the skill set it is. And sure, it's not a learnt skill, but people have a natural aptitude towards things like science (Evanthe does, for example). I have one towards being attractive, I suppose.

She's always been weird about me being a model, so has our dad. My little sister's sweet about my job though. I think she thinks it's cool. To an eighteen-year-old, it would be. I suppose to me, at twenty, it's still pretty cool. She wants to be an actress, my little sister. So she says, anyway. She's never actually done anything about it, never joined a local theatre or even been in a school play. Which sort of makes me think that maybe she just wants to be famous. Which is mad. Only a person who's never been famous would want to be famous.

TIME OF YOUR LIFE

81

I love Rain's offices. They're on Welbeck Street, and Jilly's office is the best one because *she's* the best one. Lala and I in the industry are known as "Jilly's girls," not Rain girls, even though we are technically both. Lala and I, and Chenko from the other night—we're her primary focus, and don't tell the others, but I'm definitely her favourite. I dunno why. Lala has two parents who love her, and I have only one, and he barely likes me, so maybe it's that she's sorry for me?

She cares very much about our health and well-being, which is weird for an agent, but nice. I know some girls in our industry who have agents encouraging them to throw up their dinner and chain smoke. Jilly would never tell me to throw up my dinner—bad for teeth enamel, for one—and she says all the clothes we wear are too expensive to have them smell like smoke.

I do smell a bit like smoke though—Joah loves a cigarette. I suppose he actually loves most vices…

"Do you have any perfume on you?" I ask Pixie in the lift on the way up to the offices.

She nods and fishes some out of her mini gold Duma backpack from Chanel last year, offering me her CK One. I give myself a couple of spritzes, but Pix gives me a look.

"She's still going to smell you…"

I grimace as we round the corner into the office.

It's very white, lots of plants and dramatic rugs—photos of Lala's and my most famous shoots with a big desk in the centre of it all. I'm not there for any particular reason, sometimes we just come here to come here. My mum's dead and Lala's lives in Spain now, so we're practically orphans.

Jilly springs to her feet as soon as she sees me, arms open.

"Darling heart." She pulls me into a hug and I give Lala—who's over on the sofa, magazine in hand—a smile over Jilly's shoulder.

Jilly kisses my cheek, then scowls. "You smell like smoke."

"I walked through a terrible puff of it on my way up!" I lie, and she gives me a suspicious *mm-hmm*, then she moves past me, kissing Pixie's cheek also before she turns back to me, touching my hair affectionately.

"Look at your hair, all tussled by a rock star."

"It's chic," Lala tells her.

"It's…not, darling, but okay—" Jilly gives Lala a patient smile before she turns back to me. "I heard the severity of your crush is worse than the Kelly Slater affair."

"She already said she loves him," Lala tells Jilly—sort of dobbing on me because she wants to be in Jilly's good books. Jilly's like that. Lala is literally the coolest person in every single room, and still even she wants Jilly's approval.

"To his face," Lala adds on.

Jilly stares at me, eyes wide and a bit alarmed.

"He said it first?" I offer.

Pixie throws herself down dramatically onto the sofa next to Lalee.

"Joah Harrigan said *I love you* to you?" She sighs, forlorn.

"He did," I tell Pix with a smile that gives away all my cool.

"Oh. My. God." Pix stares at me, jaw practically on the floor. "Oh my god, she's the luckiest girl in the world—" she tells no one in particular.

"Pixie." Jilly gives her a my-patience-is-waning smile now. "Do calm down."

"When did he tell you?" Pixie asks, not remotely responding to Jilly. "And where—? Was it like, after you'd had sex or like when he—"

"After he sang her a song at his show," Lala tells her.

"HE SANG YOU A SONG AT HIS SHOW?" Pixie literally yells.

Lala silently starts laughing from beside her, and I give her an exasperated look.

Biggest drama queen I've ever met, Pix. It's a crime she never went out for RADA.

"I mean—" Pix gives me a look. "Don't get me wrong, I am happy for you but I'm sad for me."

TIME OF YOUR LIFE

Jilly's back behind her desk now, chin in hand. "Is he romantic?" she asks, thinking it all through. "Is he very sweet with you, darling?"

I nod. "I think so."

I clock Lala, make sure she thinks that too.

"Yeah, I think so too," she tells Jilly with a smile.

Jilly thinks to herself for a moment. "He's rather crass, is he not?"

"He does say the F-word *a lot*," I concede.

"And the C-word…" Pixie tattles on him.

"No—" I shake my head at Jilly. "He's promised to stop that."

"Well, that's something," Jilly says with what's supposed to be an encouraging smile, but it's a bit half-baked.

"It is," Lala says, trying to counteract the energy in the room. "Sol hates that word."

"It's so lowbrow. I immediately feel poorer whenever someone says it near me…"

"Did you tell your boyfriend that?" Lala asks, eyebrows up.

I umm and ahh. "Not so colourfully, but yes, I believe my stance was made apparent."

Pixie perches on Jilly's desk, thinking to herself before she says aloud: "He is poor though, isn't he?"

I scrunch my nose up at her. "No."

"But he *was*," Pixie tells me.

I look between them all. News to me. "Was he?"

"You didn't know?" Pixie says. "He grew up on a council estate…"

I cross my arms. "How do you know that?"

She shrugs. "I read about it in *The Daily Sun*—"

I roll my eyes at her, but Lala gives me an earnest look as I sit down next to her on the sofa.

"Can you not hear his accent?"

"There are rich people in Manchester!" I pout.

"Oh, yeah?" Lala scoffs. "Who?"

"Freddie." I tell her, defiant.

She rolls her eyes. "Manchester United players don't count."

I give her an exasperated look. "Well, cut my legs from under me then, why don't you?"

"What's it matter—? You love a bit of rough," Lala reminds me with a look.

And she's definitely talking about Freddie. He's my—never mind. I haven't worked out how to tell Joah about him yet, so let's not worry about him right now.

"Is he rough in the fun way?" Pixie asks and as she does, Jilly sighs forlornly.

"I don't know why I invited you all here—I forget that I get a horrible headache…"

"Yes," I say, ignoring Jilly but only because I know she loves me so it's okay to do that. "But the perfect amount. We're just…very in-tune, like, we're oddly in sync—but he's very commanding—? Very good at the tossing about…"

"Weakest of knees for being tossed." Lala nods her head my way. "He's also very sexually thoughtful, which is nice, I think—"

Pixie opens her mouth to speak—eyes about to fall out of her head as she's poised to presumably ask how Lala even knows, when Lala preempts the question.

She gestures towards me again. "I get a play-by-play of her day whether I like it or not."

Jilly clears her throat and gives me a careful look. "I did get a call from his manager…"

"What?" I blink. "Why?"

My agent takes a measured breath. "He's…*concerned*…" She gives me an apologetic smile that I do not meet. She keeps going. "…that you're not the *best* thing for Joah's image?"

"Right—" Lala jumps to her feet, pushing her sleeves up. "What's this man's name?" she asks Jilly. When Jilly doesn't answer her, Lala turns back to me, eyebrow up, waiting.

"Mick," I tell her, because maybe Mick *could* use a visit from Lalee…

TIME OF YOUR LIFE

"Mick Who?"

And I'm about to say his surname when Jilly points her finger from across the room at me.

"Don't."

Lalee falls back down onto the sofa, pouting, arms crossed. "Cock."

"Angel—" Jilly gives me a patient, maternal smile.

"You are the fashion world's darling. And yes, there's often some lighthearted gossip about you most days in most papers in the country—what's she wearing; what's she eating; she looks *hungry*—child's play. And society in general has a fairly balanced view on you—despite the fact that you've dated several high-profile men, and even though you once dropped a tiny baggy of MDMA on the pavement out front of Holy Brompton Trinity on Christmas morning—"

Lala grimaces on my behalf, before saying in my defence, "But how else was she supposed to sit through church?"

"Ys, the general public's perception of you…you're the modelling world's good girl…"

I roll my eyes at my agent now. She's being ridiculous. "Christy is the good girl."

Every man and his dog knows that.

"Yes." Jilly nods emphatically. "And you are right behind her, darling."

"You know what—" Lala says, glancing between us all. "She's not, actually—that's what's impressive about her. She's a fucking hot mess—"

I frown. "Hey."

"Love you, Sol—you are, though. Exclusively when it comes to men. Not your fault. You were raised by a nihilistic, emotional miscreant—"

"Well—" I start but my best friend interrupts me with a head shake.

"Wasn't a question."

I give her a look. "Nor was it a point—"

"The point is"—she turns to Jilly specifically—"she's not such a good girl. She has a flaming pile of men in her rearview mirror. She's just Ysolde Featherstonhaugh, and she has that smile and those eyes, and something about that combination—"

"—Yeah!" Pixie chimes in now. "They sort of just let it slide. She's not actually as innocent as they all make her out to be."

Jilly growls under her breath. "Well, *I* know that and *you* know that, and *she*"—points to me—"knows that, but the *general public* do not."

I cross my arms over my chest, huffing a little. "So?"

"*So*—" Jilly says, before she decidedly softens her tone. "Joah is *infamously* a bad boy…"

"He's not bad!" I say immediately and defensively.

Jilly shakes her head and I do believe—though I still don't much care for the conversation—I can see she's trying to be delicate…

"That *is* his image though, isn't it? The band, darling—how they behave—they're essentially hooligans."

I frown.

"Am I wrong?" she asks, and she sounds genuine. "I'm not trying to be unkind, my sweet, I'm just identifying a potential…*branding* clash."

I shrug. "Well, why does that matter?"

Now it's Jilly's turn to look a bit exasperated.

"You are the face of several of the biggest, most prestigious brands on the planet. Your brand very much matters, sweetheart. Meanwhile—" She gives me a stern look. "Your new boyfriend is the acceptable face of hoodlums in Britain."

I shake my head again. "No, he's not."

It's all making me feel a bit sad now, actually. How Jilly's talking about him, how worried her face looks—she loves me, she's not self-serving. If she's implying Joah isn't good for me, it's because she really believes it. And I hate that.

"You know that last month he was deported from Amsterdam for drunk and disorderly behaviour?"

"Oh, yeah!" Pix nods. "I read about that—"

I look from my PA to my agent.

Jilly keeps going. "He trashed a historically significant hotel room in the city."

"No, he didn't," I say automatically, but I don't know—did he? Maybe he did?

Pixie shrugs. "According to the article anyway…"

I roll my eyes at both of them. "Why would he do that?"

Jilly nods appreciatively. "That's a really good question, Ys. Probably one worth asking him if you're going to be in a relationship together…"

I give her a little glare. "We're already in a relationship together."

Jilly raises her eyebrows. "Then perhaps you should have already asked."

I don't know why that makes me feel funny, but it does? This almost tacit insinuation that I don't know him how I think I know him.

There are so many ways you can know a person, and knowing someone isn't linear anyway.

I'd be lying if I said I wasn't a little bit aware that the breakneck speed of our romance feeds a bit into that heedless nature everyone keeps talking about Joah having—and fine, I'll give it to them— sometimes he is impulsive and impatient and impetuous—he can be those things and I can know he is those and still love him. And I know no one's said it, but I can feel it pressing in around me that people don't necessarily believe that we are—you know, *actually* in love. That they think it's just infatuation or a momentary fixation, and objectively, I understand how and why they might arrive at that conclusion—but then, they haven't seen how he is with me, how his eyes go right before we kiss, how he watches me till I fall asleep, how he holds me, how his cheek presses against mine, locked in place like a puzzle piece. I mightn't have known him for years or know what street he grew up on—but I know how his heart sounds, I know the beat of it, I know the rhythm of his breathing, I know the patterns he blinks, I know how he likes his eggs in the morning, I know the temperature he likes his showers, and I know what colour lingerie he likes me best in. There are different ways you can know a person, that's my point and that's what I'm telling myself when Pixie suddenly asks me the rudest question in the world: "Hey, what's his house like?" She asks it with a nice, casual blitheness that interrupts my reverie.

"What?"

"His place—" Pix says again. "Where he lives…what's it like?"

"Oh—" I say, because it dawns on me right then in this very terrible moment that I still haven't been there.

"You've been there, right?" Pix asks with a big smile.

Lala scowls at Pixie. "Of course she's been there—" she says, blindly defending me (which is her way), then she glances at me out of the corner of her eye to double check and her face freezes.

"Oh my god! Ysolde!" Lala yells, immediately outraged. "What!"

My hands fly to my cheeks. "Oh my god! Is that weird?"

Lala's face is all scrunched up. "It's *so* weird, Sol!"

Jilly starts shaking her head, trying to deescalate the fire I semiblame her for inadvertently starting. "It's not *so* weird…"

"Really?" I ask, hopeful, hands unconsciously covering my chest, and that's all you need to know about how I feel about him.

"Well—" She reconsiders. "No, I suppose it is *quite* weird."

My hands fly back to my cheeks. "Oh, shit!"

Pixie tries to throw me a bone. "Maybe his house is messy and he's embarrassed—"

"Or—" And I'm spiralling now. "Maybe he has a girlfriend and I'm the terrible mistress."

"If it's any consolation"—Lala gives me what's supposed to be an encouraging look—"I think I'd kill myself if you were my boyfriend's mistress…"

"Oh." I flash her a grateful smile. "Thank you, that's kind. But—fuck! No! Oh my god, I'm so stupid, this is a complete and total, unmitigated disaster—"

TIME OF YOUR LIFE

The magazines already know about us now. The were waiting for me when I left the hotel today. *Where's Joah? How long have you been sneaking around? Has he written a song about you yet? What happened with Mitchell Montrose-Bowes? Do you like bad boys now?*— imagine how mortifying it'll be if he has a fucking girlfriend he's hiding in his fucking house and I'm the last one to find out about it!

"Alright." Jilly claps her haps together, trying to corral our attention again. "Ys, calm down. You haven't been to a boy's house in Camden, it's hardly Chernobyl."

Though I'm not sure I actually entirely agree.

NINE

ysolde

"DO YOU WANT TO TALK about it?" Aleki asked on the drive over. He wasn't with me in Jilly's office; I didn't even tell him anything happened—and technically nothing did—he just knows me. It's his job to know me and read me—he's very good at what he does— and today, now, everything about me must look off-kilter, because that's exactly how I feel.

I shook my head and stared out the window, chin in my hand on this fairly gloomy day in early March.

Joah's sitting with his back to me when Aleki and I arrive. Joe's Café, Sloane Street. He's in a black leather bomber jacket, slung back in his chair, a beer in his hand, and my heart's tossing and turning in my chest because suddenly I feel funny. And stupid. God, I hate feeling stupid.

I wouldn't have met here, in public, where people can see me, but I'm worried now I'm about to find out something hateful about the boy I met almost two weeks ago and accidentally fell in love with—admittedly (particularly in context of all this) far too quickly. Lala told me that you should never break up with someone in their home or your home—half so you can get out of there quick smart when the time comes, but also so it's not tainted. You don't want to ruin a place you love, and I love Claridge's. It took me so long to feel safe again after what happened, and I finally do, and I don't want to have to move again, and so in case Joah and I are about to have a fiery breakup because it just so happens that he is indeed an arsing prick, we're doing it at Joe's Café. Which—actually, honestly, I do love. But I felt as though he'd be suspicious if I asked to meet at the Pret-A-Manger at Trafalgar Square.

I sit down across from him and his face lights up again.

"Oi!" He beams, leaning over the table and pressing his lips into mine. "Fuck—I'm happy to see you—"

It makes me happy for a second but just for a second. Kisses don't mean anything—just ask Jesus.

I tilt my head, give him a controlled smile. "Are you?"

"Yeah—" He nods, his eyes moving over my face—trying to read me. "Missed you—"

"Did you?" I say, watching him for clues, and now he's watching me back.

His eyes pinch a little. "You alright, kid?"

"Mm-hmm."

They pinch a little more. "Sure?"

I nod once, lips pulled tight in what Jo calls my "Mona Lisa–PR smile"...

He stares at me, assessing now, and I know he knows for certain that something's amiss.

"You seem weird—"

"Nope." I shake my head, flash him that same smile again, though I know full well it'll convince him of absolutely nothing.

He nods but unsure now—he scratches the back of his neck, then plucks the menu up off the table.

"You wanna grab a bite?"

"Mmm"—I shake my head—"I'm not that hungry, actually. Why don't we just go back to your house?"

I try to keep the way the question sounds in my mouth light

and airy, but I can tell by how Joah responds to it, that that wasn't a nail I hit very well on the head.

"Uh—" His face pulls. "I…guess—?"

I cross my arms over my chest, scowling at him now.

"Do you have a girlfriend?"

His brows pull together, confused. "Yes." Then—almost as though he's uncertain, and *definitely* as though he's confused—he, carefully, raises his index finger and points at me.

I roll my eyes at him. "Another one?"

"Nope." He shakes his head, fairly certain this time. "Don't take this the wrong way, but—feels like I got my hands full with this one."

"Well, what the fuck!" I sort of yell, definitely louder than I mean to. His head pulls back a tiny bit—not afraid, honestly not even startled. It hurts my ego a small bit to admit that actually, he looks slightly amused. "Are you embarrassed for your roommates to know we're together?"

"Don't do roommates, do I? I live on me own—And, Ys, *The Daily Sun*'s got a bloody timeline of our 'warp-speed romance' in it today, so guess all of England knows now. But anyway, to answer your question… Nah."

I sigh, exasperated. "Then why don't you want me to come to your house?"

He covers his face with his hands and sighs this big, massive sigh, and it's proof that I'm not mad; it's true—he hasn't wanted me in his house. I can tell.

So I sit back in my chair, arms crossed over my chest, and wait for him to speak, eyebrow up.

He straightens up and takes a measured breath. "You know that shite about notches on belts?"

My brows dip. "Yes?"

Joah rubs his hand over his mouth—he looks a tiny bit stressed, actually.

"Got actual notches on me headboard." He grimaces as he says that, and immediately upon hearing that, I think he's a tremendous

TIME OF YOUR LIFE 93

twat so I say nothing to ease his discomfort. "When I first got me house and the bed—there'd been a"—clears his throat, as though he's trying to be delicate—"*handful* of people in it, you know what I mean—?"

"At one time?" I ask. "Like, in a singular instance?"

"Uh—" His face pulls as he thinks about it. "Well, yeah, that's happened—like, in general—but nah, in *this* story, I'd just bought me first proper bed with me first pay slip, and, y'know, ended up shaggin' like sixteen girls in two weeks."

I blink a few times. "That averages out to more than one a day."

He gnaws on his bottom lip and strangely doesn't look overly endeared by my maths.

"Anyway—" He shakes his head. "Fuckin' Rich thought it was hilarious, so he starts tallyin' 'em up on the headboard after they left. And I dunno, it just sorta became a thing, didn't it?"

I crinkle my nose at him because boys are yuck.

"Well, how many notches are there?"

Joah takes this breath, like he's about to speak, but then he just keeps breathing in, nothing comes out, and then he shakes his head, looking uneasy. I don't think I've ever seen him look uneasy before, except for the time that he got cross and left my hotel room for ten seconds before he came back; he looked uneasy then too—I quite liked it to be honest.

He swallows, like there's a lump in his throat, as though he's swallowing down the actual number he's got in his mind.

"So, yeah—didn't... I didn't, well—" He's babbling now. I've never seen him babble before. "—it's twofold, innit? Figured you'd find the notches a bit...off-puttin'."

"—I do."

He gives me a look. "Right, so well done me, then—"

I pull a face. "—Well, I wouldn't go that far."

He fights off a little smile.

"And second—" He reaches for my hand. "You're not a fucking notch."

I snatch my hand back. "Because we haven't done it in your bed? Whose fault is that—?"

"No, I—" He breathes out his nose loud enough that it tells me he's starting to lose patience. "I don't want you to be one, Ys."

"Oh," I say. I go quiet for a moment. "So we're just never going to go to your house?"

"No—" He shakes his head. "Was gonna get a new bed— ordered one and everythin'. Thought maybe I could keep you… satisfied at Claridge's, till it came, but—"

"I'm satisfied…" I tell him, nose in the air.

I like him a bit again now.

"Apparently not." He gives me a quarter of a smile, then pushes back from the table, beckons me over to his lap and I oblige him because he's Joah Harrigan, and actually, it turns out, I quite hate hating him—even though I did it only ever so briefly and barely at all.

He puts one arm around my waist; the other he throws over my legs—and he's looking at me with these eyes—they're so blue, remember? But also, there's a funny, ever-growing tenderness in them that I don't think I've ever seen him sport for anyone but me. I don't think he'd like to know, actually, how he's looking at me. I think if we were walking down the street and we passed another couple and the boy was looking at the girl the way that Jo looks at me without realising, I think he'd absolutely tear that poor boy a new one—so we mustn't tell him.

I push some hair behind his ears.

"Jo—"

He says nothing, just tilts his head at me, waiting.

"How many…*notches*—do you have?"

Immediately, he's shaking his head. "I'm not telling you—you don't want my answer—"

"Yes I do." I frown, feeling a bit defensive. "I'm not a prude."

He tilts his head, puts his hand on my cheek, looks at me with those eyes he'd hate to know he gives me.

"I know you're not." He gives me a gentle smile. "Still think you

TIME OF YOUR LIFE   95

don't wanna hear my answer though, Ys. And I sure as fuck don't wanna give it. But I wanna hear yours."

"That hardly seems fair…"

"S'pose not. Go on, you first—then we'll see after that."

"I don't know—" I shrug. "Like, thirteen people? Including you?"

It's funny, actually—after I say that, ever so slightly, his grip on my back tightens, his mouth presses together, nods a couple of times, swallows—goes quiet for a few seconds—I think he's visualising it? He's gone a bit pale.

He runs his tongue over his front teeth as he thinks.

"You know all their names?"

"Yeah? Oh—" I pause, casting my mind back to New Year's Eve 1993. "There's only one I don't know."

He nods coolly. "Can I have all their names? I just want to talk—"

I give him a look because he's being silly, and then Jo goes quiet again for a few seconds and I know he's running away with it in his mind. He's very competitive, you see? And territorial, and yes, we might have arrived where we are quickly, we might have fallen down the mountain, as opposed to consciously, intentionally having hiked down there—but we're in the valley now. We are where we are, that just is what it is—and Joah, in this present moment, is absolutely beyond a shadow of a doubt, being entirely assaulted in his brain by images of me having sex with mystery men.

"Whoa—" He starts shaking his head for the millionth time today. "—fuck. No, I fuckin' hate that, like—?"

I hold his face with both my hands.

"Jo, it's not a big deal…"

He puts his hands on top of mine, gives me a look. "No, it's not. But it is, you know what I mean—?" He shoves his hands through his hair, he looks stressed now, genuinely stressed. "Am I the best?"

I give him the look I give him when he's being silly.

"The best what?" I ask, though I know exactly what he's asking.

Joah and I have a standoff with our eyes, but he's too proud to ask out loud what he's wondering.

I raise my eyebrows. "Joah, if you have a question—just ask it properly."

He closes his eyes tightly, in this funny, decided kind of way. "Fuck—nah, forget it. I'd have to top meself if I found out you shagged Brad Pitt and he were better at it than me—"

"Well." I purse my lips. "*Better* can be so subjective, because I mean, admittedly, he is very good in bed, but"—I gesture between Joah and me—"our chemistry is way better, so that makes everything better, you know?"

Joah takes a deep breath in through his nose, holds it, head falls back, eyes closed, face upwards towards the ceiling.

"Are you takin' the piss? Like, was that a joke, or are you actually tellin' me you fucked Brad Pitt?"

I frown at the sentence. "Well, 'fucked' comes across so terribly crude when you say it for some reason—"

"OH MY GOD," Joah yells loud enough that the entire restaurant goes quiet and Aleki gets to his feet a few tables away—I flash him a smile and thumbs-up to tell him I'm fine and to leave me.

The whole restaurant keeps staring and Joah realises, and his spikes go up—which I've never seen before, not properly. I've heard about it. Pixie told me he's famously abrasive sometimes for literally no reason at all, and I suspect right now he feels at least a little bit justifiably entitled to whatever spikes he's sporting.

He glowers at the faces staring at us.

"What the fuck are you lookin' at?" he asks the room collectively, then zeroes in on a specific guy in his mid-twenties. "What the fuck are you staring at, mate? Eyes on your own plate"—he says the C-word, which I hate so I won't be saying it, not even for you— "Fuck off."

"Jo—" I touch his cheek, try to centre him to me. "Calm down."

He nods a couple of times, but his eyes give him away—I'll learn that more and more—that Joah's eyes tell all his secrets and

TIME OF YOUR LIFE 97

everything else he wouldn't want you to know, and right now he's frenetic.

He rubs his hand over his mouth again. "When?"

I shake my head. "It was one time—like a year ago, at Venice Film Festival—"

"Well, shit." He sighs heavy. "That's *Legends of the Fall* proper fucked up the arse, innit? Liked that movie, didn't I? Brad *fuckin'* Pitt, Ysolde—? Jesus wept. Think I'm gonna be sick—"

"Harrigan." I tilt my head, trying to catch his eye. "You're being silly. You asked me a question and—"

Jo swallows all heavy, something about his face is pitifully desperate but almost comically so? "Gonna need you to stop talkin' now, Trouble, aren't I? Like, fuckin'—I love you, Ys"—puts his hands on my cheeks when he says that but gives me a stern look— "but, just…leave it, yeah?"

"Joah—" I laugh. "Really—considering who I am and what my job is, is it all that terribly surprising? Like—who did you think my sexual partners were going to be? The shop boy in the garage?"

He stares at me, incredulous.

"Ain't never fuckin' thought about your shags before, have I?" He pauses, reconsiders. "Well, I have—just told meself they were all shit knockoffs of me but—"

I give him my most exasperated look to date. "You are such a bloody narcissist."

Joah lets out this frustrated sound, then shoves his hands through his hair again.

"How the fuck've we ended up on this? This is the worst fuckin' topic ever—Worst fuckin' chat of me life. Who else—?" he asks me, then immediately clearly regrets it. "No. Fuck. Don't tell me." He pauses again. "Fuck it, tell me. Nah—don't!"

I'm laughing now, and he's glaring, though his eyes are finally starting to soften again.

"See what you do to me? I'm so in my fuckin' head. Never in me head about girls, not ever—and then two weeks with you and

I'm…I'm a proper melt now, that's what I am—" He gives me a look. "Like, what the fuck are we even talkin' about this for? How'd we get here?"

"Well." I purse my lips. "I asked why you wouldn't take me back to your place, and it really went downhill from there…"

"Alright, fuck it—" He sighs. "—while we're down here, you got any other questions, then?"

I nod and he looks a bit surprised.

"Oh shit—didn't think you'd say yes like—Alright, fuck—" He straightens up. "Go on, then…"

"Just one," I tell him, and he lifts an eyebrow as he waits.

I press my lips into his just because I want to and I can—what a life—then I drape my arms around his neck.

"Is it true you trash hotel rooms?"

He cocks a little half smile—I think he thinks I'll be impressed. "I've been known to trash a hotel room or two in my time."

I lift my eyebrows. "Why?"

He shrugs. "Because."

"Because why?"

"Because I can," he says, as though that's an answer, and maybe it is, but I don't like it.

I trace the outline of his mouth with my thumb—it's such a naughty mouth, it really does get him in a world of trouble. I have a feeling it will ultimately get me into many worlds of many different kinds of trouble also.

"You'd *choose* to destroy something merely because *you can*?"

And that, I suppose to his credit, does give Joah some pause.

So I add, "*Can* and *should* sometimes aren't the same things. I dare say, very often are not the same thing at all…"

"Alright, kid—" Jo gives me little shove as he rolls his eyes. "Fuckin' get down off that high horse—"

And—it's strange, I can't quite explain it—but suddenly, I'm nervous again. Different than before.

"Will you destroy me, Jo?" I ask him quietly, holding his eyes.

His head pulls back—the thought hurts him (or in the very least, offends him). "What?"

"Well, you could—" I tell him. "Could you not? One could argue I've given you that power. I love you, thus you have the capacity to destroy me." I straighten up on his lap, chin held a little high. "Will you?"

He goes solemn as he leans in towards me. "You're too beautiful."

I rest my forehead against his as my heart sinks like a heavy old anchor to the deepest part of a dark seabed.

"That's not a no," I whisper to him.

Joah's eyes lock on to mine, holds my face with his unwavering hands that are more steady than I fear he'll ever be able to be, then he looks me clear in the eye.

"No," Joah tells me.

And that—I'll realise in eventual time—will be the first time that he lies to me.

TEN

joah

YS MUTTERS, EYES FIXED ON the window, like it's got all the answers. Aleki snorts a laugh from the front seat—the smug bastard knows what's coming. I didn't even have to tell him.

We're ten minutes out from the stadium, the streets getting busier with lads in red shirts and scarves, pint-fuelled chants spillin' out of every boozer we pass. Sunday afternoon, and I'm takin' Ys on a date. Sorta. If you count draggin' her to a United game as a date. I didn't tell her, did I—? Just said I had plans for us. This is the plan.

We did stay at mine after the other day, by the way. Her little meltdown—? Fuck me, she was in her head, wasn't she? Proper spun herself out. Took her back to mine that night.

In all fairness to her, she did think the notches were funny once we got there. *Actually* funny, you know. Started counting them out loud like it was some piss-take game. Got to eighty-six before she paused, looked over at me, all wide-eyed and posh as you like.

"Are these representative of your every sexual encounter or just the ones that took place in this bed specifically?" she asked and I grimaced. She rolled her eyes, kept at it, gave me some shit for the final number in the end—and don't ask, it's none of your fucking business, is it?

Prefers her place though, don't she—classic. That girl has so much fucking stuff. It was 'round the fifth time of her asking me *do you happen to have a*—and I stopped her, because no. Shook my head. "Whatever it is, Ys, I don't have it, do I?"

She let out this little huff through her nose, that frustrated look flitting across her face like she's trying not to make a big deal of it. Classic Ys, that.

"Reckon we should just keep stayin' at yours from now on then, Trouble?" I offered, half takin' the piss. She nodded quick, smilin' all relieved, like I'd just handed her a golden ticket or summat.

So from Claridge's, it's about a forty-five-minute drive to Tottenham Hotspurs.

When we're about five minutes away, she gives me this side-eye, proper wary, like she knows I'm up to somethin' and she's already workin' out whether to have a go or let me stew in it.

"Are we going to the football?"

I give her a big, hopeful grin.

"Why didn't you just tell me?" She rolls her eyes, bit put out.

"I was being romantic?" I try. Bit of a lie, though, and she knows it straight off. Try again. "Didn't peg you for a sports girl."

"Well pegged."

"It's a really important game, Ys—" I grimace, tryin' for apologetic, but I'm not sure she buys it. "United versus Tottenham."

"Oh—" Her eyelids flutter like that means summat. "It's a Uni—we're at a United game?"

I give her a look. "Course it's fuckin' United—what else would it be?"

"Oh—" She nods more. "Yeah, it's just—"

"What?" I press, following Kekoa as he leads us through the service entrance. The stink of stale beer and concrete fills the air— proper football, this.

"Nothing, never mind," she mutters, brushin' it off. Kekoa

glances back at us, and I shoot him an exasperated look. Like, fuckin' *yeah, mate, she's still alive back here.*

"It's just tickets, right? We don't go backstage?"

I pull a face. "Not a concert, kid."

She nods, don't say owt else. Girls, man…

"Are ya pissed we're here?" I ask, half expecting her to go off on one.

"No—" Shakes her head, all quick like. "No, entirely indifferent."

"Will you be bored, but?"

She nods, dead straight. "Quite likely, yes."

"Yeah, but pretend to love it for me, will you—?"

Flashes them lethal eyes at me. "For you—yes."

Hook me arm 'round her neck, yank her in close, kiss her. Bit rough but she melts into it—always does—girls love a bit o' rough.

"Tomorrow, yeah—? We'll do somethin' you love," I say against her lips. "Like, I dunno—we'll go to that high tea you're always banging on about…"

Looks pretty chuffed with that, she does.

Takes long enough to make our way through the stadium because we get stopped a fuck tonne on the way. I mean, I always do—standard—but it's more than usual today. Cos of her.

She's a fuckin' big deal, you know what I mean? Like, yeah, we get stopped a bit in London—her scene, innit? Makes sense. But this ain't her world, you get me? We're at the football now and still, they're clockin' her almost as much as me.

Mental, innit. Proper mental.

We get to our seats—just behind the dugout, obviously. Best in the house. I settle in, toss my arm 'round Ys. Like my arm 'round her, don't I? Like the looks it gets me. Feels right, having her there. I'm used to being the centre of attention, but I don't mind it when she's the one people are starin' at. Bit proud of it, aren't I?

Stadium's pretty packed today, proper buzzing. She's lookin' around a lot, though. Funny, she's a bit like that. Always clocking exits, faces—like she's waiting for summat to kick off. Makes me wonder, you know? Think maybe somethin's happened to her.

TIME OF YOUR LIFE   103

Wanna ask her, but I don't wanna push. Still, feels like the sorta thing I should know, don't you reckon? Not cos I'm nosy or owt—just so I've got it, you know? So I know what's what.

Anyway, the lads come out onto the pitch, and there's a roar from our lot, boos from the Spuds. Proper noise. Love it.

Nudge Ys, nodding towards Freddie Fletcher as he jogs out.

"You see him there? Midfielder—number 7? Best player in the league. Easy."

She just nods, calm as you like, like it's no big deal.

He's a crackin'-lookin' lad, though. Can't deny it.

"Mad how good he is," I tell her, still watching him. "If you weren't here, I'd probably have a crack myself—"

I laugh—her too—but it's a weird one. Not her usual laugh.

Then, across the pitch, Fletcher clocks me. Eyes go wide, like he's surprised or summat. Silly bugger—fucking bleed United, don't I? Everyone knows that. Dunno what he's shocked about.

He starts headin' over. Fletch must be a Fallow fan. Love that. Knew he was a good lad.

"Oh, here we go," I mutter to Ys, giving her a big courtesy eye roll, laying it on thick. Ham it up, look all annoyed, like I'm not secretly buzzing that my favourite footballer's coming over.

Ys notices him, then—spots him making his way towards us. And then the weirdest fucking thing happens. She turns to me, takes this big breath, and swallows hard, like she's bracing herself for somethin'—

"I am so sorry," she says.

Bit confused now. "What?"

Old mate Fletcher beelines it straight to us, don't he? Hangs over the railing, casual as you like—but he's not lookin' at me. Nah man, he's lookin' at her.

"Sol," he says with a smile I fucking hate.

She gives him one of those controlled, little smiles, the kind that's all polite but keeps you at arm's length. "Fletch."

What the fuck is going on?

Freddie Fletcher—Freddie fucking Fletcher—narrows his eyes at my girlfriend, proper focused, like there's no one else in the stadium.

"You hate football, Sol…" he says, like it's some inside joke I'm not part of.

She presses her lips together, pretending to think it over, all breezy and posh. "'Hate' is such a strong word…"

"And yet you used it so often to describe the game I gave my life to…"

I'm just staring at her like a fucking idiot—didn't know this was my nightmare, but it is, I reckon. Tailor-made special for me.

"Oops." She shrugs like she's innocent but I'm realising, she sure as fuck is not.

And like, Fletcher looks amused, don't he? Like she's just put on a show for him. Hate that too.

"What are you doing here, Ys?" he asks, soft, like he's got some claim on her.

She finally gestures to me, and it's like I can breathe again. "I'm here with my boyfriend, Fletch." She says it like it's obvious, like this whole thing isn't mental. "Jo, this is Freddie. Freddie, Joah."

"Such a pleasure, man," he says, sticking his hand out at me like we're mates or summat. And fuck—course I've got to shake it, don't I? Otherwise, I'm the prick here. So, I shake it. Quick, firm, done.

"Huge fan," he tells me, all cool and easy, with that smile I'm really fuckin' starting to hate. Then he tilts his head, proper curious. "How the fuck did you get her to come?"

I shrug, playin' it off like I'm not sat here losin' me fuckin' mind. "Bribed her."

He smirks. "Brilliant."

Then, like I don't even exist anymore, he stretches his big fucking arms past me to Kekoa, lounging behind us. Offers him a hand like they're old mates.

"My man," Fletcher says, like he owns the place.

Kekoa gives him a little wink. "Fletch."

TIME OF YOUR LIFE

Then fucking Number 7 settles his gaze back on my other half. "How's your dad?"

"Pricky," she says.

"And the girls?"

Ys shrugs. Dunno what girls she's talkin' about, do I?

"Evanthe is—as always—impossibly high strung and Crumpy's... Crumpy."

Stare at her, proper over their banter. "What the fuck's a 'crumpy'?"

Both Ys and Fletch fight off a smile—pisses me off, that. Don't like it.

"My sister," Ys tells me.

She has sisters? Since fucking when?

Raise me brows a bit, not sure. "You have a sister called Crumpy?"

"No." She tilts her head. "I have a sister called *Crumpet.*"

Don't do a good job at hiding my face on that—but like, what the fuck? Rich people, man—

"*I know*—" Ys gives me a look. "Ysolde's not so weird now, is it?"

Nearly chuckle at that, when fucking Fletcher pipes up again. Bit of a yapper, isn't he? Can't seem to shut it.

"Mum misses you," he says, like it's nowt.

She gives him this tender smile. Why the fuck is she giving him a tender smile? What's tender about this?

"I'll come see her soon," she tells him, all soft and sweet. And no, she fuckin' won't—not on my watch, mate.

"Good girl," Fletcher says, like he's pleased with himself. Smug prick.

"Fletch!" comes a shout from the pitch, and I clock it's Alex fucking Ferguson. Fletch gives him a thumbs-up, all casual, like he's not just been over here stirring the fucking pot of my mother-fucking happiness.

Then he turns back to me girlfriend—again—and nods towards the pitch like she's supposed to be impressed.

"Gotta get to work—" He starts backing up, then gestures

between me and Ys. "But I fucking love this." He zeroes in on me. "I want front-row tickets, lad… VIP, backstage—the works."

Nod coolly. "Yeah, man, for sure—" Want my girlfriend all oiled up on a fucking silver platter too, you pricking bastard, piss off.

Ys smiles at him though, nodding at me. "I'd say he wants season passes but I suspect he already has them…"

Give her a reluctant nod.

Fletcher gives me a wink. "Good man."

Fuck him like.

He jogs back to the team.

Take a long, measured breath, staring at the team I love in front of me, don't wanna react. I don't fuckin' shut up about this fucking team, I know they know it, so I can't react—just stare straight ahead. So, I keep my face straight, rub my hand over my mouth like I'm keeping somethin' in, and glance at her out the corner of my eye.

"You gonna unpack that for me?" I ask, low and rough, like it's no big deal. But it is.

She keeps staring straight ahead, keeps that fucking Mona Lisa smile playing about on her lips. "No, thank you," she says.

Give her a sharp look, make her sit up straighter.

"Okay." She turns to me. "So, funny story—"

Lift my brow. "Feel like it won't be, but go on…"

"Listen—we were really young—"

My eyes pinch. "You *are* really young."

She rolls her eyes. "Younger than I am now, then."

Keep my eyes fucking pinched. "Right…"

"We used to date, that's all." She shrugs like it's nowt, proper casual about it. Then she tacks on, like it's an afterthought: "A lot."

Shake my head at her now. "What does 'you used to date a lot' mean?"

"Well—" she starts but I cut her off.

"And how the fuck isn't this common knowledge, like—"

"I mean, it's not a secret—!" she tells me. "If you looked into it or asked around, someone would have told you, probably—"

TIME OF YOUR LIFE

And I'm fucking mad now—don't wanna be, but. Not here. "How the fuck could you not tell me?" I say through gritted teeth. Try to calm meself down. Take a breath, breathe it out through me nose. "—When I bang on about United all the fucking time—"

"Well." Her hands are on her cheeks now. "I didn't think it'd please you—"

"Oh—" I scoff. "And you live to fucking please me now, do you—? Since when?"

Pouts a little, crosses her arms.

"Well, I was right—look how displeased you are."

Give her a little glare for that. Bit of a brat, isn't she?

"How long were you together?"

"Uh—" She starts thinkin' to herself but I jump in again.

"And how naked has he seen you?" I ask.

Presses her lips together for four long seconds.

"Four or so years," she tells me. "And very."

Take a measured breath. "How 'very' is very?"

"Completely."

Me head falls back towards the sky. "Oh, fuck—"

Ys shakes her head quickly. "That doesn't mean anything though—lots of people have seen me without clothes on. It's part of my job!"

Give her an exasperated look—"Ys, that's not helping—fuck—!"

She offers me a helpless shrug. "We were kids, really…"

Shove my hands through me hair—and you know what—? Fucking fuck her for this—I'm not even watching the game. I've wanted to see this game all fucking week.

"Why'd you break up?" I ask her.

"It just got"—she shakes her head—"too hard. He travelled a lot. I travelled a lot. It stopped working, is all."

I jut my jaw as I nod, muddlin' it through.

"Did you love him?" I ask her after a minute.

There's a pause for a few seconds where she says nowt and it's all I need to know without her saying a word. Does say one eventually, though… Reluctantly.

"Yes."

And fuck me, maybe I'm just a paranoid, miserable bastard, but a bit of me worries she might still do now…

She puts her hand on my arm. "That's not a big deal, though—" she tells me. Feels like a fucking big deal to me but. "You've loved other people—" she tells me. "You loved Pippa, surely—"

Give her an exasperated look. "Well, that's fucking different—"

"How?"

"Because Pippa isn't fucking Madonna!" I say louder than I mean to. Might hear some fucking chuckles from 'round us… Can't rule out it not being her fucking bodyguard, can't look at him and check because I'll have to hit that fucker if he's laughing at me, won't I—? And that sounds like a fucking headache.

Ys is trying with me, I'll give her that… She gives me a small smile. "Do you mean that Pippa isn't fornicating with Madonna or—"

I cut her off. "You know what I mean."

She sighs, sorry. "No, I know, I know, I know—I'm sorry! I should have told you but I panicked, is all! Once I realised how much you love them—"

Shake my head at her, proper pissed.

"Can't believe you've shagged my favourite player."

She eyes me, a bit condemning. "Well, you're *impossibly* promiscuous—"

"Promiscuous, am I—?" Give her a look for that. The fuckin' nerve. "You wanna pull on that thread today, Trouble?"

Does, apparently. She keeps going. "You might have shagged my favourite player too, for all we know—"

I give her a look. "You don't have a favourite player."

"Yes, I do."

I nod. "Yeah?" I lift a brow. "Who? Who the fuck is your favourite player?"

She tucks her chin, bats her eyes, and gives me a cheeky poke.

"The biggest, sexiest player I've ever known."

Fuck, I love her. Gets a smile out of me, that.

Try to play it cool like. "Alright, well done."

She settles back into her seat, lookin' chuffed with herself. "Thank you."

Sling my arm back 'round her. "Haven't fucked meself but, have I?"

Gives me a look as she tucks in.

"Well, now I know you're lying."

GOALS, EXES, AND DRAMA: YSOLDE'S RUN-IN ROCKS JOAH AT SPURS GAME

By Fiona Tate, Entertainment Correspondent, The Daily Sun

When you're dating the world's biggest supermodel, drama follows you everywhere—apparently even to a football match. Fallow front man Joah Harrigan found this out the hard way at Tottenham Hotspur's home game yesterday, where he and girlfriend, Ysolde Featherstonhaugh, found themselves in the middle of a headline-making run-in with her ex, Manchester United's golden boy, Freddie Fletcher.

Featherstonhaugh, 20, widely regarded as the face of a generation, turned heads from her prime seats just behind the dugouts at White Hart Lane, where she joined Harrigan, a die-hard United fan. But the outing took an awkward turn when Fletcher—United's star midfielder and a longtime fan favourite—reportedly spotted his ex during warm-ups and made a beeline for her.

Eyewitnesses say the encounter was "polite but loaded."

"You could cut the tension with a knife," said one source. "Freddie smiled at her in this way that only an ex can—like he knows exactly what he's doing. Joah just stood there, looking like he wanted to be anywhere else."

Featherstonhaugh, ever the picture of grace, reportedly kept her cool during the interaction, offering Fletcher little more than a smile and a quick word. "She's a pro," another onlooker noted. "Ysolde looked unbothered, but the dynamic was impossible to miss. Joah looked genuinely rattled."

This isn't the first time Featherstonhaugh's past has sparked headlines. Whilst the model has famously kept her private life under wraps, whispers of her romance with Fletcher—said to have taken place before her meteoric rise to fame—have lingered in the industry for years.

As for Harrigan, the famously cocky singer, sources say the encounter may have thrown him off his game. "Joah's always got that devil-may-care attitude, but this was different," a source close to the scene spilled. "Imagine running into that ex—the one who's a football superstar—at a match. Brutal."

Still, the couple didn't let the drama overshadow their night. Post-game, Harrigan was spotted with an arm protectively slung around Featherstonhaugh as they left the stadium together. Ever the showman, he reportedly gave a cheeky grin to photographers, whilst he flipped them off as they were climbing into their car.

Love, football, and exes—a messy triangle that's proving more dramatic than any 90 minutes on the pitch.

ELEVEN

joah

YS HAD ASKED IF I had plans this afternoon, and I did—a radio thing at *Top of the Pops* that ran shorter than expected. Once it's done, I head to Mayfair to surprise her.

She'd given me a key to her room, hadn't she? Pretty cute, that. Never used it before. Feel like a bit of a big man when I open the door with it now.

Soon as I do, I hear voices. Weird. Who the fuck's here—? Never has people over, Ys.

I walk farther into her suite, hear the voices coming from the dining room, and poke me head 'round the corner—

It's her, two girls, and some old geezer sitting across from Ys. One of the girls is next to him, the other beside her.

Ys spots me, and at first, her face lights up for a split fuckin' second, but then it goes to worry or some shit. Then she reins that in too. Smiles big at me, but it's not a real one. Know her smiles now, don't I? This ain't one of 'em—

The man eyes me up and down, and I'm not gonna fuckin' lie— don't like him. Hasn't said a word yet, but I already know.

"And who is this?" he asks after a few seconds of silence.

TIME OF YOUR LIFE

"Dad, this is Joah. My...boyfriend."

The dad looks at her—fuckin' news to him, I can tell that much.

"Joah," Ys says, lookin' at me with them proper intent eyes. She's askin' me summat, but I ain't got a clue what yet. "This is my father."

I nod my chin at him. "Alright then?"

The dad nods back. Don't reckon he's too keen on me either, mind.

"And these are my sisters—"Ys points at them vaguely. Doesn't name them. Fuck, she's in her head. One of the sisters is obviously older and matronly. The other, nicer face, prettier too, she's clearly the youngest.

"Oh my god," the younger one mutters—but not quiet like, loud enough so everyone in the room's got an earful. "He's even hotter in pers—"

"—Crump," Ys cuts her off with a look—a big sister one. Fucking means business, you know what I mean—?

I walk farther into the room, shaking me head at me girlfriend. Feel fucking bad that I missed whatever this is—

She stands up from the table. I slip my hand 'round her waist, give her a peck.

"Sorry," I tell her. "Didn't know—would've skipped the radio thi—"

"No." She shakes her head. "It's fine."

I give her a nod, but there's summat in all this, buried somewhere, that's not right. Don't sit well with me. Don't like it.

Not a chair for me, by the way. Pisses me off, that.

So I nod at Ys, make it clear she's sitting on my lap now without saying a word. Reckon I might want her close anyway.

Pull her down proper onto me. Dad clocks it, his face like thunder, staring with them pinched-up eyes.

"You're the singer."

I nod. "Yep."

He stares for a few more seconds, then turns to Ys. "I didn't know he was your boyfriend."

"Oh, well." She shakes her head. "We happened rather quickly—"

"—Clearly," he breathes out, sounding unimpressed. "When?"

Fuck, I hate this prick. She looks proper stiff, all tense and dead weird. Does my head in.

"Just a couple of weeks ago."

"I'm Crumpet," the little one says suddenly, offering me her hand. That one wants to act, I reckon Ys said.

I take it. Catch Ys's eye, do my best not to laugh out loud at the most ridiculous name I've ever heard in my whole fucking life.

"Hey." Give the little sister a smile. "Joah."

"And that's Evanthe." Ys points to the older one, who gives me a polite but not all that welcoming smile.

"And my father, John," she says finally.

I stick my hand out for him, and you know what? That motherfucker stares at it a good fucking three seconds before he takes it.

"You can call me Mr. Featherstonhaugh," he goes.

"Yeah." I drag my tongue slow over my teeth, let the silence hang a beat too long. "Not happening, John."

Feels like maybe every girl in the room sucks in a breath, sharp like. Feel Ys go stiff in my lap, her little body tense as owt.

John straightens up. "So, are you as bellicose in real life as you are portrayed in the media?"

Lift my chin a bit, tilt my head. Some fucking nerve, innit? "You tell me, mate."

"Jo—" Ys murmurs, her eyes full of worry.

I press a kiss to her shoulder, let her know I've got this. Not gonna deck him. Not yet, anyway.

"What d'you reckon?" I ask, lookin' at her with a bit of a grin. "Am I *bellicose*?"

She gives me a look, a tiny speck of amusement breaking through. "*Sometimes*."

Johnny boy rolls his eyes, proper testing me now. Gettin' on my last bloody nerve.

TIME OF YOUR LIFE

"Lovely," he mutters, like the smarmy git he is.

"He is that too," Ys says, straightening up. Protecting me, I think. Fuck, I fucking love her. "Very lovely, and funny and clever and protective. And antagonistic. He just loves a grump…"

Dad's not impressed at all by that, is he—?

"Why is that?" he asks.

"Dunno, John—" I shrug at that bleeding prick of a man, stare him down. "Just a lot of shit pisses me off, I s'pose…"

"Uh." Ys clears her throat, trying her best keep everythin' movin', bless her. "Joah's headlining Glastonbury this year."

"Oh god!" Crumpet yells, proper jumps off her chair, like summat scared her out of it. "Can you get me tickets? Please? Please!"

"Yeah," I chuckle. "Easy done."

She's buzzin' off that. Turns to Ys. "And I can come with you?" she asks her big sister.

Ys nods. "Of course, Crumpy."

"Maybe," the dad pipes up, all firm-like, trying to make some sorta point—dunno what point—a fuckin' stupid one but, know what I mean?

"Anyway, Ysolde," he says, dabbing his gob with his napkin like a fuckin' aristocrat. "What's going on in your world? How's work?"

"Well," she says, glancing 'round the table before her eyes land on me. Holds 'em there a second. "I was chosen to be the cover of *Vogue*'s September issue."

I stare at her, completely gobsmacked. Holy fucking shit. Then it hits, and a massive grin cracks over my face. Buzzing, I am. Proper buzzing. Dead chuffed for her.

"Ys." I grab her face with both hands, couldn't stop myself if I tried. "That's fuckin' massive."

John—that wee bastard—sits back in his chair, doesn't seem like that news moved the metre at all for him. "You've been on the cover of *Vogue* before."

See it, don't I? That flicker of hurt flash across her face when he don't clock how big a deal it is. Quick as owt, she blinks it away, but I saw it.

"The September issue's, like, the biggest honour *Vogue* can give you—" she starts to explain, her voice steady, even though I know she's pissed he don't get it.

The dad smirks, proper smug. "Didn't know *Vogue* were in the business of bestowing honours these days."

I pinch my eyes at him, proper hard. Reckon there's a fuck tonne of shit this bloke don't know, no lie.

Ys don't say a word, just sits quiet, and he ploughs on, givin' her one of those fake, indifferent smiles. "Well, that's very nice, Ysolde. Oh—!" His face lights up. "Did you hear? Evanthe's got a boyfriend. Did she tell you?"

In a split second, Ys slaps on a smile, all painted delight for her sister. But I catch it—just before she pulls the mask on—see how much it fucking stings. And fuck that. No one's hurting my girl. Not her old man, not anyone.

I shake my head, stare him down, and let out a sharp laugh. "What the fuck?"

The dad pulls back like I've slapped him across the chops, all wide-eyed, bit floored. Like no one's ever dared to speak to him like that.

Ys springs off my lap, grabs my hand in a flash. "Can I talk to you?" she says, not waiting for an answer, already draggin' me up and outta the room before I can give the bastard any more lip.

When we're out of earshot, she spins 'round, givin' me that exasperated look. I shoot one right back at her.

"Are you havin' a laugh?" I stare at her, proper stunned. "What the fuck was that, Ys? He treats you like fuckin' shit."

"I know," she mutters.

I shake me head. "And you just take it."

She nods. "I know."

Hottest girl in the world, best one on the planet, right? Don't make any sense. "—But you're...you."

TIME OF YOUR LIFE 117

"I know." She drops her head, lookin' all embarrassed. "But he's my dad."

And I'm not sayin' it out loud, but I ain't so sure. Might share his DNA, but he ain't no fuckin' dad.

Give her a look, don't I? "One more word outta him, I'm gonna knock your dad's fucking block off, kid."

"Jo—no—I told you the night we met he didn't like me—"

"I know, but—the more I know you, the less fuckin' sense it makes—You're perfect."

She gives me a tired smile. "You're sweet."

"Oi, don't say that shit to me—" I scowl at her. "I'm a fuckin' rock star, alpha bullshit, manly man."

She smirks like she thinks I'm a right laugh. "Fucking rock star, alpha bullshit, manly men can be sweet..."

"Yeah." I look down at her, sceptical. "How'd you know?"

She shrugs. "Because mine is."

So I sling me arm 'round her neck and snog the life outta her for that, don't I?

Then, behind us, someone clears their throat.

I pull back a bit from Ys, but I don't stop holdin' her, do I? Don't really feel like I should, y'know? I know who's clearing their fuckin' throat and I ain't gonna let her go 'round him again.

Her dad's standin' there, sisters behind him—

"We're going to go," he says.

"Oh," Ys replies. Just "oh," and I'm ready to deck him again, the tosser.

"Long drive," the dad says.

"Sure." Ys nods. "Of course."

She forces a smile, and fuck him—no one forces a smile out of her.

"Where the fuck do you live, then?" I give him a look, make sure he knows I know he's bullshit, head to toe. "Penzance?"

John's eyes narrow at me. "Berkshire." He turns to his daughter. "Speak soon."

He walks out of the hotel room.

"Have a good rest of your week—" Ys says to Evanthe, who gives her a cool smile.

"Congrats on the boyfriend—" I say to her cos I don't like the look she just gave my girl. "Big fuckin' stuff—"

Ysolde's hand flies to her mouth to stifle the laugh tryin' to escape, but Crumpet lets a giggle slip. Evanthe shoots both her sisters a filthy look and skulks off.

Crumpet grins at me. "You're pretty funny." She looks past me to Ys. "I like him."

Ys gives her a proud, little smile, and then the sister gives her a hug. "Love you."

"Love you more," Ys says back.

Then they're gone.

As soon as the door shuts, I stare at her, eyes wide, can't fuckin' believe it.

"What the fuck did you do—skin his fucking cat?"

She gives me this little laugh—really, just a puff of air. Looks sad, doesn't she?

"I look like my mother."

"Oh" is all I say. Fuck. Put my arms 'round her again. "Oi, how'd she die?"

"Cocaine overdose," she says, and I dunno what I was expectin', but all I can think to say is "Fuck."

She don't say owt back, just nods.

"Shit—" I shake me head. "Your old man don't strike me as the party type—"

"He wasn't—" She shakes her head. "She was, though. A model too, actually."

"Fuck off." I give her a smile. Had no idea.

"Yeah." She nods, proud of her mum. "You'd probably recognise her face if you saw it… She was the first Black model to have her face on *British Vogue* in 1966."

"Wow—" I nod, impressed. "Ys—she'd be so fucking proud of you—"

TIME OF YOUR LIFE 119

"Thank you." She smiles, looks a bit knackered now, though.

"How'd they meet?"

"Well." She tilts her head, thinkin'. "He's very rich—"

I cut in, "—With a name like fucking *Featherstonhaugh*, spelt how you twats fucking spell it… You don't say…"

She smiles, amused. Keeps goin'. "And she was here alone; her family lived really far away—"

"Yeah?" I nod. "All the way out in fuckin' Berkshire—?"

That gets her. Proper laugh from her for that.

"I think he saw her and wanted her because she was beautiful but didn't really want her for *her*. Thought she'd settle down more than she did—"

"Was she a rubbish mum?" I ask. Dunno why.

"No." She shakes her head quickly, almost defensive. "No, but I don't think being a mother came naturally to her, necessarily—"

I nod a couple of times, tilt me head before askin' the next one.

"How old were you when she—"

Don't know why I can't say it? Fuckin' idiot, I am—she says it for me.

"Died?"

I nod.

She thinks back.

"I was…six. Crump was four. Ev was…eleven?"

I frown. Hate the thought of owt hurting her. Six is a baby.

"How old was your mum?"

"Thirty-two."

Head pulls back and I feel a wave of sick I don't fully get. "Fuck. Ys—"

Shake me, makin' sure I catch her eye. "Oi, listen—I need you to know, right? Your dad is a fuckin' piece of shit, right? All this shit, it's his loss—yeah?"

She swallows, nods sorta barely. Eyes look glassy—fuck, I ain't never seen her cry before. Dunno what I'd do if I did—? Die, probably—? Just fuckin' die. Can't stomach the thought. Lovin' someone is well fucked, innit?

But I'm right though, know what I mean—? His loss, no doubt. But my absolute fuckin' gain.

TWELVE

ysolde

"OH, GOD—" LALA SAYS, PANICKING and averting her eyes. "Look away—"

"What?" I do try to look away, but I don't know what I'm looking away from, so it's not incredibly effective.

We're at Tramp. Everyone on the planet is in here tonight, except for my boyfriend (he's on his way from a photo shoot for *Rolling Stone*). I'm actually out by myself tonight! I gave Aleki the night off. He wasn't mad on it, but we made a deal—he'd drop Lala and I off, and I had to be with Joah or Richie the entire night. He must like Jo more than he wants to tell me. Kekoa hasn't left me with anyone else since what happened happened.

Anyway, Lala's elbowing me with great urgency now. "Look down! Look down!"

"Why!"

"Well, hello there," says the smarmy voice of my dumbest ex.

I give Mitchell Montrose-Bowes a long-suffering smile.

Lala fucking hates this one. Hates. Tolerated him when we were together, ready to set him on fire once we'd broken up.

Lala hangs her head in defeat as Mitch leans in and kisses my cheek. He moves in to kiss Lala's, but she dodges him and it's overt and hilarious. Lala can sometimes strike people as abrasive, but that's mostly because she is exactly that. And I love her for it.

Mitch gives her an impatient smile "Always a pleasure, La."

"La," she says to him.

"What?" Mitch looks between us, confused.

"LaLa. There's two."

Mitch rolls his eyes. "I was shortening it."

She nods with a fake empathy all over her. "And I wasn't having a fucking bar of it."

"Fair enough." He shrugs before he turns to me. "It's not true, is it?"

I lift a bored eyebrow at him. "What isn't?"

"There's no way you're fucking about with Joah Harrigan."

My head pulls back. "Excuse me?"

Mitch shakes his golden head of hair, like I'm the silliest billy in all the land.

"He's beneath you," he tells me.

Lala grabs two drinks from the tray of a waitress passing by us—they're not walking around serving drinks, by the way. She just hijacked someone else's beverages. But it's Lala Caravella, and who's going to stop her from getting exactly what she wants—? Not I, to be sure.

Lalee hands me one of the drinks, takes a long sip of hers, zeroes in on Mitch.

"Well, *you* were beneath her and she fucked you, so—"

Mitch gives her a fake smile and flips her off; she mirrors him, does it all right back.

"So it's true then?" Mitch asks, eyebrow still up.

I stare at him a few long seconds. "I know you know it is."

"I'm just shocked—" Mitch shrugs. "He's very working-class, Featherstonhaugh."

"So?" I cross my arms over my chest. I hate this shit—I don't much care for anyone being talked down upon, but Joah?

TIME OF YOUR LIFE 123

Mitch shrugs like he means nothing by it, but he does. "Just didn't know you were into that sort of thing."

"You really shouldn't talk about him—" I shake my head.

Mitch looks pleased to think he's perhaps struck a nerve in me. "You're protective of him?"

"No—" I shake my head, but yes, obviously—"He doesn't need my protection. I just think that if he heard you were running your mouth about him he'd—" I mime a throat being slit before I smile uncomfortably. "I don't think you could take him."

Mitch looks offended now. "I fought a fucking lion in my last movie—"

I roll my eyes. "Your *stunt double* fought a lion—"

Lala cuts in. "—And didn't he lose, like, a massive chunk of his arm—?"

Mitch gives us this *yeah and—?* look. "That's why we use stuntmen."

"Yeah, I don't think Joah's going to fight your stuntman though, MB—" I grimace. "I suspect he'll just pop you right in that pretty little nose you paid for."

Mitch's chest puffs up, defensive mode: activated. "That's an unsubstantiated rumour—"

"We don't need it substantiated, Mitch," Lala cuts in. "Your nose literally changed shapes. We're not daft."

"I beg to differ," he says to Lala and I start trying to pull her away.

Last thing any of us need right now is my best friend getting into a tiff with my ex-boyfriend.

"Your new movie's shit!" Lala calls to him.

"Yeah, well—you two look like whores in the YSL campaign," he calls back.

"Well." I give him a little shrug. "You're the expert on that, so"—Lalee and I keep backing away—"I'll take your word for it."

And then I back into someone who yelps "ow," then shoves me off them.

I swing around and find myself face-to-face with Meghan Miller, the girl Mitch cheated on me with.

Lala nods, impressed. "Brilliant timing, wow—"

"What are the chances—?" I say to Lala before I look back at Meghan. "Meghan. Hateful as always."

She rolls her eyes at me, then flips her hair over her shoulder. "I got the L'Oreal campaign. Heard you went for it—sorry."

She pretends to grimace.

"Oh, no—Darling, you're confused—" Lala shakes her head as she says to me under her breath, "But what else is new?"

Lala clears her throat, giving Meghan a sorry smile. "Ys was offered that campaign—she passed on it. That's why you got it. She's the face of Versace now, didn't you hear? How would you hear, I suppose—" Lala's waffling on to herself now. "You run in such different circles. L'Oreal and Versace, they're not really the same thing, are they?"

"Down, girl," I whisper to my guard dog of a best friend.

Lalee points to Mitch. "Isn't that what you said to Meghan that night?"

"Look—" Mitch gestures behind me. "Here comes your Working-Class Hero now."

I give MB a final, disparaging look before I dart over to Jo, quick as I can. He's quite perceptive, Joah—I wouldn't want him catching wind of any of the last five minutes and kicking something up.

"Oi," Joah says, slipping his arms around my waist, brushing his mouth over me—but he's watching MB.

"Hi—" I intentionally hold his eyes for a few seconds, try to tell him *I'm fine, it's fine*—I catch Richie's eyes behind him, give him a smile. "Hi—"

He gives me a little nod, points to Jo, signals that he's been drinking.

I can smell it on him, actually. Shit.

I try to distract him, glancing between the brothers. "How was it?"

TIME OF YOUR LIFE

"Fine—" Jo nods, not looking away from MB across the room. "Who the fuck is that?"

"Who?" I pretend like I don't know.

"That fucking blond lad your best friend's mouthing off at— you know, the one you were yapping to when I walked in—"

"Oh—Mitch?" I laugh it off. I feel a tiny bit nervous, actually. "He's no one. Just my ex-boyfriend."

Joah scowls at me. "Fuck off—! How many ex-boyfriends you got?"

Richie lets out an exasperated breath on my behalf. "Fuck, Jo—"

I tilt my head at my head. "Interesting question. About 268 less than the notches on your bedframe. Should we keep talking about my exes, Jo?"

Joah thinks to himself. "Yeah. Nope."

"So—" I look between the Harrigan boys. "I wanna hear about this shoot—! It was with Jill Furmanovsky, right?"

"Yeah!" Rich nods. "She's fucking incredi—"

"Nah—" Jo says, already moving past me towards Mitch. "I wanna meet that fucking geezer—"

I chase after him quickly. "No, you don't—"

"Aye, I do." Joah positions himself in front of Mitch. "Oi," he says to get MB's attention, except he gets Lala's too. Joah flashes her a smile—it's a bit bleary. "Hey, La." Then Jo looks back at Mitch. "And who the fuck are you?"

Mitch looks past Joah to me for a second—honestly, he looks nervous.

Honestly, I'm beginning to wonder if he should be.

"I'm Mitch," he says.

Joah squints at him. "Why does your face look familiar?"

Mitch glances around, looks annoyed he has to say why that might be out loud. "I'm an actor?"

"Nah—" Joah shakes his head without missing even a beat. "Can't be that, can it? I don't watch shit films."

Jo flicks a cocky little eyebrow of his up, and if I wasn't busy feeling incredibly stressed about whatever the absolute fuck is going on, I probably would have thought that all quite sexy.

I shrug, trying to keep it light and breezy. "Maybe he just has one of those faces…"

"Jo, do you know what—" Lala says, and she has her sparky eyes on, which is no good for me. I suspect at any given moment, my capacity would be absolutely maxed out with either sparky-eyed Lala or a drunk Joah, but both—? Fuck. And she doesn't know. She doesn't know Joah's drunk. And she's not hypervigilant to the way people hold themselves or their eye movements because she hasn't had to be, which is why she's being a brat—not malicious—when she says: "Mitch was just telling Sol how you're beneath her."

Joah squares up. God, he's tall—he slouches a lot, actually. Still incredibly tall with a slouch, but when he's standing up straight, oh my god.

Jo's eyes pinch. "Was he fucking just?"

I cover my face with my hands. "Lalee—"

Lala nudges me apologetically. "Sorry, I just hate him so much—" She nods towards MB.

"What you reckon, La—Should I show Mitch what it's like to be six feet beneath the ground?"

I turn to Rich now, eyes big and a bit desperate.

"Yes!" Lala says, excited because evidently she's incorrigible.

"Jo…" Richie says, sounds like a big brother. Joah looks back at him, looks annoyed he's there, actually.

"No, you should not—" I say pointedly to Joah, standing directly in front of him, hands on my hips. Then I look at Mitch over my shoulder. "And Mitch should leave."

He looks cross about that. "But I didn't do sh—"

"Listen—" Richie slings an arm around Mitch, sort of guiding him towards the door. "Stay if you want man, free country and all that shit, but my brother's had a few tonight and he's fucking unhinged at the soberest of times, so I'm encouraging you—for *your* sake—*fuck off.*"

TIME OF YOUR LIFE

127

"Yeah!" Lala beams. "Fuck off!"

Mitch does, thank god. Don't think he leaves as much as he gets out of Joah's line of sight.

Joah stares at Lala for a couple of seconds, a new fondness for her on his face. "You're a fucking good egg, La."

"Yes!" She's delighted. "Thank you! Not everyone gets that—"

Jo nods towards the fire escape.

"Wanna have a fag outside?" He gestures towards me. "This one don't smoke."

"Yeah, alright." She starts walking away.

Jo turns to me. "Alright, Trouble?"

I give him a smile. We kiss. He goes after my friend, and I hear him say as they leave, "My friend is well keen on you—"

"Is your friend sexy?" I hear Lala ask.

"You tell me—" And Joah points to someone in the crowd who I can't see.

Rich and I trade looks, and I take a great big breath as we walk in silent step over to the bar.

"Whiskey. I don't care what kind," he tells the bartender. Then he looks at me. "What do you want?"

"Tom Collins, please," I tell him.

Richie hands me my drink. I take a sip.

"Why is he drunk already?" I ask. The night's quite young, that's all.

Richie rubs his hands over his mouth like he has something to say but doesn't quite know how to say it.

"Oi, listen, right—It's been fucking mental how tame Jo's been since you met."

Whoa. I don't know what I thought he was going to say—I didn't think it'd be that.

"What?"

Richie shrugs. "He was drunk and high every night before he met you. Got into a fight at least once a week—"

I'm looking at him like I think he's a liar. I think I *do* think he's a liar, actually. He just shakes his head, though.

"I mean, Ysolde—you had to know that. It was in the papers every fuckin' day."

"The papers lie," I remind him.

Richie shakes his head. "Don't needa with him. Truth's fucked-up enough, innit?"

I don't know why he's saying any of this. I shake my head—is he implying something—?

"I didn't ask him to stop anyth—"

"Nah, I know." Rich shakes his head quickly. "You're just the kinda girl you change y'self for, don't need to ask…"

I frown, not really tracking.

"Then why is he drunk?"

I don't love it when men drink, actually. Don't care when *I* drink—I know that's a double standard, but I don't care. I like my men strong and in control and sound of mind.

Rich gives me a long look. He's quite restrained, I think. I think he has lots of things to say, and he chooses not to say them.

"He's a complicated lad, my brother…" He nods to himself. "Lot of feelin's."

I say nothing—because, what? He keeps going.

"Lot of unprocessed pain—"

I look at him suspiciously. "Are you being funny?"

Richie pulls a face. "Are you—? Or has he just not shown you his true colours yet—?"

I don't like the implications of that. Actually, I'd go as far to say that I resent the implications of what he just said. "I know all his colours."

"So you've seen him high, then?" he asks, staring at me intensely.

"Well—" No, is the answer, truthfully. But I think I'd probably have lied to shut this man up, but he cuts me off before I get a chance.

"And who's he punched when he's been with you?"

I shake my head at my boyfriend's big brother. "What are you doing?"

"I'm giving you a fucking heads-up, Featherstonhaugh—because

TIME OF YOUR LIFE

I don't reckon you know our kid as well as you think you do." His eyebrows go up now. "And I can fucking smell it on him, you're gonna meet him tonight."

I think he's just trying to scare me. I don't know why.

I've heard that they have crazy fights. Joah hasn't said as much, but Pix told me. She said the Harrigan brothers are infamous for their fights. Maybe this is part of it. Maybe Joah's this sort of, innocent bystander to an emotionally manipulative mastermind?

I give Richie an annoyed look and push past him, going and standing at the bar on my own instead.

I never go to and stand at bars on my own, really. For one, Aleki would kill me. And two, I don't really like talking to strangers… But I'd fancy my chance with a stranger over another minute of Richie Harrigan's mind games, I think.

I order another drink and then take a long sip of it.

"You alright?" says someone, sidling up beside me.

I barely glance at them. "Yeah. Fine."

"You know him?" The guy nods his head in Richie's direction— who's looking at me, actually. Staring. Bit of a scowl on his face.

"Uh—yeah." I nod. "My boyfriend's brother."

He nods a few times, something about the nod makes me feel like he might have already known that.

"You're Fallow's girlfriend," he tells me.

I pinch my eyes. "I'm Joah Harrigan's girlfriend, yes."

He shrugs. "One and the same."

I give him a bit of a bored look. "If you say so…"

He watches me a couple of seconds, takes a sip of his own drink.

"Richie can be a bit of a prick," he says and that gets my attention. Maybe I'm weak, I don't know—we all like to be vindicated.

"Right?" I look at him properly for the first time. God, he's kind of familiar. Handsome. Blond. Short hair.

"Is he a bit of a pot stirrer or something?" I ask.

"I've always found him to be that way." The guy nods. "Yeah…"

"Really?"

"Yeah—" He nods again. "Stirs shit up for your boyfriend, I think. Frames it like Joah's the bad seed, but I'm not so sure—"

I give him a little scowl. "No one thinks Joah's the bad seed…"

"Baby, everyone in his bar and their fucking mother thinks Joah's the bad seed, besides you."

And then he unscrews the lid of his little vial necklace, does a line of cocaine right in front of me. He offers me some wordlessly. I shake my head.

"Sorry—who are you?"

He smiles, looks 80 percent amused, 20 percent pissed off. "Do you not know who I am?"

I lift an eyebrow. "Should I?"

He nods coolly. "Most girls do…"

I shake my head at him, unfazed. "I'm not most girls…"

He nods again. "I can see that…" He pauses, looking me up and down. "Your boyfriend knows who I am."

"Oh—" It suddenly all clicks. "You're Bright Line."

He looks pleased I recognise him. "Finn." He offers me his hand. "Williams."

I take it, reluctantly. "Ysolde."

"Oh." He chuckles. "I know exactly who you are."

Hardly surprising. "Most people do…"

"Yeah." He nods casually. "I've actually come all over your chest before."

And it's weird, I don't entirely process what he's said immediately. It feels a bit like there's a CD in my brain and the track is skipping. I stare at him, completely confused.

"I beg your pardon?"

He's smiling now. Looks pleased. Happy to have rattled me. "There's this photo of you in *The Face* and you're…" He trails. "You know—" He grimaces and gestures to my breasts, mouths *naked*. "Fuck, Joah must hate that. He's such a jealous prick sometimes, isn't he—?" He's grinning. "It'd drive him mental that anytime I want, or anyone wants really, they can—"

TIME OF YOUR LIFE

"Please stop—" I cut in.

He doesn't though.

"—find a photo of you with your tits out and have a g—"

And then—oh my god, literally out of nowhere, there's a hand wrapped around Finn Williams's throat as he's shoved violently backwards into the bar.

"Finish that sentence, bruv—" Joah says through gritted teeth. "I fuckin' dare ya"—Jo squeezes a bit tighter—"Come on, big man, let's fuckin' hear it now…"

"Jo…" Richie says quietly, edging closer.

Joah sort of shakes Finn. "Fuckin' SPEAK!"

He starts making sounds that aren't good sounds, you know—there are sounds people make when they're not getting air. I'm familiar with that sound, unfortunately. I made it once myself.

"Jo—" I shake my head at him, quick and urgent. "I don't think he can"—my voice breaks—"breathe?"

Gritted teeth, Joah shakes his head "Don't care."

"I care!" I grab his arm, trying to shake the Bright Line guy loose from his grip. "I care, Joah—"

Jo glances at me, looks enraged. "Why are you protecting him?"

"I'm not protecting him—" I shake my head quickly. "I'm protecting *you*." Joah watches me for a second, his chest is heaving. "Let him go—please?"

Jo stares at Finn Williams dead in the eye and squeezes yet again, tighter.

"—Talk shit to my girlfriend one more time, I'm going to rip your fuckin' spine out through your stomach."

Then he throws him away by his neck. Jo turns around, hooking his arm around my neck, pulling me away towards the exit and then—

Fuck.

Finn William launches at him. Genuinely, completely tackles him. Knocks me right over.

And then the bar erupts into chaos. I hit the floor hard, my palms stinging against the filthy floor, and I know it's stupid but the first thing I think is—*fuck, I'm going to have bruised knees for the swimwear shoot I have in Paris next week. Jilly's going to kill me.* I'm still thinking that impossibly stupid thought when I'm plucked up from the ground and planted back on my feet.

Richie tilts his head, staring at me. "You alright?"

I nod quickly, but I'm not really, I'm completely rattled—*what the fuck is going on?* My heart's pounding because—holy shit— Finn's on Joah now, fists flying everywhere. Jo's swinging wild, drunk and furious, landing one to Finn's jaw that makes him stagger, but not before Finn comes back with a hook to Joah's ribs. That hurts him, I can see it on his brow.

"Joah!" I scream, but he doesn't hear me—or if he does, he doesn't care. They just keep fighting.

Then—thank god—Richie barrels in, shoving his way past the crowd that's already forming to see the spectacle.

"Oi!" he yells, but it's then I realise, he's not there to stop it—he's here to back his brother. I don't know what it is about them—mob mentality—I think something must have happened when they were younger? Maybe they got into lots of fights or something? Made some bad friends—? But Pixie's mentioned this before—an attack on one of them is an attack on both of them. Unless they're the ones attacking each other, I suppose.

Anyway, Richie grabs Finn by the shoulder, spinning him 'round just as fucking Mitch Montrose-Bowes—of course it's fucking Mitch MB—dives on in, slamming a fist into Richie's gut.

"Fuckin' hell, mate—" Richie growls, doubling over before straightening, catching Mitch with a nasty uppercut. And it's pure carnage now. They've gone completely barbaric. Fists flying, glasses smashing, someone around me yelling something about getting the bouncers, and I'm not really doing anything except—when did I start crying?

"Jo!" I scream again, my voice breaking, but he doesn't hear me. He's too far gone, slamming Finn down on a table. Finn comes back with a fist to Joah's perfect jawline, splitting his cheek open, blood blooming instantly. Joah spits—actual blood—then he grabs a beer bottle from a nearby table without even looking.

"No—!" I shout, but it's too late.

The crash of glass echoes over the room as Joah cracks the bottle over Finn's head. Shards fly everywhere—sharp, glittering—and Finn stumbles, clutching at his head, blood dripping between his fingers.

The room goes deadly quiet.

"Shit, Jo—" Richie looks a bit scared, actually—breathing hard, staring at the wreckage in front of him. Mitch is dragging Finn back, both of them bloody and staggering, and Jo's standing there, chest heaving, bottle neck still clutched in his hand like a weapon. His eyes are wild, unfocused, until they find mine.

"Joah…" My voice is shaking.

For a second, he just stares at me, like he's waking up from a terrible fever dream—then his face hardens again, and he jerks his head towards the exit.

"We gotta go," he says, voice rough, grabbing my hand, pulling me through the crowd as everyone watches, silent and stunned.

I let him pull me. My hands are trembling. My heart's racing. And as we burst out into the cold night air, Richie and Lala behind us—Lala's on her impractically large mobile phone, no doubt calling Jilly. She's good in a crisis, Lala. Always has been—Joah starts shaking his head as we pile into a cab.

I don't know who hailed it.

"It's not my fault—" Jo says. "He jumped me."

"I know." I nod, though I'm not sure I do know that.

"And he said vile things to you—"

I nod a lot really quickly. "He did."

I don't even think Jo heard the worst of it, actually—

Joah looks at Richie with big eyes, worried, asking for help without asking.

"It's gonna be fine, Jo," Richie says calmly, and I think Joah believes him. He nods a handful of times—looks out the car window. His chest is still heaving as he absent-mindedly picks up my hand and kisses the back of it.

Across from me, his brother stares at me, hand pressed into his mouth. Then he shakes his head as he leans forwards towards me, whispers so no one else can hear him, "Told you."

BRAWL AT TRAMP: JOAH HARRIGAN CLASHES WITH RIVAL ROCKER

By Fiona Tate, Entertainment Correspondent, The Daily Sun

BREAKING: A night out at London's famed Tramp nightclub spiralled into chaos when Fallow front man Joah Harrigan and Bright Line's Finn Williams erupted into a heated brawl.

Witnesses say tensions flared after Williams exchanged words with Harrigan's girlfriend, supermodel Ysolde Featherstonhaugh, with some sources claiming the rival rocker made inappropriate remarks about her.

"Joah just snapped," said one attendee. "Next thing, fists were flying, and Harrigan smashed a bottle over Finn's head."

The situation worsened as Harrigan's brother, Richie, entered the fray, reportedly clashing with actor Mitchell Montrose-Bowes, another one of Featherstonhaugh's rumoured exes. "It was total chaos," said a bartender. "Glasses were breaking, people were shouting—everyone was stunned."

Security stepped in to break up the fight, escorting the bruised and bloodied rockers from the venue.

With tensions between two of British rock's biggest stars boiling over, this is one feud that's bound to escalate.

THIRTEEN

joah

LAST NIGHT GOT AWAY FROM me, didn't it?

Bit of a clusterfuck, that.

Don't really remember much of it, if I'm honest. Woke up this morning in Ys's hotel room—bruised ribs, no shirt, and no Ys beside me. First time that's ever happened since we met.

She was pissed, wasn't she? Or scared? Fuck, I hope she wasn't scared. I'd rather she tear into me, know what I mean? Proper pissed is better than her lookin' at me like that—like I've ruined everythin'.

Anyway, shit's properly fucked, and I've "really done it this time"—Mick's words, not mine, as he paces up and down Ys's floor like a man possessed.

Ain't seen this many people crammed into her suite before.

Me and her. Richie. Lala. Kekoa—who's properly pissed off. Mick. Her agent, Jilly. Fry. Chops.

Mick's on the phone, shouting at someone like his life depends on it. Jilly's over in the corner giving Ys a right proper bollocking. It's full-throttle bedlam.

I walk out cautiously—not like me, is it? Ain't never cautious. But these lot look well pissed.

TIME OF YOUR LIFE 137

Me brother clocks me straightaway, gestures my way with a grin that's owt but friendly. "There he is—man of the fuckin' hour. Nice of ya to join us."

Glance 'round. Room's got the vibe of an intervention, don't it? Not interested in one of those, thanks.

Ys spots me, and she's on me in a second—eyes wide, darting across the room like it's her life's mission. Throws herself into my arms, and I swear to god, it's fucking weird to be loved the way she loves me. To love her back the same way… To be relieved when I've got her in my arms—? Didn't know I wasn't relieved before until I've got her now, and then it's like—fuck. Everythin' feels proper good, you know? And if that ain't a metaphor for fuckin' all of it—I dunno what is.

Her agent steps forwards, sticking her hand out like this is a business meeting or some shit.

"I wish it were under better circumstances, but it's good to meet you. I'm Jilly."

I shake it.

"Joah." I nod, try to give her a smile—don't reckon it makes it to me eyes, though.

"Joah," she repeats, all formal. "You want to walk us through what happened from your perspective?"

I rest my chin on top of Ys's head, shake my head, and give her a shrug. "Dunno, really—don't remember."

That don't win me any points with the old bird, does it? She takes one of those deep, measured breaths through her nose, all controlled and proper. "Why's that?"

"Because I was bladdered."

Another sharp breath through her nose—think she might bloody hyperventilate at this rate. She catches Ys's eye, then looks at Mick, like, *fucking handle this, would you?*

Ys is staring at my face, proper fixated on the black eye, brow bent in the middle all worried—it's cute, don't mind it.

She touches it, gentle-like, and I don't wince like—not a fuckin' prat, me, but Christ—hurts like fuck. Ys knows me too well, mind. Clocked it, even though I'm trying not to show it.

"Are you okay?" she asks, voice all soft and sad. Hate it when she's sad. Fuckin' hate it. Makes me feel worse than the black eye ever could.

I reckon she was sad last night. Pretty sure I remember her crying—crying in the taxi on the way back, crying in bed next to me too. Dunno what about—? Me, I s'pose.

"He's fuckin' fine—" Mick scowls at her. Don't care for that tone, do I? Shoot him a look, like *wind your neck in, mate*, but he doesn't give a shit. He's fucking livid. "He's not the one bottled in the goddamn head, is he?" Mick tells her.

I roll my eyes—can't fucking help it, can I? "It was a bottle of fuckin' Fosters, mate—hardly a weapon."

Richie gives Mick a look, full-on exasperated, like he's had enough of all of us. "*That* he remembers."

"What was the fight about?" Jilly presses, all business.

"He was talkin' shite to her." I point a finger in Ys's direction. She don't say a word, just stands there, quiet.

Mick's eyes go wide, proper fucking dramatic. "If you bottled Finn *fucking* Williams in the head because you were jealous your girlfriend was *talking* to him, Joah—swear to god—"

"No—" I cut him off with a sharp look, one that says *fuckin' watch yourself, mate*. "I heard him talkin' shit to her."

Mick turns to Ys. "What'd he say?"

Her chin tucks down, and she still doesn't speak.

Never seen her this quiet. It's weird. Throws me. Don't like it.

"Might be helpful for us, Ys—that's all." Jilly again, softer this time, like she's trying to coax it out of her.

"Because—" Jilly keeps telling her. "Rather strangely, Finn Williams' camp haven't released a statement yet—"

"Well—" She crosses her arms over her chest. "He did say *something*, but I wouldn't have thought it was worth being bottled in the head over—"

TIME OF YOUR LIFE

She gives me a bit of a look when she says it, but she's not really cross, is she? Reckon she's a bit fucking pleased, if we're being honest. Loves being fought for, this one, you know what I mean?

I hook my arm 'round her neck and tug her in towards me.

"It was a *Fosters*!" I say again, exasperated now that no one's fucking getting that part through their fuckin' heads. My girl gives me a look like I'm a twat, but I reckon she just dunno what a Fosters is. Posh girls, man…

Ys looks back at Jilly.

"Joah didn't hear it anyway."

"Well, what did he say?" Jilly asks.

Ys says nowt.

"Go on—" Kekoa tells her.

Ys glances 'round the room, proper cagey. To be fair, there's a lot of fuckin' faces here. Then she looks at me—shakes her head.

It's weird. She's uncomfortable, yeah—but it's more than that. Like she's embarrassed or summat? Ashamed?

"Tell me?" I say, quiet. She still looks unsure, and I pretend that don't sting, but it fucking does. Can tell it's not about me, though, whatever this is.

Shift myself in front of her, blockin' out the lot of them. Try to make it feel like it's just us, just me and her. Tilt my head a bit.

"Hey, Trouble, it's me. You can tell me anythin'."

Her eyes, they're heavier than normal. Reckon I'd say, with some confidence, I ain't never seen 'em all that light anyway. She breathes out through her nose, like she's gearin' herself up, then leans in close—whispers, quiet as a fuckin' church mouse, what that shitbag said to her last night.

And my jaw—? Goes fuckin' tight.

I glance at her. "Are you paraphrasin'?"

Ys shakes her head.

"That verbatim, then?" I clarify.

She nods, barely but.

"Right—" My blood is fuckin' boiling. I look over at my brother, nod my head towards the front door. "Rich, get your shit, we've got a job to finish—" I look at her bodyguard now. "You too, mate. You're gonna want a head on a platter for this one—*trust me*—" I look between my manager and hers. "Where is he?"

"Joah, mate—" Mick sighs, bit of an eye roll. "What are you gonna do?"

"I'm gonna fuckin' kill him, is what I'm gonna do—Where is he?" I ask again. When Mick, the fucking piece of shit, doesn't answer me, I turn to Lala. "Lala?"

Lala looks caught—put her in a shit position just now, I know that. She knows where he is—think she wants to tell me too. Reckon she'd help me kill him herself if she knew what he said to her best friend.

"Lala, no—" Ysolde gives her a *don't you dare* look. Then she turns to me, gives me one in the same vein but sterner. "No. Thank you. But no."

Shake my head. "No one gets to talk to you like that, Ys—"

Gives me an exasperated look. "You bottled him in the head, Jo. I think he got the message…"

Jilly clears her throat as she clamps her mobile phone to her chest, glancing around the room. "I'm on the phone with Peregrine Spindle—*The Daily Sun* are willing to spin the article in our favour—that you were protecting her, defending her, quote some of the less desirable things Williams has been known to say in the past about women, but heads up—" She's talking to Mick specifically now. "Perry said the story's going to be everywhere either way."

Rich lets out this sigh. "Fuck."

"I don't care—" I shake my head. "Fuckin' run it."

"I care," Mick says.

"I care too," says Fry, Chops nodding along next to him.

Shake my head at me mates, fucking little traitors. "You dunno what he said to her…"

"Yeah—" Rich scoffs. "No one does, fuckwit, she only told you."

TIME OF YOUR LIFE   141

Give him a glare for that but he's right—fuckin' hate it when he's right. I look over at Ys. "Can I tell them?"

Looks horrified, she does. "No, you cannot tell them!"

"Maybe"—Lala pipes up, talking directly at me—"you should just get out of town for a few days. Lay low?"

Mick nods along. "That's not a bad idea, is it?"

Guess I see the merit of it, and there's worse ways to kill time, I s'pose.

Look over at Ys, nod my chin at her. "Wanna go away for a week or two?"

She grimaces. "I have to go to Paris tomorrow."

"Oh—!" Jilly nods along. "The Chanel swimwear campaign." Shakes her head like it slipped her mind. "That's right."

Shrug, lookin' at Ys. "I'll go to Paris."

Jilly grimaces straightaway. "I don't know—" Zeroes in on Ys. "It's a work trip, darling…"

Give ol' Jilly a manky look for that. "I'm not going to like…fuck it up."

She takes a measured breath. "Not on purpose, I'm sure."

"Richie will go," Mick announces.

I stare him down. "What?"

"Richie will go too." Mick nods now, like it's already fucking decided. "Keep an eye on him."

"The fuck he will," I say at the same time my brother says, "No, Richie fuckin' won't."

"Joah—" Mick gives me a look.

"No—" I shake my head. "Fuck that. I don't need a fuckin' *minder*—"

Rich makes this *pffft* sound, fucking pisses me off.

"What was that?" I stare at him. I could go a fight right now. Bit sore from yesterday, but I'm still fucking pissed off, and I feel a bit like throwing a punch, don't I? "You wanna swing that sound by me again, big man?"

Rich steps towards me, ready—always ready, both of us, for a fight, aren't we—? Kind of had to be, though. Square my shoulders, go to move towards him and Ysolde stands in my fucking way.

"Joah. Shut. Up." She overenunciates and the whole fucking room goes quiet.

Weird, because Rich tells me to fuckin' shut up every other minute, but her saying it carries a weight in this room that I don't understand or fucking like, frankly.

Ys turns 'round calmly and rests her eyes on Jilly. "Will it help?"

Jilly shrugs, shaking her head. "I don't know—"

Ys don't accept that. "You know everything. You have impeccable discernment." She lifts an impatient brow now. "Will Joah getting out of London help?"

Jilly sighs. "I don't know whether it'll help *you*, my priority, but *objectively*, yes I think it would help him...to go...*somewhere*... else...that isn't here. And behave *well*...and *lay low*."

"Okay." Ys nods, decided. "Well—let's, then," she tells me.

"Yeah?"

"Yes," she says like she's the fuckin' boss. Feel like maybe she is, though? When the fuck did that happen, ey? "And Rich can come—"

I pull a face. "No!"

"Yes." The boss rolls her eyes at me. "That's not a big deal." She shrugs. "It's probably good if he's not here either. Maybe you'll drift from Britain's consciousness..."

"Yeah, alright—" I roll my eyes at her. "Let's see how that goes."

CHIVALRY ISN'T DEAD: FALLOW FRONTMAN DEFENDS GIRLFRIEND IN NIGHTCLUB CLASH

By Peregrine Spindle, Entertainment Editor, The Daily Sun

In an age when decency and honour often take a back seat to scandal, Fallow front man Joah Harrigan proved last night that chivalry is alive and well.

The rocker found himself at the centre of a nightclub altercation at London's iconic Tramp when rival musician Finn Williams allegedly made disparaging and highly inappropriate remarks about Harrigan's girlfriend, world-renowned supermodel Ysolde Featherstonhaugh. According to witnesses, Williams's behaviour left Harrigan with little choice but to step in.

"Joah didn't go looking for a fight," said one source close to the scene. "But when someone disrespects the woman he loves, he's not the kind of man to stand by and let it happen. He acted to protect her dignity."

The situation escalated after Williams reportedly continued to provoke Harrigan, leading to a brief physical altercation. Whilst no one condones violence, those present were quick to point out Harrigan's measured restraint. "He could have done far more damage if he wanted to," said one onlooker. "But he kept it focused. He just wanted to send a clear message: Don't cross the line with Ysolde."

Harrigan's team has declined to comment on the incident, but insiders suggest the rocker is "deeply protective" of Featherstonhaugh and regrets that the situation became physical. The couple, who have been linked for several weeks, left the venue together shortly after the fight, with Harrigan reportedly keeping a close arm around his girlfriend as they exited.

Fans have been quick to rally behind the singer, hailing him as a modern-day knight in shining armour. "He was just standing up for her," said one onlooker. "We need more men like Joah Harrigan in the world."

For Joah Harrigan, it seems love and loyalty are nonnegotiable— even in the face of controversy.

JOAH HARRIGAN: THE LOUT WHO GOT LUCKY

By Marcus Firth, Arena Magazine

It's hard to understand how Joah Harrigan, the boorish mouthpiece of Manchester's beloved Fallow, has managed to fool anyone into thinking he's worthy of his rock star crown. In a sea of genuinely talented musicians, Harrigan sticks out like a sore thumb—and not in a good way. With his snarling Mancunian drawl and cocky swagger, he's carved out a reputation as one of music's most obnoxious front men—but dig a little deeper, and there's very little of substance propping up this so-called star.

Let's start with the obvious: Fallow's success owes much more to Richie Harrigan, Joah's older, possibly taller and infinitely more talented brother. Richie, the band's primary songwriter, is widely regarded as the true genius behind their hit tracks. His lyrical prowess and musical ingenuity have been the backbone of Fallow's rise to fame, leaving many to wonder if Joah's contribution extends beyond his overblown stage antics. Without Richie's creative brilliance, Joah might still be shouting into a microphone at dingy pubs, a far cry from the arenas he now occupies. And as for Joah's vocal abilities? At best, they're passable, but are they all that different to a semi-talented bloke belting out tunes at a backstreet karaoke bar?

Joah's mediocrity, however, doesn't end onstage. His behaviour offstage is just as notorious, cementing his reputation as the enfant terrible of British rock. Harrigan seems incapable of navigating a night out without descending into chaos—whether it's picking fights, hurling insults, or creating a spectacle that only adds fuel to his tabloid notoriety. Paparazzi lenses have captured him stumbling out of Soho nightspots more times than can be counted, often with a different woman clinging to his arm. His string of fleeting romances is as prolific as it is unremarkable, painting a picture of a man more interested in collecting conquests than any kind of real connection. Even his high-profile relationship with supermodel and London 'It Girl' Ysolde Featherstonhaugh feels less like genuine affection and more like an elaborate PR distraction. Not even the allure of dating one of the world's most glamorous women can gloss over the tarnish of Harrigan's public escapades.

Speaking of image, Joah's so-called status as a style icon raises more questions than it answers. Is he truly stylish, or is he simply coasting on his undeniably good looks? His unwashed hair, eclectic and often questionable collection of jackets and parkas, and his beat-up Converse might be hailed as "effortlessly cool" by some, but strip away the chiselled jawline and smouldering gaze, and what remains is a man who could easily be mistaken for someone who's just rolled out of a bin. It's a harsh reality that Harrigan's allure owes more to his face than his fashion sense, leaving him a far cry from the genuinely stylish front men he's so often compared to.

And yet, despite all this, Joah Harrigan continues to be heralded as the face of Fallow, the so-called voice of his generation. But how long can the charade last? At some point, fans will wake up and realise they've been sold a second-rate front man riding on the coattails of his bandmates' talent. Until then, we'll just have to endure more of Joah's boozing, brawling, and belligerence, wondering how on earth he's managed to fool us all for this long.

FOURTEEN

ysolde

THE SHOOT WENT SMOOTHLY.

Joah wasn't there. Not that Joah being there means it wouldn't have gone smoothly, don't read into that—I mean—never mind.

The shoot went well.

Separately, Joah is doing okay too. It's been a few days since what happened at the club and he's calmed down a bit.

When I spoke to Jilly last, she said the papers weren't talking about Jo any differently than they normally would—you know, silly, rowdy rock star, drunk and got carried away again. Can't imagine it will have won Jo any points in the eyes of my father. Can't imagine Jo would give a shit about that, though.

We've been staying at Hôtel Plaza Athénée—beautiful. One of my favourite hotels. We spent a couple of days just shopping and going to museums and restaurants, and it's a strange, forced holiday that I didn't know I needed but am thoroughly enjoying.

Rich is both a painful and a welcome addition. They're weird together, Joah and him. Kind of fascinating to watch. They're either entirely in sync, closer than close, or they completely, totally despise each other.

And it's always the strangest things that sets each other off. Like, they had a massive row because a waitress asked Rich what he'd like to drink, and Joah cut in and ordered first. Or yesterday, Rich walked into our room without knocking and Joah lost his fucking mind.

We were on Avenue des Champs-Élysées at the Louis Vuitton flagship yesterday—they both liked the same button-down and oh my god. *Complete* children.

And then, an hour later, they're sitting in a bar, watching the football, finishing each other's sentences, teasing one another about things that go over my head—old inside jokes between the brothers.

I get back from a facial from Joëlle Ciocco—heaven, by the way. Get one if you can—and find Joah on the balcony.

He's a vision in that sunlight, though I suppose he's always a bit of a vision, isn't he? There's something about his face, like he always looks like he has a secret that's going to get the both of us in trouble. It's inherently sexy. And those terribly famous, impossibly blue eyes are cast a bit golden now in the fading Parisian sun. Of course, as we all know—his mouth is bottom heavy, and I love that, actually—but it's more so today. Poutier or more serious or something.

And it's because his face is so lovely and so distractible I don't clock immediately that something's amiss. Only when I kiss his cheek and he doesn't look up at me do I feel in me that something's astray.

He's reading something—a magazine?—intensely.

Right then, Rich rounds the corner, sees the magazine in Joah's hand, and beelines towards him.

"Don't read that—" He shakes his head, reaching for it, but Joah jerks it out of his reach.

"I told you not to read that—" Rich sighs. "Jo—"

I look between them. "What is it?"

"Nowt," Rich tells me in a voice that tells me, actually, it's rather something.

TIME OF YOUR LIFE

149

"An article," Jo says, still reading it.

I look for his eyes, I don't find them. "About what?"

"Me," he says, but his voice sounds funny.

I glance up at Rich, my eyes are more nervous than I want them to be. Truthfully, perhaps so are Richie's.

"What does it say?" I ask neither of them specifically. I'm asking either of them, I suppose.

Rich shakes his head again. "Jo, don't."

Joah finally looks up, eyes sharp—fighting eyes—I'm starting to know them now. He points an angry finger in his brother's face. "Don't fuckin' tell me what to do, man—"

I put my hand on Jo's shoulder. "He's just trying to help—"

"What's reading it going to do, Jo?" Rich says to him. "You'll just feel like shit."

I look between them again, and I'm getting a bit frustrated now. "I mean—what the fuck does it say?"

Jo clears his throat. *"It's hard to understand how Joah Harrigan, the boorish mouthpiece of Manchester's beloved Fallow, has managed to fool anyone into thinking he's worthy of his rock star crown."*

My heart sinks.

"Jo—" I start but he shakes his head.

"Not done."

"Let's start with the obvious—" Joah reads a bit theatrically now. *"Fallow's success owes much more to Richie Harrigan, Joah's older, possibly taller and infinitely more talented brother. Richie, the band's primary songwriter, is widely regarded as the true genius."*

"Jo—" Rich interrupts, but Joah talks over him loudly.

"Without Richie, Joah might still be shouting into a microphone at dingy pubs—"

Joah looks up from the article, giving Richie and I both a pointed look. Then he keeps going.

"Not even the allure of dating one of the world's most glamorous women can gloss over the tarnish of Harrigan's public escapades."

I cut in. "Joah—"

He holds up a finger to silence me.

"—*strip away the chiselled jawline and smouldering gaze, and what remains is a man who could easily be mistaken for someone who's just rolled out of a bin.*"

"No—" I shake my head. "Okay, stop. That's enough."

I try to pluck the magazine away from him, but he holds it out of my reach—except fuck him, because I'm nimble, so I clamber over him and pry it out of his hands and fling it over the balcony.

"Jo, none of that's true." I sit myself on his lap, push my hands through his hair. "You know that."

He stares at me a bit blankly. Looks lost, actually. That frightens me.

"Do I?" he asks.

I put my hand on his cheek and look very squarely in his eyes. "Yes."

"Alright. If you say so." He nods, then he stands up—and he doesn't completely shift me off of him, he just—stands? I don't tumble off his lap, I catch myself and I'm fine and it's nothing, but it's maybe the least aware he's ever been of my physical presence. "Back in a sec."

And then he saunters away.

I perch nervously—or *uncomfortably*, I should say—I'm not nervous. Why would I be nervous, you know? I'm not, that all just threw me for a second is all.

"You good?" Richie says, watching me closer than I like.

I nod.

He nods back, slower though, thinking something through.

"Buckle up," he tells me.

I roll my eyes. "Don't."

"What?" He shrugs like he doesn't know.

"Don't do that." I shake my head at him. "You don't know it's about to go sideways…"

"Yeah, I do," he says coolly. "And so do you—" He nods at me. "You're learning. That's good."

I cross my arms over my chest. "You're so dramatic."

TIME OF YOUR LIFE 151

"*I'm* dramatic?" He scoffs. "I'm not the one doing lines in the bathroom on me own because some twat wrote a shit article about me—"

My heart drops a foot in my chest.

"He's not doing that."

"Yes, Ysolde." Rich gives me this *you know I'm right* look. "He is."

"What am I doing?" Jo asks as he rounds a corner, itching his nose with his finger.

"Nothing—" Rich says to Jo, then catches my eye. "Just proving my point."

"Alright—?" Joah says, glancing between us. "Shall we?"

I give him a cautious look. "Shall we what?"

―――――

Not two hours later, and definitely two and perhaps a bit bottles of scotch later, Joah pushes back from the table we're sitting at in the small hole-in-the-wall bar we've found ourselves at.

"Gotta piss," Joah says, staggering away, hopefully towards a loo.

"Charming." I flash his brother a smile, before I glance around our surroundings.

I've never been to a place like this in Paris before. Honestly, I didn't know places like this *existed* in Paris, which makes me realise I've experienced only a very privileged and curated version of Paris. Rich picked it. I think on purpose. We won't run into anyone we know here. No sneaky photographers lurking, waiting to catch my heartbroken boyfriend out. He is heartbroken by the way. Utterly shattered. He pretends he doesn't care what people say about him, but he does. Very much.

This is a terrible part of loving someone, isn't it? That they become your heart that lives outside of your body and they exist in the world, and the world we live in tries to beat everyone and everything down, and today it picked him, and it's working.

There's always been a sparky light in Joah's eyes. I saw it the very first night we met. Maybe over time I've embellished it, but in the eye of my mind's memory, there's this magical light inside of his eyes that I think I watched the world dim a bit today.

Do you know how that feels? To watch something you love be destroyed?

My heart's aching for him, that's what I'm thinking about when I realise Richie's just sitting there, quietly, watching me.

He nods his chin towards me. "Oi, what'd he say to you?"

I frown. "Who?"

"Finn."

I let out an incredulous laugh. "I'm not telling you…"

"Why?"

I stare at him, can't really believe he's pushing me on this. "Because it's terrible?"

He shrugs. "We're practically family."

I pull a face. "We…*aren't.*"

He squints over at me. "We are friends, though, right?"

I squint back, truly thinking about it, I suppose. "I don't know…"

"Fuck—"He shakes his head. "You're a piece of work."

"Excuse me—" I cross my arms, looking him up and down. "You're very antagonistic of my boyfriend—"

He laughs once, dry—like he can't believe it.

"*I'm* antagonistic of your boyfriend—?" He shakes his head. "Fuck, how thick are your love goggles…"

I give him a look. "You love stirring up shit for him!"

"*He* loves stirring shit up for him," Rich says, matching my look but only for a second because out of the corner of our eyes, we each see Joah exit the bathroom.

Two girls at the bar stop him as he passes.

"Excuse me—" one of them says in a French accent. "Are you Fallow?"

Joah grins, cocky—his eyes are blurrier than I'm comfortable with, truthfully. He looks over at Rich, calls to him, "Hear that, kid? *Am I Fallow?*"

TIME OF YOUR LIFE

153

Joah and Richie stare at one another across the bar, then Joah looks away, back to the French girls, nose in the air.

"Yeah, I fuckin' am."

Rich sits back in his chair across from me, rubs his mouth as though he's a bit tired. "Yeah, it's me. *I'm* antagonistic."

"He's drunk."

"Yeah." Rich nods. "He usually is."

I glare at him for that—I'm about to say something back when I hear the other French girl ask, "Can we get your autograph?"

"Yep." My boyfriend nods, leaning back against the bar. "Don't got a pen but."

The girls fish around in their handbags. One of them glances up at him, eyes pinched. "You are...Joah—"

"That's me," he says.

She nods appreciatively. "You are so—uhhmm—" She pauses, looking for the word, I think. "Canon—?" she says to her friend, then shakes her head. "What is the English word?"

"*Hot?*" offers the friend.

"*Sexy.* Do you know?" she says.

"Both work." Joah nods, loving it—frankly. I don't mind; it appears he needs the ego boost.

Then—you won't believe it—"Crimson and Clover" by Tommy James & the Shondells starts playing.

And it's so strange, Jo looks over at me from where he's standing with those two girls, gives me this lost, bleary smile—this look like, *I can't believe they're playing our song*—then he proceeds to turn to his two French fans and belts it out for them. Dramatically, all for show. And whilst it's not romantic, I know, I can tell he's not being romantic— though, they are, mind you, absolutely loving it—I don't know why, it does somehow still take the sheen off of when he sang that to me.

I watch it all, my heart sinking in this weird way that I don't understand at all. What's it sinking for? What's being sunk? What in this moment crushed me—I don't know the answer, but something did.

I don't look away from Jo and the French girls when I ask his brother, "How often does he dedicate songs to girls in the audience?"

Richie holds up a singular finger and points it at me, then he nods his chin towards Jo. "That's not the same thing."

"No—" I shake my head. "I know."

"Don't worry about it," Richie says as he picks up his scotch, takes a big, deep sip. "You've just got a front-row seat now…"

I give him a confused look. "To what?"

Richie looks past me over to his brother, nods his chin that way. "Welcome to the Joah show."

FIFTEEN

ysolde

IT'S A FEW HOURS LATER and we've gotten Jo home, poured him into bed a little bit before midnight. I fell asleep next to him quite quickly, and I thought that'd be the end of it. Moment passed, crisis avoided.

Alas…

I wake at around 2 a.m. and roll over to check on Joah, and I freeze. His side of the bed is empty.

"Jo?" I call for him. 'Cause he's in the bathroom, probably— right? He's just in the bathroom.

"Joah—?" I call a little louder.

He probably can't hear me. He said their concerts are so loud, he's actually on track for being completely deaf by forty. I call for him again.

Still nothing.

And then I see powdered residue on Joah's nightstand.

I get a wave of sick.

Lala says I'm quite good in a crisis, but I'm not so sure; I think she's wrong—my heart feels like a stone and I can't think properly, and my brain's going down too, my heart's pulling it under.

I used to find powder on my mum's nightstand too. And on the kitchen counter. And sometimes on the car dashboard.

"Richie!" I yell, which sort of frightens me, because I don't consciously do it, it just happens.

I'm moving towards his room even though I didn't tell my legs to do that, and he meets me halfway—grabs me with a hand on each of my arms—gripping me in the dim light of the hallway.

"What's wrong?" His brows are low, automatically worried.

"He's gone."

Richie's face pulls. "What?"

"Joah's gone."

He shakes his head. "What do you mean—?"

"I mean *he's gone.* He's not in our bed, he's gone—"

He stares at me, frowning, puzzling something out in that busy, weird head of his.

He's bigger than I thought—? Like, buffer. I don't know why—? I suppose in fairness, I hadn't really thought about him *without* clothes on before, and he doesn't wear clothes that really show him off…but he's not…*not* hench?

"What?" Richie's face pulls all confused because I'm absolutely fucking staring.

"What?" I blink a lot of times. "Nothing."

He gives me this look like I'm being weird, but I'm not—I'm just tired and worried.

Rich rubs his eyes, tired. "When was the last time you saw him?"

"When we went to sleep?"

He sighs. "Are you sure he's not in the bathroom?"

I give him a look.

"Sorry—" He shoves his hands through his hair. "Okay. Come on—grab your coat—let's go."

Five minutes later, I'm in my nylon trench coat from Prada, nothing underneath except my black lace camisole and hotel slippers, running around the Eighth Arrondissement with Richie Harrigan, in his oversized black hoodie looking ridiculously dishevelled, hands shoved deep into his pockets, and all I'm really thinking about is the white powder on Joah's bedside table.

People take drugs, I get it. Sometimes I do, but not often. Most people around me do, it's fine—Lala doesn't really either—at least, she doesn't take a lot of coke—I think she does that for me. Coke's the one that makes me most nervous. It just frightens me a bit, that's all. It doesn't matter when other people do it, but when the people I love do it, it feels a bit like my throat starts closing up.

"He's knows when's…when…right?" I ask technically Rich, but I don't look at him when I do.

"What?" he says, walking still.

"Joah knows when to stop," I say, trying to convince myself that it's true.

Rich stands still, looks over at me under the flickering light of a streetlamp. "We're going to find him."

I nod, don't say anything.

He tilts his head. "Don't worry—"

I cross my arms over my chest. "I am worried."

He shoves me playfully. "Well, that's going directly against what I said, innit?"

I almost smile at that. Not quite though. Rich sighs, heavy. Like he's sorry. "Jo does this." He glances down at me. "I told you, he's been good with you… He's not…been…himself."

"So this is him being himself?"

"Reckless? Impulsive? Selfish? Stupid?" Jo's older brother scoffs. "Yeah, yeah—sounds about right…"

I roll my eyes, annoyed at him now. All those bad things roll too easily off his tongue.

"He's your brother."

Rich lifts an eyebrow. "You don't have rubbish things to say about your sisters?"

I stop walking. "How do you know I have sisters?"

"I don't know—" He sniffs a laugh. "I'm paying attention?"

Jo didn't know I had sisters. That's a bit funny, don't you think?

"I have bad things to say about one of them," I clarify.

Rich shrugs. "So I have rubbish things to say about one of my brothers too."

I bump him on purpose with my shoulder. "You only have one brother."

"Thank god—" He rolls his eyes. "One's enough. Full-time job running about after this idiot—"

I stand still again, stomp my foot because I'm tired of it. "Stop."

He doesn't though, keeps on walking ahead.

"I mean—You'll see..." He shrugs, resigned. "You're seeing right now."

I stare after him, trying to get a grip on their dynamic, because it is weird. They know each other impossibly well—the other night I watched Rich jump blindly into a fight, fists already swinging purely because Jo was in the fray—but there's an undertone between them too. Resentment, I think.

"Are you jealous of him?" I call after him.

That stops him walking. He turns, both eyebrows up in the air now.

"Am I jealous of—Hah." He's offended. "No."

I shrug, unconvinced. "You seem jealous of him."

"Do I?" Something flickers in his eyes—he's not just offended now, he's angry. And something else—I can't quite place it. "What the fuck does he have that I might want?"

And then his eyes quick as a whip flicker down me, and I wonder—? But, no. Surely, no.

But there is some resentment in him though, I can see it.

Probably it's not for—never mind. I clear my throat.

"He's the front man. Is that what this is about?" I ask him, eyebrow up. "Do you wish you were the front man?"

His jaw pulls tight.

"I'm not jealous of Jo," he tells me. "Jo's jealous of me."

"Yeah, okay." I sniff a tiny laugh, maybe that was meaner than I meant to be.

TIME OF YOUR LIFE

Rich holds my eyes, unflinching he says, "He is but…"

I roll my eyes. "Okay."

I start walking again.

"You know he can't write for shit—" he calls after me, jogs a few paces so we're back in step. Says nothing for four or five seconds.

"None of our songs are his."

I look over at him, surprised. "What?"

I didn't know.

"It's me," he says with a shrug. "I write everything."

I didn't know that actually. Joah's never said as much. I've never asked, I suppose. I just presumed—

Still, he's being a bit more disparaging than I like, so I give him a stubborn look.

"If you genuinely believe that you writing everything equates to none of the songs being his, you've grossly underestimated how important your brother has been to the success of your songs."

Richie's jaw goes tight again, eyes darken—he's cross now. Well and truly.

"Yeah, alright—" He nods coolly. "We don't need to talk anymore."

I nod back. "Great."

We walk in silence the rest of the time, poking our heads into whatever bars we pass that are still open. And by now it's been a while, more than thirty minutes and still, no sight of him.

We've wandered down Boulevard des Capucines and taken a right on Rue Daunou.

"Let's try here," Rich says, nodding at an underwhelming glass door.

I say nothing but follow him inside.

We look around; it's dim and hard to see—nothing stands out and then I see Rich double take towards the back corner.

It's him.

Him and some questionable-looking gentlemen, actually.

I go to step towards him, but Richie stops me.

"Maybe it should be me?" He says it some certain way, and I can't pick what it means. I think he's worried. I'm not sure who for though.

I breathe out my nose, impatient. "Why would it be you?"

Then I push past Rich and beeline over to Jo.

I lay my hand on his arm, gently.

"Jo—?" I say quietly. He doesn't immediately look up. "Jo."

He looks up at me, eyes bleary, blinking. "Hi."

His face shifts as he recognises me.

"Hey." I smile gingerly. It's forced. I make myself, because he's high as a motherfucking kite.

"Whoa." He chuckles, sitting back in his chair. "Hey, boys—" He pulls me down onto his lap gruffly—you know when men forget their strength? He's not just forgotten his strength, but like—his birthday, his name, probably my name—

"This is my girl!" He gives a big smile to who I presume to be two Parisian drug dealers.

I push his hair gently behind his ear. "Your girl would very much love for you to come back to the hotel now…"

I give his friends a cursory, apologetic smile, but Jo shakes his head. "Nah."

And I can feel Richie sidle up behind me. Weird that I can feel his presence, maybe? I'm not sure I've ever felt it before. Not that that means anything that I can feel it now—just that he is present, that's all.

I shake my head at Jo, sighing. "Please?"

"Nah, I'm good," he says, nodding towards the men across the table. "I'm here with my friends, Trouble. I'm good."

"I don't think you are so good, Jo," I tell him gently, standing and trying to bring him to his feet also—to no avail though.

His face goes dark; he doesn't look like himself for a moment. "So who the fuck asked you?"

He's never talked to me like that before. It sort of takes my breath away.

TIME OF YOUR LIFE   161

"Oi," Richie growls from behind me. "Fuckin' get up." Richie grabs his arm, yanking him out of the booth. "It's time to go."

"No," Jo says, eyes as unfocused as he is unsteady on his feet. "I'm fuckin' good."

Richie scoffs. "The fuck you are. Let's go, Jo. Now."

I don't know whether it was the "now" or just the combination of everything up until now, but Rich demanding Jo leave goes down like a tonne of bricks and he shoves Rich. Hard.

Richie shoves him back without even think about it, like it's a pure knee-jerk reaction, but he's sober as a judge, so it's not a fair fight.

"Stop—!" I scramble between them. "Please stop!" I turn to Rich, give him these eyes to tell him that I'm fine. "I'll talk to him. Just give me a minute." Richie gives his little brother a long, irritated look before he skulks not-too-far-away.

Jo watches him leave like a dog watches another dog walk by its house.

I stand on my tiptoes, put both my hands on Joah's cheeks. "I don't want to watch you do this."

"Just go then—!" He gestures towards the door. "You don't have to fuckin' be here. Go—"

"No." I shake my head firmly. "I love you, you love me. You're obviously going through something at the minute, and so you're acting fucking insane, and so I *can't* leave you, but you've already had enough"—I eye the powdery white on the table in front of him—"and I'm asking you *please don't make me watch you overdose.*"

My eyes go bigger and rounder at that. I try to tell him without *actually* having to tell him why it would be tremendously cruel and inappropriate for me to have to say aloud why I need him to get a handle on himself. "Please?" I say quietly.

And then it clicks.

All the anger and self-concern dissipates off his face and he swaps it straight for remorse.

"Fuck." He takes a big breath, then starts nodding really

quickly. "Yep. Shit." He pulls me away from that table, towards the exit. Blows right past his brother—like he doesn't even see him.

"I'm sorry," Jo says once we're on the street. He grabs me by the wrist, yanking me in towards him—he smells like everything under the sun. Sweat, alcohol, cigarettes, just like—generic-bar scent.

"Do you hate me?" he asks.

"No," I say, muffled by his chest but maybe it's unconvincing because he doesn't buy it.

Behind Joah's head, Rich nods his head towards the Main Street. *Let's go,* he mouths.

I give a very subtle nod back.

"You hate me—" Joah groans. "Fuck!" He covers his face with both his hands. "Fuck, I'm such a fuckup."

"You're good—" I tell him, squeezing his hand. "We're good. Everything's fine."

But I'm not really sure that it is.

Forty-five minutes later, Joah is showered and back in bed. I take a long shower after that myself. I feel as though I have a million different kinds of germs and feelings and thoughts trapped in my hair and on my body.

I come back out feeling a little bit more like a human, but still, admittedly, a fairly weathered one tonight.

I go to Richie's room—I don't know why—I've not gone to his room once so far on this whole trip, but I do tonight. Sort of without thinking about it.

I poke my head in.

He looks up from his bed—shirtless, grey sweats on, sitting on top of the covers all leant back against some pillows.

He's watching late-night TV, and he puts it on mute when he sees me.

"He went down okay?" he asks like we're talking about some

TIME OF YOUR LIFE 163

impetuous child we're babysitting. I suppose—considering all things this evening—that's not all the way that far from the truth.

"Yes."

He nods his chin towards me. "You should get some sleep," he tells me.

"I can't—" I shake my head. "I'm nervous he'll run off again."

Rich gives me this funny look, as though I'm silly for even thinking that.

"I've got this." He waves me off. "You sleep. I'll stay up. Make sure he stays."

I pause, uncertain. "Are you sure?"

Rich says nothing, just gives me this solemn nod, and I know—I don't know why or how—that this is neither the first, nor the last time that Rich will be on the night shift for Jo and his antics.

I give him a grateful smile, then turn to go back to our room.

"Hey—" he calls to me.

I turn back around, an eyebrow up.

"What was that before?" he asks.

"What was what?"

He nods towards our room, vaguely in Joah's direction. "What did you say to him?"

I pause, the reason caught on the tip of my tongue, because the truth is, honestly, actually, I haven't told all that many people about what happened.

I don't know why… Like, sharing my pain with them might lessen it, and I think it's important I feel it, lest I ever get too drunk or too carried away and silly with my friends—then I remember.

I purse my lips, and he sits there waiting for my answer all the same.

"My mother died when I was six from a cocaine overdose," I say rather matter-of-factly.

Rich's head pulls back. "Fuck."

"Yeah." I give him a sad smile.

"Ys—" Richie calls to me as I'm about to close the bedroom door. "Ys—?"

I pause, waiting.

"I'm really fuckin' sorry that happened."

I swallow heavy. "Me too."

SIXTEEN

joah

DON'T GIVE ME THAT LOOK, right—? So I got fucked-up in Paris—who hasn't?

It was fine. No one knows I did, press never found out about it.

Felt a bit rubbish, though—that late-night dander? When Ys found me at the back of that pub—I was pretty fucked-up when she found me, so I don't remember a tonne, but how she looked when she said whatever she said about not making her watch me get high, how her face looked—that cut through all the other shite.

That little worried dip in her brow lives in my brain now like a fuckin' billboard. Don't want it there, if I'm honest. It's fuckin' annoying, like—Forgot this about being in a relationship, didn't I? It's why me and Pip broke up. Cos I'm fuckin' selfish. I know that—don't like thinkin' about other people, and you know what? I'm thinkin' about someone else right now all the fuckin' time. It's hard. Fuckin' hard to filter everythin' I do through the lens of how it might make some girl feel who I just accidentally started to love one day.

And I do love her, not saying I don't—but it was on accident, and I think that's key for remembering. Because I didn't plan for this. Wasn't this thing I've spent the last few preparing for, it just fuckin' happened, didn't it? You know all that shit about sowing wild oats; I've got so many fuckin' oats to sow, man—and I can't now, can I—? Cos I've met this girl I fuckin' love and I don't wanna hurt, and ya know what's fuckin' fucked-up—? Still hurt her anyway, didn't I? Without even trying, you know?

Which is fuckin' hard, and scary, like—

Didn't know what to do that next morning. Knew we probably should talk about it—not evolved enough to *actually* know how the fuck to start a conversation like that though, know what I mean?

Stayed in bed next to me the next mornin', so she did—not like her—barely ever wake up with her still in bed next to me.

Ysolde takes these monster showers in the morning, I reckon in the vicinity of like forty-plus minutes. Likes to make a pot o' tea and read a *Vogue* or summat. Don't like to read it in bed, but. Asked her why once—said it's because it's work. Don't like to bring work into bed or some shit—I dunno.

All I know is the mornin' after I got high in Paris, she's in bed when I wake up.

Pretendin' not to watch me, but 100 fuckin' percent watchin' me—can tell by the way she pretends to notice me waking up, like it's a surprise to her.

Gives me this perfect smile, but it ain't easy for her. I know what her easy smiles look like—that ain't one of 'em.

Strained with worry because I'm a piece of shit—which, to be fair to myself, I did fuckin' warn her about, didn't I? Night we met, I told her I was a piece of shit, and I am, aren't I? Did fuckin' lines in bed next to a girl whose mum died of a coke overdose? Fucked-up. Even I know that. Kinda like I couldn't help myself, but—know what I mean? Needed something to take the edge off, shut my mind the fuck up.

She rolls in towards me. That bend in her brow back. "Are you okay?"

"Yeah." I nod, like it was nowt—because it fuckin' was nowt, you

TIME OF YOUR LIFE 167

get me—? Didn't actually do owt wrong, did I? Not in the scheme of things.

Objectively, I got fucked-up and didn't hurt no one. It's only bad in context of *her*, like—

Kinda hate that…that I can't be meself or do what I wanna do because I love some girl now? That's fuckin' stupid.

"Are you sure?" she presses.

"Yeah." I shrug. "I just—the article got into me head, that's all."

She nods. "It was a shitty, silly article." Tilts her head, lookin' for me eyes. Let her find 'em. "And not remotely true."

I nod back. Dunno if I believe her actually, but like fuck am I ever admitting that out loud.

So I say instead, "Yeah, I know."

"Do you really?" she asks, and fuck her for knowin' me like that. Reckon I don't fuckin' like being known.

She swallows, looks a bit nervous again—fuck.

"Then why did you—" she starts but I cut her off.

"Cos I'm a fuckup, Trouble." Give her a shrug—try to soften it with a smile, but it don't land. Am a bit sorry about it, I s'pose. Not gonna say that though, am I? "I fucked up. That's all."

Shakes her head a lot, don't she?

"You're not a fuckup," she tells me. Says that like I've fuckin' hurt her feelin's callin' meself that.

Loves me too much, man. Don't fuckin' know what to do with it.

Girls with shit dads, you know how they are—? Usually just a bit of fun. But I like this one too much for her to be just that.

Understatement, that. Tits up in love with her, aren't I? So then what? What's left?

The truth of it still fuckin' stands, don't it?

I am—without a doubt—an absolute fuckin' fuckup.

And I'm scared I'm gonna fuck her up too. "Yeah I am, Ys." I press my mouth into her forehead. "And don't you fuckin' forget it."

SEVENTEEN

ysolde

I HAD TO GO AWAY for work this week and it was a funny feeling... I don't like to be away from Joah. I get this weird, sort of sick feeling like there's a knife twisting in my stomach when I'm away from him. I've never had that with a person before, but the whole flight over from London to New York, I have that strange nauseousness you get that's specific to loving a person and being some distance from them.

But now that I'm here and he's not—I suppose if someone were to ask me with a gun to my head how I feel, I'd perhaps very quietly admit that I'm a tiny bit relieved.

Which sounds terrible, I know it sounds terrible, and it could be misconstrued but it shouldn't be—

Joah's just a very intense person. Loving him is incredibly intense. My honour, absolutely. It can be a lot sometimes I think, that's all.

The shoot goes incredibly well—it was Lala and I and a few of the other girls for Versace. A brilliant day—I kind of needed it, actually. I didn't realise I did. I didn't realise that my brain was a bit tired just from everything going on back home, I suppose. I have a weird life, I know that. It's nice to be amongst people who understand it and Cindy, Claudia, Christy—those girls do. They had a million questions about Joah, of course—everyone does. And my cheeks flushed as I talked about him, and my heart fluttered as I told them secrets about him and how he is with me, but a strange thing—and I think it doesn't mean anything—but I did feel a tiny bit tired of talking about us.

That's never happened before.

Usually it's just a thrill? Usually, it feels like I'm bragging, getting to talk about being loved by him. I don't know why, but today it didn't feel like a brag. And I don't want to read into anything but I feel like Lala saw it on me or in me, whatever the difference was.

Later, back at The Carlyle, Lala crawls into my bed in her robe—we always have sleepovers when we're in foreign places together. We have since we met. She has her own room, obviously. I just don't love sleeping by myself, I suppose. I also just like being with my best friend, you know?

She falls back on the pillows and sighs. "Fuck that was mental today, wasn't it?"

I look at her, grimacing. "With that guy?"

"Yeah." She nods. "Kekoa was freaking out—"

There was a bit of a non-incident, ultimately, where someone from *US Weekly* snuck on set to try and snag a few photos of Jo and I—the problem being, of course unbeknownst to him, Joah wasn't there. The second and primary problem though was that he looked a good bit like Mark Draper, so unfortunately for him, he was tackled and apprehended by my security guard.

I flash Lala a smile, and I try for it to be real, but it's sort of forced because I don't know how anything to do with that could ever be all the way funny to me, even when I might want it to be. "That vein in his head—*gigantic*."

Lala watches me closely. "You were alright, though?"

"I mean—" I shrug. "It wasn't him, so—"

Mark Draper's in prison.

"Still—" Lala gives me a gentle smile. "Might have rattled you."

I shake my head and shrug as though what happened last September is nothing but dead leaves from the trees of my past falling on my shoulders, brushed off easily and nothing to me.

It's a lie, though.

It's a wool coat I'm wearing in a stormy sea, and it's pulling me under and I can't peel it off my body no matter how hard I try.

I can't say that though, can I? So I smile instead. "Only for a second."

"Good." Lala smiles, and I'm grateful she bought that. Her face lights up with a thought. "Hey! How was Paris?"

"Yeah—" I smile big, but I feel it falter. "It was—" My voice trails and it would have been unmissable to a layman, let alone my best friend.

She frowns. "What?"

"Nothing." I shake my head. "It was fine."

Lala's eyes pinch and I roll mine, huffing before I explain. "Joah read this awful article about himself—and he sort of spiralled one night, and got really drunk and…high, and went missing for a while, but—"

Her face pulls. "Oh my god."

"No, it's fine—" I say quickly. "Rich and I found him."

"No, Sol." She gives me a look. "That's fucked-up."

I purse my lips. "Is it?"

Lala gives me this—*are you serious?* look and raises an eyebrow. "Does he know?"

"About my mother?" I clarify.

She nods, eyebrow still very poised. "Yes."

"What the fuck?!" She sits up straighter.

"No—" I shake my head quickly. "I think he was just going through something—he felt bad for it. I know he did—"

She crosses her arms over her chest, looking ever so mildly appeased. "Did he say sorry?"

I mirror her—arms crossed, nose in the air. "Yes," I say.

TIME OF YOUR LIFE   171

Well, *technically* yes. Right after it happened, yes, when he was high. But not soberly, not the morning after.

Actually, we barely talked about it after it happened, which I thought was perhaps a bit strange, but then—I don't know—? I'm hardly an expert in relationships. The longest standing relationship I've had with a man is Fletch, and we were together when we were so young, so it's different. It's easy to talk to Fletcher, and he's so direct anyway—Joah's not like that. Joah's completely in his head all the time, barely saying what he means ever, because he's so preoccupied by appearing like the rock star he actually organically already is.

I did feel as though we should have talked about it properly, but he didn't want to. And he already felt so weird and bad about it. He kept calling himself a fuckup, isn't that terrible? He said it as though it were off-the-cuff, but I have a feeling—just from the way his eyes looked—I think that he really believes it?

Lala's looking at me, eyes dancing over my face, searching for something, but I don't know what.

I shift, self-consciously. "What?"

"You fall hard and fast, Solly. Always have," she tells me.

"So?"

She tilts her head, then keeps going. "You were fucking obsessed with Kelly Slater the second you saw him—but this… You and Jo, it's something else."

I peer at her out of the corner of my eye. "What do you mean?"

She shakes her head, like she's trying to make sense of it herself. "I don't know what I mean. I've never seen you like this before—" She squints at me like she's trying to peer through a mirage or something. "I've never really seen anyone how you are with each other, not this quickly at least."

My eyes drop from hers. I'm not really sure that she's saying it like a compliment. I suppose I'm not really sure what she's saying at all.

Lala ducks a little to catch my eye again.

"You're intensely connected—don't you think?"

I open my mouth to disagree—I don't know why, I just feel like maybe I should? She cuts me off.

"Sol, your entire countenance changes when Joah leaves the room—same with him. Like, he looks immediately agitated when you aren't beside him—and it's like—" She shakes her head and breathes out this breath I didn't know she was holding. "God, I mean—that's kind of incredible... But then, also, it's like—"

She stops speaking, presses her lips together.

I wait, eyebrows going ever and ever up. "Is it bad?"

"No." She shakes her head quickly. "I don't think it's *bad*." She pauses. "Maybe dangerous though."

I pull my knees up against my chest. "Why dangerous?"

"Well, I'm not sure—" She shrugs. "I think you're"—she's looking for the word—"tethered to him now, or something—? You're locked in, you know? Final answer." She gives me a silly smile, like she's trying to make the heavy things she's saying a little bit lighter. "All roads lead to Jo..."

And at that, I give her a look—because... All roads lead to Jo? No. Tethered? Please.

"Lala, I'm twenty."

She shrugs innocently. "Well, maybe I'm wrong!"

But the quietest voice within me whispers: *She's not wrong.*

I watch my best friend—whom I know so very well and who cannot, for the fucking life of her, conceal her true feelings—very closely as I ask this terribly significant question.

"Do you not like him?"

"No, Ys!" She reaches for my hand immediately, shaking her head—it's earnest, I can tell that much.

"I like him...more than I wish I did"—she shrugs—"I can tell how much he loves you. I love that. And I love that he'd fucking kill a bitch for saying something vulgar to you... I adore how much he adores you, it's very transparent on him"—she purses her lips, thinking—"maybe in a way that he doesn't even realise..."

"What do you mean?"

"I don't know—" She pushes her hair over her shoulders. "Like, he's obsessed, babes. How often could Joah fucking Harrigan be this smitten with a girl? Like, it's not happening, Solly—It's gotta be weird for him."

I cross my arms again. "Why would it be weird for him?"

"Because it *is* weird," she says, unflinchingly.

"Hey—" I frown.

"Sorry." She gives me a gentle smile and squeezes my hand as she tries to pick her words more carefully this time. "I mean, it's just a very intense and passionate kind of affinity you have for one another. I've never seen you love someone how you love him, and I think that's incredible. But as the person who's spent the last five years being your protector... Ys, you *have* to understand—that's also terrifying, you know—?"

I think my face must look discouraged because Lala pushes some hair behind my ears as she gives me small smile.

"Something can be great and scary at the same time, you know..." She elbows me gently. "Most worthwhile things are."

EIGHTEEN

joah

ME AND THE LADS ARE at Chinawhite. Bit weird being out without Ysolde but—fuck it, I guess, here we are.

This sorta shit makes a fuck tonne less sense once you're not lookin' for someone to fuck like, don't it?

It's just me, Fry, Chops, and Harley sittin' in a corner. He came with that model he's on the pull with, but ain't paying her much attention. Dunno why. She'd go alright. Ys says she's pretty up-and-coming on the fashion scene, says she's out of Harley's league. Then again, I don't think Ysolde understands how proper fucking good Harley Parks is at what he does, know what I mean? There are producers and then there are *producers*, and you can tell whether you had the first kind or the second the fucking minute a record plays through the speakers.

Anyway, Rich is here too—him and Lox are on the outs at the minute—dunno what about this time—can't keep up, but he's well looking for a shag. Been on the tune with these two girls in the corner—good for him.

And me? I'm just mindin' me own business, kind of wondering what I'm even fuckin' doing here—only thing stopping me from going home is that I fucking hate the idea that Ysolde's in

New York right now, god knows where, with god knows fuckin' who, doing god knows what—and I'm just here, like, twiddlin' me thumbs? Fuck off.

And I don't think she's hooking up with someone else, like—be for real, who's she fuckin' instead of me, you know?

Still, though. Summat fuckin' tragic 'bout the idea of my girl out on the lash in New York while I sit home like some sad little twat. Can't be havin' that, can we?

"Excuse me," someone says, interrupting my train of thought. I look up. There's this bird standin' there—looks familiar, couldn't tell ya why. Pretty fuckin' hot though, I can tell you that much.

"Hi." She smiles.

I don't smile. "Alright."

"I'm Meghan. Miller," she says, sitting down next to me, even though I definitely didn't ask her to. Name's familiar. *Have we fucked before*, I wonder.

I look her up and down. "Alright, Meghan Miller—?"

"I know who you are," she says, voice low.

"Yeah." I nod, unfazed. "It'd be pretty fuckin' weird if you didn't."

"I know Ysolde," she says.

"Oh, fuck!" I smile, walls immediately fly down now. "Do ya?"

"Yeah." She nods coolly. "I also know she's away."

Oh alright, I think to meself. *Interesting.*

"Do you know that?" My eyes pinch. "And what about it?"

She gives this little shrug, all sweet-like, but I reckon she's about as sweet as a bag of spanners. "I know people get lonely when their partner is away…"

I take her in, eyes fall down that body she's got. She's this leggy, messy, very shaggable girl with intentions as see-through as her fuckin' dress.

Nod my chin at her. "Are you suggesting anythin'?"

"I'll do anything you like," she says, unflinching.

I look over my shoulder, make sure no one else is in earshot for this. Coast is clear.

"I want you to go to the bathroom—" I say to her quietly and she nods, eyes smoky with want now. "Go to the sink. Stand in front of the mirror—" She nods again. "And I want you to look at your reflection in the mirror, yeah—? That's important—"

"Okay." She swallows, voice husky.

"And then I'll come, stand behind you—" Her chin drops to her chest, keeps her eyes on me—and I've gotta fuckin' give credit where it's due, she is proper stupid fit, in this sorta manky way?

"And then what?" she says, eye-fucking the shit out of me.

"And then—" I pause because I'm a fan of the dramatics. "—we'll both stare at your reflection while you try to explain to me on what fuckin' planet you think I'm fuckin' this"—I gesture to her—"when I'm already fuckin' that." I nod my head in the hypothetical direction of my girlfriend.

Meghan Miller's jaw drops—almost felt a bit bad actually. Looks proper gutted, don't she? Stands up so quickly she nearly falls over as she tries to scurry away.

"Did you make that girl cry?" Rich calls over to me, bit amused by the thought.

"Dunno—" I shrug. "Probably."

He laughs. "Why?"

Shrug again. "She had a crack."

"So?" Harley says, leaning into the conversation. "Isn't she away?"

Annoys me, that. I know he knows her name. Fuckin' everyone knows her name.

Except me, the night we met. But I'm me, so—

Pinch my eyes at him. "Yeah?"

Chops leans in now. "And you're…not…hooking up with other girls?"

My brother doesn't speak, but I can tell he's listening.

Reckon he and Ys are sorta mates now after Paris. Guess that's nice, innit? Dunno, me and his girls, him and my girls, it ain't never been pretty. I think Lox is a pain in the fucking arse, and he thought Pippa was a bit of a gobby cow.

TIME OF YOUR LIFE 177

I can tell he doesn't mind Ysolde but.

"No," I say, make sure he hears me for good measure.

Fry chuckles—does me fuckin' head in when my personal life becomes a fuckin' family affair with the band.

"Since fuckin' when?" Fry says.

Since her, you piece of shit is what I want to say, but I don't.

Try to laugh it off instead.

"Dunno, man"—I shrug—"It'd be a bit of a headache, you know?"

"Fuck," Harley chuckles. "You're whipped."

He nods his head in the direction Meghan Miller darted.

"Mind if I have a crack?"

I glance 'round, subtle as I can, nod at the model next to him, Ys's friend. "Are you not here with her?"

I reckon she's pretending not to know what's happening, but I can tell by her face—I'm getting better at reading girl faces now, I reckon—that she knows. Eyes are wet, or summat.

Harley shakes his head quickly and dismissively. "Nah, mate— we're not serious."

Dunno about that, though. How she's been looking at him—? Reckon she might think they're serious. Or did until just now, you know what I mean?

But then—none off my fucking business though, is it?

Give Harley a shrug.

"Have at it," I tell him before I nod at the door. "Imma head off."

I stand, catch me brother's eye.

"Where are you off to?" he asks.

"Headed home, just—"

Rich looks surprised. "You good?"

"Yep." I nod.

"Nah—" Fry says, chiming in again. Little fucker. "He's fuckin' lovesick, man."

I roll my eyes at him. "Fuck off."

"You are though, lad." Fry flashes me a shit-eating grin. "The old

Joah would have been all over that—" He nods to where Meghan Miller was sat.

And you know what, fuck it—he's right. Like, sirloin tastes fucking great if you never had Wagyu, you get me? But once you do, you're fucked for all other steak.

I shake my head at him like he's an idiot who's wrong, not someone pointing out a change I hadn't consciously decided to make, you know?

"Still the old Joah..." I give him a tight smile as I back away.

Fry scoffs a laugh again and gives me this look. "If you say so, mate."

NINETEEN

ysolde

I DID HAVE THIS FUNNY little panic whilst I was away that maybe something would happen whilst I was gone.

And perhaps maybe a little bit of that is because MB cheated on me, but also because I'm not an idiot. I know how these things work. And you shouldn't be naive either…

On those magazines you read with those titles "Celebrities: they're just like us!"—no, we aren't.

Sorry, but we aren't.

We couldn't possibly be because our entire paradigm is different to yours.

There're studies on how an increase in power correlates directly to increased risky or unethical behaviour.

There are a lot of theories as to why this happens—narcissism, increased opportunity, group norms, high stress, addictive personalities—a million reasons. I personally think it's more because of the necessity of want—how important desire and desiring for something is for humans… When you're a celebrity, you have most things that you want. You don't want for much. I think you have to start wanting extra things.

I, on and off, see a psychologist, can you tell?

I'm not seeing her much at the minute. Don't read into that, though.

All of that was to say: I know for normal people, cheating is this big, horrific deal—and I can objectively see how it is—but I will say, in my circle, amongst my peers, many of you would be alarmed or at the very least aghast with how prevalent it is.

Does that make it right? No, of course not. Is it ideal? Never. Have I been the other woman on one or two occasions? Perhaps. Did I return from New York with a weird sense of dread in my stomach preempting the delivery of news I didn't want to hear under any circumstance? Also perhaps.

I don't know that there's much Joah wants for, you know?

There's a knock on my door before I hear the key and it opens.

In walks the most beautiful bouquet of flowers I've maybe ever seen—pink and orange tulips with chamomile flowers dotted throughout. My favourites. I don't even think I told Joah that.

He peers over them, evidently pleased with himself.

"Trouble." He grins at me as he offers me the bunch. I take them—I feel shy all of a sudden? Silly, I know, but he does that to me.

Then he opens his arms, wraps me all up in them, and I think he breathes out—like, sighs. Happy sighs.

"Fuck, I'm happy to see you." He kisses the top of my head, then pulls back a bit. "How'd you go, were you amazin'?"

I shrug. "Hopefully."

His eyes search over my face. "You look fuckin' incredible, is somethin' different—? Or have I just forgotten how fit you are?"

I bat my eyes at him. "The latter…"

He gives me this half-baked smile. "Shame on me, ey…"

I pull him into the living room, push him onto the couch and then sit on his lap.

"How was your week?"

"Yeah—" He nods. "Fine…"

"Get up to anything fun?"

He shrugs. "Had an interview with an Australian magazine? Bit boring."

"How's Richie?" I ask.

He gives me a look. "Very boring."

I roll my eyes at him, and then he sits up a bit straighter, like he remembered something.

"Oi—I got a funny story. So I was at a bar with the boys—"

I nod, waiting for more. "Yeah?"

"And this girl had a crack, didn't she?"

And my heart sinks. Fuck, he's going to say it. Has it sunk on my face—? Can he tell it's sunk?

I swallow, nervous—though I try my best to sound normal. "Well, fair play to her I suppose, one must shoot their shot—"

"You know her," he says, smiling still.

"Oh." I frown, a bit interested now in a non-masochistic way. "Who was it?"

"I dunno"—he shrugs—"Meghan somethin'."

The frown deepens. "Miller?"

He snaps his fingers. "That's there, yeah—"

I have a hard time keeping my face in check. I clear my throat, heart racing now. "Meghan Miller hit on you?"

"Yep." He nods.

"Well—" I clear my throat. "What happened? Did you—"

He cuts me off, actually looks completely horrified. "No!"

"Oh, really!" My eyes go wide. I probably sound too surprised. That's terrible of me, isn't it?

"Of course I fuckin' didn't."

My shoulders slump a little. "Sorry—"

He thinks to himself for a moment. "Think I made her cry, I reckon."

"Why?" I blink, then shake my head, trying to understand. "And how?"

Jo grimaces at his own private thought. "Turned her down a bit theatrical, like—you know?"

My eyes pinch.

"I…would like *more* information…"

He rolls his eyes and launches into the story, about how she was impossibly forthcoming with her intent to shag my boyfriend because she knew I was away (and on a campaign she'd never get in a million, trillion years, I'd like to say, thanks) and how he cannonballed through her confidence in a way where she'll probably genuinely, *truly* need therapy, and I try not to laugh, but it's an uphill battle.

"Oh my god—" I stare at him. "That's…so much meaner than I thought you were going to say—wow."

He shrugs, unbothered.

I settle in on his lap, pushing some hair behind his ear. His eyes go soft for me in a way I think he wouldn't actually like if he knew his eyes were doing it.

"Do you know—" I give him a tiny smile, pretending like there's not a little bit of sting attached to it still. "She's who my ex-boyfriend cheated on me with?"

His face shifts.

"Didn't know that—" Shakes his head. "Would've been fuckin' meaner if I knew."

I smile, amused. "How?"

"Dunno—" He shrugs. "I'll have a think and get back to you. Oi—" He elbows me. "I wanna hear about New York."

"Yeah—" I shrug my shoulders, breezily. "It was good, a really easy trip—"

Jo nods. I keep going.

"The shoot was so good, and it was so fun to be with Lala and the girls, and I mean, Jo—the campaign is iconic. Like, I actually think it will end up being quite culturally iconic—you're going to love it."

He gives me this restrained smile, like rock star him is trying to play it cool, but real him doesn't want to.

"Course I fuckin' will—" He nods his chin at me. "You girls have any big nights out?"

I shake my head. "Just a couple of dinners."

"No dramas?" he asks, eyebrows up, and I wonder if he knows something. I wonder if Lala or Kekoa said something to him? He and I have never really talked about Mark Draper properly. I'm sure in passing we probably have, but not in great detail. I don't like to recall it in great detail, that's all.

I clear my throat delicately and flash him a quick smile.

"Well, there was that brief interlude where we momentarily thought that my stalker had found me, but—"

"Whoa, whoa—" Joah holds his hand up. "Your—*what*? Your stalker?"

"Yeah." I shrug like it's nothing. "You know, the—"

His face has gone serious in a way I've never seen.

"You ain't never told me about no stalker."

"Oh," I say quietly, then swallow. "Well, anyway—" I shake my head quickly, hoping we can just blow right past this. "It was just a weird series of events in the end. He's still in prison." I give him an encouraging smile but Joah doesn't look all that encouraged.

"In prison?" His head's pulled back now. "What the fuck is he in prison for, Ys?"

"Um—" I purse my lips. "Stalking me."

"Christ—" Joah takes a steep breath. Everything about him has gone eerily quiet. "What the fuck happened?"

"He just like—" I shake my head dismissively. "You know, broke into my house, and...used some of my stuff, and made he and I dinner in my kitchen and—"

He blinks a lot—I haven't seen him do that before—he's struggling to process it. I get it.

"Did he touch you?" he cuts me off.

God, I hate that question. I hated it the first time the detective asked me, I hated it the second time when Lala asked me, I hated it the third and fourth time when Jilly and then my sisters (not my father) asked me, I hated it the fifth time when Fletch asked me, and I hated it the sixth time when I had to talk through that night with a trauma therapist and she asked me too.

I still hate it now. Maybe more so. I didn't belong to anyone when it happened—I don't know whether I've ever really belonged to anyone ever before this, not really—not how it feels to be Joah's, and I think that makes this worse now. Because before the violation was just my own to bear, but now also his.

"A bit," I tell him quickly before I drop his eyes. "But it could have been worse. And it's—" I shake my head. "I don't know. I had to play along, you know—? I-I didn't want to upset him—" I swallow and Jo's eyes look beyond devastated. "So I don't know whether it'd even be classifiable as nonconsensual touching."

He tilts his head and gives me a look. "It was fuckin' nonconsensual touching, Ys, alright—"

"It wasn't much—" I shake my head. "Just he kissed me and my neck and, I don't know—like, touched my arm—put his arm around me on the couch—"

Joah looks like he's going to throw up, but I'm just telling him the story now, it's all tumbling out. "And then the postman came, and I told him I needed to answer the door, and he asked why, and I said because the postman would worry if I didn't and there was nothing to worry about, right—"

Jo's nodding along slowly.

"So I answered the door." I shrug a little. "And I don't know, the postman—I think I must have whispered I needed help, but I don't remember? But he...knew. Somehow, he understood. He pretended it was fine, but he left and called the police and they got there just in time—" I nod to myself, crossing my arms over my chest. "It was certainly...headed...in a direction that I wasn't mad on—" I force a smile.

He was getting violent by the time they arrived, and I won't say how—I don't think Joah could stomach knowing how—but do remember that earlier I said that I've heard before firsthand the sounds of someone running out of air.

TIME OF YOUR LIFE 185

"They found rope and duct tape and lighter fluid in his bag, and like fifty letters he hadn't sent. I think that's why he's in prison." I nod. "I used to get letters from him, that I didn't think very much of initially because I was stupid—"

"—No." Joah shakes his head. "Not stupid."

"Yes," I tell him, sure of it. "Stupid. And I thought I was untouchable. I'm very touchable, it would turn out." I flash him a quick smile, trying to lighten the mood but to absolutely no avail.

Joah presses his hand into his mouth, eyes are fretful. First time I've maybe seen it viscerally on his face, how much he actually loves me. I knew he loved me, I could see that already, but this here on his face, I don't know—it's a quantifiable amount. Strange that I can see it so easily now when something's hurting him. What does that say about us? About him?

"How did he—" Jo starts, then stops himself. Shakes his head, tries again. "Where did he—?" He swallows, takes a measured breath. He's trying so hard to stay calm, but his mind is completely swimming. "When, Ys? Like, where did it start?"

"We don't know—" I tell him, shaking my head. "Apparently I met him a few times at events or—I don't know, I'm not sure—" I shrug. "You know, we meet so many people, I could never place him—" I think back to those strange brown eyes he had, that have always since struck me as far too dark for his very light skin. "He was strange though—one of those—*I was sending him messages through the TV screen* types…"

Joah's staring at me, but I think technically it'd be more off into space. He looks like he's going to be sick, actually.

He blinks a couple of times as he looks at me—properly looks. "I'm so sorry, Ys."

"For what?"

He shakes his head. I think his eyes are teary, maybe? I've never seen him teary. "That I wasn't there—"

I put my hand on his cheek. "We didn't know each other, how would you—"

"It don't matter—" He's full of a remorse that isn't his to carry. "I should have been there."

"Jo—" I tilt my head at him. "You couldn't have been there. And thank god you weren't, he might have hurt you—"

"Nah—" he says, decidedly. "That fucker'd be dead."

I say nothing, just nod once. He's struggling with it, I can see it all over him.

I've never seen him frightened before. He keeps getting lost in thought, eyes somewhere else far away.

"Oi—" He looks at me suddenly, almost like he's remembered I'm right here. "Let's cancel dinner."

"What?" I pull a face. "Why?"

"Dunno—" He shrugs. "I just—let's order in, yeah? Can we?"

"Well, yeah, but—" I hold his face with both my hands. "I'm okay, you know?"

"No, no, yeah—" He shakes his head dismissively. "I know."

"I promise, Jo." I hold his eyes. "I'm good."

"No, I know." He nods, sure. "And now you're mine, so you always fuckin' will be."

TWENTY

joah

SO, THAT WELL FUCKS ME up, dunnit? Worst thing I've ever heard in me whole fuckin' life.

Proper does my head in. I think about her all the time—that's not new, I've been like that fucking since the second I met her, and it was annoying then—but now? She's not just in my head; I'm worried about her now. Where is she, is she safe? What's she doing? Who's she with? I've done a fucking full one-eighty with her body-guard now, haven't I? What a lad. Huge fan. Doin' god's work, ain't he?—keeping her safe, and all.

Y'know before I found out about that shit with the stalker, I didn't much like being away from her, but fuck it, now she's coming everywhere with me.

Like this interview I've got this afternoon with *Rolling Stone* at Abbey Road. We're recording our next album there—which, fuck, I know—*fuckin' epic*, but like—dunno why we're meeting there, but we are. Reckon Mick must've told them we're further along with the album than we are. Not even got goin' yet, have we?

I walk into the studio, Ys holding my hand, trailing in behind me.

Mick pulls a face, nods his chin in her direction and fucking says out loud, "What's she doing here?"

Whole room goes still—not a ton of people, you know? Us, Rich, the interviewer, I s'pose but he's all the way on the other side of the room, makin' himself a coffee. There's Mick's little PA who he's 100 percent fucking whose name I can never fuckin' remember for the life of me—couple of others—dunno, don't care.

I pinch my eyes, stare over at my manager.

"Sorry, mate—" I shake me head, all mock-apologetic. "Must've got me wires crossed… Thought this was supposed to be an interview for Fallow."

He takes a measured breath through his nose. "It is."

Give him a nod. "And I am…?"

His nostrils flare as he answers, don't they? "Fallow."

"AND SHE IS ME," I proper yell, loud enough that Ys jumps in fright next to me. I jab a finger in her direction. "She goes where I go, and you don't bat a fuckin' eye."

"Jo." She puts her hand on my shoulder, rubs it a bit, trying to calm me down. "It's fine—he didn't know I was coming—it's not a big deal."

I barely look at her out of the corner of my eye. "It's a big deal if I say it's a big fuckin' deal."

Rich moseys on over. "What's going on?"

When I say nowt, Ys glances from me to Rich.

"Uh—" She clears her throat. "Jo just found out some—" She's choosing her words carefully. Reckon I catch her trying to look for the interviewer. Smart. "—*difficult* news about me—" She flashes him a quick smile and summat in the edges of it makes my heart feel fucking squashed as I remember again that someone tried to hurt her, tried to make them hers and not mine. "I think he's maybe having some trouble processing it," she tells my brother, and ain't that the fuckin' understatement of the century.

Rich's face falters to a worry. "You alright?"

"Yeah, she's fuckin' fine, man—" Shove him. "Piss off."

TIME OF YOUR LIFE 189

Dunno why that shits me, but it does. One thing you gotta know about me and Rich is we turn on a fuckin' dime, you know? Don't no one know me how he knows me, same goes for him—but fuck, do I hate him sometimes, the nosy shite.

Rich gives me a warning look, his jaw all tight, then—fucking get this—he turns to me girlfriend, throws her a fuckin' look, like they're mates.

"Rich—" Mick says, eyeing him. "Why don't you"—he nods towards a door—"take Ysolde to—"

"No—" Shake me head. "Don't take Ysolde fuckin' anywhere—"

Ys turns to me, puts both her little hands on me chest. "It's—" Gives me that smile she does when she thinks I'm being fuckin' dumb. Bit rude. "I'm fine—"

"But—" I start.

She shakes her head. "I'm fine, Jo. I'll be with Rich." Flashes me one of them proper reassuring smiles. "You know I'll be fine."

I nod a couple of times, tell her without saying a word that she can go with him.

Mick shakes his head—looks stressed, he does. But like, fucking hell—what else is new?

"What the hell is going on with you, man?"

Brush it off. "Nothin'."

"Not fucking remotely convincing, but alright." Mick gives me an impatient look. "Listen. Anythin' here, all of it, they'll use—" He nods towards the *Rolling Stone* journo. "Eyes everywhere, Jo—The interview hasn't started but it has, know what I mean?"

He shoots me a look, and I roll my eyes. Course I know what he means—reporters are sneaky little fuckers, aren't they? I nod, grudging.

"This is a big one, Jo," Mick says, dead serious. "What they write about you, *it sticks*."

He pauses, then adds, "Forget your girlfriend for a second—"

I go to bite back straightaway, reflexive, but he cuts me off sharp. "Think about your career, mate."

I breathe hard through my nose, jaw tight. "Yeah, alright."

I trudge over to the reporter, already clockin' him. Dunno how I feel—he's got this look about him, like he fancies himself a big man, might be the type to make things proper fuckin' awkward for no reason.

"I'm Shane Westman," he says, sticking his hand out. "Good to meet you."

I take it, give it a quick shake. "Same, mate."

He motions to the chair behind me, like I need directing where to sit.

"Right, Joah, appreciate you takin' the time today..."

"Yeah, man. All good."

"*Probably Never* is being hailed as one of the most iconic albums in British music history. How's that feel?"

I give him a look, dead unimpressed. Bet it's written all over my face, innit?

"How d'you reckon?" I fire back, quick as owt.

Mick coughs, proper pointed, and gives me that look—*play fuckin' nice, Joah.*

So, I slap on a grin, put a bit more effort in. "Time of my life, mate. Fuckin' unreal."

He nods, doesn't miss a beat. "I've got to ask—how're you handling this next level of fame? The crowds, the scrutiny, the constant eyes on you?"

"Yeah, look—fuck, it's a lot, innit? People don't get it, but it is. It's a fuckin' lot."

That piques his interest, I can tell. He looks at me, leans in like he's about to uncover summat profound.

"A lot to handle, sure. But isn't that part of the deal? You've got fans worshipping the ground you walk on—screaming crowds, sold-out shows. It's everything a rock star dreams of, isn't it? Or...is it starting to feel like too much?"

I don't say owt, just stare at him. This prick don't have the first fuckin' clue what too much for people like us looks like, so he can jog on.

TIME OF YOUR LIFE 191

He clears his throat, all business. "There've been whispers about your relationship with fans. Some say you've pulled back, gotten colder. Is that fair? Or is fame just hitting different now?"

"Nah, fuck that—that's not part of the deal. The deal's music, mate. That's all I signed up for. And bullshit—I ain't pulled back shit." I pause, smirking. "I mean—fuck, sure, I used to shag more fans—s'pose that's different."

I chuckle at me own joke, don't I?

This Shane lad raises an eyebrow, leans back, proper intrigued now.

"You bring up shagging fans—there's been plenty of talk about how accessible you used to be. But you're saying that's changed?"

"Course it's fuckin' changed."

His eyes pinch a bit, like he's sniffed somethin' interesting. "Should we talk about why?"

"Nope," I fire back, dead blunt. She's off-limits. No one's fuckin' touching her ever again.

Journo sniffs out this single laugh, nodding like he's clocked summat. "Do you miss it?"

"Do I miss shagging fans?" I glance 'round, proper can't believe it. "Is this what *Rolling Stone* is writing about these days? Fuck, mate—" I shake my head at him. "Wind your neck in."

"Do you worry that if you keep seeming less accessible, you'll lose them?"

And y'know what? That one fucking stumps me. Hadn't really thought about it before, not properly.

He presses on, though, doesn't let up. "Fans fuel the machine, don't they? They buy the records, sell out the shows, keep you—keep Fallow—in the spotlight."

I nod along, slow. "Sure."

"Don't you think they feel like they've earned a piece of you?" He tilts his head, proper smug now. "I mean, isn't that what being a rock star's all about—giving people a bit of the fantasy?"

Somethin' snaps behind my eyes. "Fuck the fantasy, man! Fuck the fans—"

The words are barely out my mouth before I clock what I've just said. Mick clocks it too—his eyes go wide, proper panicked, and he shifts towards us like he's about to step in.

And fucking Shane? He looks like all his Christmases just came at once.

"Fuck the fans?" He almost laughs, all incredulous, like he just struck gold. For a journo, he kinda fuckin' did.

"Nah—" I shake my head fast, heart pounding. Shit. This is bad. "I mean—not *all* the fans."

He nods, dead smug now. Knows he's got me on the ropes. "Which fans are you fucking?"

I drag a hand over my face, try not to show how fucked I feel inside—though I reckon it's written all over me. This is a mess, innit? And I'm angry, proper fuckin' mithered. Don't wanna talk about fans right now, not when a fan's the one who fuckin' did it to her.

"Look, I'm not slaggin' 'em off, right? It's not like that—But some of 'em... some of 'em don't know where the line is. Forget we're not theirs, like."

He leans back a bit, watching me, testing the waters like he's fishing for summat more. "So it's the entitlement that gets to you?"

"The entitlement, the fuckin' delusion of it—like I'm not secretly telling you I love you when I'm singin' 'Drift Away,' know what I mean? Or like my girlfriend's not sending you messages through the telly when she's walking a fuckin' Gucci runway."

Shouldn't have said that—I didn't mean to. Just came out. Fuck, shouldn't have gone there. That's piqued his interest, hasn't it?

"So, it's the fantasies, then?" he asks, leaning in. "The way people project their own stories onto you, onto her—turning your lives into something that's theirs, not yours."

I run my tongue over my teeth, sharp, agitated. "Sure," I mutter, keeping it clipped.

My single-word answer seems to make him happy, for whatever reason. Dunno why.

TIME OF YOUR LIFE

"Do you ever feel like you're trapped in those stories? Like no matter what you do, you're stuck being someone else's idea of Joah Harrigan?"

I scowl at him, proper hard. "I'm me own man, aren't I? Don't give a fuck what anyone thinks of me. I'm the singer of the best fuckin' band in the world. End of story, know what I mean? Like, what else is there?"

He smirks a bit at that, proper smug—I reckon if we were in a boozer and I saw this lad about, I'd crack him over the head with a snooker stick.

"Best band in the world—okay, sure. But, Joah, you say you don't care what anyone thinks, yet here we are. The frustration, the edge—it's coming from somewhere. So, what's really eating at you? Is it them not getting it? Or is it something else entirely?"

I don't say owt, just shift in my chair, lock my eyes on him. Let him think he's a big shot if he wants—I'm not afraid of him.

After I let the silence hang for a good twenty seconds, Shane the Prick glances 'round, looks uncomfortable, then clears his throat like he's trying to regain footing.

"Alright. Let's shift gears," he says, lifting his eyebrows like he's got a proper groundbreaking idea. "Your girlfriend—Ysolde Featherstonhaugh—her name's everywhere lately. Do you feel like your relationship is becoming just another part of the spectacle? Or is it different—something you can keep just for yourselves?"

Feel my jaw tighten, proper hard. "Next fuckin' question."

And would you believe it? The prick looks amused at that, like he's enjoying himself. Smug bastard.

"Touchy subject?" he says, smirking like he's already won. "Funny, because from the outside, it looks like you two thrive on being seen. All the photos, the red carpets—it's like you're inviting the spectacle in. Or"—he leans forwards, proper smug—"is it just that you can't control the narrative anymore? That scares you, doesn't it, Joah? Being out of control?"

God, I'd fuckin' love to hit him. He knows he's winding me up, I can see it in his face. Don't wanna react—can't react, I know that—but fuck me, I wanna.

And then he presses, one last shove.

"Is that what all this is really about? The fans, the fame, her—are you losing control?"

And then—fuck, I don't even know I'm doing it, it just happens. I'm on my feet, finger pointed right in his smug fuckin' face. "You know what? Fuck you, mate. Fuck this—I don't need this fuckin' interview. This is bullshit—"

Mick's there in an instant, rushing over like he's trying to douse a fire. "Joah—calm down."

"No—" I shake my head, proper fuming. "Fuck this. I'm done."

I move away from Shane the Prick, looking 'round, heart fuckin' poundin' like mad. "Where's Ysolde?"

He don't get up, that journo—just gives me this look.

"Joah, come on, we're just talking here… You've got nothing to prove—"

Mick grabs my arm, voice low and urgent.

"Joah, mate, don't. Just breathe, yeah? We'll wrap this up."

I yank my arm away from him. "Nah, I'm done with this shit."

I turn back to the reporter, point to his Dictaphone on the table.

"You wanna write somethin'? Fuckin' write this—I don't owe you, or anyone else, a fuckin' thing. Not my music, not my life, not her. None of it."

And then I'm off, out the door she went through before this whole fuckin' mess kicked off, calling her name.

She doesn't answer, though, and I feel it—this weird, crawlin' panic under my skin. Proper unsettlin' like. Where is she? Why can't she hear me? That image—that fuckin' image that's been runnin' laps in my head since she told me a few days back what happened—it barges its way in again.

I shake my head, proper hard, like an Etch A Sketch, tryna clear it, but it's no good. Can't unsee it. I'm angry about it—fuckin' fuming I am. And that interview? Shit. Mick's gonna have my head for that. The label'll have to pull strings to bury it. If it goes to print? Fuckin' bloodbath. Mick'll sort it—he always does.

But I shouldn't have done it. Knew I shouldn't have the second I got out of bed this morning. Felt like shit—been feelin' like shit ever since she told me. Dunno why, just…fuckin' do.

Not her fault, I know that but still, I'm kind of fuckin' pissed at her, I dunno why—know I shouldn't be. I know it's probably stupid and fucked-up, but she's in my head, and I can't fucking get her out of it, and, you know what? I hate it sometimes.

Like she's in my mind, under my skin, in my blood for fuck's sake. I feel how much I love her like fuckin' coursing through me, all the fuckin' time, and I don't like how it makes me feel. I don't like thinkin' about her more than I think about me fuckin' self.

I ain't never done that before, not with no one. I'm a fuckin' rock star, I am the main event. Always have been, thought I always would be—then I went and fell in love with a fuckin' goddess. *Accidentally*, mind you. Was talkin' shit the night I met her, wasn't I? Tellin' her I was a bit in love with her the minute I saw her—guess there was some truth in that, I s'pose. Didn't mean it at the time but, did I? Just wanted to shag her, which was the beginnin' of the end really, wasn't it? Can't shag a girl like that and walk away.

I'm still dartin' 'round fuckin' Abbey Road, calling her name, gettin' more and more wound up every time she don't answer.

"Ysolde!" I yell again, shovin' open another door—and there she is. Sittin' on a couch, legs tucked under her, head thrown back, laughin' proper hard with me brother.

And it shits me, dunnit? That I'm out here fuckin' up my life, losin' me head worryin' about her, and she's in here havin' a fuckin' laugh.

Her face lights up when she spots me, like she's got no clue what's been goin' on.

"How'd you go?" she asks, all breezy.

I stare at her, say nowt, just drag me eyes over to Rich, glaring at him hard enough to burn a hole through his head.

"Let's go," I snap, dead blunt. That's all I say.

She gets up straightaway, and her whole face changes—nervous now, like she's clockin' the mood. "Was it not good?"

"No, it was shit. Let's go."

She glances back at Rich—gives him this look—and I feel me stomach twist. What the fuck is with them two and their fuckin' looks? What's that about?

I nod towards the door, sharp. "Fuckin' now, Ys."

TWENTY-ONE

ysolde

HE WAS IN A WEIRD mood after that interview. For days, really.

Strangely in his head about it. Stroppy and moody, and it's never felt strained between us but it suddenly felt strained.

But still, he stayed. I almost couldn't get rid of him, actually.

Not that I was trying to, but—I do a spin class at David Lloyd. And *Joah came to it*. Joah hates exercise. He does it still, because he has to—*apparently*—but mostly he just runs on a treadmill—complains a lot of the time—and he maybe does some weight training, a tiny bit of the time, and *definitely* complains about that when he does.

Richie told me a funny story about how at one point when they first blew up that Jo wanted to get really fit and so he got a personal trainer, but that Jo got so cross at him telling him what to do, that he and the trainer got into a physical fight—surprise, surprise—he didn't even make it through their first session.

Anyway, he came to my spin class. I don't know why. *How weird is that?*

And I love being around him, don't get me wrong, but there's suddenly an intensity that I don't entirely understand. I'm not sure whether he does either. Because sometimes I feel as though almost he's a bit cross at me? Like, irritated or something. It might be in my head—? Probably it is because I don't feel it all the time, just some of the time.

Joah leans back on my bed, glances over at me. "What do you got on this week?"

"Um—" I purse my lips. "I have to fly to Milan on Tuesday for a fitting and then Wednesday I need to be back in London for a meeting with Rain—"

"—Fuck." He cuts me off, sitting up a bit.

I frown at him, waiting to understand.

"I'm in Manchester, Trouble—" he tells me. "Tuesday on for rehearsals. I can't come."

I give him a confused smile. "That's…fine."

"Nah—" He shakes his head, something clearly running through it. "Shit. Will you be alright, but?"

"I'll be fine," I say again.

Joah nods, a bit as though he's trying to convince himself that he believes it. "If it was anythin' else I'd put it off, but—"

"Joah." I cut him off with a look. "What's going on?"

"Dunno." He shrugs quickly, looks away. "Nowt."

"Why are you suddenly my shadow?"

He sits back, proud and offended—his two most ready and accessible emotions.

"Fuck you," he says.

It's the fire in him, you know—? That has him react like that. He's all impulse, do first, think later. It's something I'm learning about him, actually—more and more. Obviously, he has an ego—talk to him for two and half seconds and you'll know that, but he's also incredibly proud. Pridefulness is a peculiar thing, don't you think?

I say nothing. That's another thing I'm learning. If you give him a minute, let his own reaction settle in him, he'll come around like he does now.

TIME OF YOUR LIFE

His eyes go sorry and he shakes his head. "Dunno—I just—fuck—I feel proper sick even thinkin' about somethin' happenin' to you—"

"Jo—" I sigh. "Nothing's going to happen to me."

He stares at me, incredulous. "Somethin' already did."

"And I'm still here!"

He shakes his head. "But what if—"

"—No," I cut him off. "No *what ifs*. I'm still here."

He goes quiet, just watches me.

"Joah, you need to let it go. I myself am still learning every day to let it go, but it's going to be so much harder if you're holding on to it for me."

He breathes in through his nose, eyes look almost glassy—definitely, they look afraid. My heart sort of pangs with a curious surge of tenderness for him.

I give him a careful look. "Is that why you've been so weird?"

Jo scowls at me. "I ain't been weird, piss off—"

I give him a look. "Three days ago you came and sat at the back of my class at Pineapple Dance Studios."

"Yeah?"

"So you don't like dance. *Or* classes. *Or* pineapples."

He gives me a look before he nods his chin at me. "Do like you in tight clothes though, don't I?"

I roll my eyes at him as I roll in towards him.

"When we met, this had already happened to me. I know it's new information for you, and I love you for caring how much you care, but—I'm okay."

"Okay." He nods thoughtfully.

I lift up a hopeful eyebrow. "Okay?"

"Yeah." He nods again, his eyes searching over my face. Then sort of out of the blue, he grabs me, kisses me really big and deep—a peculiar kind of desperate—like there's something hidden at the bottom of the kiss and he's trying his best to find it. He pulls back eventually.

"Sorry if I've been fuckin' weird," he says.

"It's okay." I smile at him, pushing my hand through his hair. And then I wonder—"Is *this* why you tanked that interview?"

Jo grimaces, rolling back on his back as he stares up at the ceiling. He looks immediately stressed. "Yeah…I dunno—I was so fuckin' in me head about it—"

"Joah—" I frown.

Shit—I feel completely terrible. That's all my fault.

He exhales sharply. "And the journo was asking these questions, like—pryin', you get me?" Joah shakes his head, thinking back to it. "Don't think he knew nowt, but like—"

"He couldn't know," I tell him. "No one knows. We kept it under very wraps."

Jo nods, and then my heart twists with panic. I glance at him out of the corner of my eye. "You haven't…told anyone…have you?"

"Nah," Jo says in this quick, dismissive way that makes me realise I was crazy for even wondering it—he'd never—then he slings an arm around me, dragging me in close. "The lads are sniffin' about—cos of the interview. Dunno, I—" He shrugs, frowning. "I mean, Mick'll sort it, but I proper fucked it, didn't I? Like, they're all askin' why? What happened, like—"

I purse my lips. "Do they know it's because of me?"

Joah presses the tip of his tongue into his top lip—does that when he's thinking—I like it. I think it's cute. Don't tell him though. He hates being cute.

"Dunno." He shrugs. "Maybe? A lot of me these days seems to come back to you, don't it—? So…maybe?"

I frown a tiny bit. "Are they cross?"

He thinks about it for a second, then reluctantly shrugs. "A bit. Mick's fumin'—"

I swallow, a little pit growing in my stomach now. "Is Richie?"

Joah rolls his eyes, amused now. "Richie don't got no teeth, don't worry about him—"

TIME OF YOUR LIFE 201

Richie does—for the record—I'm quite sure, have many, many teeth. They both just love to dismiss one another.

I press a finger into my mouth—wondering something—I don't really want to ask the question on my mind but I feel like perhaps I should.

"Should I...*not*...come to the Manchester show then... maybe?"

"Nah—" Jo reflexively shakes his head. "Come."

I nod, relieved. "Okay." I breathe out a breath I didn't know I was holding, actually—right as Joah's eyes pinch in thought.

"Well, maybe—"

"Oh," I say, trying not to sound a bit hurt. Silly how I could be hurt at my own suggestion, yet here I am.

"Dunno, just that, like—" Jo's muddling it through in his mind, that much is obvious. "Everyone is kind of pissed off at me." He gives me a grimace. "And kind of you."

I frown now. "*I* didn't do anything."

"Nah, I know." He gives me a look. "Buncha pricks though, aren't they? Ain't your fault. But it's just a bit—I dunno. I don't want them to give you shit—"

I watch him for a few seconds before I ask, "You don't want them to give *me* shit? Or *you* shit?"

He pulls his head back, looks annoyed at that. "Oi."

I regret it straightaway. I shouldn't have said that; it probably wasn't fair.

"It's fine." I tell him, quickly.

He looks at me, suspicious now. "You sure?"

I nod. "Yep."

He looks at me, uneasy. "You seem pissed—?"

I shake my head. "I'm not pissed."

Though I am, between you and I, possibly the tiniest bit pissed.

I wonder if he knows it? And I wonder if it's feeling too tricky with the boys that he actually just doesn't care in this instance.

"I get it." I give him a small shrug. "It's my fault somehow."

He groans. "Ysolde—fuck—" Big sigh. "Come on, that's not what I'm sayin'—"

I lift an eyebrow, silently waiting for him to tell me what he *is* in fact saying.

"Just—I dunno, like—it's a lot, you an' me, all of a sudden. We're fuckin' everywhere. Used to be me an' the lads, now it's you an' me."

Which—by the way—is objectively a fair assessment. That's true. There is an undeniable public fascination with Joah's and my relationship.

He keeps going. "Reckon they'll think if you're there, it'll be about you. Or us, not the band, an'—"

And maybe I'm paranoid, probably I am—I just…have a feeling. I don't think I believe him—?

"And Mick's bein' a right prick. It'd get him off me back, make him think I'm takin' work serious, y'know—"

"No, yeah—" I nod along anyway. "I understand."

He nods back, then he tilts his head, looking at my face carefully. "Are we good?" he asks.

"Yeah." I nod back, but really, I'm not so sure.

TWENTY-TWO

joah

"JO." ME MUM'S GRINNIN' AT me as she swings open the front door to the house me an' Richie grew up in. We bought her a place last year, we did. In Chorlton, proper nice. She wouldn't go, though. Stubborn as a mule, me mum. That's where I get it from.

Mum's cheeks are rosy like always—she grabs me by both sides of me face—beamin', she is.

She pulls me in, plants a kiss on each cheek. "Missed you."

I step inside, givin' her a hug. She pulls back, lookin' at me like I've just offended her.

"This new girlfriend of yours not feedin' you?"

"She's a supermodel," I say, givin' her a look. "She's not fuckin' feedin' herself."

Mum smacks me on the arm. "Not in my house with that language."

"There goes his whole vocabulary," Richie pipes up from the settee, loungin' about like he owns the place.

I flip him off. He flips me off back.

Mum sinks into her favourite armchair, lookin' at the pair of us all soft-like.

"My boys are back," she says, all proud.

I roll me eyes at her, and she nods towards the kitchen.

"Dinner's on. Your favourite," she says, lookin' all proud of herself.

I can't help smilin' at her. "Smelt it the second I walked in the door."

Lancashire hotpot.

She nods, dead chuffed. "Got enough to feed an army. Presume I'll be—" She cuts her eyes to Rich. "Loxy comin'?"

He nods.

"And the boys?" She glances between us. "Last I saw Fry, he looked a bit—well—are you not payin' him?"

"Mum," Richie groans, throwin' his head back.

"Alright—" She lifts her hands, all innocent-like. "None of me business."

I give her a look. "He's paid, Mum. Just got one of those—what d'you call it? Fast—"

"—Metabolisms," she finishes with a nod. "Well. Lucky him."

Rich snickers. She's always been funny, our mum.

She points upstairs. "Got some fan mail in your bedroom—" She pauses, thinkin'. "Boxes, actually."

I screw me face up. "How'd you get 'em?"

"Cos you told Mick Sloane to throw 'em away, Joah!"

I roll me eyes at her.

"—and I thought to meself, ah, well, we can't be havin' that. So I told him to send it here, an' that when you come home—*if* you ever come home"—master with the guilt, me mum…—"that I'd make you go through it."

I stand up, dander over to her.

"Gonna make me, are ya?" Kiss the top of her head. "You and whose army?"

Then she reaches down and takes her slipper off her foot, giving me the eye.

I duck quick as she swings at me, laughin' as I dart upstairs to me room. Can hear her and Rich chucklin' behind me.

TIME OF YOUR LIFE

205

"I wish you'd stay here—" she calls after me. "But I understand that you're a big shot now, too tall for his single bed."

Told ya. Fuckin' masterful.

"—I've been too tall for that bed since I was sixteen," I call back.

Mum's the best bird in the fuckin' world, ain't she? Like, sorry Ys—fucking close second—but there's no one who's met my mum who don't love her.

'Cept one.

Me old man. He was a piece of shit, but. I've said that before. I s'pose proper grammar'd have me say, "My old man *is* a piece of shit," cos he ain't kicked the can yet or nothin'. But he's not around, so what does it matter?

That's not a bad thing—it's a fuckin' miracle, I reckon.

Cos he weren't just a piece of shit. He was proper bad news.

Used to smack me mum about.

It weren't just the one time. It was all the time, wasn't it? You'd hear him come through the door, already half-cut, kickin' off about some shit—work, money, her. Didn't matter. Any excuse would do. Me an' Richie, we learned early how to get in the way, take the brunt of it so she wouldn't have to. Didn't always work, but. He'd get his digs in anyway if he couldn't get his hands on her, call her all sorts of names like it was sport.

Richie'd take the hits. Back then he was bigger, shoulders an' all. Me, I wasn't much good for takin' it, so I got good at givin' it back. Knew how to make him pause, at least. A kick to the shin, smack with somethin' heavy if I could grab it fast enough. Didn't care how manky it was—rather him mad at me than her.

But that last time—the last time we saw him—that was the worst of it. He comes home pissed, screamin' blue murder cos he's lost some quid on summat stupid. Walks in, smashes the photo on the mantel—our family photo, the only decent one we ever had. Glass everywhere, bits of the frame hittin' the floor. Mum tried to calm him down, like she always did, but he grabs her arm, twists it till she's cryin'. Proper cryin', not just holdin' it in like usual. It was out of its socket, we'd find out in the end.

Richie stepped in, like he always did. Shoved him back, told him to leave her alone. But he goes and gets himself thrown into the table—hit his head, went down hard.

And I'm stood there, watchin' it happen, and somethin' in me just snapped. I grabbed the fire poker, didn't even think about it, just swung it at his back. Me dad staggered but he don't stop, does he? Just turned on me instead.

Next thing I know, I'm up against the wall, his hand 'round my neck, liftin' me like I'm nothin'. I couldn't breathe, like—couldn't even move. I thought, *This is it. This is how it fucking ends.*

But then—I dunno—Richie was up again, tackled him from the side, knocked him down. We were both on him then, throwin' punches, kickin', whatever it took. He staggered out the door, swearin' he'd come back, but he never did.

Mum was on the floor with me after, holdin' me like I was a kid again—s'pose I was, kind of—? About thirteen, I reckon I was. I remember her cryin' into my hair, and all I could say over an' over, was, "Don't let him come back."

We left that night. Took everythin' we could carry, and I fuckin' couldn't carry shit. I was shaking' like a leaf that night, wasn't I? Whatever we could fit into me mum's shitty old Ford Escort mk2.

Still see it, y'know? Every now and then. The way his face looked, the way Richie looked after it too. Broke somethin' in both of us like. We got through it, though, didn't we? Dunno if we came out whole, but.

Ain't told Ys all that.

Ain't really told anyone, to be fair.

Don't think it's anyone's business, like—

I know it's shit. It's why I don't like comin' home, though. Reminds me of him. Of before, when I was some shit-kickin' kid who couldn't look after himself or his mum, needed Richie to fuckin' bail me out.

TIME OF YOUR LIFE   207

Hate that. Hate that Richie had to save me. Hate that he took the brunt of it too—took my punches like. Makes me feel like I owe him. Don't wanna owe owt to no bugger, know what I mean?

Bit of that's why I didn't want Ys to come. Didn't want her seein' where I came from, gettin' clues about me life I don't want her knowin'. Don't want her knowin' any of this shite. Wouldn't want her thinkin' there's any kind of weakness in me, y'know what I mean?

And if we're bein' honest, reckon I think about her too much. Like, it's a bit fuckin' pathetic, innit? She's kind of all I think about, like—Know it ain't her fault—well, it is, but it isn't.

Just wanted a minute to meself, y'know? Not a crime, that. Still feel a bit shit 'bout it though, don't I? Dunno why. Don't wanna talk about it.

I sigh, sit meself down on the bed, and start goin' through the post—fuckin' loads of it, isn't there—? Last thing I wanna do, but I don't want that fuckin' slipper, do I?

Most of it's sound. Bit mental that people care this much, eh? Like, can't grumble about it, can I—? Mental, but.

Some of it's proper weird, though. Makes me think of Ys and what happened, and then I start feelin' fuckin' sick and stressed, so I stop. Lay back on me old bed, starin' up at the ceilin'—how'd I ever fit this thing?—don't remember it being this small, do I? But it is. Funny thing about growin', innit. Don't really know till after you're done that you were.

And I'm not tryna have a mither, but it ain't dead soft either. Feels like home, but—know what I mean? Just summat about it.

Dunno how long I stay there for.

It's Richie saying "Oi," as he knocks on the door, two quick taps, that pulls me out of me head.

"Look who's here," he says.

I sit up fast—can't believe my fuckin' luck that she's come anyway, even though I told her not to. Don't even care that she ignored what I said—I'm just fuckin' glad she's here.

I'm up on my feet, ready to hug her, but it's not Ysolde standin' in me doorway.

I look at Richie quick as a whip. What's he playin' at?

"Hey, Jo," she says, smirkin', givin' me that look she always does—sizin' me up.

I breathe in through my nose, steadyin' meself. "Hey, Pip."

Fuck.

TWENTY-THREE

ysolde

I'VE JUST FINISHED MY MEETING with Jilly and the head of the agency, Margaux Welles, at Lagans Brasserie. Pix was with us too—I brought her along in case there was anything I needed to action, but it was just a catch up, really. Margaux just likes me, Jilly said. Actually, after that meeting, I'm quite sure Margaux actually more likes my boyfriend, but that's neither here nor there and who can blame her.

If I wasn't dating Joah, I'd probably have a lot of questions about him too. I mean, fuck—I *am* dating him and I still do.

Pixie gets along with everyone on the planet, and her and Margaux got along crazy well—chatting away, primarily about my boyfriend and his music, which was strange to witness but sort of nice because then I didn't have to talk about us.

Jilly warned me about it… She said it'll feel like a pain to have flown back in from Milan for it, but that it's important to keep her sweet.

After Jilly and Margaux leave, I send Pix home and I stay on by myself—I'm not by myself much these days.

I'm not even really by myself now. Aleki's in a car out front waiting for me. We're both reading the same book at the minute—we started doing that a few months ago. At the minute we're reading *The Bridges of Madison County*.

He's ahead of me because every time I try to read, Joah plucks it out of my hands and tosses it away.

"What are ya readin' for?" He'd give me a look. "Don't like reading."

"I'm not asking you to read—" I'd tell him.

It's around then that he usually plucks the book from my hands. "If you've got time to read, you've got time for snogging."—Which is honestly really, really hard to argue with when you have the soul-penetrating blue eyes of Joah Harrigan right in your face.

So, admittedly, yes—reading has fallen to the wayside lately, and I'm using now to catch up.

I'm three coffees deep when a voice I can't quite place but do know, says my name.

"Ysolde."

I look up only to see Mick Sloane.

I'm not honestly overjoyed to see him. Why would I be?

This is the first time I'm seeing him properly, I think.

It's not at nighttime, we're not at a show, it's not through the blur of stress that Joah's murdered the lead singer of Bright Line, it's not when he's ready himself to bottle me in the head for being the reason Joah fucked up an interview with *Rolling Stone*—and even still, I'm not mad on him.

And I don't mean to be unkind…but he doesn't…*not*…remind me of a used car salesman.

"Mick." I force a smile. "Hi."

There's just something sort of desperate to him. Sweaty?

And he always looks a bit red? Not sunburnt, though—I mean, gosh, it's London in March, what sun?—he just always looks a little bit red in the face. Which is unfortunate because he sort of has red hair. Strawberry-blond hair, technically. But when I told Joah that his manager had strawberry-blond hair, Joah said, *"Don't fucking tell*

TIME OF YOUR LIFE 211

him that," and I asked why, and he said, *"Because it'd break his spirit."*
To which then I said that that was crazy, strawberry-blond hair is beautiful, and then Jo said that he didn't reckon it would really be on Mick's list of priorities to be beautiful, and I said, *"Well, you never know,"* and he laughed and kissed me.

"How are you?" he asks.

"Fine." I nod.

He glances around us. "What are you doing here?"

"Oh, I just had a meeting with Jilly and Margaux Welles—"

"Head of Rain." He nods, impressed. "I know her well."

Though I suspect he actually does not.

He nods at the plate in front of me. Caviar. Beluga, obviously.
He smirks. "Model's diet?"

I give him an unimpressed smile—which, sorry—maybe I shouldn't have—it's a man's world, I know. I just don't really like my diet being questioned by a little man with a pinkish hue.

"Something like that," I say.

He nods. "You coming to Manchester?"

I breathe in through my nose, shaking my head. "No."

"Oh." Looks genuinely surprised by that. "Why?"

"Because—" I close my book now, dog-earring the page I'm on. "Joah said...not to..."

"Oh." Mick's mouth pulls into a confused frown. "Why?"

I shrug. "I suppose there's been so much—like—you know—
whatever... I didn't want to detract from their show—"

He nods sympathetically. "That's sweet—" he says, looking at
his cell phone. It's one of those new little Ericsson GH337s. Quite small, actually. I like it—I hadn't seen it in person till now, but I could fit that in bags.

He finally drags his eyes up from his phone back to me. I don't know what he's looking at, really—what could even be on there that's that interesting? I feel like he might just like to feel important.

"You wouldn't, though," Mick tells me. "You should go."

I feel bad for thinking he just wants to be important now that he's being nice to me.

I sit up straighter. "Really?"

"Yeah." He nods emphatically. "Yeah, you're his girlfriend. He loves you—You should be there—!" He nods to himself, some distant cogs in his head turning—I can sort of see behind his eyes. "He'd want you there," he tells me before tacking on an encouraging smile at the end. "You should go."

And I won't lie—I'm kind of completely delighted. This has warmed him to me plenty.

"Okay." I'm smiling now, properly.

People like it when a supermodel smiles at them—he likes my approval, I think. He looks chuffed.

"Do you want me to put you on a flight up there?" he offers.

"Oh—" I pause, contemplating the offer. That would be so great actually. "Would that be annoying?"

"No—" He swats his hand through the air. "Least I can do."

Least he can do for what? I wonder for a second, but then he says, "I'll call Jilly with the flight details."

"Okay!"

"Don't tell him though, okay—" He gives me a warning look. "Jo could use a nice surprise."

I nod in agreement, and Mick gives me a wink. "I'll see you up there."

TWENTY-FOUR

joah

——

PIP KIND OF LINGERS AFTER that. Reckon I should've told her to piss off, but I s'pose I don't mind her being about. Like putting on an old pair of trainers—bit worn, bit knackered, but they fit.

And no one really gives a toss. We walk around town, and yeah, eyes are boggled, but they're boggled at me—Joah fucking Harrigan. Not because I'm with Ysolde Featherstonhaugh, the face of the decade or fuckin' whatever. Different buzz, know what I mean? This is just me, and it's nice. No whispers trailing behind us, and if they're cameras, they're just here for me. That's Manchester for ya. And Pip, I s'pose. Just…easy.

"What's she like?" Pip asked as we walked along the canals near Castlefield.

We'd had lunch earlier at The Oxnoble. Dunno why—no reason, really. Just because I could. Because I was me, and I can do whatever the fuck I want, know what I mean?

"Who?" I said, even though I knew exactly who she meant.

Pip hadn't let me off with that, though. Gave me a look. "Piss off."

Made me laugh.

She don't look owt like Ysolde, you know? I don't have a type. Just "girl," I s'pose. Pip is nearly white blond, dark eyebrows, very pink mouth. Ysolde's mouth is well pink too, but it's different, innit? Her skin's brown. Pip has this—I dunno, what do they call it?—fairy look about her. Pixie-like. Always has.

"You'd hate her," I told Pip.

She glanced up at me out of the corner of her eye. "Course I would," she said, then looked straight ahead again. "She's fucking you."

What was I meant to say to that? I hadn't known what to say—fuck, like—she was well underplaying what me and Ys were, but it felt shit to rub that in Pip's face, so I didn't clarify. I reckoned that's probably why I didn't clarify—right?

"So." She pursed her lips. "How'd it happen?"

"Saw her in a bar." I shrugged. "Talked to her."

She nodded, unimpressed. "Riveting stuff…"

I said nothing. Bit good at that I am, lately.

"She tall?" Pip asked.

I nodded once.

She scrunched up her face. "Yuck."

Didn't like that—summat about it had sat weird in me chest. But I didn't know how to set Pip straight either, because it was her, wasn't it?

"Nah." I shrugged like it was no big deal. "Legs up to her eyeballs."

"You're a boobs man," Pip said.

I sniffed a laugh. "Yeah, but she don't really got those…"

Dunno why I told her that—fuckin' regretted it straight after.

Pip watched me for a few seconds. "You've changed."

I cut her a look. "Fuck off."

"You have," she insisted, then stared straight ahead again. She walked a few paces, eyes on the ground, before asking, "Will I meet her?"

"Nope." Told my shoes.

TIME OF YOUR LIFE

That caught her attention. Pip had looked up at me again, interested now. "She not coming?"

Shook my head.

"Why?"

"Dunno—" I shrugged. "Bit of a circus whenever she's about—"

Pip nodded her chin at me, not buyin' it, like—"You love a circus."

Said nowt, didn't look at her even—did that *staring straight ahead* thing meself.

"Ah," she chuckled under her breath, like she got it. "You only love a circus when you're the ringleader."

Let out this long, slow breath out me nose, gave her a bit of a side-eye.

But she's right, know what I mean?

Say what you want about Pippa, but she knows me fuckin' well.

It's true, what she said. Is it summat to be proud of? Nah, but fuck it—I s'pose neither am I.

When I walk into the green room at The Haçienda with Pippa, Richie's leant back on the sofa, arm slung 'round Loxy, and he clocks us straight off. Looks from me to Pip and back again, gives me this look.

Proper fucks me off too, dunnit? Like he thinks he's dead clever, like me and him are havin' some secret, knowing chat about me girl, but he can fuck right off with that.

Reckon he thinks he's mates with her now after Paris. But she's mine, not his, and whatever he thinks is going on, whatever shit he thinks I'm doin' with Pip, I'm not. I've been good, haven't I? Been a proper good lad. Been such a fuckin' good lad that I reckon I'm a bit of a prat now actually, but that's beside the point.

"Any word from Ysolde?" Rich pipes up, tryna make a point. "How's she doing?"

Fuckin' annoying, man. He's always annoyin', but this—? It shits me proper. Him, and then, like—still, even when she's not here, dunno how but my fuckin' show's still about Ysolde. How's that, know what I mean?

"Haven't spoken since yesterday, man," I tell him, trying to make a point of me own. Dunno who I'm making it to, really.

Probably should still give her a call. I will. After.

"Don't worry about her, lad—" Mick says as he strolls into the room, cracking open a beer. He takes a long sip. "Just focus on the show, mate. She'll be right." Then he squints from the other side of the room—putting it on, isn't he? Like, he's old, yeah—but his eyes ain't that bad. "Oh, is that Pippa?" he quips, breaking into a grin, arms open, making a beeline for her.

"Hey, darling," he says.

She grins up at him. Always got on, those two. "Hey, Mick."

"How you been?" Mick flashes her that charming, manager-smile of his.

"Yeah, I'm—" Pip starts, smilin' back, and then she glances at me—how she shouldn't. Reckon if we're being fuckin' honest, she looks at me in a way that says summat that ain't all the way true. Not this time, at least.

And fuck, Richie clocks that too, don't he…sittin' over there looking like he's about to say summat—mouth open, already gearing up to start running his mouth, when somethin' on the telly catches his eye—

It's footage of Lala, strutting down a runway at some show, lookin' fuckin' sharp as ever.

Rich nods his chin at the screen. "That's our kid's mate."

Chops groans. "Fuck, she's fit—"

"She's well fit," Fry chimes in, and Richie nods, bit too fervent for Loxy's liking—Clocks that, she does, then gives him a sharp elbow to the ribs.

"Pack it in, Rich." Loxy scowls. "You wanna take a walk down Deansgate after this, see how fit I am with my heel in your arse?"

TIME OF YOUR LIFE 217

"Nah, Lox, swear down—" Pip shakes her head, smirking. "Even I wouldn't kick her out of bed."

"What you and Joah get up to in your boudoir's none of my business," Loxy fires back, folding her arms.

"We don't got a boudoir," I tell her, rolling me eyes, throwing meself down on the couch next to her.

Pip follows, sliding in on me other side. Closer than she should, probably.

"Whose fault's that, eh?" she mutters, dead low so only I can hear. And fuck, my stomach's straight up in my throat. Dunno why—? That ain't never happened before. Never cared before how another bird talked to me. Dunno why I suddenly do now?

"Richie—" One of the guitar techs pokes his head into the room, looking like it's life or death. "There's a weird buzz coming from your amp. Need you to sort it before the show—"

Rich groans like a kid who's been told to do his homework.

"Go on, don't be shit—" Loxy says, giving him a shove.

He groans again, louder this time, but gets himself up and trots off, mutterin' summat I don't catch.

"Oi—" Chops pipes up, catching my eye from the corner. "But would ya?" He nods at Lala, still on the telly, strutting her stuff.

"Fuck off," I say, shaking my head reflexively. "Nah."

"Fuck off yourself—" Fry laughs, slapping his knee. "As if you wouldn't."

"I wouldn't." I shrug.

Loxy snorts, proper loud, and don't I hate being laughed at? And then her and Pip go and swap this look—like they're takin' the piss and I'm the mug—that shits me even more.

Pip leans back into the couch all casual, eyes me—knows how to get under me skin, you know? "Fuck, she's got you on a lead, don't she?" Says that like it's fact.

My jaw goes tight—give her a scowl. "Piss off."

"Nah," Fry chimes in, nodding along like he's got me pegged. "You're well under the thumb, mate."

I'm under the thumb? Fuck off, I'm not.

Don't like this shit. Like it even less now that Lox starts laughing now too, proper loud. "State of you—" Lox chuckles. "Proper gone, innit?"

I shake my head at the lot of them. "I dunno what the fuck you're all on about, but you're chattin' shit."

"Alright, kiss me, then," Pip says, dead casual and it sends my fuckin' head for a loop.

I stare at her for a couple of seconds—try to get my ducks in a row.

"What?" Shit. This is bad. "No."

And my ducks—? They ain't in no fucking row. Because it's a dare, innit? I'm fuckin' stitched up either way. Like—either I don't kiss Pip and then everyone's on a fuckin' mad one about how I'm Ysolde's fuckin' lapdog now, or I kiss her, and that's me cheatin' on Ys, innit?

"Why not?" Pippa shrugs all innocent-like, but it's shite. She's not innocent—ain't never been.

I run my tongue over my teeth, buying time.

"Cos I don't want to."

She gives me this look, though, like she don't believe me for a second. "You always want to…"

But I don't wanna right now, do I? Or—do I? Shit. Are they right?

If it wasn't for Ys, would I kiss Pip? Yeah, probably. Like, why the fuck not?

Fuck—if it wasn't for Ys, I probably would've wanted to shag Lala too.

So—fuck—are they right? Am I fuckin' under the thumb?

I dunno how many goddamn times I have to say it—I'm Joah Harrigan. No one's got me on a fuckin' lead.

But I think I'm on one. *Shit.* Am I fucking on one? I don't wanna be.

Hate it, me. Fuck that. I'm a fuckin' rock star, not some soft-arse

TIME OF YOUR LIFE   219

twat moonin' over a girl. "Yeah, alright then—" I say to Pip, nodding at my lap. "Come on, then."

Just a kiss to get 'em all off my back, you know?

She climbs on like it's nowt—muscle memory or some shit, and that feels…I dunno, weird now, don't it? Familiar like, but off. And she makes a proper song and dance of it too, because that's her. Always been like that.

Arms 'round me neck, batting her lashes for a few seconds, then—fuckin' hell—she pounces. Literally. Proper pounce.

First girl I've kissed since I met Ysolde… Won't lie to ya, don't love it. Don't hit how it used to like.

It ain't bad, is it? It's just fuckin' sirloin to Wagyu, know what I mean?

Dunno how long we kiss for—not like I'm fuckin' swept up in it or owt, but cos I'm in me head, you know? Thinkin' 'bout how this is sorta fuckin' weird. What am I kissin' this bird for, you know—? When there's this girl back waitin' for me in London— the one I'm fuckin' obsessed with. Best snog I've ever had, best shags of me life, and a face I can't get out of me fuckin' head. What the fuck am I on like?

And it's now—right fuckin' now—while I'm thinkin' all that, that I hear Chops sayin' my name only about a thousand times.

"Jo—Jo. Joah. Joah—"

It ain't even me who pulls back—it's Pip—stops kissin' me to lean over and smack Chops quiet, and it's right as she leans Chops' way—that's when I see it.

That's when I see her.

"Fuck," I mutter under my breath.

"So," Ysolde says, arms crossed, starin' at me like she's about to set the fuckin' place alight. "*This* is why you didn't want me to come to Manchester."

"Ysolde—" Mick says, taking a step towards her, and she gives him the iciest fucking look I've ever seen in my life.

"Fuck yourself," she snaps, and—maybe my head's just spinning, maybe I'm imagining shit—but did he smile? Did Mick smile when she said that? What the fuck's that about?

Don't matter. It don't matter because Ysolde walks bang into the room, no hesitation, and straight over to Pip.

"Pippa—? Hi." Ysolde just sticks her hand out, all polite-like. Pip just stares at it, then at me, then up at Ys—who's towering over her—before finally, awkward as fuck, shaking it.

"It's so good to meet you—" Ys says, smiling in this way I ain't never seen before. It's weird. Thought I knew all her smiles. Guess she's never needed to take this one outta the toolbox before. Not 'round me, at least. Not till now.

"I've heard about you." Ys goes and she does that same polished-to-fuck smile again—Pip can't even meet her eyes.

I could gip, couldn't I? That's when she looks at me, eyebrows up, face all conversational, like she's just chatting.

"No, Jo—do you know what? She's prettier than you made her sound."

And you could hear a fuckin' pin drop in that room, couldn't ya?

Pippa's eyebrows shoot up, her mouth falls open, and she gives in to gravity, sliding right off me lap.

"But you're right—" Ysolde keeps going, voice all light and airy. "I *am* more attractive. Just, you know, in that"—waves her hand through the air—"silly, conventional kind of way." She scrunches her nose and shrugs like we're a pair of daft little duffers. Feel about fucking two feet tall, don't I?

"So—" Ys glances between me and Pip. "What are we doing?"

"Ys—" I start.

"No." She shakes her head, still all smiles. "No, that's not a name for your mouth anymore."

Eyebrow lifts, curious, like she's dissecting me. "Was this always the plan, Jo?"

I sigh. "Ys—"

And then summat behind them eyes of hers proper snaps. "Not. For your mouth. Anymore," she says, slow and sharp,

TIME OF YOUR LIFE   221

over-annunciating like I'm thick.

Am fuckin' thick though, aren't I?

Start shaking me head. "I can explain…"

"I'm *quite* sure you could," she says, that smile sliding back into place, fuckin' eerie, innit? "But it's already incredibly self-explanatory." Then, like I'm not even worth it, she pats me on the arm. A pat—like she's wishing me luck on my fuckin' A levels. "Anyway—have fun finishing this up. She looks like a hard worker. That tracks."

And just like that, she turns and fuckin' swans out.

Fuck—it's like all the air's been sucked out the fucking room. I'm on me feet and after her in under two seconds, but—innit just my fuckin' luck—she runs into Richie in the hallway.

Hear him before I see him.

"Hey," he says to her. "You alright—?"

Round the corner, and Richie takes one look at me—and dunno, do I have hair that looks I've had a snog, or something, like, how's he know?

"Ah, fuck—" he sighs, pinching the bridge of his nose like he already can't be arsed with what's coming next.

"Ysolde—" I reach for her but she jerks away.

"Stay the fuck away from me," she says, and her voice sounds raw now. Eyes are sad too. She was fronting in the room before. I can see her now.

"Ysolde—" I go to grab for her, but she jerks back like I've got the plague. I shake me head, try again. "Can we just—"

But she fucking shoves me. Full-on shoves me. Proper hard, too, like she means it.

"Stay. The fuck. Away from me." She's yelling now—yelling. She ain't never yelled at me before, not like this. My head's spinning. What the fuck's going on? What did I just do?

"I hate you," she spits, and it cuts right through me, don't it?

Don't handle this shite well. Back me into a corner—don't matter who y'are, even if you're the love of me fuckin' life—I'm gonna come out swingin'.

"I told you not to come!" I shout back—don't like being yelled at meself, is the thing. Don't like being talked to like that by anyone, you know what I mean?

"So you could do this?" she asks, eyes all wide with betrayal.

No, is the answer I don't tell her out loud. Dunno why.

She shakes her head at me. "Fuck yourself."

Over it now—don't much fucking care for being shouted at in the hallways of me own show—all these eyes on me like I'm the villain here, like I'm the fucking fuckup. Maybe I am. Don't give a shit, even if I do.

Shake my head at her, the whole ship's already going under—might as well sink with it.

"Don't need to," I say, my chin up, all cocky. "That's what she's for, innit?"

Said it to hurt her, didn't I? And it does—I see it land—wait for the rush to come, the one I get when I'm in control and everyone else can get fucked, I don't care—doesn't come, but. Not this time.

"Apparently so." Ysolde gives me a threadbare smile. Then she nods back towards the green room. "Go get her, tiger."

Give her a weird fucking salute as I turn and walk away—dunno why—felt like a good exit at the time, but actually I think I'm just a prick.

Round the corner, don't go back in that fucking room—stay close as I can where she can't see me, make sure I can hear it all. Fuck, my heart's beating fast—we've never had a fight before, but this feels bad.

She looked proper sad, didn't she? Proper fuckin' sad. Fuck. What've I done?

"Are you alright?" my brother asks.

"Yeah," she says, but I can hear she's lying.

"Sorry," Rich says.

"No, it's good—" says it, but it's shite, that. "It's fine."

"Do you have a place to stay tonight—" Rich asks. Fuckin' annoying how good he is of thinkin' about things ain't never cross my mind. "Are you—"

"I'm good," she says. "I'm all set."

"Oi, here." Sounds like he hands her something. "That's me number. Ring me if you need owt, yeah?"

"Thanks, Rich," she says, quieter this time.

"I mean it," Richie says, his voice carrying as he walks away, heading my way. "Call me," he calls back, dead serious.

He rounds the corner.

"Don't fuckin' tell her to call you," I snap, warning him with a look.

Rich snorts, proper amused, rolls his eyes and keeps walking back to the green room.

"I ain't takin' the piss—" I shout, going after him. "You can fuck right off."

Rich don't even glance back, the prick. Just strolls over and plants himself next to Mick, like I'm not about to set the place on fire. Fine.

Pippa's in the corner, huddled up with Lox, lookin' like a kicked puppy. Don't care. Bit shit, I know, but I can't care right now, can I?

"What the fuck's she doing here, Mick? Eh?" I jab a finger his way, my voice bouncing off the walls. "Why's she even fuckin' here?"

Mick shrugs, useless as ever. "I told her to come," he mumbles.

I stare at him like he's off his head. "Why the fuck would you tell her to come?"

"Because—" He shrugs again, all limp and pathetic. "She's your girlfriend."

"Yeah, and you fuckin' hate her," I spit, my voice sharp enough to cut glass.

Mick rolls his eyes, long-suffering. "I don't *hate* her," he sighs, dead annoyed. "I was trying to be nice."

Glare at him, proper livid. "Well, bang-up fuckin' job there, mate. Nice one. Gold fuckin' star."

"None of this is his fault, mate," Rich tells me, and fuck him—I spin his way.

"Where is she? Where's she gone?"

Rich just shrugs, cool as a fucking cucumber, like none of this matters. "I dunno."

"Well, I need to know!" I shout, my voice cracking with it. "So fuckin' find out!"

"Are you off your fuckin' head?" Richie gets up onto his feet again and right into my face now, proper close, his voice low and sharp. "Mate, you must think I'm someone else—"

"Shut the fuck up and find out where she is," I bark, pointing a finger at him.

Rich takes a step back, slow as you like, and gives me this smarmy little grin that makes my blood boil. "I don't reckon she's your girlfriend anymore, mate."

The words hit me like a gut punch. Is that true? Fuckin' hell, do you reckon that's true?

Shove me hands through my hair, pulling at it, desperate now.

"Where's she staying?" I ask, my voice tight, looking from Richie to Mick like they've got all the answers. "Where's she going?"

"I dunno!" Richie snaps, all exasperated, throwing his hands up like he's the one with the problem.

And then it clicks—fuck.

"—Is Kekoa here?" I blurt out, the thought making my chest tighten.

Mick stares, proper confused. "Who?"

"Her fuckin' bodyguard," I grind out. "Did she bring him?"

Please, fuck, tell me she brought him. At least then she'd have someone with her, someone to keep her safe—

"Oh, him?" Mick scratches at the back of his head like a muppet. "Nah, she didn't bring him."

Cos she was coming here for me, wasn't she? Told me she didn't need him places when she was with me.

Fuck. This is all so fucking fucked.

She's here. Alone. She fucking hates being on her own. Where's she gonna go?

TIME OF YOUR LIFE

"Shit." I press my hand to my mouth, feel like I'm gonna gip. "Cancel the show."

"What?" Mick stares at me like I've just punched him.

Chops and Fry shoot to their feet, both talking over each other.

"What?" Fry yells, as Chops shouts, "No fucking way!"

"I have to find her!" I shout, chest tight. "I'm not going on!"

Richie's right there now, all up in my face. "Yeah, you fuckin' are."

"Nah, fuck it—" I shake my head, blood boiling. "This is on you, Rich. I'm not fuckin' going on—"

"On me?" Richie scoffs, face all twisted. "How the fuck's it on me?"

"Bringing her 'round." I jerk my chin at Pippa. "You knew what you were doing. Piss off, like—"

"Yeah, right," Rich says, a smirk pulling at his mouth. "I made you hook up with her…"

I stare him down, fists itching, then turn back to Mick.

"Make the call, Mick. I'm not going on."

"Yeah, you are," Rich says, cracking his back like he's king of the place. "Our insurance don't cover you being a melt, so—"

"Does it cover you being a prick?" I snap back, fire in my voice.

Mick exhales through his nose, rubbing at his face. "Sadly, no."

"Find her," I bark at him, pointing straight at his chest.

Mick gives me a look—trying for something paternal, but it don't land. Never does. Fuck fathers.

"I'll find her, Jo," he says, voice low. "But you've *got* to get on that stage—" He shifts, proper serious now. "Joah—we can't do this again."

Grab the bottle of scotch off the table, twist the lid, and take a swig. Burns all the way down.

I wipe my mouth.

"Fine."

TWENTY-FIVE

joah

THE GIG WAS ALRIGHT. RECKON it looked better than it felt—for me, at least, you know what I mean? The crowd were buzzin'—proper packed in, shoutin' their fuckin' lungs out. Could see 'em singin' every word like their lives depended on it, arms up, eyes wide, sweating buckets. I think I sounded alright—? I can usually tell by Richie's face if I sound shit, and I think I was alright tonight. The boys were solid too. One of those shows people'll probably talk about, say it was electric or some shit. And it was, I s'pose. But me? I weren't there.

Like, yeah—I played every chord, sang every word—fuck, that's the job, innit? Might as well've been a puppet on strings, but. Head somewhere else the whole fucking time. I'll give you one guess where.

Like, where the fuck is she? Are we actually done for? Does she really fucking hate me? Ain't never said that to me before, has she—? And where the fuck is she now? What's she doing? Is she alright? Dunno if she ate today—? Fuck—like, she don't really eat when she's upset, does she? My stomach's in knots, proper twisted, thinkin' about her in this city she don't know without me.

Do you know what's proper fucked? Even though I feel sick with it, I'm still fuckin' pissed at her too. Because like, every cheer, every roar from that fuckin' crowd—it just bounced right off me, like I couldn't even hear it, know what I mean? And it's her fault because she was in me fuckin' head. Drives me fuckin' mad. She's in me head when she's my girlfriend, and she's still in me head when she's not. Like, I can't win, can I?

And like—a bit of me is scared I proper fucked it—do you reckon I did?

Dunno. She's not been angry like that before—not with me—don't fuckin' tell her, but like—I'm kinda scared of her. Not actually, but kinda. Hot girls when they're angry are like, I dunno—diabolical.

Probably, I can fix it but, yeah? When can't I? If I wanna fix something, I can fix something, you know what I mean? Girls—they always get over it.

But, then—I dunno—*is she girls?* She ain't a normal girl, I know that. But she does love me, don't she? So—like, fuck—that's gotta count for something, yeah—?

My mind's fuckin' swimming.

Bleedin', like—*Where the fuck is she?*—that's all that's banging 'round me head as I walk offstage.

"Oi, mate—" Mick's lingering outside me dressing room, slapping me arm like we're all pals. "Fuckin' great show."

"Fucking—no. Stop, I don't care—" I snap, shaking me head at him. "Did you find her?"

He pulls in a sharp breath through his nose, looking like he's bracing for a smack. "Wanna—" He jerks his head towards the door. "Let's—"

I follow him in, slam the door shut behind us, the echo bouncing off the walls. "What the fuck's going on?"

"Right, so—" He's rubbing at his mouth like he's got an itch he can't get rid of, looking proper knackered. "I had one of the boys follow her out the venue—"

Nod, leaning in like that's meant to mean something. "Yeah…?"

"Said just, keep an eye on her, like—make sure she's right…see she gets to a hotel safe—"

"Okay…" I keep nodding, like it'll calm me down or some shit. Good. Glad he did that. Makes me feel a bit better, I s'pose.

But then Mick takes this deep breath, like he's winding up for something, and then…fuck all. Just holds it in, like he's suddenly forgotten how to talk.

Me head pulls back. This weird, nervous twist starts up in me gut, like I already know I'm not gonna like what's coming next.

"What?" I ask, voice sharp now.

He shakes his head, proper cagey. "Listen, I don't wanna—"

"Nah." I nod at him, heart thumping harder. "Go on."

Blows that breath out like he's been holdin' it a year. "She got a taxi to The Cliff."

My eyes go wide. "What fuckin'—?" Words are spilling outta me before I've even got a grip. "What's that supposed to—Like, what fuckin' cliffs?" We don't even have cliffs in Manchester? Barringer's, maybe? Currier Point? How the fuck would she even know about them?

Mick's staring at me like I've just gone daft.

"No, mate—" He gives me this look, proper slow and deliberate, like I'm the thick one here. "As in *Salford*."

Takes me about two seconds get me head 'round it—nah, no fucking chance.

Shake my head at Mick, my stomach already twisting up. "Fuck off."

That's where fucking United train, innit? My chest's tight, my throat's even tighter—oh, I'm gonna gip.

Mick nods once, proper slow, like he's trying not to spook me or some shit.

"Freddie Fletcher came out—" I don't mean to do it, but fuck it, I sigh.

"And, mate—" He looks sorry for me. Fuckin' hate it when people are sorry for me. "They looked pretty friendly…"

TIME OF YOUR LIFE

"What do ya mean?" My head's shaking, words tumblin' out. "Nah—no fuckin' way—What the fuck do you mean—?"

"Dunno, Jo—" Mick shrugs, his shoulders all limp like he wants to disappear. "It wasn't me there, mate. Just—" He hangs his head, proper pathetic. "He said they looked like more than friends."

Do you know what—? Fuckin' fuck her.

"Yeah, right." I nod. Fuck her. I'm done. Done with her, done with relationships and shit—never again.

"Alright—" I nod at the door behind him, jaw still clenched. "Fuck off now."

Mick tilts his head, giving me one of those looks, like he's trying to be a dad.

"Jo—"

"I said fuck off." Louder now, cutting through the room, letting him know I'm not fucking about. "And send Pip in."

Mick fires me off another paternal look. "Joah…"

Stare over at him in fucking disbelief. "Did I fuckin' stutter?"

He sighs, big and heavy, like he's the one with the problem here. Then he walks out, closing the door loud enough to make a point. Not a slam—can't slam doors on your wages, can you? But it's loud.

Can't fucking believe her, can I? One fight, and she runs straight back to her ex? And not just any ex—nah, it's got to be *Freddie* fuckin' *Fletcher*, don't it? What the fuck am I supposed to do now—? Can't swap teams, can I? But I can't support him either—no chance I'm singin' "Glory, Glory Man United" with the image of him fucking Ysolde in me head. Fuck that.

There's a case of Stella in my room—part of the rider—but she's not gonna cut it tonight. Should be a bottle of Balvenie knocking about somewhere. I rifle 'round for it, knock over a stack of merch and free shit people leave in here for me in the process, but I find it eventually. Unscrew the top, don't even bother with a glass.

Plough through half the bottle before the door creaks open and in walks Pippa. She's fucking filthy at me.

I've pissed this girl off more times than I can count—don't reckon I've ever seen her like this, but. She's livid. Proper raging.

Nod me chin at her. "Oi."

She closes the door behind her but doesn't move, just leans against it, arms crossed, glaring.

"How were we?" I ask, casual as you like. And yeah, I ask it on purpose. Bit of a reminder of who the fuck I am—Joah fuckin' Harrigan, remember? Lead singer of Fallow. She's here having a strop at my fucking show, know what I mean?

She shrugs, dead casual. "Fine."

Fuck off, we were unreal, and she knows it.

"Where's your girlfriend?" she asks with a glare.

I stand up, take a step towards her, the bottle of Balvenie in my hand. Take a swig to take the sting out of what I'm about to say: "Not my girlfriend."

My chest fucking lurches as the words come out, dunnit? Like me own body's fuckin' rejecting whatever's happening.

Pippa scoffs, full of contempt, shaking her head. "You're a piece of shit."

"Yeah." I nod, swallowing it down. That's fair, I reckon. Take another swig, then hold the bottle out to her.

She grabs it, takes a big, long pull, and then fixes me with that glare of hers again, one eyebrow arched like she's daring me to say something stupid.

"I'm not as pretty as her?" she asks, voice sharp, cutting.

I roll my eyes, dead casual, like she's being ridiculous. "She's a supermodel…"

Pip's scowl comes back with full force. "Fuck you!"

I tilt my head, watching her close. "Yeah, do you wanna?"

Her eyes pinch, confused now. "Do I want to what?"

"Fuck me." I say it plain as owt, like it's not a big deal. Doesn't flinch me. At least on the outside.

She makes this noise, proper disgusted like. "No."

"Yeah, you do," I tell her, all calm because I know it for a fact.

Take a step closer. She takes another swig of the scotch, eyes narrowed, not moving away. "Come on…"

Shoves the bottle back at me, all gruff-like, and our hands brush when she does. That's on purpose. Her eyes flash up at mine, glaring but full of fire.

"I hate your girlfriend."

I shake my head at her, fuckin' cool as owt. Say it again because I need to hear it again to believe it—need to get it through me fuckin' head. "I already told ya… *Not my girlfriend.*"

Pippa rolls her eyes like I've said the dumbest thing she's ever heard.

"I fucking hate Ysolde Featherstonhaugh," she says, spitting her name like it tastes bad.

I take another swig of the scotch, nodding back at her slow.

You know what? Fuckin' me too.

TWENTY-SIX

ysolde

I WASN'T EVEN ALL THE way sure that Fletch would be there, but I figured it was my best bet. That I'd at least know *someone* there. Tommy Langford, who's been Fletch's best friend for forever, he's on the team too. Or Elliot Harper, who he used to flat with for a bit when they were just starting up. There'd be someone there—someone in Manchester who wasn't connected to my stupid fucking boyfriend. Ex. *Ex*-boyfriend.

Just…connected to my ex-ex-*ex*-boyfriend. Much better.

I pull up outside The Cliff in a taxi around the same time Tommy's walking in—an act of God.

He spots me.

"Oi." He grins. "What are you doing here?"

"Is Fletch here?" I ask. I don't really feel like chatting. I'm eleven minutes away from having an absolute, full-body shutdown and I need to go somewhere where no one can see me collapse. I'd like to think I'm hiding that fact well, but Tommy's face bends in concern. "Yeah, he's—" He nods his head towards the building. "Do you wanna c—"

TIME OF YOUR LIFE 233

I shake my head and he nods a couple of times, getting it. Or perhaps not getting it at all but so deeply convinced he's ill-equipped for whatever might be about to happen next that he just backs away towards the door.

"Alright. Stay here." He looks confused. "I'll go grab him."

I'm standing out there—teeth chattering—probably not cold enough for that, if I'm honest, but I've always been colder than everyone else.

About 9°C outside right now, dark too.

There's a man across the street who followed me from the venue—the stalking victim in me is a tiny bit paranoid about him, but I think I recognise him, and the part of me that wants to believe that Joah isn't a complete sack of shit wonders if he sent him to make sure I'm okay. That, or spy on me.

Either way—when it gets back to Joah that I came here, he's going to shit a brick. Good. I actually hope he shits two. And gets an anal fissure whilst he's at it.

"Hey," says that other ex-boyfriend of mine. The good one. The one I probably shouldn't have broken up with in the first place. He reaches for me. "Are you—?"

And then I immediately start crying.

Freddie Fletcher's face falls heavy with a worry he's had for me since the moment we met.

I'm safe with him, you see. I've always been.

Our mothers were best friends, did you know?

He holds my face in his hands, looking at me properly.

"Hey, hey, what happened?"

He pulls me in towards him, holding me against him.

"Solly." He kisses the top my head because he's just like that. "Talk to me."

I pull back a little, shaking my head at him.

"We've been trying to avoid unnecessary drama in the papers, so he told me not to come because it's been a lot lately—"

"Right—" He nods, waiting.

"So I didn't. But then I did—" I pause for dramatic effect. "To—you know—*surprise him*—"

Freddie grimaces. "Uh-oh."

"He just wanted to hook up with his ex." I sniff.

His face falls on my behalf. "Shit."

I start shaking my head. "And I didn't bring Aleki—"

"—Why?" he asks, tone sharp. He knows about Mark Draper.

"Because—" I give him a look. "I don't really need to when I'm with Joah. There's always so many people around them anyway, plus there's usually security—he was just sort of doing nothing—he needed a holiday!"

Freddie shakes his head. "Don't like that."

"I was going straight from the airport to Jo! And—" I shake my head again. "I don't know where I am. I haven't booked anywhere, I don't have a place to stay—"

He gives me a look like I'm silly as he tosses an arm around me. "Yeah, you do."

———

It took some convincing because I didn't want anyone to see me and for rumours to start already that Jo and I are over—*are we over?* I suppose we are. We are. We definitely are—but Fletch promised that the boys at the club wouldn't say anything when we had to go back to the locker room to pick up his stuff.

There were a few whispers when I walked in. I think you could probably tell I'd been crying. People can always tell when I've been crying. Lala says it's because my eyes go like sphalerite. Pix says it's because my mouth goes extra pink and boys want to kiss it better. I don't know which is true, if either is—the point is, Manchester United do stare when I walk in with their right midfielder.

He grabs his stuff, says bye to his friends, and we walk to his car in relative silence. A black Porsche 911.

He opens the passenger side door for me, bends over, buckles me in, and he hovers—our faces all close how they've been a

TIME OF YOUR LIFE

million times before this and probably will be again a million times after it too.

He's really beautiful, Fletch. Obviously, you know that—you've seen him. We've all seen him. He's the biggest deal in the world when it comes to football. In the papers they say that god gave with both hands when it came to Freddie Fletcher.

He's really tall. As tall as Joah, definitely (which, do remember, is very tall)—with this lean, athletic build that makes everything he does look effortless. His skin's this really warm, lovely brown that somehow seems to catch the light even when he's not in the light, and he's got these impossibly sharp cheekbones and dark eyes that always look like they're sizing up the whole room. His hair's short and curly, neat but never too done. He's got this natural presence, you know? As though he were born to take up space. He is. Always has been. Annoyingly gorgeous, too.

We pull up outside his house in Worsley. Less than fifteen minutes from where they train.

It's quite posh—definitely a bit big for just him—he said on our way there that he doesn't mind it because usually he's got a couple of the reserve players that can't afford much themselves staying with him, which is very like Fletch. He's just inherently good.

We walk into his home and I'm sort of impressed—he said his sister picked everything. I'm not sure whether that means he likes it. I know he likes his place in London more than this one, and I know that he did most of the choosing for the London flat, but Lauren wants to be an interior designer, and Freddie's never been that good at saying no to her.

We take a sharp turn into his living room.

"Oh my god—"The room is completely kitted out. Moody grey walls, massive windows, a marble coffee table polished to a mirror shine. A gigantic TV so big it's basically a cinema screen. Beneath it, there's a sleek, black cabinet with a state-of-the-art sound system and a stack of CDs arranged like art. The lighting is soft, the rug is plush, the shelves have just enough books and memorabilia to look intentional, and there's actual good art on the walls. But there's no sofa, no chairs…not a single thing to sit on in sight.

I laugh in disbelief. "Fletch."

"No, listen—" He tosses his car keys down on the table. "I ordered a new couch—so I got rid of the old one—but then the new one was delayed so—"

"So—" I cut him off. "This is pathetic! Ninety thousand pounds a week, they pay you."

"I know, I know—" He hangs his head in shame.

I shake my head at him. "What would your mother say?"

"Well, she wasn't lovin' it either." He shrugs, helpless.

"No—" I give him a look. "I would think not."

He chuckles as he sits down on the floor, his knees propped up.

"It's fine—" He pats the space in front of him. "Good for you to sit on the floor. Come down off that high horse every once in a while—"

I put my nose in the air. "I'm not on a high horse."

"You live on high horses." He gives me a look. "Speaking of— what's Evanthe up to these days?"

I flick my eyes, amused. "Oh, she has a boyfriend, haven't you heard—?"

"Oh—" He chuckles. "I heard." He pulls a face. "The way your fucking dad cares about that makes it sound like she belongs in a bell tower."

I squash a smile. "No, you know him—he's stuck in the '30s— only proper thing a woman can do is be a wife, and she went off and became a doctor…"

Fletch gives me a playful look. "Better than a model…"

"Well," I shrug in lighthearted defeat. "Anything is. Even acting."

He smirks. "Crump still on that train, then?"

"Oh, well supposedly it's her lifelong dream…" I breathe out my nose. "I think it's just…the *being famous* part she wants."

He nods. "Think it's that for a lot of people, probably."

TIME OF YOUR LIFE

"While we're on the topic of the fame-hungry—" I pinch my eyes at him. "Where's…*Minty*?"

He gives me a long-suffering, sort of loaded look.

Minty is Fletch's on-again-off-again girlfriend. They started basically as soon as we stopped.

She went to the same school as us. She's a year older than Freddie, who's a year older than me.

"Ibiza," he says. "With the girls."

She's kind of a WAG. Acts like one, even if she isn't actually technically one.

"And are you guys…?" I lift an eyebrow as I ask my very open-ended question.

"I dunno—" He shrugs with a grimace.

I give him an unimpressed look. "You *don't know*?"

"No—" He shakes his head. "It's on and off and on and—I don't know—" He shrugs. "It's hard. You know, I'm away a lot—"

That's why we broke up. He and I—our careers both sort of took off at the same time. He went away a lot. I went away more. We started fighting all the time—which feels—*I know, impossible*—how can you fight with this man? Believe me, you can, there are ways. I found all of them. It's just that at the minute, he probably strikes us all as particularly angelic in light of Joah.

I give him a nod. "I recall."

"That—" He eyes me. "And my fucking ex keeps popping up randomly." Our eyes catch, each of us knowing full well that I *am* the fucking ex. And I *do* pop up randomly. In varying degrees of oftenness…

"She doesn't love that," he tells me.

"Oh." I cross my arms over my chest. "Would you like your ex to…*stop*—?"

He gives me a long look, pinches his eyes back at me. "I didn't say that."

"Well, listen—" I sit up straighter and flip my hair over my shoulders. "I don't know whether you know this, but I've never been the *biggest* fan of Minty—"

He rolls his eyes. "You don't say?"

"She was so indifferent towards you in school. She was only interested in kissing you once you'd signed with United as a trainee."

"—I know." He groans.

I shrug, light as a feather. "—Me? I've been trying to kiss you since I was thirteen."

He squashes a smile. "You have been kissing me since you were thirteen."

"Yes." I bat my eyes at him. "I suppose I have."

"So why stop now?" he says, just with this playful, little quarter-smile. Nods his head his own way, signalling for me to come to him, and I do.

I crawl across the floor and into his lap, press my nose against this.

He holds my face in his hands and stares at me, eyes all big and gentle.

"We should probably stop doing this."

"Okay," I say, swallowing heavy. "Now?"

That quarter-smile goes to a full half.

"No." He laughs, and then he kisses me.

God, and you know what, kissing Fletch is like a blanket being thrown around your shoulders on a cool night. Immediate warmth; immediately, I'm comfortable; immediately, I'm okay.

Was I not okay before? I hadn't realised. I thought I was. Maybe I was—? Maybe I was more than okay, and it's only now that it's over and we're done for that I'm not okay.

Am I okay?

I think I'm okay.

I'm with Freddie, so I'm fine—even if I'm not fine.

Even if every morsel of my brain feels how your skin does when you touch a hot element and your hand's burning—like how even if you can't see the burn, you can still feel it—? In your skin, under your skin, and there's an ache in me that I'm here doing this with someone who isn't Joah, which is stupid—because *I'm twenty*! Did I think we'd last?

I'm such a fucking twat—nothing lasts. Ever. And Joah's an artist (don't tell him I said that, his head's already too big). But artists, they're good with their words and they're good at making you think you're special and making you feel special, but I'm not special. What Joah and I had—*evidently*—was not special, so. Here I am, again. Literally again because I've done this a trillion times with Freddie, but also metaphorically again because I do...do...*this*. I get tricked. I fall in love too quickly, and it doesn't just burn out—it burns through me. I don't like how that feels—that gaping hole in the centre of me—And do you know what? Between us, this might be the worst one yet.

I think probably every time up until now I've thought *okay, I think that boy is the one*, but this time, with Joah, I don't know—I suppose a tiny bit of me believed it in a different way. I think we just felt different.

But this just proves my sad little point...feelings are shit and liars.

Feelings are for the weak, and though it pains me to admit—I am the weakest of the weak.

Can't be alone for even a minute without a boy by her side to make her feel better, I read that about myself in a magazine once. It stung a lot, only because I realise it was completely, utterly true.

And do you know what's worse? It's really only better for a second, isn't it? It's just pressure on the wound. The wound's still there underneath the hand that's covering it, that's making the bleeding stop—and the hand can't stay there forever. Hands never do. But I suppose better for a second is still somehow better than just worse all the time.

Besides—nothing's ever worse with Fletch. At best, it's fantastic, at not-best, it's neutral.

With him, it's just autopilot, you know? We've been on cruise control with this kind of thing for what feels like half my life.

It was Freddie, by the way.

Freddie is who I *actually* lost my virginity to. I was

fifteen—maybe even not quite that—we were by ourselves, there was a snowstorm—we were at his house. Tom Petty had just released *Full Moon Fever*, and Fletch had it on cassette.

It wasn't planned. He did have condoms, though—so it must have been on his mind a little bit.

We were on top of his bed—not under the sheets—we laugh about this all the time now. Because neither of us had had sex before, we didn't know what would happen—and certainly neither of us knew how to wash sheets, so we didn't want to have sex in the bed in case—*you know...* So we did it on *top* of the bed. Which was a really bad idea because duvets are significantly harder to wash than sheets. I think we flipped it over in the end.

Do you know, I think afterwards, after we did it, that's one of my favourite nights of my entire life. Still now even (and I've had some pretty good nights since), but he and I tangled in his duvet, sitting on his floor, wrapped up in each other...? Pretty hard to beat. We stayed like that until morning when his parents and sister were finally able to make it home.

"Free Fallin'" still makes my stomach do backflips.

And he's *so* good at it, that's worth noting. So good at knowing me and preempting me and what I want and need—definitely more than I'm able to for myself.

I've asked him about it before, why and how he's so good. He just smiled and said that he just pays attention.

There's something so sexy about that, isn't there?

So unbelievably different to what it's like with Joah.

Jo is all passion, all-consuming, everything-all-at-once intense, his hands are busy-busy everywhere. I'm usually quite tossed about—and don't get me wrong, I actually *love* it—it's very fun. The funnest sex I have ever had in my life I have had with Joah.

But I wonder—how many other people is he having fun sex with?

TIME OF YOUR LIFE   241

Afterwards, I lie on my back, staring at his ceiling.

"You alright?" Fletch asks, rolling in to face me.

I glance at him. "Yes, fine." I force a smile. "Brilliant."

He squints at me, assessing. "You're in your head."

Our eyes hold. No point lying to him. "Just a bit."

He watches me close before he asks his next question. "Are you sad?"

I suspect he already knows the answer.

I swallow, my eyes drop from his. "More than I wish I were."

"Should we not have done—" He nods his head back in time. "…that?"

"No—" I smack his arm. "Of course we should have." Then I give him a stern look. "And we'll be doing that again."

His head rolls back and he stares up at the ceiling again. "Ysolde—"

"Fletcher…"

He looks at me again, an eyebrow up. "Sol."

I mirror his face. "Fletch."

He laughs, then shakes his head. "I don't like to hurt you."

"You *didn't* hurt me." I give him a look. "*Someone else* hurt me. *You're* making me feel better."

"This"—he waves a finger between us—"is very dysfunctional."

I nod appreciatively. "Correct."

Then he gives me a *right, so…?* look. "So maybe we shouldn't?"

I glance at him like he's being silly. "We already have"

His face stays serious. "But maybe we shouldn't *again.*"

I roll my eyes at him. "Take your clothes off."

"Sol—"

"Fletch—" I copy his tone. "Take your clothes off."

And do you know what? That boy shakes his head at me. Half because he's a good guy, half because he's on a power trip. The nerve of him, either way!

I give him a look as I sit up now—remind him I am in fact a supermodel.

"This is going to be so embarrassing for you…" I tell him, brushing my hair over my bare shoulders. All of me is bare though, I suppose.

"For *me?*" he quips as he props himself up on his elbows, watching me—properly watching me. My plan's already working—how could it not? I'm literally a naked supermodel and that boy is staring at me like he's a cartoon coyote and I'm a rib eye with legs.

"Yes." I nod. "For you."

"Yeah?" He smirks, staring at not-my-eyes. "How's that?"

"Well, in ten seconds when you're positively begging for me to have sex with you, you'll just feel silly."

"Really?" He licks his bottom lip, amused. "Go on, how's that happening, then?"

I stand there in his living room in nothing but knickers I put on for Joah. "Close your eyes."

He rolls them first, but then he does what he's told.

I pluck a CD from his stack and pop it into the player.

"She's a good girl, loves her mama—" blares over the speakers. *"Loves Jesus and America too—"*

His eyes spring open before they go to slits. "Brat."

"Yes." I nod in agreement, smiling triumphantly.

He breathes in through his nose, looking annoyed. "Ysolde…"

I blink sweetly at him. "Yes, Fletch?"

He stands to his feet. "Take your clothes off."

TROUBLE IN PARADISE? SPARKS FLY AT THE HAÇIENDA

By Fiona Tate, Entertainment Correspondent, The Daily Sun

Whilst Fallow lit up The Haçienda for the first of their highly anticipated hometown shows, whispers of behind-the-scenes drama overshadowed the performance. Front man Joah Harrigan was spotted arriving with Pippa, an old flame, sparking curiosity amongst those backstage.

Noticeably absent, however, was Harrigan's girlfriend, supermodel Ysolde Featherstonhaugh. Fans were quick to speculate about her no-show, but it didn't take long for her name to pop up elsewhere. Featherstonhaugh was later seen entering The Cliff, the famed Manchester United training grounds.

What exactly brought her there remains unclear, but it's safe to say the story doesn't end here.

TWENTY-SEVEN

joah

DON'T REMEMBER MUCH OF LAST night, do I? Got well pissed. Definitely fucked Pip. Don't remember it, mind—but she was naked in my bed this morning, just—rolled over and kissed me like we're summat we well aren't.

Pinched me eyes at her. "Did we—?"

"Yeah." She smiled, dead pleased with herself, wasn't she?

Nodded once. "How many times?"

She frowned. "You don't remember?"

"Nope." Shook me head at her. "Don't remember a fuckin' thing."

She rolled her eyes, proper dramatic. "Just once."

Bit surprising, that.

"Said you wanted to take things slow…"

Things? What fuckin' things—?

Gave her a look. "Don't sound like me…"

"I know." She laughed like she thought it was mad too.

See, took about two bottles of scotch to get me head to fuckin' black out. Only way to stop seeing it—Ysolde getting fucked every which way, all over the Theatre of Dreams.

TIME OF YOUR LIFE

Roll into The Haçienda 'round six, on me own. Pip's bound to be kicking about somewhere, but she's latching on in a way I fuckin' don't want her to. Told her to go on ahead without me.

Make me way into the green room, peel off me sunglasses. Overhead lights are fuckin' blindin'—squint up at 'em, fumbling for the dimmer till I get 'em down to summat reasonable.

Don't clock it straight off, but the whole fucking room's watchin' me.

"Alrigh', sunshine." Richie grins from the far end of the room.

"Fuck yourself," I say, heading straight for him anyway. Toss meself down next to him, legs sprawled.

Rich throws me a flat smile. "Don't you look fresh as owt…"

Give him a little once-over, slow enough to make it sting. "Aye, well, you look like shite, so s'pose that's why I'm the front man."

He sniffs a laugh, but I know that proper fucked him off.

"On it last night, were ya?" Rich presses.

"Oh, he was on it," Pippa chimes from across the room, eyein' me in this way I wish she fuckin' wouldn't. Didn't even clock she were there, so that tells ya plenty about I'm feelin' about Pippa Sparrow at the minute.

"Oooh…" Loxy coos, perched next to her.

Don't like they're mates. Both of 'em do me fuckin' head in on their own, but together—? Christ. Couldn't tell ya if it's the hangover or the fact I'm staring down the barrel of day two without the only girl I reckon I've ever properly loved, but either way—fuck me. They're painful.

"Oi." I nod at Pippa. "Get us a tea with lemon, will you?"

She nods, beamin' now—happy to be needed.

Just want her to fuck off, don't I—?

And don't give me that look—she knew what this was. Broke up with me girlfriend fuckin' *yesterday*. She's a fucking idiot if she thought last night was owt more than a quick shag to get one up on Ysolde.

"Oi, Jo—" Chops nods his chin at me, and I can tell from his face he's fuckin' pissed about somethin'. Takes it the most seriously, our kid. Fucking loves the music.

"You missed sound check," he tells me, all stern-like.

I breathe out, bored. "I sound checked yesterday."

"Yeah, and *now* it's today."

"Crackin' work, Sherlock—" Pinch me eyes at him like he's thick. "Dead astute, that…"

"Joah—" He keeps at it. "Mate, today's a new day with amps that buzz, mics that hum, and a fuckin' kick drum that's gone walkabout!"

Roll me eyes. "Mate, we got one record—we sing the same fuckin' songs every night. Give it a rest." Grimace at him a bit. "Sorry 'bout that kick drum, though. Fuck, you better find it."

Richie snickers next to me as Chops huffs off, muttering to himself.

In walks Heddie with a rack of clothes.

I sigh when I see her—don't even know why. Feel knackered just thinkin' about her. Probably shouldn't. Probably should take her back to me room later, you know? Keep me mind off things…

She plucks a couple of jackets off the rack and strides over, grabs me hand, and pulls me to my feet. Starts fussing about, shiftin' me 'round without saying a word.

Don't say owt back meself, just watch her moving 'round me—watch her ignorin' me on purpose, wondering what the fuck she's playin' at.

Unzips the jacket I'm wearing, puts me in a different one like I'm her very own paper fuckin' doll.

Then she looks up at me for the first time, voice low, says, "Heard you and that girl broke up."

"Which girl?" I ask, playing dumb.

She rolls her eyes. "You know—*that* girl."

Dunno why that pisses me off—Heddie calling her *that girl*. Maybe cos she's not just *that girl*, is she? She's the only girl on the fuckin' planet who's ever mattered.

TIME OF YOUR LIFE

Give her a hard look. "You know her name." I stare her down—dunno why—just fuckin' angry, I s'pose. Maybe I'll lean into it, be who they reckon I am anyway. What is it they call me again—*belligerent?* Aye, go on then.

"Say it," I tell her.

She shifts, uncomfortable. "What?"

"You know her name," I snap. "If you're so fuckin' chuffed me and her're done, least you can do is say it."

Heddie shoves a pair of jeans into me hands.

"You're a prick." She gives me a glare before she turns and runs off.

"Yeah—" I call after her, then glance 'round the room at everyone staring like I've grown a second head. "Why's everyone so fuckin' surprised by that these days?"

"Cos you've gotten prickier," Richie says, calm as you like.

I scowl at him. "Piss off."

He watches me in that way I fucking hate. "You alright?"

Asks it like he actually gives a shit.

"I said *piss off.*"

Rich runs his tongue over his teeth, proper annoyed. He don't like being talked to like that. I know I'm gonna fuckin' pay for it later—dunno how, but I will. I can always tell.

"And you've forgotten, little brother, that you're here cos *I let you be.*"

Hate it when he says shite like that. Mostly cos it's a load of fucking bollocks, but also cos I'm a bit worried it might be true.

Richie nods his chin at me. "You talked to her?"

"None of your fuckin' business," I spit back.

He breathes out through his nose. "So *no.*"

I look at him, proper incredulous now. "Fuck off!" I snap, louder this time.

Everyone says I'm the prick, right? I'm the one with the fuckin' bad rep and the ego the size of a lorry but it ain't just me, you get me? He's got a bit o' proud in him and all, and most the time, Richie don't bite, but if I push him far enough—fuck. And he gets that look in his eye—I know it—pushed that boat out a bit far tonight, didn't I?

Rich chuckles, proper smug—pushes himself up off the couch as he stares me down.

"Tonight's gonna be fun."

———

The Haçienda's rammed tonight, sweat hanging thick in the air, walls vibrating with the noise. Second night, sold-out crowd, and we're fuckin' flying, man. Should've been flying, anyway. Trying not to be too in me fuckin' head, but I am.

I miss her. Don't miss people, do I—? But I miss her. Wish she was here, wish she was backstage waiting for me or at side of the stage watchin' me—and then I fuckin' hate meself for all of it. Hate her for it too. Two nights in a row, somehow me fuckin' show's all about her.

So get this. We're halfway through the set—I've just finished "Freight Train." It's all going pretty good, like well good, considering I'm a bit high and not all the way sober, you know what I mean?

And then I see her.

Her. Ysolde. In the wings. Other side of the stage from me, watchin'.

Not us, alright—? You can fucking be sure of that. She's not watching *the band*, she's watching *me*. And of course she is, like—who the fuck else would she be watching, yeah?

And you'd think I'd be chuffed, wouldn't ya? Seein' her. That she's here, that she came back—wanted her to come, didn't I?

Careful what you wish for, but—cos she's not alone.

She fuckin' brought him.

Our eyes catch—jolts through me, this mad electricity, and I look away fast—fuck.

Dunno what to do. What do I do—? I'm a fuckin' deer in the headlights out here, so I just sing the next song on the setlist.

TIME OF YOUR LIFE   249

Fuckin' tank "Cheap Thrills," don't I? Cos I just keep lookin' on over at her—and you know what? Fuck it, I'll say it—I *am* scared of her.

The way she stares at me—holds my fuckin' gaze—makes me feel like a wee lad again. In the worst fuckin' ways, like she can see straight through me and I'm about two-foot-fuck-all, you get me?

She's staring at me like she thinks I'm shit. Maybe I am—? *So what's she fuckin' here for then?*

Only one answer, innit. To fuck with me.

And it's workin'.

Properly workin'.

I'm lookin' over at her so much, I'm fuckin' up the song— forgettin' the lines, losing me place—and she just keeps on staring, watchin' me set meself on fuckin' fire.

And she's there, battin' her eyes, happy as fuckin' Larry.

It's workin' so much that—get this, yeah?—I stop singin' half-way through the fuckin' song. We're three minutes in, tops, when that little fuckin' siren leans back into Freddie motherfucking Fletcher, who tosses his arms 'round her, bold as brass.

And me—? Had fuckin' enough, you know?

I smack the mic stand over, barrel straight towards her—Chops and Fry exchanging their little *oh shit* looks, Richie's just snorting a laugh cos, of course, he fuckin' is.

"Oi!" I yell at her, pointin' right at her. "Are you out of your fuckin' mind?"

She stares at me, all wide-eyed and innocent, blinkin' like she's got no idea what's happening.

"I beg your pardon?" she says, proper posh, voice like honey.

I jab a finger at Fletcher now, heat rising in me chest. "You're gonna bring *him* here—? Parade him 'round at *my* show?"

Now, I don't reckon the crowd can see what's happenin'— probably just saw me storm off mid-song, shoutin' like a fuckin' nutter. Don't look great, do it? Don't fuckin' care, but.

Ysolde lifts those shoulders of hers, easy fuckin' breezy, like this is all nothin'. "No one's parading... If anything, it's the *opposite* of parading—we're *literally* hiding in the shadows."

"Get out of my fuckin' shadows!" I yell, voice cracking with how mad I sound. She rolls her eyes, and the way she does it... She's baitin' me—she's fuckin' baiting me! That's new, innit? Ain't seen this side of her before. Did I break her or just push her too far—I dunno?

Don't hate it, either way. Don't mind a girl with a bit o' fight in her—this could get real fuckin' fun, know what I mean?

She crinkles her nose. "Well, but they're not *your* shadows."

My jaw goes tight. "They fuckin' are tonight."

"If *anything*..." She tilts her head, casual as you like. "They're *Fallow's*..."

Grit me teeth. "*I am Fallow.*"

She lets out this little laugh—dunno why, but it proper twists the knife.

"You are...*so* conceited." Shakes her head. *Fuck me, I love her head.* "Joah, you're *part* of Fallow—" And get this—she turns to Fletcher, yeah—? Drops her voice a bit but not enough to stop me hearin'. Wants me to hear, she does... "He doesn't even *write* their songs." She pulls a face, like she's fuckin' embarrassed for me. And you know what? Fuck her. How the fuck does she know that? I never fuckin' told her—don't fuckin' tell anyone that, do I?

"Be nice," whispers the greatest footballer alive, way too close to the ear of the girl I'm fuckin' wrecked over.

"No," she says, lockin' eyes with me, all defiant and shit.

I shake my head at her, feel me chest burning, then glance 'round wildly.

"Who the fuck let you in here—?" I look for Mick. "Find out—Mick!—" Scrambles towards me, he does. "Find out and fire them—"

Whip back 'round to her, waving at the exit. "You two can fuck off."

"Nah," my brother pipes from behind me. "They're my guests."

TIME OF YOUR LIFE   251

I freeze. Turn 'round, slow. "What?"

He shrugs, all casual-like. "I invited them."

Shake me head. "No, you fuckin' didn't…"

Rich just smirks, leaning into his mic, the absolute prick. Ignores me completely. "Manchester, are you having *a fuckin' night!*" he shouts to the crowd. They go mental.

Then he looks back at me, smug and calm as ever. "I did."

I take a sharp breath, tryin' not to lose it completely. "You invited *my* ex-girlfriend to *my* show?"

He pulls a face, like he disagrees with the basic fuckin' premise. "I invited *your* ex-girlfriend to *my* show…"

I hear Chops mutter to Fry, "Right, so apparently we're not in the band anymore…"

Like—piss off with that. Read the fuckin' room; it ain't the time.

I glare at Rich, teeth clenched so hard it hurts. "Why?"

He shrugs again, like it's nothin'. "We're mates, me and her…"

And then—I dunno—somethin' snaps.

Don't even think about it, don't choose to do it, I'm just doin' it… Reckon my fist was in his face before the words were even out his mouth proper, and Rich staggers back, grabbing the mic stand to stop himself goin' down.

The crowd goes mental, screaming like it's part of the show. For about a half a second, Richie looks stunned. Then his expression shifts—everyone reckons I'm the fuckin' hothead. Like, yeah, I'm impulsive, but Richie? He fuckin' stews. His anger's well deep, like volcanic.

He shoves me hard in the chest. "You're a fuckin' child, you know that?"

"And you're a fuckin' snake," I shoot back, going for him again, grabbing his shirt this time.

It's all a blur after that—Richie swingin' for me, me landin' a proper good shot at his ribs. People in the back shouting, the crowd screamin' louder. The boys stop playin' entirely about now.

Rich is on me like a dog with a bone, though. We crash to the floor, fists flying, elbows cracking against the stage. Feel a sharp sting on me mouth—taste blood—don't stop, but. Can't, can I?

Neither can Rich, I don't think. Hard to, once you start, you know—? Neither me or him, we ain't never been good at sayin' when.

And then Freddie dives in, draggin' Rich off me. "Oi, boys—! That's enough—"

Richie tries to lunge at me again, but Freddie's got him, proper struggling to hold him back, but cos when Richie's on one, he's fuckin' on one.

"You're a fuckin' headcase," Richie pants.

"And you're a cunt," I spit back—promised Ysolde I'd stop saying that word, didn't I? Ah, well. I wipe me split lip with the back of my hand—blood smears across me knuckles, but I dunno—I don't know if I'm done fightin' him yet.

"Come over here and say that to my face," Rich snaps, staring me down.

I step towards him, fists clenched, and then—Ysolde—she jumps in front of me.

"Jo, stop!" she pleads, eyes wide, all urgent. Hand on me chest, warm and firm, and for a second—because I'm a fucking div—I forget how to breathe.

Forget the fight altogether, don't I?

All I can see is her face—eyes wide, starin' up at me, pleadin'— and somethin' else there, too. Uneasy, maybe? Is she scared of me?

Maybe.

But for different reasons, I reckon.

Looks worried, she does. I hate that. Fuckin' hate it when she's worried.

"Get them off the fuckin' stage!" someone shouts from the wings. I feel security movin' in, their hands all over me. Can hear the boos startin', ripplin' through the crowd, louder and louder, right up until Rich and I are fuckin' manhandled, shoved off into backstage.

And do you know what—? Still, all I can think about is her

TIME OF YOUR LIFE 253

hand on me just before—fuckin' calming me, steadying me, anchoring me to the goddamn planet, I reckon.

Look over at her, clock she's gettin' shoved about by security too.

"Don't you fuckin' touch her!" I yell at the dozy cunt hangin' on to me girl's arm. I'll have his fuckin' job for that.

And then there's a finger in me face. "Don't you fuckin' start—" Mick is well livid.

We're backstage now, yeah—? And I'm dead serious—I ain't never seen Mick redder in his motherfuckin' life.

"What the absolute fuck is wrong with the two of ya?" he growls. "Have you lost your fuckin' minds?"

And me—? I know I proper fucked up here, so I don't say a thing—neither does Rich.

You know who does, but? Ysolde.

"I—" she starts, voice all quiet, shaking a bit, that's there. "It's my fault, I think—"

Mick spins on her, wild-eyed, tone he's got no business using. "You don't fucking say?"

And it's quick as owt, you know—Freddie yanks her behind him, squarin' up now for a fight himself, but me—? I'm already yellin'—

"YOU DO NOT TALK TO HER LIKE THAT!" My voice fuckin' rips outta me—Ysolde jumps, you get me? That's kinda loud.

"Fuckin' fuck off," Rich spits at Mick, proper venom in his voice. Then he turns to Ys, softer now. "It wasn't."

And that's fucking annoying, too, innit?

"No—" I shove him again. "Piss off—you don't talk to her."

Rich snorts, like he thinks I'm playing, but I ain't.

"Fuck you, man—for real, like—proper fuck you," I snap, shakin' me head like mad, pointin' at her. "You don't get to fuck 'round with her, Rich. You don't get to use her against me—"

"Why not?" Rich quips, brows up, darin'. "You use everyone else, don't ya?"

"Cos *she* is the fuckin' love of my life, isn't she!?" I yell and it cuts through the air like a blade.

That whole back area goes quiet as a fuckin' church. Mate—you could hear a pin drop.

Richie's got this look, sorta smilin', like he's well pleased with himself or summat—dunno why.

Ysolde—she's still as owt, eyes wide like it's fuckin' news to her. You know what? S'pose it's news to me too.

Mick rubs his tired eyes, mutters summat under his breath, and walks off, sighin' as he pulls out his phone.

Freddie Fletcher, the jammy bastard, sniffs a laugh, like he thinks all this is a joke.

He claps a hand on me brother's shoulder. "That was fun—" He nods at Rich. "I like you…"

Rich sticks his hand out—they shake, like they're fuckin' best mates.

Then Fletcher turns to Ys, cups a hand 'round the back of her head, pulls her in close—fuckin' hate that—he kisses the top of it.

"I'll catch ya, Ys." Gives her this look, like he knows her… clocked her game or summat. "Well played. I'm in London next week. I'll call ya—"

She nods, smilin' a tiny bit. Looks embarrassed. Bit cute on her but.

Then he turns to me, tilts his head. "See ya, man. Sorry for—" He nods towards Ysolde, grimaces like it's all just some big misunderstanding.

Then he fucks off.

Ysolde and I just stand there for a good few seconds in total fuckin' silence, starin' at each other.

Grab her hand, drag her into my dressing room—yank her inside, door slamming shut behind us as I press her up against it.

Kiss her like I ain't never fucking kissed anyone.

Like, life-or-death shit, you know what I mean? I reckon she could be the death of me.

TIME OF YOUR LIFE

Dunno how long it lasts, do I—? Could be seconds, could be two fuckin' hours. Could be forever, for all I care. I'm just…lost in her—willingly too, recklessly, fuckin' happily lost. Don't matter where if she's there, know what I mean?

It's her that pulls back a little—course it is.

"You're bleeding," she says, voice soft.

I shake me head. "I'm fine."

"No," she says, firmer now. "You're *bleeding*."

"I said *I'm fine*," I say, louder, more annoyed.

Guess me and her fight now, ey?

Stares at me, eyes big. Don't like to be talked to like that—not used to it, I s'pose. She wipes her mouth, then—feels like a knife twisting in me chest—like she's fuckin' wipin' me off her.

She straightens up, all calm now. "Do you want me to go?"

"No," I tell her.

"Are you sure?"

Shove my hands through me hair, start shakin' my head. "That was bad."

She nods once. "Yes."

Blow out a long breath, try not to let on that I'm about to fuckin' shit it. "How bad?"

"Um…" She purses her lips, tilts her head slightly. "Uh—*quite*."

Gesture back to the ghost of fucking Freddie past. "What'd you fuckin' bring him for?"

And then like, the fuckin' balls on this girl, man I swear—she stares over at me like I'm daft. "…To torture you."

"Aye." Glare at her for that, don't I? "Well done."

"Thank you." She nods once, looks too fuckin' pleased with herself for that—catch her fightin' off a smile. Dead pleased with herself.

She grabs my wrist, drags me to the settee, shoves me back onto it. Then she kneels up, tissues in hand, hovers over me as she dabs at my busted lip.

I shake me head, thinkin' back on it all. "I can't fuckin' believe Richie…"

And I see summat flicker across her face—some thought she has but swallows down.

I nod me chin at her. "What…?"

She shakes her head. "Nothing."

"No, what?"

She presses her lips together, trying to decide whether she'll say it. She clears her throat quietly. "You do know *you're* the problem, yes?"

Fuckin' bullshit.

"Fuck off," I tell her.

"You are," she tells me, all matter-of-fact-like.

Give her a manky look. "No."

"Yes."

"No…" I scowl.

"*Absolutely*, you are."

I thump my chest. "*I'm* the talent."

She gives me a look. "Joah, you're *both* talented."

"I'm the front man."

She looks at me, eyebrow up. "So?"

"So there's a reason you're fuckin' here with me and haven't spent the last two months over at his place suckin' his cock—" I say well off-the-cuff, all fuckin' angry that she's on his side and not mine—it comes out me mouth without a thought and I've fuckin' said it before I even know I'm sayin' it, and her face like—fuck me, I'm a dead man. She's proper ragin'—straightaway, she's pushing up from the couch to get away from me, and so I grab her wrist, shakin' me head fast as I can. "Wait, wait, shit! Sorry. I'm sorry. I didn't mean—I shouldn't have—I dunno w—I run my mouth when I'm—"

She bends down close to my face. "I don't know who you think you are or, more importantly, who you think *I* am, that would lead you to believe that I would *ever*, under any circumstance, allow you to speak to me like that, but that is your first *and final* warning."

"Yeah, alright." I nod like a schoolboy. "Fair enough."

TIME OF YOUR LIFE

257

She gives me a steep warning look.

Put my hand on her waist—don't want her to go anyway.

"See, that's why I like you…"

She looks at me, unimpressed. *"Why?"*

"Cos you call me out on my bullshit."

She shrugs like she don't get it. "Richie calls you out on your shit and you don't much like him for it…"

"Yeah but—" I push some hair behind her ears. "I ain't fuckin' Rich, which really softens the blow of all that yellin' you're doing."

"Well." She straightens up, keeps dabbing my bloody mouth. "You're a prick who frequently deserves to be yelled at. Also…" She pauses. "…I don't think we're fucking anymore."

I lift an eyebrow. "Yeah?"

"Yes."

Tilt my head at her. "Just snogging in doorways?"

Gives me a proud, stubborn look. "You caught me by surprise."

I nod a couple of times. "Should I not have kissed ya?"

She stops with the dabbing, holds them bloody tissues in her hands, brows all bent in the middle like she's got summat heavy on the mind.

"Well, I don't know—" She swallows. "Because you called me something out there before in the hallway, where—"

"Oh fuck—" I groan. "Caught that, did ya?"

"Well." She bites down on them lips—ones I wanna be kissin', mind. "You said it loud."

Mouth twists, nod once. "Oh good. Everyone hear that then, or—"

"Yep." She nods.

"Mint." I rub the back of my neck with me hand. Fuck. Bit embarrassing. She looks pleased, but—maybe worth it, then.

Nod my chin at her. "Probably should have a chat, ey?"

Her eyes look big again. Hopeful or nervous—? I dunno.

"Where are you stayin'?" I ask her.

"Where are *you* staying?" she asks back.

"The Midland."

"Me too," she says.

"Oh—" Pull me head back in surprise. How didn't I run into her? "You got a room there?"

She stares at me, eyes unwaverin'.

"No," she says, and I swallow heavy.

My heart starts poundin' in my chest again, don't it—? Fuck, I love her.

She gives me a tiny smile.

We grab my stuff and walk out into the hallway—not hand in hand, but shoulder to shoulder, and fuck it like—take what I can get, know what I mean?

Walk past Richie's open dressing room and Ysolde pauses, pokes her head in.

She stares over at him, all reclined back on the settee, Loxy tendin' to him like he's a fuckin' fallen soldier or summat.

"You okay?" Ys asks.

Loxy looks at her over her shoulder. "He's fine." Tone's sharp.

Rich gives Lox a look, not havin' it.

"I'm glad *you* think so," Ysolde says, eying her—bit bolder this time 'round, ain't she? Not faffin' about bein' polite and proper. "But I was asking Rich."

Rich swallows a smirk. So do I—don't really swallow mine but.

"I'm alright," Rich tells her.

She tilts her head. "Yeah?"

"Yeah." He tilts his chin up. "You?"

Ys glances back over her shoulder at me, then back to Rich—does this little smile—Christ, but I love her, don't I?

"Oi." I nod my chin at him, slingin' an arm 'round Ysolde. She shoves it off her straightaway and I don't miss a beat when I put it straight back there where it fuckin' belongs. She fights off a smile, but know she likes this shit.

Rich watches us—looks, I dunno—invested?

"You off?" he says to me.

TIME OF YOUR LIFE

"Yep." I nod. "Good show tonight."

"Yeah," Rich says.

Then we both chuckle. And Ysolde is lookin' between us back and forth like we're a tennis match—mind fuckin' blown.

"You guys are completely mental," she says, can't believe it.

I roll my eyes at her.

"Laters," I say to him.

Gives me a small wink.

She don't have brothers, so she don't get it. She don't need to get it. We get it.

TWENTY-EIGHT

ysolde

I'M VERY RESTRAINED THE ENTIRE car ride to the hotel. Like, sure, it's only about a three-minute drive, but I'm in the back of the car with *the* hottest boy in the world who accidentally just declared to an entire hallway of people that I'm the love of his life—and I don't snog him once the whole three-minute drive. I sat as near the car door as humanly possibly because if I sit too close to him, I'll smell him and if I smell him, I'll be all over him.

Joah doesn't smell like anything you could buy in a bottle—as though he'd ever wear anything like that anyway. He just smells like him—which is kind of hard to describe. Maybe a little bit leathery, even though he really doesn't wear leather all that often. I suppose, truthfully, the thing he smells most of is—ever so faintly—cigarettes and probably less faintly, alcohol. Always beer, sometimes scotch. And I think something else—it's harder to place though—I don't know—maybe a bit how the ground smells after it rains—? Clean but rough at the edges.

Breathing him in is like taking in a breath near a fire—it makes you warm. The smell of him makes me warm down to my fingers.

TIME OF YOUR LIFE

He stares over at me, mouth pressed together. "Why you sittin' so far away?"

I shrug demurely. "Just am."

He nods his head towards himself. "Don't wanna come over here?"

I shake my head, resolute. "No."

(Yes.)

Joah's eyes pinch. "So am I gettin' you your own room at this hotel?"

I take a couple of breaths, watching him. It makes him nervous. I like making him nervous. "No," I say eventually, and don't tell him I noticed, but he breathes out a little relieved breath—that completely adorable man.

And then—listen, what happens next—it's not our fault.

The car pulls up at the hotel—Joah looks out the window and sighs. "Fuck."

There's a crowd waiting for him. Thick, too. His fans are mental. Mostly women, but some men.

"Ready?" he asks me, but he looks over it already.

I nod and the doorman opens it for us.

Security from the hotel wait for us to emerge. Joah exits first and screaming erupts loud enough that it startles me.

Joah reaches back into the car, takes my hand, and pulls me out—security leads us though the crowd, but that crowd—god—they sort of fold in on us—? Grabbing him, grabbing me—a man grabs me at one point and Joah shoves him off so much more roughly than he should have. You stop becoming a person when you're a celebrity, you see?

You become public property. We're just...*things* right now, we're not people.

We get into the lobby, every single eye in the place is on us but not in a way that feels nice or cool or has any level of cache, more— either they're sorry for us or they're irritated by our presence and the scene we just inadvertently caused.

Jo doesn't let go of my hand until we're in the lift and the doors close.

As soon as they do, he glances down at our hands still in one another's, and—bam!—it must look choreographed, but actually, we're just insanely in sync. He rushes me, bangs me back into the lift wall at the same time that I climb his waist like a tree house.

His mouth drags across mine, down my neck, across my chest—the lift doors open—we don't stop. He just carries me out of there, me on his waist, kissing the absolute shit out of me, stumbling towards the door—one hand still around me, the other fishing in his pocket to find the room key. He bangs me against the door again, then he opens it and we fall through it—nearly hit the ground but he's quite strong and I'm fairly light, so he catches me— kicks that door shut, then he tosses me down onto his bed, takes his own shirt off, then hovers over me, waiting.

I grab him by the neck and pull him down on top of me. His hands start to wander and his kisses grow to more, and right as I think we're probably about to get to the good stuff—he pulls back, shaking his head.

"No, no, no, no—we should talk."

"*Really?*" I stare at him in disbelief.

"Aye."

"*Now?*" I blink.

He gives me a look. "Trouble…"

I press my hands into my cheeks as I sit up.

"Yeah, okay." I tug my little Vivienne Westwood miniskirt back down where it belongs.

And then we just stare at each other. I'm waiting for him to say something, and it probably takes me a full fifteen seconds to realise I think he's waiting for me to say something back.

"Well?"

"Well what?" He shrugs.

I shake my head at him. "You're the one that wanted to talk…"

"Yeah." He shrugs, helpless. "I dunno what to say but—"

TIME OF YOUR LIFE

I give him a look. "I don't know—? Perhaps that you're sorry?"

His head pulls back. "For what?"

"For hooking up with your rancid ex!" I yell, and Jo starts shaking his head again.

I feel mean calling her that. She's really quite pretty, but I *really* don't like her.

"You don't understand—"

"I think I do," I tell him.

"No—" He sighs. "I was just making a point."

"Were you?" I lift up an eyebrow. "Which?"

Joah's face freezes, then it scrunches up.

"Nah, we don't needa talk anymore." Gives me a smile.

I press my lips together, pinch my eyes at him. "Which point might that be, Joah?"

He swallows, then sighs. "I was tryna prove that I ain't..." He takes a breath, then says it quickly, "—under your thumb like."

I blink at him several times.

"Sorry—you kissed your ex-girlfriend to prove that you're not"—I pause, raising my eyebrows to make sure he knows that nothing he's said alleviates any of the responsibility I feel he should be bearing—"*under my thumb*?" I blink a few more times. "You were trying to prove that?"

He nods, just owning it now. "Yeah."

I give him a look. "Because it would be so bad if you were?"

"Yes." He nods firmly.

"Why?" I ask.

"Because I'm me!" he shouts.

"And *I'm* me!" I yell back. "You realise men adore me, yes? The world over—I am beloved by men—close your eyes and point to a man, Joah, and I swear to god, he'll trade places with you—"

Joah looks at me incredibly serious and shakes his head. "I don't wanna be under no thumbs, Ys."

"Okay." I shrug, and then I don't know what to say after that, because what can I say? I didn't actually do anything, I don't think?

It's not like I actually put him under my thumb, it's just how he feels, and I can't control how he feels. I don't think I'm terribly bossy or demanding, do you—? Am I? I don't feel as though I have been.

So then we just sit there—lie there?—for a few agonising seconds in complete and total silence.

"Oi—" He looks over at me. "Did ya fuck him?"

I pause. Uh-oh. I mean, *yes—obviously*. I can't imagine *he's* going to be all too pleased to hear that though. So I pivot.

I lift an eyebrow. "Did *you* fuck *her*?"

Joah and I have a standoff with our eyes and then his hands fly to his face, and he groans.

"Oh, fuckin' hell—I can't believe you fucked my favourite player."

I roll my eyes at him. "I had already fucked your favourite player!"

"Christ—!" he grumbles. "Don't remind me."

"*You asked*—!" I stare at him, wide-eyed. "I didn't just *volunteer* the information—it's not like I was like, *oh, we did it on the floor*—"

"Argh!" Jo yells to make me stop talking. "Don't fuckin'—like, you say it and then I see it in me head, Ys—!" He's a bit frantic, honestly… "I'm bang on at fuckin' visualising things, you get me—? And I don't fuckin' wanna see that."

I nod. "Okay."

He swallows. Eyes pinch. "…How many times did you do it?"

My head rolls back. "You *just* said—"

"How many times!"

"I don't know—" I shrug. "Like, four?"

His face goes still, eyes wide. He may actually even pale a bit. "*Four?*" He blinks. "Four! Fuck on off."

"I was really cross at you—" I shake my head. "And…he's really good at it."

He points a finger at me, like—*that's a warning*. I roll my eyes.

"Why—?" I look at him nervously. "How many times did you sleep with Poppy?"

He gives me a look. "*Pippa*," he says.

I obviously already knew that. Fun to pretend I didn't though, so I shrug. "If you say so."

He rolls his eyes at me, then breathes loudly out his nose, jaw tight now.

"Once."

"Once!" I repeat in disbelief, staring at him with boggly eyes. "*Actually?*"

He runs his tongue over his teeth. "Yeah."

"No!" I breathe in, confused—shake my head a lot.

He gives me a look. "Stop."

"That's mad." I tuck my chin at him. Genuinely, I'm shocked—

"Oh my god"—I let out a little laugh. "You must like me *so* much."

He nods, serious again, eyes locked on me. "I do, aye."

He rolls back, staring up at the ceiling.

"And I dunno what the fuck to do about it."

I'm still watching him, though. I frown. "Why do you need to do anything about it?"

"Because I fuckin' hate this, Ys—" He shoves his hands through his hair, then glances over at me. "I don't like how I feel when I love ya."

"Oh—" My head pulls back. I'm blinking a lot—am I blinking a lot? "Okay." I swallow—my mouth feels really dry. I think I'm nervous. "Well—*How*...do you feel when you love me?"

"I dunno—" He shakes his head. "Just...don't like that you're the thing that matters most to me."

I breathe out a breath that sounds like a laugh. I wonder if it makes me sound more okay than I feel? I feel like he just ploughed into me with a bin lorry. "Right."

He knows he's upset me, I can tell. He's looking for my eyes straight away and he sort of finds them. They're dimmed, though. How could they not be?

"But you do—" he tells me, eyes all locked on mine. "You *are* that thing. But—" He shoves his hands through his hair, looks stressed about everything. "I don't want you to be that thing." He covers his face with a pillow. "Feel like a right fuckin' soft-arse muppet—"

I roll in towards him and peel his hands off his face. "No one thinks you're soft—"

He raises a brow. "Just a muppet?"

"Sometimes—" I tell him with a look.

"I was in me head, Ys." He shakes his head at himself—looks embarrassed or something—and it's then that I think I spot it—for the very first time, I think I see it in him—maybe he doesn't actually believe that he's all that and a bag of chips.

"Everyone kept sayin' you had me on a fuckin' leash, that I was your lapdog and all that shite. I don't wanna be under no one's thumb, you get me? I'm a fuckin' rock star, Ys—"

"Right." I nod once and give him a cautious look. "You know none of it's real though…"

He scratches his neck. "What's not?"

"Fame," I say, though I'm quite sure it's quite obvious. "Everything we do… None of it's real—"

His chin tucks. I've offended him—or he's angry, or…I can't quite tell.

"My music's real," he says.

"Joah!" I roll into his body, groaning into the place between his shoulder and his neck that I love so much. "You're so insufferable, sometimes! That's such a twatty thing to say!"

"No, it is—" He pushes me back a little, making sure I'm looking at him. "It fuckin' is."

I roll my eyes, which doesn't remotely stop him.

"People might forget my name, might mix me up with me brother for the next thirty fuckin' years, but—" He leans in, his voice incredibly, positively sure. "Fuckin' hear me when I say, they'll be playin' my songs till I'm dead, Ys." Proud glint in his eye. "I know they will."

And there was something in the way he said all that, something

TIME OF YOUR LIFE

in the way he *needed* me to be sure of what he was saying, which that told me *actually*, he himself didn't even know it to be all the way true—just that he very much needs it to be. To be remembered, to be significant matters to Joah in a way that goes beyond the way we all want to be more than nothing—his desire to be known and properly adored and esteemed—I think he wants it in this genuinely fundamental way. How we all need air and water and food, I think he needs to matter.

I nod a couple of times, try to mentally prepare myself as best I can to ask a question I know I probably shouldn't, because the answer—I know it's probably going to crush me.

"Is there a world where you could be okay if no one remembered your songs or your name except for me?"

"No," he says without even a thought. And I was right. Crushed.

He gives me a sorry look, touches my face ever. "Know I should say yes, Trouble, but no—Sorry." There's an urgent desperation in the eyes of the man I love who looks so very much right now like just a boy. "They need to remember me."

I don't know why, but something about that feels like such a death sentence. I'm not sure for who. Him? Me? Us? Someone's not making it out of this thing alive, I fear.

"They will," I tell him with a smile, but I don't think the smile's all that convincing.

He tilts his head, looking frustrated. "Fuck, I made you sad again."

"No—" I keep trying to look more okay than the soggy, stepped-on pudding I feel like right now. "It's just—" I wave a finger between us. "Fire and water." I give him another smile that's trying (but failing) to be brave. "Still doesn't bode well for us, really."

He holds my cheek in his hand. "We work."

"Do we?" I'm not so sure.

"Ys." He props himself up a bit. "I love you more than owt I've ever fuckin' loved—"

"Yeah—" I roll my eyes. "And you just told me you don't want to."

"Still fuckin' do, don't I!"

"How do you think that makes me feel, Jo?" I shake my head.

"I mean, *fuck*—!" He lets out a sharp laugh. "Should make you feel fuckin' incredible, Ys. Cos I can't not love you, can I?" He gives me a look. "Even when I fuckin' hate ya… Even—" Lifts his eyebrows, nearly completely right off his forehead. "*Even* when you've just fucked my favourite midfielder—"

I pause. I think I would like the upper hand again. I don't know when quite he took it from me, but I should like it back.

"Four times," I remind him, and Jo wrestles this annoyed smile off his face, drags his tongue over his teeth.

"Fuck you."

I laugh and he grabs me by my waist, pulling me in towards him.

"Come here."

TWENTY-NINE

joah

SATURDAY AFTERNOON, ME AND YSOLDE—just bein' shit-kickers today, we are. Best fuckin' way to spend time, that. I know—proper gip—but fuckin' nowt with her, like? Don't get better than that.

We've been knockin' about the Heath, ended up on one of them posh streets that circles back in on itself, park in the middle. She's been bangin' on all day 'bout how her favourite house in the world's here, so I tell her to show me.

"There it is." She points to it from about fifty metres away, like she don't wanna get too close. "That's my dream house."

Her face goes this way I ain't never seen before. Daydreamy like—all fuckin' reverent.

Now to be fair to her like—it's a nice fuckin' house. And I dunno, there's summat about it, like it's been sat there for a hundred years, waiting for some fucking perfect little family to move on in. All red brick and white window frames, proper posh like—but not that dead cold, toff kinda posh. Garden wall, but it ain't too high—inviting enough. They ain't tryin' to keep you out, know what I mean?

"Wait—" Pinch my eyes, trying to see. "Is that—? There's a sign up—"

She follows my gaze.

"It's open for inspection," I tell her, beamin'.

"Oh—" She shakes her head. "No, we don't have t—"

"Why not?" Give her a shrug. "Let's go in."

I pull her that way; she's shakin' her head right up till we're basically outside it.

"Come on—" I nod at the door.

"Why?" She shrugs. "It's not like I'm not going to buy it."

And if I were better at pickin' up on things (which I'm fuckin' learnin' I'm *really* not), maybe I'd clock that there's summat here— somethin' way above my fuckin' pay grade.

"Why not?" I shrug back. "You could."

She gives me this look, like I'm daft. "I couldn't."

Summat there on the edges of her eyes but—fuck, I dunno— bit like hopefulness, innit?

And seein' that look on her face—fuckin' better than coke. Addictive.

I'd take a bump of that every day of me life, if she'd let me.

So I decide to feed it. Want that hope to stay right there on that face of hers, don't I?

"You literally could," I tell her.

She shakes her head again, eyes gone all wide now—but there's somethin' different in 'em this time. Seen it on her before like—bit like she's waitin' for somethin' bad to happen.

"I can't live in a house, Jo."

"Why?" I say, not getting it, right up till the second I fuckin' do. Proper bellend, I am. "Oh," I say quietly, and she takes this big breath that's more like a sigh than owt else.

Hope's gone from the face—and fuck, I miss it already. Want it back.

"Well—" Give her a shrug. "What if I'm there?"

Her little head pulls back, don't it?

"*You'd* want to live *here*? In *this* house—?" She looks 'round, confused. "On this quiet, posh street?"

TIME OF YOUR LIFE

271

"Maybe?" Peer 'round the street again. And yeah, like—it don't fuckin' scream 'Harrigan,' does it...? But she do. "If you're there."

She smirks. "Liar," she says, but that hope's back—right there on her face. And I want it to stay forever, don't I? You know what, like—? I fuckin' am lyin', but. Sounds like a fuckin' nightmare. But Christ, she looks happy at the thought. And fuck me, that's scary as owt. "We both travel too much..." she tells me technically, but I reckon she's really just tellin' herself.

"Come on—" I nod towards it. "Let's just have a look."

Grab her hand, lead her up the stairs, an' it's funny—get this feelin', dunno, like—In some other world, maybe. One where I'm not me, not famous, where my fuckin' priorities are just...normal. Like normal people priorities, yeah? And fuckin'—whatever else, then... Yeah—I can kinda feel it, I s'pose.

The front door's black—but like, rich black, somehow. Don't like when people say black's black. It ain't. There are different types and this fuckin' black door's posh black, innit? Got a bloody lion's head knocker right in the middle, all brass, not overly polished—wish I didn't like it, but fuck, I kinda love it.

Walk inside, and she's peering 'round eyes wide—summat about her face that makes me chuckle, looks like she's snuck in here on her own devices, like she shouldn't be in here.

I watch her takin' it all in, get lost in that weird, dreamy hope in her eyes.

"Hi there—" The estate agent rounds the corner. "Can I help y—"

Stops dead in her tracks when she clocks we're us. Fit enough, she is. Blond, neat hair, good face—probably would've had a crack a couple months ago, no doubt.

She blinks twice, swallows once. "Are you—?"

"Uh—" I chuckle. "Nah—" Shake my head, but give her a little wink to say actually, yeah. "Just look like 'em."

She smiles, charmed, because I'm me.

"Phoebe Woodhouse—" She extends her hand. "And you are...?"

"I am"—thinkin' on me feet is what I'm fuckin' doin'—"Mr....
Jones." I give her a quick smile.

Ysolde's balkin' at me, well confused as Phoebe Woodhouse
turns to her, offering Ys her hand. "And you are—?"

Ysolde stalls, so I toss me arm 'round her. "*Mrs....*Jones."

"Pleasure." She smiles at us both. "Are you in the market for a
home?"

I nod. "*The Joneses* are, yeah."

"Well,*Joneses*, you've stumbled onto a real gem here. Built in the
late nineteenth century by Horace Field, I believe this house specifically was built in 1895 but has obviously been very well tended
to…"

Ysolde looks 'round, summat a bit like wonder—proper
kidlike—dancin' about in her eyes. "I didn't realise it was so old."

"Timeless though." Phoebe smiles. "Don't you think?"

Ysolde nods.

"Semi-detached, five bedrooms, three bathrooms, original
hardwood floorings, all new appliances and obviously"—she waves
her hand 'round the fuckin' sun-soaked entryway we're all standin'
in—"flooded in unbelievable natural light."

Ys flashes her a smile, walks cautiously deeper into the house.

"So, Mr. Jones—" Phoebe says, smirking. "What is it you do?"

"Uh—" Think about it for a second. "—*finance.*" Then I point
at Ysolde. "She's…a…yoga instructor."

She glances over her shoulder, confused.

I shrug. "Explains the body," I tell her, then turn back to Phoebe,
keepin' it goin'. "Don't pay much, but fuck me—would you look at
that arse?"

Ysolde's head snaps 'round again, eyes wide. I snort, proper
amused—Phoebe cracks up, too.

"Do you have any kids?" she asks us.

"No," Ysolde calls back as we walk through to the kitchen.

"Yeah," I tell her. "Boys. Two of 'em. Just wee sprogs, like—
month old."

TIME OF YOUR LIFE   273

"Wow." Phoebe nods, playing along. "I mean—" She looks at Ysolde. "You look amazing."

"Uh—" Ys glances down at herself. "Thank you. I bounced back very...*quickly*...apparently?"

Phoebe smiles, walking ahead.

Ys grabs me hand, looks up at us. "You want boys, do ya?"

"Aye." Nod, like she's a right div. "Course I do. I'm scared of girls."

She rolls her eyes. "No, you aren't."

"Well—" Give her a look. "Can't be fuckin' two of ya's, can there? I'd be proper fucked then, wouldn't I?"

She smirks, shakes her head as we step into the next room.

Some fuck-off fancy room, baby grand smack bang in the centre.

"Alrigh'—" I nod at the piano, catching Phoebe's eye. "Can I—?"

Phoebe nods, gesturing for me to sit.

I play piano, did you know? Dunno if Ysolde does, mind. Mustn't, cos her mouth falls open soon as I sit down an' start playin' "Imagine."

Lennon's a fuckin' legend, innit?

Look at how my girl's lookin' at me right now—that man's gettin' me laid from across the fuckin' beyond.

Ys stares at me, eyes all—fuck, I dunno—she loves me like, that's all. Best feelin' in the world, that. Havin' the person you love, love you back. Think you're the fuckin' sun.

Don't sing, though, do I? Ain't no fuckin' soft lad.

Stop abrupt after the first chorus, give Ys a smile. She walks over, puts a little hand to me face, eyes all soft, proper serious but.

"You are the talent," she says and fuck, that's me well done, know what I mean?

Like, that's it. Best compliment of me life. Fuck all the others. Don't need 'em.

Weird, havin' a total stranger clock a moment like that between me an' Ys. But then—that's bein' fuckin' famous, innit?

Phoebe shows us the bedrooms—one's a nursery.

Ys runs her hand along the edge of the cot, eyes gone dreamy again but sorta sad. Sorta lost.

"This is a great neighbourhood for a young family," Phoebe says gently, watching us from the doorway.

I look over at her. Forgot she was there. "Yeah?"

"It really is—" She nods. "It's safe. The schools are great. The Heath's right there…"

"He's just pretending—" Ys shakes her head, like—fuck knows, like she's worried someone might actually believe it. "We don't really have kids."

"I know." Estate agent gives her another proper sweet smile. She's a good bird, Phoebe. Don't mind her.

"I know who you are." Phoebe whispers it to Ys, gives her a little wink.

Ys' cheeks go a bit pink. "Oh."

Then she brushes past us, back into the hall, down the stairs—like the dream's gone bust.

"Sorry—" I toss Phoebe a shrug. "Spooks easy, her."

Ys is waitin' for us at the bottom of the stairs, hands in her pockets, eyes big and wide. And as I walk toward her—Fuck, you know what? I see it.

That other world.

Where I'm not me, but she's still her, cos she's fuckin' perfect.

Where she's barefoot in the kitchen, and there's toy cars fuckin' everywhere, crayon drawings on the wall, kettle always on, fire always lit.

And it's enough for me.

Don't need the whole fuckin' world to know my name. Don't need to be remembered by no one but her and them two boys.

But I do.

And I know that makes me a fuckin' piece of shit.

Do need it, but.

When we reach the bottom, Phoebe tilts her head at Ys. "You

know, people buy houses for the lives they hope to create all the time…"

"Oh, I—" Ysolde shakes her head. "I can't…I can't live in—I have to live in a hotel."

The estate agent looks confused.

"Something ha—" Ys stops herself. "I just have to live in a hotel."

"Okay," Phoebe says, not pushing. "If you ever change your mind—" She hands me her card, then gives Ys and me a proper good smile. "It was lovely to meet you, Joneses."

We walk back out front, stand outside the gate—her on the outside, lookin' in. Makes my heart fuckin' pang for her. Throws me sometimes, like—how much I'm still gettin' to know her. How much about Ysolde I don't understand right till I do.

An' this is one of them times.

I mean, it's not nothin'—probably set you back two mil, easy. But that house—it ain't drippin' in money, is it?

Not all fuckin' gold an' marble, know what I mean?

Her dream home's a home.

Proper lived in.

And her face right now, starin' at it—it's hers, you get me?

And summat about that fuckin' tells me somethin' 'bout her that scares me to me bones.

Cos that's *her* house. I fuckin' know it is.

Dunno that it's mine, but—?

That house speaks to summat in her. Somethin' she don't even know she wants.

And I dunno. Don't reckon I'll ever be able to give her this, know what I mean?

And I wanna give her everythin'.

"Oi." Scratch me cheek as I take her hand, cross the street.

Nod back toward the house. "That what you want, Trouble?"

"No." She shakes her head quick.

Watch her a couple seconds. "You said it's your dream house."

"Yes…" She nods. "*Dream.*"

"You could have that house, but—" Nod back at it.

She gives me a tight little smile. "But I don't have that life."

I lift me brows. "Aye. Could, though."

"How?" She shakes her head, shruggin'. "With you—?"

Dunno why her sayin' that feels like someone's cracked me over the head with a fuckin' saucepan.

"Well, I don't—" Fuckin' flounderin', I am.

She looks past me, over me shoulder—lookin' for a distraction. "Oh! Ducklings."

JOAH HARRIGAN: THE ROLLING STONE INTERVIEW

HIS MOST UNHINGED, UNFILTERED, AND IMPATIENT INTERVIEW YET

By Shane Westman

Before diving into this interview, it's worth addressing what transpired after our conversation. At Fallow's Manchester show, midway through their set at The Haçienda, Joah Harrigan and his elder brother, lead guitarist Richie Harrigan, shocked fans when a physical fight broke out between the two onstage. The incident made headlines worldwide, prompting speculation about the band's unity. When reached for comment, Joah declined to address the situation, as did Richie. Mick Sloane, their longtime manager, waved it off: "Shit happens. They're brothers. They know each other's buttons too well. Both love to push 'em."

But even before the Manchester incident, the tension surrounding Joah was palpable. Sitting down with him at Abbey Road Studios just days earlier, his restless energy and simmering frustration were impossible to ignore.

———

Midafternoon in a plush London hotel suite, and the silence is palpable. The kind of place that seems designed to swallow sound, today it's charged, broken only by the occasional drag of Joah Harrigan's cigarette and the low hum of my tape recorder.

Dressed in baggy 504s, a (I'll be nice) "lived-in" white T-shirt, and an oversized denim jacket, Fallow's enigmatic front man doesn't so much sit on the velvet sofa as occupy it, legs splayed, shoulders tense. At 23, Joah exudes the effortless charisma of a man who's used to commanding attention. Across from him, I'm armed with a notepad and the unenviable task of peeling back the layers of one of the most compelling, unpredictable rock stars of his generation.

But even before the interview began, it was clear something was off. Harrigan's usual swagger seemed fractured, his jaw tight and his eyes darting towards Ysolde Featherstonhaugh, 20—his supermodel girlfriend whose presence has become as much a part of his mythology as his music. She'd followed him in, an unshakable figure herself in the room, despite the tension radiating off him.

At one point, Sloane pulled him aside.

"Anything here, all of it, they'll use," he warned, his voice low but firm. "Eyes everywhere. The interview hasn't started, but it has. Know what I mean?"

Joah gave a curt "yeah." But it was clear his mind was elsewhere. As Ysolde exchanged a look with Richie, the unspoken weight in the room was almost suffocating.

"Yeah, man, look," he says once we begin, running a hand through his hair. "Fuck, it's a lot, innit? People just don't get it. But it's a lot."

"A lot to handle, sure," I reply, leaning in. "But isn't that part of the deal? Fans worshipping the ground you walk on. The screaming crowds, the sold-out shows—it's everything a rock star dreams of, yeah? Or...is it starting to feel like too much?"

He exhales sharply, the smoke curling around him like a restless spectre. He says nothing. I've struck a nerve.

"No, fuck that, that's not part of the deal. The deal's music, man. That's the only thing I signed up for."

"So you're pulling back from fans, then?" I ask.

Harrigan looks impatient, I can tell I've started to grate him.

"I ain't pulled back shit, man. I mean..." He chuckles, the sound dark and self-deprecating. "I used to shag more fans, I guess that's different now."

The comment lands awkwardly, a sharp contrast to the growing

TIME OF YOUR LIFE

tension in the room. He shifts uncomfortably, as if realising he's said too much.

"You bring up shagging fans." I nod along. "There's always been plenty of talk about how relatable—how accessible even, you used to be. Are you saying that's changed?"

And there's that nerve again—he scowls at me. "Course it's fuckin' changed."

I ask him whether we should talk about why, and it's a quick, firm no from him. I'll circle back to that rumoured why he walked in hand in hand with later.

"Do you miss it?" I ask.

"Do I miss shagging fans?" The front man balks.

"Are you worried you'll lose them if you keep seeming inaccessible to them?"

He goes quiet. Have I stumped the great-and-mighty Joah Harrigan? Days of wonder.

I press on. "Fans fuel the machine, don't they? They buy the records, they sell out the shows, keep you—keep Fallow—in the spotlight..."

Harrigan's nodding along.

"Don't you think they feel like they've earned a piece of you?" I press, tilting my head. "Isn't that what being a rock star is about— giving them a bit of the fantasy?"

Something snaps behind his eyes. "Fuck the fantasy, man! Fuck the fans—"

The words are barely out of his mouth before the weight of them hits. His manager clocks it instantly, his eyes wide with panic, and he shifts towards us as though to step in.

"Fuck the fans?" I echo, leaning forwards, incredulous.

"Nah—" Joah shakes his head fast, his jaw tight. "I mean—not all the fans."

"Just some of them?" I clarify.

Harrigan drags a hand over his face, frustration and something close to regret flickering across his expression. "Look, I'm not slaggin' 'em off, yeah? It's not like that. But some of 'em...some of 'em don't know where the line is. They forget we're not theirs to keep."

"The entitlement, then?" I ask, careful not to let the moment go. "That's what gets to you?"

"The entitlement, the fuckin' delusion of it," he snaps again. "Like I'm not secretly telling you I love you when I sing 'Drift Away,' know what I mean? Or like my girlfriend's not sending you messages through the telly when she's walking a fuckin' Gucci runway."

His words hang in the air, heavy and bitter, and it's clear he knows he's gone too far. The tension radiating off him is almost palpable now, and when I push forwards again, it's as though he's daring me to break him.

"So it's the fantasies, then?" I venture. "The way people project their own stories onto you, onto her—turning your lives into something they can own?"

Joah's laugh is sharp, humourless. "I'm me own man, aren't I? I don't give a fuck what anyone thinks of me. I'm the singer of the best fuckin' band in the world, end of story, know what I mean? Like, what else is there?"

"Right." I give him the most encouraging smile I can muster. "The best band in the world—you're famous for your confidence... but, Joah, you say you don't care what anyone thinks, yet here we are. The frustration, the edge—it's coming from somewhere. So what's really eating at you? Is it them not getting it? Or is it something else entirely?"

The shift is almost imperceptible, but it's there. A twitch of the jaw, a flicker of something raw and unguarded. "Next question," he mutters, his tone a warning.

I press forwards, knowing I'm on dangerous ground. "Your girlfriend—Ysolde Featherstonhaugh. Her name keeps cropping up in all the headlines lately. Do you feel like your relationship is

TIME OF YOUR LIFE

becoming just another part of the spectacle? Or is it different—something you can keep just for yourselves?"

His jaw tightens farther. "Next fuckin' question."

His words are ice, but I don't stop.

"Touchy subject, huh? Strange, because from the outside, it looks as though you two thrive on being seen. All the photos, the red carpets—it's like you're inviting the spectacle in. Or..." I move in towards him slightly, voice low. "Is it just that you can't control the narrative anymore? Does that scare you? Being out of control?"

The explosion is immediate.

"You know what? Fuck you, mate. Fuck this—I don't need this fuckin' interview. This is bullshit." Joah leaps to his feet, his voice shaking with fury. Mick, his manager, rushes over, hands up in a placating gesture. "Joah—calm down."

"No—fuck this. I'm done." Joah's eyes flash as he glares at Mick, then turns to me, pointing at the recorder like it's personally offended him. "You wanna write something? Write this: I don't owe you, or anyone else, a fuckin' thing. Not my music, not my life, not her. None of it."

The door slams, the sound ricocheting through the too-quiet suite. Smoke from Joah's last cigarette still hangs in the air, sharp and acrid, like the aftertaste of his words. And just like that, the front man of the world's biggest band walks away, leaving behind a trail of smoke, shattered composure, and the kind of chaos that no headline will ever fully capture.

THIRTY

joah

STOMACH'S BEEN ON THE FUCKIN' floor since I read that article.

Fuckin' brutal, no?

Everyone's freakin' out—don't, me. Not most times.

Today, but? Fuck.

Felt bad, you know? Like—I know I run me mouth. Always have. Known for it. Know I do it. Knew I did it then. Fucked up thinkin' Mick'd clean it up, didn't I? Some shit I say, it's just water off a duck's back, like.

Might be a fuckin' duck, but this ain't water, is it? Not this time.

It's fuckin' crude oil—everywhere on me. Stuck to me.

And all the Fairy Liquid in the world ain't shiftin' it.

"Was your head fuckin' cut, Jo?" Rich yells at me. "What were you mouthin' off about the fans, anyway—?"

Mick nods in my direction, deadpan. "Mouths off about everythin'."

"*But not the fans!*" Richie shouts, proper wound up now. "*Never* the fuckin' fans!"

I sigh, stressed as fuckin' owt. "I had a fuckin' weird day, man."

TIME OF YOUR LIFE

"A weird day—?" My brother balks at me like I've lost me fuckin' mind. "You've fucked our band for a *weird fuckin' day?*"

I shake me head, tryna find my way outta this. "Ysolde just—"

Mick lets out this groan I hate, one of those *here we fucking go* noises, and on any other day, I'd call him out on it. Don't reckon I got a leg to stand on right now, but.

"What?" Mick snaps, sharp as owt. "What the fuck did Ysolde do now?"

Richie smacks Mick in the gut. "Fuckin' enough with the Ysolde shit." He turns to me. "She what?"

"I—" My voice trails off. "Can't…say."

Mick stares at me, pure disbelief on his face. "What?"

"Just—" Shake me head, frustrated. "Somethin' happened. Me, I had just found out—fucked me up, that's all."

"Well, what happened—?" Rich crosses his arms, starin' me down like he's waitin' to be impressed.

"Summat, alright." Shoot him a proper fuck-off look. "It was bad. I was in me head, just—"

But Mick—course he ain't lettin' it slide. "What the fuck had you in your head that fuckin' bad?"

And listen, right—don't give me that look—ain't my story to tell, I fuckin' know that. But they're both fuckin' yellin' at me—Mick stood there, hands on his hips like he's about to tell me off in front of the class. Don't like bein' yelled at, do I? Don't like bein' blamed for shit that weren't my fuckin' fault. And that interview—? Not my fuckin' fault.

I'd just found out the worst fuckin' shit about my girl, yeah? And I was well fucked off about it.

They wouldn't let me bail. Tried, you know? Tried to palm it off—Mick said no fuckin' way—*he* said no.

So I went. And it was a fuckin' shit show.

But that weren't my fault, was it?

And if they knew what I know—if they knew what I'd just found out—

They'd fuckin' get it.

They'd know it weren't my fault.

Right?

Ys gets to mine a few hours later. Lets herself in—got her a key cut. Not a big deal to you, maybe. Is to me. No one's got a key but me and the cleaner. Don't even fuckin' know where me own keys are half the time. She beelines straight over, drops onto me like it's instinct. "I'm so sorry. I've seen the papers."

"I fucked it—" Shake me head at her, proper gutted. Lads've been gone for a bit now, and to be honest—I've spiralled a bit since.

Just me, in me own thoughts, on me own—realisin' how fuckin' bad it all is.

How fuckin' stupid and ungrateful I sound.

Fuck the fans—?

What's the matter with me?

"Like, I'm in such deep shit, Ys—" Shake me head again, proper defeated. "It's a fuckin' disaster."

"Actually, though?" she asks, all gentle-like, tryna coax me outta the pit I've dug meself into.

I nod. "Sound like a fuckin' ungrateful piece of shit." Drop me head into me hands. "Like I hate me fans—"

"*How*—? You *love* your fans." She shakes her head, all confused. "How did that even—"

"Because—!" Throw me hand her way, frustrated as fuck. "I was so in me fuckin' head about ya—about what happened, you know? And that fuckin' psycho and what he did to ya. I was fucked off at fans that day. And that fuckin' reporter—kept hammerin' on. Fans, the fans, the fuckin' fans. And I snapped."

"Oh, god." She slumps. "Well, what can we do—?"

"Nowt." Tryna keep me voice steady, but she'll hear it anyway, won't she?

"Mick already tried to squash it—didn't work. It's out."

TIME OF YOUR LIFE

She puts her hands to me face, gives me that look—soft, too much in it. Hate that fuckin' look. No, I don't. But I reckon she might love me too much, you know?

Dunno I deserve it right now.

"I'm sorry," she says, quiet.

I sigh, shakin' me head. "I'm fucked. Unless—" Mick'd suggested somethin' before, but I told him to fuck off with it. Shake me head again—more at meself. "Nah—"

"No—" She sits up a bit, brows up, hopeful for summat. "What?"

Keep shakin' me head, brushin' it off. "Nah, never mind—"

She pokes me in the ribs, persistent as ever. "Tell me."

"I dunno—" Shrug weak, like I already know it's a shite idea.

"Maybe if you told everyone what happened—?"

She blinks, confused. "Why?"

"It would explain why, just—"

"Could you not just say you had a bad experience with a fan the day before or something—"

"Nah." Shake me head. "Mick says we need specifics. Too vague otherwise—"

"Oh." She nods, like she gets it. Then stops. Face shifts. "Hold on. Does Mick know what happened to me?"

"Well—" Grimace. Wince a bit. "Like—"

She balks, proper horrified. "Did you tell him?"

I sigh, shoulders slump. "I was tryna explain to him and Rich how it got so fucked-up—"

Her face falls, completely. She rolls off me lap, hands straight to her face. "Oh my god, Jo—*Rich* knows—?"

"I'm—" Fuck. Hate it when she's upset. Proper hate it. Don't want her worryin' about this. "—It ain't a big deal, Ys."

She pulls back, blinks a bunch—like I've just fuckin' smacked her.

"Like—" Fuck. Shake me head, frustrated with meself. "That's not what I mean… What happened, it—"

She's watchin' me now, sharp-eyed, dead fuckin' still. Like she's waitin' for me to dig meself deeper.

"Ysolde, what happened to you is the biggest fuckin' deal in the world to me. Fuckin' obviously—that's why I'm in this fuckin' mess—"

She rolls her eyes at that. Losin' her, I can tell.

"But them knowin'—" Keep goin', tryna get it right. "That don't matter. Who gives a shit, like?"

Her, I reckon. She might.

She's sat there—on her hands—all quiet. Bit weird. Looks like a scared kid, almost. Makes me stomach twist.

"Is it really that bad?" she asks, voice small.

I nod to the article on the table—*The Daily Sun*. Big red letters screamin' **THE FALL OF FALLOW**?

She stares at it—that fuckin' article—an' I can see the cogs turnin', them little wheels movin' behind her eyes.

She bites her lips together.

"I'll do it," she says quietly. "I'll tell them what happened."

"No—" Shake me head fast. "Really?"

She nods.

Give her a look. Careful.

"You sure?"

"Mm-hmm." She swallows.

"Are you really, actually, properly sure?" Need her to mean it.

She looks at me, straight on. "Will it help you?"

Press me lips together. Few seconds. Tryna find the proper words.

"Think it might save me whole fuckin' career."

"Then yes—" She gives me this look—told you before, didn't I? She loves me too much. "Of course, yeah."

Hook me arm 'round her neck, yank her in. Bury me face in her hair.

"My fuckin' hero."

IN HER OWN WORDS: YSOLDE ON FEAR, FAME, AND FINDING HERSELF

By Alexandra Kerridge, Marie Claire UK

When Ysolde Featherstonhaugh opened her front door on an otherwise unremarkable autumn evening last year, she could not have imagined the nightmare awaiting her inside. The space she had carefully curated into a sanctuary—her Primrose Hill home with its pale wood floors, stacks of well-loved books, and delicate, sun-dappled corners—had been violently intruded upon.

Mark Draper, an obsessive fan whose fixation had escalated from unsettling letters to something far more sinister, was waiting for her. The dining table was set with a candlelit meal he'd prepared using her own groceries. Her scarf was clutched in his hands. Her world, once luminous, had been dimmed in an instant.

In recounting the incident to *Marie Claire*, Featherstonhaugh, 20, speaks with a quiet strength well beyond her years, her polished demeanour only barely masking the gravity of her ordeal. "He thought we were destined to be with one another," she says, her voice measured but resolute. "He believed I'd been sending him messages in my interviews or in the way I looked at the camera—apparently we'd encountered one another before, but truthfully, I didn't even know he existed until that night."

Draper's arrest was made without fuss and flew under the radar—Featherstonhaugh's own request, preferring to focus on her safety and recovery. It's only now, months later, that she's finally ready to speak about what happened.

"Talking about it felt impossible at first," she admits. "I didn't want to be defined by what he did, by the fear he caused. But I've realised that sharing my story might help others feel less alone."

Featherstonhaugh's vulnerability and grace are what make her so magnetic, a quality her fans have cherished since the earliest days of her career. But being vulnerable in the public eye has also exposed her to the worst of human behaviour—a reality that's been complicated further by the fallout from Featherstonhaugh's rock star boyfriend, Joah Harrigan, 23, and his now-infamous *Rolling Stone* interview. His comment, "Fuck the fans," sparked immediate outrage, threatening to sully the reputation of the biggest band in Britpop history.

For Featherstonhaugh, who has always prided herself on her connection with their audience, the backlash towards Harrigan was particularly painful to watch.

"You have to understand, Joah is extremely impulsive—on top of being deeply protective of me. He didn't mean it. It wasn't about the fans—certainly not his fans." She shakes her head, eager to clarify. "That doesn't excuse it, of course. But fame isn't always as simple as people think. It can be overwhelming, suffocating, even. He found out something really terrible right before that interview and he hadn't had time to process it at all. Unfortunately then, he began to process it sort of in front of the entire world. And quite badly, at that."

Still, Featherstonhaugh is determined to steer the narrative back to what truly matters: gratitude. "The fans have been nothing but incredible to me—to him—!" she says, her sincerity unmistakable. "They've supported me through so much—I'll never ever take that for granted."

Her resilience is evident not only in her words but also in her actions. Within days of Draper's arrest, Featherstonhaugh hired full-time security and had moved to a new location. She has since immersed herself in work, channelling her emotions into creative projects that reflect her growth.

"I've had to learn how to be again," she says. "I refuse to let fear dictate how I live my life. Yes, I've had to make adjustments, but I'm still here. I'm okay. I'm still standing."

It's that unwavering determination that has endeared Featherstonhaugh to millions. Whether she's gracing magazine covers, attending industry events, or simply engaging with fans online, she carries herself with a warmth and authenticity that makes her seem both untouchable and deeply relatable.

"I've always believed that vulnerability is strength," she tells me as our conversation draws to a close. "Sharing this part of my life hasn't been easy, but if it helps even one person, then it's worth it."

As I watch Featherstonhaugh gather her things and rise from her chair, I'm struck by the quiet dignity she exudes. She's a woman who has faced her darkest moments and emerged stronger, not despite them but because of them.

In a world where fame often feels superficial, Ysolde Featherstonhaugh reminds us that it's possible to be both extraordinary and human. And in doing so, she's not just reclaiming her story—she's rewriting it entirely.

THIRTY-ONE

ysolde

THERE'S A BANGING ON THE front door of my hotel suite, and there's only two people on the planet who would bang on my door like that. Three, I suppose. But Joah has a key.

I open the door to find one of the other two on the other side of it, clutching a *Marie Claire* in his hand.

"What the fuck is this?" Fletch asks, pushing his way into my room.

Kekoa pokes his head around the corner of my sitting room and spots it's Fletch. He lifts his eyebrows, asks *are you okay* without actually asking a thing. I flash him a little thumbs-up and he leaves us.

I look up at Freddie, and though I know exactly what he's refer-ring to, I still say, "What's what?"

He shakes his head at me, looking annoyed. He shoves the magazine into my hands.

"Ysolde, what the fuck is this story doing published in fuckin' *Marie Claire?*"

I shrug. "I decided to give an interview on it."

"No—" He shakes his head. "You said you'd never talk

TIME OF YOUR LIFE

about this…that you *didn't want to*—that it was no one else's business—"

"Fletch." I cut him off. "It was time…"

"Yeah—?" He lifts an eyebrow. "Funny that timing just happened to coincide with the fucking boy of the month mouthing off and getting himself into some heavy shit?"

I tilt my head at him. "That's not fair."

"No—" Fletch agrees. "It's not, but that didn't fucking stop him, did it?"

I give him a look. That's not what I meant and he knows it.

It's true though, what he's saying. I'd never had the desire to share what happened—to relive what happened—I don't know why? As though saying it aloud makes it truer? Which is crazy, because it is true—I know it's true; it happened; it was bad. No matter what, it was bad—but for some reason, the thought of sharing it made it feel worse?

So Fletch is right, I never had any intention to speak about it.

But things change. Priorities change, you know—?

Fletcher shakes his head.

"This is bullshit, Sol—that he'd—"

Then there's more banging at my front door.

"That him—?" Fletcher straightens up as he walks towards it. "Fucking hope it is, I have a couple of—"

"—he has a key," I call after him as Fletch swings open the door, and in blows Lala—wearing a lilac dress from Chanel 1994 RTW collection and Pix close behind her in a black, red, and hot pink Helmut Lang top from his Fall RTW line last year.

Lala pauses in front of Fletch, looking him up and down—then over to me, then back at Fletch.

"Interesting," she says more about him rather than *to* him, then she turns her attention to me. "What the fuck?"

Pixie flits over and hugs me. "Are you okay?"

"Yes." I nod quickly. "I'm—" I swallow. "Yeah."

"She's not," Lala tells the room.

"She is!" I insist.

Pixie looks at me confused. "You've kept this so quiet all this time…"

"I can change my mind…" I tell them all, all of them staring at me—I feel like they're cross at me, but that's mean and I don't know why they would be. "I'm allowed to change my mind!"

"Of course you can!" Pix kneels in front of me, holding my hands. "It's your mind to change, it's your story to tell—you… just…" She purses her lips. "You changed it quite drastically, quite suddenly."

"Do you know what—?" Lala says loudly. "*I* changed my mind."

She doesn't even need to say any more because I already know where this is going.

I give her a long look—doesn't stop her.

"Fuck him," she tells me, shaking her head. "He says he loves you, but that's fucking bullshit—"

Aleki is standing in the doorway, nodding along. I don't know when he joined in. I suppose it's a little family affair now.

Lala keeps going. "You don't put yourself first if you love someone else."

"He didn't make me do it," I tell them all. "He asked—I said yes."

"He should never have asked!" Fletch yells.

"His career was in the fucking toilet!" I yell at the ceiling.

"How do you know?" Freddie says, staring at me.

I look over at him—I don't ask *what* aloud but look at him, waiting for more.

"How'd you know his career was in the toilet, Ys? Because I love you, you're my oldest friend in the world, you're not that fuckin' astute."

I frown. "Hey."

Lala inhales sharply through her nose. "If you're about to tell me that that motherfucker told you his career was in the toilet—"

"—*Not verbatim!*" I cut in.

TIME OF YOUR LIFE

Pixie gives Lala a *calm down* look before she settles her gaze back on me. "Well, what *did* he say, then?"

"Umm—" I purse my lips, shrugging my shoulders. "Nothing really, just that it was fucking disaster."

Lala rolls her eyes big. "Which is an insanely unfair thing to say to someone when you're asking them for a favour—Like, of course you fucking said yes. How the fuck were you supposed to say no?"

"I wouldn't have said no anyway!" I yell.

"And *that*"—Lala points at me accusatorially—"is the problem, Solly. *That* right there." She tilts her head. "Remember when I said it scared me—?" She lifts her eyebrow. "This is why. Because *you* love him—" I open my mouth to protest, but she cuts me off. "—And he loves you too! I'm not saying he doesn't okay—?" she clarifies before delivering the fatal blow: "But not as much as he loves him."

"That's not true." I shake my head. I don't know why I say that though, because I think actually, really, truthfully, she might be right. I think it is true. I think I've known it for a while. I suppose you could argue he all but told me as much himself.

Lala sighs. "He got you to tell the world about the worst day of your whole fucking life to throw himself a line…"

I sit on the sofa next to Fletch, my shoulders slumped now. "You're making it sound worse than it is."

Freddie bumps me with his shoulder. "It's pretty bad, Ys."

Lala points at Freddie. "He would fucking never."

I look up at Fletch, who says nothing, and still, all the same, I know it's true. He really would never.

Lala shakes her head. "I can't fucking believe Jilly let this happen—"

"She said it was my choice!" I shrug, feeling less and less confident in my decision with every passing second.

"Right." Pixie nods. "But did she say it like, 'darling, it's your choice!'…or was it more like…'…it's your choice?'"

I stare at her blankly. "I don't know what that means!"

"The second one," Aleki says, and I give him a very sharp look, and all he does, that man, my bodyguard, whom I employ and whose bills I pay, gives me a flick of his eyebrow, like—*I said what I said.*

"Listen—" I shake my head at them all collectively. "I can't talk about this right now, I've got to—"

My best friend lets out an accusatory gasp and points a finger at me.

"Don't you say 'see Joah'! Do not you *fucking dare* say you're seeing Joah…"

I frown at her. "We have plans."

"Cancel them," Fletch tells me.

"What!" I blink at him. "No! *Especially* no, coming from you! My ex-boyfriend telling me to cancel plans with my current boyfriend, it's very self-serving."

"Nope." He shakes his head, unfazed. "Self-serving was you coming to my house two weeks ago, fucking me four times because you had a fight with your boyfriend, and not calling me since."

Lala's hand flies to her mouth in shock.

"Oh my god, you messy slut, I love it," Lala says once she's recovered. "Four times?" She queries, looking at Fletch with her head tilted. "That's some stamina! Look at you, stud! Didn't know you had it in you."

Freddie looks mildly offended. "I'm a *professional* athlete."

Lalee gives him a wink. "Yeah, you are."

My head drops back to the ceiling. "Lala."

"Sorry." She snaps back into focus but whispers to me, "Want details on that later though, please—"

"Don't see him," Pix says, quietly. She looks genuinely sad for me. A bit like her hero just fell off his pedestal. He did, I suppose.

"Seriously, Sol," Lala tells me. "Blow him off."

"No!"

"Yes!" she counters. "Like, fuck him—!"

TIME OF YOUR LIFE

295

"Yeah—" I give her a look, lowering my voice. "That's loosely the plan, La."

Fletch groans and, admittedly, that doesn't impress Lala either.

"You've *got* to be fucking kidding me. You are on strike!" She points to my crotch. "*She* is on strike!"

I roll my eyes at her. "Lala."

"No listen, Sol. That man—" She pauses, reconsidering. "*Boy.* Let's call a spade a spade—" She gives me a look to make a point. "He *fucked you over* so he could stay afloat." I start to shake my head again, but she keeps going. "He should be absolutely fretting that he's lost you because of this, Solly."

"I agreed to it!" I yell, exasperated.

She looks me square in the eye. "And *that* is your tremendously gracious heart and mildly weak character's burden to bear. *His* burden, however, is—*or should be*"—another pointed look from her—"that he *dared* fucking asked you the first place."

Hold on… Is she right? Fuck. Is she right?

I haven't really thought all that much since it happened—him on the couch, he looked so sad and desperate—like he was drowning and I had a lifeboat.

I just wanted to help him, I didn't think about how it wasn't helping me—I hadn't thought about how it made me feel unsafe and weirdly exposed all over again. Joah was drowning, he needed help, I could help, so I did. But at what cost?

Me, I suppose. I'm the cost.

"I'm calling him," Lala tells me, and I say nothing because I don't know what to say anymore. I'm still reeling a bit.

"What are you going to say?" Pixie asks.

"That we're going out tonight," Lala says to me, eyebrows up. "*Without* him."

I glance over at Fletch. I don't know why. He feels like a good pulse-check in the room, I guess—usually, anyway. Right now all he gives me is a shrug.

"I'm telling you—" Lala says as she riffles through her purse and plucks out her little black, leather address book. "That boy needs to have the fear of god put in him that he's fucking lucky to have you and *maybe* he actually even doesn't anymore…"

"Lala—" I shake my head at her. "I'm not breaking up with him."

She picks up the phone in my room and starts dialling his number.

"Well, that's your choice—but either way, right now, he should be squirming in his skin, Sol—"

She pauses.

"Joah," she says into the phone. "Hi. It's Lala—I was just calling to let you know, Ysolde can't come see you anymore."

THIRTY-TWO

joah

YS CAN'T COME SEE ME anymore. That's what her fuckin' mate says to me on the phone.

What the fuck?

Take a breath. Jaw goes tight.

"Alright." Clear me throat. "Why?"

"We're going out," Lala tells me. Even though she can't fuckin' see it, me eyebrows shoot up. What the fuck's goin' on?

"*You're goin' out?*" I repeat back, trying to keep it calm.

"Mm-hmm," Lala hums, like this is no big deal. "Girls' night," she says. "Kind of."

Press me lips together. Fuckin' *girls' night?*

"*Kind of?*" I echo, proper sharp now.

"Yeah," Lala chirps, light as a bloody feather. "Kind of."

You ever seen girls get on their fuckin' high horse? Don't reckon they even know how annoyin' they are—overbearin', nosy as fuck. Lala's never been a brat till now, but fuck me, she's gunnin' for the crown tonight.

"What the fuck does 'kind of' mean?"

"I dunno, Jo," she says, tone turnin' smug. She ain't never called me Jo before. Reckon we're not close enough for it, either. "Use your imagination."

Then I hear summat—Ys's voice, I think. Faint in the background. She's protestin', like she's tryna grab the phone off Lala. It's her. I fuckin' know it is.

Now I'm fuckin' fumin'.

"Oi, let me talk to her."

"No," Lala says, and I swear I hear a fuckin' smirk in her voice.

"Yes, Lala," I growl, teeth gritted. "Fuckin' now."

"Mmm—" she hums. "I wouldn't take that tone with me, boyo. My tolerance for you is crumbling like a fucking McVitie."

"Put my girlfriend on the fuckin' phone."

"No," she says, proper unfazed. And then the line goes dead.

Can you fuckin' believe it? She hung up.

Holy shit. I'm fuckin' ragin'.

Grab me keys, don't I—? Head straight over. Takes me thirty minutes and then I fuckin' leg it up to her suite.

Get there—she's already fuckin' gone.

And I don't know where Lala lives—didn't fuckin' listen, did I? Somewhere in West London, but what the fuck am I gonna do— Knock on every door from Kensington to Notting Hill till I find her?

Dunno what this is. Don't know what the fuck's goin' on. Last we spoke, me and Ys were golden.

And now—? What the fuck?

Drop meself on the settee in her lounge. Weird feelin'—sick fuckin' feelin'—like maybe I fucked up, like—?

But how? Don't even know when. What the fuck did I do, you know what I mean?

The article worked, didn't it? That was the plan.

And then I get a niggle—which, do you know what—? Never had one before. Not about relationship shit, anyway. Don't reckon I've ever cared enough to feel one. Never loved anyone enough to even notice if I did. Don't fuckin' like that she gives me niggles, man. Proper wet, soft lad shit, that. But fuck me, this niggle's gettin' louder.

Did I fuck up? Was that article selfish? She said aye—that's not my fault. *She fuckin' said yes.* And thank Christ she did, because—shit, it was bleak there for a minute. But the tide turned today. She turned the fuckin' tide for me.

Because she loves me. She did this for me because she loves me.

And you do right by the people you love. And she did right by me.

You know how waves come in sets, they say? Fuck me, here comes the second one...

Another sick feelin'—but it's bigger this time, innit? Worse.

Feel a pit grow in me stomach, mouth dry as a fuckin' Weetabix.

Wonder if—*fuck*—maybe, I dunno—? Maybe I didn't do right by her?

GIRLS JUST WANT TO HAVE FUN (AND STIR UP DRAMA)

By Fiona Tate, Entertainment Correspondent, The Daily Sun

Ysolde Featherstonhaugh, 20, stepped out with her glittering inner circle last night, marking her first public outing since the shocking revelations of her terrifying ordeal with her stalker broke.

Joining the international supermodel and global style icon for the evening were her closest confidantes: Lala Caravella (21), freshly crowned the face of a major luxury beauty campaign; former child star turned It Girl Riley West (22); pop music's favourite American, Chloe Bosworth (23), known for her breakout hit "Velvet Touch"; up-and-coming model Arina Melnichenko (20); and one other unknown friend.

The girls were seen painting the town red, kicking off the night with dinner at The Ivy, before heading to the legendary dance floor at The Met Bar, where they partied until the early hours. Sources tell us the group was in "high spirits," spotted downing shots of tequila and giggling conspiratorially as they posed for Polaroids.

But whilst the girls' night seemed like the ultimate celebration of friendship and freedom, one thing was glaringly obvious—Featherstonhaugh's very famous other half, rock star Joah Harrigan (23), was nowhere in sight. Could there be trouble in paradise?

Tongues began wagging when Ysolde was spotted sneaking out of the club at 2:30 a.m. with none other than American heartthrob and scandal magnet Jamie Cross. The 25-year-old crooner—known for his leather jackets, brooding good looks, and penchant for older women—was seen laughing and walking hand in hand with Ysolde as they climbed into the back of a waiting car.

"They looked cozy," an onlooker dished. "Ysolde was glowing, and Jamie couldn't stop smiling. It felt like they were in their own little bubble."

Whilst it's far from the first time Jamie's been linked to a famous beauty—his past flames include a supermodel and a very married Oscar nominee—fans were quick to question what this means for Joah and Ysolde. The couple, who had a whirlwind romance that took them and London by storm over the last few months, are no strangers to drama, but insiders claim this could be a sign of deeper cracks in their relationship.

"Joah's been on edge since the fallout from the Manchester show," a source close to the couple revealed. "The fight onstage, the *Rolling Stone* interview—it's all taken a toll. Ysolde's been trying to support him, but the tension between them has been impossible to ignore. She's young, she's beautiful, and she's not going to wait around for Joah to figure himself out."

Others speculate Ysolde's recent traumatic experiences may have shifted the dynamic between the pair. "She's been through so much," says a well-placed insider. "Joah's protective, but he's always been known to have a selfish streak. There are whispers that he's struggling with how much attention Ysolde's been getting lately—and that she's tired of making herself less so he can feel like more."

As for Ysolde and Jamie, could this be the start of a new rock-star romance? Or was it just a harmless encounter between friends blown out of proportion by the gossip mill? Time will tell!

THIRTY-THREE

joah

NEXT DAY, ME AND THE lads are havin' lunch with Mick—meant to be regroupin' after that fuckin' shit storm of an article—but really, just fuckin' grateful to get to take me mind off whatever's going on with me and Ys.

Been a day now, maybe more. Last time we talked was last night—just before Lala was bein' a proper bitch to me on the phone. But now—after a whole fuckin' day of wallowin', backstrokin' through me own head—realise I didn't even talk to Ys much yesterday, either.

Had so much shit with the band—fuckin' *Rolling Stone* called me to apologise. Miracle, that. Was busy, that's all. Me and Ys were meant to grab dinner later—that was the plan. Till me girlfriend got hijacked by her fuckin' mate. Been really fuckin' in me head about it, haven't I? Hate that. Proper melt these days, aren't I? Hate how much I give a shit about her. Especially when she won't fuckin' call me back.

Called her suite 'bout a fuckin' thousand times—nowt. Called the hotel—said she ain't come home yet. Tried her mobile—fuckin' useless. Don't even know why she's got one—never answers the

TIME OF YOUR LIFE

thing any day of the fuckin' week. Me head's proper done in at this point. Just me, sat at home, panickin' and spirallin'. Fuckin' hate that I'm like this over her.

So, aye. This lunch? Fuckin' welcome distraction, it is.

The Atlantic, Piccadilly. Bit swanky for me, but Mick's a knob an' he fuckin' loves it. He's payin', so fuck it. Everyone's got a drink in hand when Mick raises his glass. "To avoidin' crises."

"Here, here." The lads clink. All in good spirits, aren't they?

Rich is sat across from me, eyes on me. Never been one for celebratin' when it's just me draggin' meself outta a hole I dug in the first place.

"You know what," Mick says after a long gulp of his Harvey Wallbanger. "Decent of her to take this all on the chin for ya, all things considered—" Nods to himself, like Ys has just done him a fuckin' personal favour.

"Not a bad girl in the end."

Me head pulls back, proper confused. "What the fuck are you on about?"

"Yeah—" Mick shrugs, shoulders movin' like it's nowt. "You know, I can't really fuckin' believe it."

Glance at Rich. Uneasy. Hate that about meself—when shit feels rocky, still look at me big brother. Such a fuckin' soft lad, these days. State of me, I swear.

Fix me eyes on Mick, frowning. "Believe what?"

Mick freezes, goes all still, he does. "Wait..." He looks 'round the table. "Have you not seen it—?"

Fry's face scrunches up. "Seen what?"

Mick zeroes in on me. Proper nervous like. Lift me an eyebrow, waitin'.

"Oh." Mick clears his throat. "Jo—I'm—Shit." Sighs, reaches for the shopping bag hooked over the back of his chair. Fishes somethin' out. Hands me this rolled-up magazine. I just look at him, flat, then down at it in me hands—stomach fuckin' caves in, don't it.

Her on the cover. Laughin', holdin' hands with that fuckin' American—What's his name? *Jamie somethin'*. Birds go fuckin' nuts for him. Don't like his music much meself, but wouldn't have said he was shit or owt. Till now. Now—when I see him on the cover of the fuckin' *Daily Sun*, arm slung 'round my fuckin' girlfriend, dead of night, both of 'em laughin' as they're gettin' in a car and fuckin' leavin' together—*now* I fuckin' have summat to say.

Girls' night? Fuck off. Is this what "kind of" meant? It don't make sense. Like, what the fuck is happenin'? What the fuck is she playin' at? She wouldn't just fuck about with some fucking cunt, would she? Why would she like—? Fuck, yeah—okay. Since yesterday, been gettin' this weird feelin', like—fuck, maybe I did proper fuck it with that article. Didn't hit me till Lala called, runnin' her fuckin' mouth. But this is a piss-take, yeah? This has to be a piss-take.

Push back from the table, don't I?—just need to get away from the lads for a minute. Don't want 'em to see how much I fucking care. And fuck, I do care. Gone fuckin' soft, me. Care about that fuckin' girl more than it's good for me.

And you know what? I've cared about shit before. Don't like being embarrassed, do I? Who does, know what I mean? Like, I've felt shit when I've looked stupid, or when summats gone tits up and it's embarrassin'. And this—no lie—is fuckin' embarrassin'.

But, fuck—I know that's not why I care, how I care. It's her. It's just her. She's mine, you know? Or—she's fuckin' supposed to be.

"Oi—" Rich calls after me as I sidle up to the bar.

Order two double shots of scotch. Drink 'em back-to-back. Order another.

Bartender throws Rich a look—bit uneasy. Still pours it, though, cos who the fuck's not gonna serve me, you get me?

"Jo—" Rich starts.

"—Don't." Cut him off, sharp.

"Talk to her." Voice low, like he's tryin' to be the reasonable one here.

I down that double in one. "Nope."

"Joah." He says it again. Grabs me shoulder this time. "Call her."

"No—" Glare at him. Scowlin'. "Fuck that."

Are you kiddin'? Can't even fuckin' see straight, man—Fuck her.

Proper done with her now, I am. She's gonna sack me off—blank me for two days—then let me find out she's on the pull with other lads like this. Nah. Fuck her.

"Jo." Rich shakes his head. "Mate, there's probably an explanation—"

"What?" I ask, eyebrows up. "What's the fuckin' explanation, then?"

"I dunno—" He shrugs. "You know the paps, lad—they're fuckin' rats. They just want a story—they're probably just mates, Jo." He sounds sure of it. "She wouldn't do that to ya."

"Look where his fuckin' hands are on her, man—!" Yell louder than I mean to—gets caught in me throat cos—fuck. If I think about it—*really* think about it—Start shakin' me head. Nope. Can't be thinkin' of it.

Lower me voice. "Fuck, like—" Shove me hands through me hair. "Look how they're laughin', Rich."

Gonna gip, reckon. Not from the scotch. From her.

Bitch.

"Jo—" Richie shakes his head. "She's not like that…"

"Yeah?" Lift me brows. "That's weird cos she fucked Freddie Fletcher four times in the fuckin' what—? Sixteen hours we were broken up for up in Manchester."

Richie breathes out his nose, gives me that sick-of-me look. "Joah—"

"So fuck off, Rich." Shake me head at him. "I don't wanna hear it."

His jaw goes tight—shakes his head, walks off.

Dunno how long I stay there—drink a lot, proper fast.

I know the lads are stayin' close by—everyone's on high alert now. Probably a good call. Feel like startin' shit, don't I? What I wouldn't fuckin' give to have…what's-his-name—? That Bright

Line fucker—? The one I bottled in the head—? *Williams.* What I wouldn't give to have that motherfucker walk in here right now.

Better not, though. Might fuckin' kill him if he did.

When I get like this—and yeah, I ain't never been like this before, cos this is fuckin' worse—but I've been fucked off before, haven't I? Had my share of bad fuckin' days. Who hasn't like—? I know meself enough to know I need to get this energy out.

Gotta fight someone or fuck someone.

Don't have a preference, do I? Whichever opportunity presents itself first, know what I mean?

And then I see her.

That girl, the one I made cry. Shagged Ysolde's toff of an ex— you know who I mean?

And I know what you want me to say—that I was fuckin' strong enough to walk away. But I ain't. Don't even want to. Nah, she's exactly what I need right now.

Don't need another drink to convince meself either. Don't need no convincing.

I walk over to her—she's sat with her mate.

Mate's not bad either.

"Oi." I nod at the crying one. Not cryin' now but you know what I mean.

She looks at me, confused—cautious, you know? Fair enough, I s'pose.

"You good?"

She frowns. "Yes?"

I nod, don't smile—don't have any smiles in me right now, do I? Turn to her mate instead, offer her my hand. "Joah."

The mate blushes straight up, don't she? Shakes my hand anyway.

"Tara." Clears her throat, all nervous. "Whitmore."

Tilt my head at her. "Alright, Tara Whitmore."

"Where's Ysolde?" the crying one asks, makin' a point.

Can't knock her for that, can I?

"Dunno," I say, staring straight into her eyes. "Don't care."

Don't think I'm meant to notice, but the mate pinches her under the table, all fuckin' excited.

I nod my chin at the one I made cry. "I forgot your name."

She rolls her eyes, acting like she's offended, but let's be real—she's just happy I'm chattin' to her.

"It's Meghan," she says.

"Miller." I nod slowly. "I remember now."

She straightens her shoulders, those catlike eyes lock on me.

Run my tongue over me teeth, nod my chin at her again. "I was a prick to you, Meghan Miller."

Her nose goes in the air, all proud and shit. "Yes, you were."

Press my lips together, shake my head. "Sorry about that. Dunno what got into me—" Then I give her this look, the one that's never not worked before. "Can you think of a way I could make it up to ya?"

She smirks, already pleased with herself but nowhere near as fuckin' pleased as she'll be soon.

"I'm sure I could come up with something…"

THIRTY-FOUR

ysolde

NOW LISTEN, I WOULDN'T CONSIDER myself an overly religious person—I don't know how much of the Bible is real, but something doesn't have to be all the way real for key parts of it to still remain perfectly true. It's good to be selfless, it's good to be kind, it's good to put other people first, it's good to forgive, to be humble...

Those are things that are celebrated traits and championed within our species, not just in that book, but in almost every ancient religion.

In the Qur'an those who are selfless are praised, and in Tao Te Ching those who are selfless are rewarded. Confucius considered kindness (technically ren, but we'll call it benevolence) as the highest virtue, and then the Stoics believed that we're all part of a larger human family, and we should be good and just to each other, all of us, all the time. In Hinduism, the Gita teaches that forgiveness and tolerance are divine qualities, and Zoroastrian ethics encourage reconciliation and harmony.

Which is all to say—even if you don't believe in all that much of the Bible, I think we can agree that the wise, old ancients all sort of agreed that there's this baseline of things it's good to be and a baseline of things it's bad to be.

TIME OF YOUR LIFE 309

Pride is a crazy thing, isn't it? In my line of work—in his—it's par for the course, really. Kind of assumed, but there are varying degrees. There are limits.

What I'm trying to say is, in the old story that the ancient Jews and Christians were told about the fall of mankind, I think there's a reason that the original sin—the *actual* original sin, not that thing with that poor woman and the apple—the real sin that fucked everything up—I think there's a reason the ancients made it pride.

Joah's proud. I know that. I've known that since the night we first met; you can smell it on him a good mile off. And it's strange and it's hard to put definitive parameters around it, but there's a difference between being proud of yourself and being prideful.

Joah Harrigan has every reason—every fucking reason in the world—to be proud of himself. And with the career he's had, there is of course an anticipated amount of ego.

The miserable truth is, ego, sometimes, to a certain extent, can be very sexy. Right up until the moment it isn't, and in my short twenty years on the planet, I'm yet to figure out when that threshold *actually* is and from whence is that fateful point it's crossed. All I know so far is that when you reach it, you reach it. When you've crossed it, you've crossed it—and it's near impossible to come back from.

I haven't called him, okay? I'm proud too.

And the more time I was with Lala and the girls, the crosser I began to feel about the article—and I don't even know if I think they're right. I don't know if I believe Lala when she's saying that Jo was drowning and I swam out to help him, and he just clambered on top of me and used me as his float—never mind that then I'm drowning and it's my face under the water... I don't know if I think that's true—I don't know that it could be?

And even if it isn't, I feel more and more sure that he was rather in the wrong for asking me in the first place.

So I went out with Lala and the girls, and I had a really fun night where I wasn't sad or weird or in my head all wondering whether my boyfriend threw me under the bus on purpose, or if it just happened on accident, just.

Whilst we were out, we bumped into our friend Jamie—he's an American; we didn't even know he was in town. Lala and I party with him often in New York, and he is literally the funniest, sweetest man on the planet. Girls lose their mind over him; he's absurdly sexy—brown eyes, perfectly styled brown hair, ridiculously fit from head to toe, and—unbeknownst to nearly everyone outside the industry (and possibly even some *in* the industry)—he is also incredibly gay.

So when I saw the red tops running their stupid gossip how they always do, I thought nothing of it—magazines like those say shit about shit all the time. Like, if I actually paid daily attention to all the rumours *The Daily Star* and *Mirror Weekly* run about me, I'd be the pregnant, long-lost grandchild of Anastasia, empress of Russia, in a secret relationship with Lala and Joah's just my beard.

So I see the articles about Jamie and I circulating, and it doesn't flag me as concerning, okay? And maybe with retrospect, I might see that that's on me. That's my fault. A stronger woman would have called him, but I'm not a strong woman. I think I'm actually quite a weak one when I'm backed against a wall.

It's the night after my girls' night, and there's a party we're all going to at Groucho. I presume Jo will be there because we talked about it earlier in the week—he was complaining that he didn't even want to go because he thinks the person whose birthday it is, is a bit of a twat, but anyone who's anyone in music in London has to go because they're all sort of at the mercy of Oli Raines.

I like him though, so I was always planning on going anyway, and truthfully, whatever weirdness might be between Joah and me, I presume when I get to the party and I see him, it'll disappear because most bad things do when he and I are face-to-face. I don't know why?

He's this sort of magnanimous, black hole of a man, and all the bad things and all the scary things and any of the small, tiny things that might have been things that maybe could have possibly been very slight concerns of mine that may have crept into the darkest corners of my mind very late at night—all those things, when you're in front of him—none of it matters. Who he is swallows it all. I think I said something about that the night I met him, didn't I? Gravity.

That's what I anticipate when Lala and I arrive at this party. I'm in this Versace spring 1995 RTW black bustier dress that's genuinely, possibly actually the perfect dress, and I wear it a bit knowing Jo will love it, and I love it when he loves what I'm wearing, I love it when his eyes fall down me, I love it when he gets in his head about smiling too much at me, and I know he'll be annoyed by how much he'll like this dress, so that's what I decide to wear.

Have you ever walked into a party and known within a few seconds of being there that absolutely every single person there is talking about you?

I have. It just happened.

"What the fuck?" Lala whispers to me, uncomfortable as she glances around. "What's going on?"

I shake my head. "I have no idea."

And then Fry catches, a weird look in his eye.

"Alright there, Ys?" He gives me a strange smile.

I don't know why it's strange exactly, but it is. I suppose we're not that close, he and I.

"Yes, Fry. Fine." I smile at him. "Is my boyfriend here?"

"Your boyfriend?" he says, nodding. "Is he your—well—" He shakes his head. "Right. None of my business—"

I look at him confused. "What's none of your business?"

He shrugs quickly. "Nothin', I dunno."

Lala looks at him, irritated now. "Is Joah here or not?"

"He's here, alright," that Harley man says, sort of smirking. I'm not mad on him, honestly. I think he's a bit of a dick. Chenko says he's very good in bed though, so I guess good for her—? Except not that good for her because he's here with someone who *isn't* her?

I look him up and down, as well as the girl he's with who's nowhere near as pretty as Arina Melnichenko.

Harley points towards a back corner, tilt my head as I look for Jo—I'll be pleased to see him, actually. I do miss him.

He's revoltingly beautiful—how beautiful he is sort of softens so many of his sharper edges, though, please don't tell him I said that—we both know he'd just mouth off about how *rock stars aren't fucking beautiful.*

And it's now, now as I am thinking how happy I'll be to see him, how much I've missed his mouth and those improbably blue eyes and the rest of his (secretly) beautiful face, when I see that very face snogging Meghan Miller.

Had you told me that is what I was going to witness tonight, I'd have presumed immense pain would befall me. My imagination would have predicted a sensation not dissimilar to my knees being capped as I'm standing right there. Just searing pain, completely, entirely, radiating-all-through-me everywhere—and rest assured, that will come—but right now, there's nothing.

Lala's whole entire body tenses up next to mine, she's blind with rage immediately, but me—I'm... *probably in shock, really*—? But I'll just say in this present moment, I feel rather calm. Even as I walk over to him, calm.

I'm standing in front of him and Meghan Miller and their revolting little public hookup for a good ten seconds before Lala aggressively clears her throat, and Joah pulls back, looking over at me with blurry, high eyes.

I look to my right and spot Richie nearby, watching on with a sad look on his face. Worried, I think. He should be.

"Interesting," I say to Jo with a tight-lipped smile.

He rolls his eyes. "Don't be weird—" He shakes his head. "Don't make this weird."

Lala scoffs, cannot believe it.

"You think *I'm* the one making this weird?" I gesture to myself. "Me?"

TIME OF YOUR LIFE   313

"Yep," he says, blinking in a way where his eyelids drag too slowly over his eyeballs.

He's really fucking high, and that does make my heart pang. I wouldn't want him to know that though, so I shrug.

"No, you're right—What's weird about you hooking up with Meghan Miller in a club in front of like, four hundred people we both know—?" I laugh airily.

Joah's eyes pinch. "'Bout as weird as you being papped on a date with Jamie fucking Cross when you were supposed to be havin' a fuckin' 'girls' night'…"

Oh shit. I blink a few times, seeing where our wires have gotten crossed.

"Jo—" I start, but he cuts me off.

"You know what? Fuck you," he spits. "You're pissed at me for the article—? Fine, that's fine—"

"—What? No, I—" I'm blinking a lot. Doesn't matter. He's talking over me anyway.

"—but just fuckin' 'round behind my back—? Fuck you."

My head pulls back. "Are you—are you being for real…right now—?" I shake my head. "Are you cognizant that you are actively hooking up with a girl who isn't me?"

"Yeah—" He shrugs. "Fuckin' tit for tat."

"Joah—" I try to stay calm, try to tell myself that he's hurt, he's misunderstood my relationship with Jamie—it's easy to forget under all his bravado that *sometimes*, about *some* things, Joah really is really insecure. "There's more than you—"

"—nah," he cuts me off again. "Fuck yourself."

"You're being irrational," I tell him.

"No, I'm not." He slings an arm around Meghan Miller, who's looking too pleased with herself, and with the look Lala is giving her, if I were her, I'd be sleeping with one eye open.

"I'm fuckin' fine," Joah declares.

I breathe in through my nose. "You will regret this…"

"Nope." He gives me a cold, tight smile. "Just regret you."

And there are those kneecaps. I nearly buckle when he says that, but luckily—I suppose?—he keeps going. "We're done, you and me—" Nods his chin in another direction. "Fuckin' piss off."

"Yeah, okay." I give him a single nod and a warm smile, then I turn.

"Are you okay?" Lala whispers quickly as we walk away. "We can go—"

But we don't need to go. I have a better idea because, like I said before, I'm not overly religious and I'm not very good at forgiving people either.

"No," I tell her and give her a controlled smile.

"What are you doing, Ys—?" She shakes her head, already she can tell I'm up to something. Of course I am. I'd never let a man do that to me in public and get away with it. Not even if I thought that man was the complete and total utter love of my whole entire absolute life. "Where are you g—" Then she stops talking as I stop walking, having just planted myself right in front of Richie Harrigan.

Lala's head pulls back, confused.

I bat my eyes up at him. "Hi."

He takes in a long breath through his nose. "Alright?"

"Do you like my dress?" I ask him, and his eyes fall down my dress—he looks annoyed about it.

"Aye," he says.

I smile up at him, pleased. "Did you have a good week?"

Rich tilts his head, says, "Ys, don't—" at the same time as I hear Joah yell, "Oh fuck on off!" And then he barrels on over, grabbing my arm and yanking me away from his brother.

"Oh!" I blink at him a few times in mock surprise. "I'm sorry, are you no longer fine—?"

"That's not the same thing," he says through gritted teeth.

I smile as though I'm not following. "What isn't?"

"You fuckin' my brother."

Richie's head pulls back. "Sorry—do I get a say in this?"

"Oh my god." I laugh airily at Jo. "You're crazy! I said *hi*."

TIME OF YOUR LIFE   315

Joah's jaw goes tight. "You said 'hey' with your sexy eyes."

My jaw drops in faux-shock as I look between the brothers. Rich concedes with a grimace, "You did."

Joah gives his brother a bit of a shove and points a threatening finger in his face. "Don't you fuckin' look at her eyes and fuckin' call them sexy—"

Richie smacks his hand out of his face. "Don't put your fuckin' finger in my face if you want to keep it, lad."

"Oh—" Joah laughs, dry and drunk. "The big man's here today!"

"Jo—" Rich says, trying to deescalate things. "You're dr—"

"No, fuck, man—" Joah says to him, his eyes slits. "You wanna take a swing at her, fuckin' see what happens—"

And then I grab Joah by the arm and yank him a step away. "Oh my god, do you hear yourself—?" I stare up at him. "How *impossibly* unhinged you are? You have spent the last—*god knows how long*—hooking up in a rather public setting with a girl who isn't me, despite the fact that you and I are—*were*, I should say— *were* in a relationship—and *you're* upset because I said *hello* to your *brother*."

"Yeah!" Joah nods, stubborn. "Why the fuck even would you do that?"

I give him a look as though I think he's the biggest dope on the whole planet, then turn and walk over to the bar.

Lala orders me a tequila straight.

"Now what?" she asks.

I give her a look out of the corner of my eye.

"Give him a minute…" I tell her.

I understand men. I know how to make them dance for me on strings like little puppets. Am I proud of that—? Fuck, I don't know. It's 1995—I don't have many trump cards in my pocket as a biracial woman, feminine wiles are about all I've got, so sorry, boys, it's a dog-eat-dog world.

Lala looks confused ever so briefly, and then right on cue, Richie Harrigan wanders towards me, eyes pinched. Lala blinks away her surprise and she sort of slides a foot or two away—striking up a conversation with someone she wouldn't usually talk to, but she's taking one for the team, I suppose.

"Fuck, you're trouble." Richie laughs and my heart pangs because that's what Joah calls me.

Called. Called, you silly girl.

"Maybe." I shrug, smiling up at him. "Sometimes."

"Daft cunt, my brother is," Rich says, nodding.

"Yes."

"But—" He gives me a look. "He *is* my brother."

I look at him, exasperated. "I. Said. Hey."

Richie tilts his head to the side, gives me this *come on* look.

"We know each other pretty alright by now, you and me, don't ya reckon—?" he says.

I shrug. "I suppose…"

He runs his tongue over his teeth. They both do that. I'd never noticed that they both do that till now.

"There was a look in your eye," he tells me, but he isn't cross about it.

"No, there wasn't," I tell him, my nose in the air and definitely, 100 percent lying.

"Aye, there was," he tells me, a bit sternly. "You're wound up, Ys. Worked yourself right up, which"—he gives me a confused, almost questioning look—"bit fuckin' rich, that, considerin' Jamie Cross an' all…"

I roll my eyes at him. Jamie's not out.

If Joah had called me and asked me, I would have told him—fuck, Jamie himself would have told him. But I'm not telling anyone his secret for nothing. And now Joah's for nothing.

"But still, like," Rich keeps going, "*that*"—he nods his head back over to Joah, who now has Meghan pressed up against a wall, kissing her in a way that, if I were to pay attention to it, would make me violently ill—"is fuckin' tasteless. So sure, yeah—fuck him. But, like—you're also…I dunno—" He shakes his head, fighting off a smile. "Christ, you don't fuck around, do ya, Featherstonhaugh—? You got some fight in ya."

My nose goes back in the air. "I don't know to what you're referring."

"I mean—" Rich gives me a pointed look. "If I'd said, 'Aye, go on then,' would you have dragged me into the bogs there an' then?"

I straighten myself up. "I don't even know what 'bogs' are."

He drags his hand over his mouth, wiping away a smile that probably—admittedly—shouldn't be there. "Yeah, you do."

"Yes, I do." I laugh once and then so does he, then I shake my head, watching him out the side of my eye. "And you would have had a good time."

He nods coolly. "I know I would have," he says—fuck—it's the strangest thing? I think I blush a bit. Weird.

Richie looks a tiny bit pleased, but there's something else there on his face too. Some type of trepidation… "Ys, I can't have that kinda time with ya."

"Why—?" I roll my eyes. "Do you guys have some rule about 'cross over'?"

"Nah—" He shakes his head. "Just don't fuck about with anyone our kid's in love with."

I stare over at him, my heart suddenly feeling all heavy.

"He doesn't love me," I tell him.

"Yes," Rich says solemnly. "He does."

"No," I insist. "He *says* he does, but he doesn't."

Rich shakes his head. "He *says* he does, doesn't *act* like he does because he don't know a fuckin' thing about it—but he does." He gives me a look, trying to make his point. "Loves you as much as someone can love another person when they've never really seen… you know, love like—"

I blink up at him, a bit thrown by that actually.

"That was absolutely far too soft for you, Richie Harrigan!" I scrunch my face up at him. "What's going on? You never defend him—"

He shrugs, unbothered. "I'm on E."

"Ah." I sniff, amused. "That makes sense."

And there's this strange, weighty pause between us, and he's watching me—eyes suddenly heavy.

"I would. Just so y'know." He nods to himself. "If ya weren't his like…"

My heart's gone funny. Beating so fast, I think it trips itself out of rhythm. Have you ever had the feeling that you're playing with fire? I haven't—not till now. There's something about it, actually.

"I'm not…" I say, my voice barely louder than a whisper. "Now. Not anymore."

"Nah—" Richie shakes his head. "Y'are. Mightn't wanna be, but you are."

He gives me this strange look and this sort of resigned shrug—a bit like he's sorry, a bit like he could be sad about it—then he nods subtly to his left.

"There's an American actor in the corner who's been staring at your legs since the fuckin' second you walked in."

I lift my eyebrows. "How do you know that?"

Richie moves in close to me, his mouth by my ear—by far the closest we've ever been to one another. "Because I've been watchin' your legs since you walked in."

Our eyes catch how they probably shouldn't, then he clears his throat.

"Real pretty boy—" He motions his chin towards the American again. "More your speed."

He starts backing away.

"What do you know about my speeds?" I call after him.

"I know ya speeds—" He rolls his eyes at me. "We're mates, remember? You and me."

And then he disappears into the crowd.

I take a second to take a breath and compose myself because that was—nothing. That wasn't anything, was it—? I'm just tired. Looking for male attention, that's all.

TIME OF YOUR LIFE

Which, speaking of—I'm in desperate need of it right now—what with Joah about to get Meghan Miller fucking pregnant in the corner over there.

So I look over my shoulder, and there he is—that American actor. Impossibly famous. He's won an Academy Award for the last three years in a row. He's outlandishly gorgeous, all golden and everything. Very blond hair, very golden skin, very golden eyes—and he is, to Richie's credit, absolutely drinking me in.

I make sure our eyes catch—hold his gaze for a good three seconds—then I turn away, back to the bar.

And I'm about to look back over my shoulder, to go for eye-fucking round two, when I'm rudely interrupted by the most annoying man on the planet.

"You okay?" Mitchell Montrose-Bowes asks me. "You look sad."

I don't look sad, I don't think. He's probably sad because Joah's probably fucking Meghan in the bathroom by now.

"Go away, MB."

He looks offended. "I'm just asking if you're—"

I give him a sharp look. "I am sad but I'm not sad enough to go home with you, so fuck off."

"Whoa—" His head pulls back. "Would you believe me if I said I was just worried about you—?"

I give him a dubious look and he elbows me gently.

"You know, once upon a time I loved you."

I take a sip of my drink as I roll my eyes. "So you say."

MB stares straight ahead, mouth pressed together, like he's thinking of what to say.

"Joah Harrigan thinks he's king fucking shit and everyone knows it."

I feel a wave of sadness, try to swallow it down. "That's because he is king shit."

MB nods a couple of times and puts his hand on my shoulder—which is weird—like, nice, he's being nice, but it's weird to me that he's being nice.

"Ys—" he says. "If he's king shit, you're queen shit." Then he walks away and I'm alone again.

Fuck, I hate alone. I hate alone so much. The world gets so noisy when I'm alone.

I went on this waterslide once, where it was basically just a vertical drop where the floor falls out from under you, and you're just falling, really…getting sort of slapped around by the water, but it's the sound—that rush sound of all the air, all that nothing I was moving through at light speed all around my head—that's how it feels when I'm by myself. That's the sound I hear when I don't have someone to love me.

I order another drink and drink it too quickly, but I think that's going to be my vibe for the next little while—I need to take the edge off of how my heart's feeling.

At least until—"Excuse me," says an American voice.

I turn to look at the voice, and I don't know why I'm surprised—but it's him. The actor.

I sort of forgot about him for a minute there—the drinks helped—don't know how, not when he looks like that.

He gives me the easiest of smiles to have ever been smiled in the history of time and smiles. "Hey," he says.

I straighten up, try to look substantially more together than I feel in my body. And heart. And mind.

"Hello."

"I'm River," he says, offering me his hand. "Casablancas."

I take his hand, and he puts his other one on top of mine, shaking it firmly.

All my body goes warm. Again, that could be the alcohol, though.

"Hello, River Casablancas."

He smiles. "And you are…?"

I give him an amused look. "You know who I am…"

"Yes, I do—" He chuckles. "I do, yeah. You got me." Then he tilts his head, looking at my face. "Whoa, you're like—" He shakes his head, speechless.

TIME OF YOUR LIFE

"—Beautiful." I nod. "I know." I give him a glib smile. "It's riveting stuff."

His head pulls back, surprised. "You don't care about being beautiful?"

I shrug. "Not really."

He looks confused. "Even though it's gotten you… *everything*—?"

I stare up at him in defiance. "Do you care about air, River?"

His eyes pinch, curious. "Not particularly."

"Even though it keeps you alive?"

He nods, sort of getting my point. "I guess I'd only care about it if I was running out of it."

"So tell me I'm beautiful when I'm sixty and the world is tired of my face," I tell him, unwavering.

"Yeah, okay." He nods, smiling. "Deal."

And there's something about that that feels a bit like that's a challenge.

"So how does someone compliment you, then?" he asks, and he's asking it genuinely. "Properly, I mean."

Truthfully, that stumps me. "I don't know, actually."

"Well." He gives me this casual smile that feels like he's a pool on a hot day. "—If you figure it out, I'd really love to give you one."

"—OI, YS!" Joah suddenly belligerently yells from across the club. "PLAYIN' OFF EASY AGAIN, ARE YA? SLUT!"

And almost immediately, I see Richie appear and hook an arm around Joah, dragging him away—and I'm standing there—don't even know what to do, don't even know how to process what he just said to me—And River? His head's pulled back, and I can see genuine anger across his face on my behalf.

"What the fuck—" he says, and I see him square up. "Hey—!" he yells back to Joah, and I quickly grab his arm, telling him no.

"Don't," I tell him earnestly. "Thank you, but don't—"

His eyes are locked on Joah, unfazed. "I'm not scared of him—"

"He's high," I tell him dismissively. "And the last time he got into a fight, he bottled the person in the head, so, god—please, just leave it."

He processes that information with a few blinks.

"Fuck," he says.

I nod back. "Yes."

His face tugs, uneasy. "Boyfriend?"

I roll my eyes. "Ex. *Obviously*."

"A recent one?" he guesses.

I nod carefully.

River tilts his head, shaking it gently. "Listen, I don't want to get in the middle of anyth—"

"Then, what the fuck are you doing—?" I ask, arms crossed, impatient.

"Lying!" he says quickly, reacting to my tone. "Fuck—!" He laughs as he starts backtracking. "That was a lie. That's what you say—I'm trying to impress you!" He lets out this strange breath that's a bit like a laugh. He looks a bit nervous. It's cute. "I'll get in the middle of—fuck—anything for you. I don't care."

"Better." I eye him as though I'm suspicious, but do you know what? Fuck it—I'm all in. Might as well.

He keeps shaking his head, not really acting like the cool American movie star he was a minute ago. "I'm sweating—literally sweating—just talking to you. You're the most beautiful girl I've ever seen in real life and that isn't even a compliment to you!" He looks exasperated. "—Which is—like, fuck—! I'm fucked."

"Well." I give him a very intentional look. "Not *yet*. But, presumably soon…"

He pauses—smiles a lot, then licks it away. He takes a breath.

"Ysolde Featherstonhaugh, can I take you back to my hotel?"

"No," I tell him, and the disappointment that spreads over his face is completely fucking adorable. I gaze up at him sweetly. "But I will take you back to mine."

TO BE CONTINUED IN...

part two

time of your life: probably never

Acknowledgments

This book was written in the crazy haze of a month. I didn't mean to write it, but I sort of knew I needed to. I know acknowledgments are usually to thank people, and I will, because there are many to thank, but it's my book, so fuck it, I'm going to acknowledge some other stuff, too.

2024 was a hard, almost impossible year. We moved states and left people we love, our little girl and I had an accident and she nearly died, and my cat *did* die. A lot of things didn't go to plan. I lost control a thousand different ways and the rug was pulled from under me so many different times in so many different ways, I've lost count. I've never cried more, I've never been more stretched thin, and I've never been so scared—though simultaneously, I've also never been so thankful and grateful. The conversations I'm in, the tables I'm at, the opportunities I'm given, who I get to work with, the people I get to meet, how much strangers on the internet allow me and welcome me into their lives—I am so thankful and so grateful. Not just professionally…but also, like—where I live, how I live, who I get to be in love with, the children I get to raise, the animals I get to care for, the people I get to call friends and family—I am, by every definition of the word, blessed. Blessed is sort of a weird word sometimes, and I struggle to say it—maybe it's because of #blessed, or maybe I just have more in me I that have to work through... Who knows, it's not really the point.

I grew up in a pretty religious environment. It took a long time for me to reconcile what I saw in the pews (or behind those frosted doors) and the rhetoric spewed from many of these self-proclaimed "Christians" supposedly in the name of the one true God. Supposedly we share that God, but I don't think we know the same one. We couldn't. As I type this in 2025 living in the United States of America, if you asked me whether I was a Christian, I think I'd say no. Not because I don't love Jesus any-more, because I do. It's because there are a lot of people these days who bear that name not to honor Him, not out of reverence for Him, not because of what He's done, but because a book was written 2000-3000 years ago (depending on which part we're talking about), and they like to weaponize certain parts for their own agendas. This book isn't remotely religious —if you're read-ing this, at this point, you're probably like, *what the actual fuck is she even talking about?* I'm not trying to preach, that's not my intention—my intention is this: I have experienced the goodness of God in my life, and it would be remiss not to acknowledge as much.

Now to acknowledge the less ethereal and more overtly tangible...

Benja, you carried a lot that month to let me write this. Thank you.

Emmy, we were so stumped by the cover at first—but once we knew what to do, boy oh boy did you do it. Thank you for bringing Ysolde and Joah to life so perfectly.

Amanda, Madie, and Molly—for being the ones who would read everything I wrote as I was writing it and would then proceed to gas me up accordingly. Every day for a month. As we all know, I unfortunately really do work so much better when I'm being told that my work is good—I truthfully don't think that this book would be here if you hadn't all encouraged me over the finish line.

Hellie, for when I called you and said, "I think I'm accidentally writing a novella, it's going to be 65,000 words," and you said, "You know, that's actually just a book." This book was a mad dash till the final minute, and I appreciate you and how well and hard you work for me and my stories all the time.

To my publishers and team at both Bloom and Orion, when I called you in January 2025 and said, "Hey, I have a new book. It needs to come out in July…of this year"—thank you for not hanging up, and thank you for—as always—getting it, going with it, and making it happen as magnificently as you both always do. Extra thanks to Christa for just always making impossible shit happen for me and my books. This is a fun one.

And lastly, I sort of said this at the start of this book. Jessa, my girl, you had an absolute shitter of a year. It nearly broke you. You did it anyway. That's important to acknowledge too.

About the Author

This time—*literally* (as she is actively typing this out) this time last year, Australian-born, self-confessed Anglophile Jessa Hastings told her husband she would never move to Tennessee… She regrets to inform you that this here author biography is in fact being written from her desk in Nashville, and much to her absolute shock and wonder, she really loves it here. Thankfully, also in Tennessee are her husband, two children, her still very beautiful but increasingly clingy dog (she hasn't done a wee not in his presence in about five months), and her two cats, which is one less than the last time she had to write one of these things. She misses that cat called Whiskey every day. She regrets to inform you that she's still not a very good sleeper, still has a very busy brain, still cannot do her hair, and still feels quite certain she would die if a cut-up piece of banana touched a slice of orange. She is fairly sure that this book in your hands is her eighth published book, thus the math would imply that this is her eighth attempt at writing an author biography. She is empirically aware that they are getting worse, and she is sorry about that.